MONKWORKS

MAGICAL DEVICES

A NOVEL BY

ROBERT VINCENT RYAN

BAYTON NAYBY BOOKS

Contents

To Todd and Jill,
for your amazing gifts of inspiration, insight, and love.

It's the end of one age,
and the shape of another
is not yet clear.

What will this new age bring?
Who will own the future?
Who will be left behind?

Tough questions for a treacherous time,
because no one can guess
how the story will end.

PART 1: *MAGIC FOR THE MASSES*

ONE: NOT A COMPLETE ASSHAT

They'll be all over me when I emerge from the tunnel. It's literally a rite of passage. If I can't evade the thieves, bounty hunters and nefarious creeps from assorted realms out to steal the magical devices I carry, then I fail as a Monkworks Field Tester.

I'm standing in a fake torchlit, real stone and iron corridor way beneath Floendahl Abbey, gearing up for my next mission. There is no fire atop burning sticks to light my way, just magic replicas that stay lit indefinitely without soot and smoke. It's part of the miracle that is the Abbey's Monkworks manufacturing facility: Why use the real thing when fake works so much better?

My pack contains the usual survival gear, both magical and mundane, plus four *Floe* prototypes that I am tasked with evaluating somewhere out in the Three Kingdoms. *Floe* is this mysterious force that only the secretive monks of the Abbey possess. They somehow harness its magical properties within the Monkworks facility to power the enchanted devices they sell. Rock? Metal? Aether? No one who knows is saying.

By the time a new magical device is far enough along in its development to get to me for field testing, it has passed every internal hurdle its monkish creators can devise. Then it's up to me, and other Testers like me, to ensure it works in real life situations or to, quite literally, die trying.

Imagine this: You launch an arrow to deploy a magical rope bridge across a bottomless chasm, get halfway out there over the abyss, only to feel the supposedly failsafe cords snapping apart. This is why the monk who recruited me likes to call the Tester job 'exit level.' Is it me, or do all Floendahl monks share an off-putting sense of humor?

If a device fails during testing it gets sent back to be fixed. The unfortunate Tester? Not so much. But it's not like any of us would be missed for long, since Testers are pretty low down in the Abbey pecking order. But still, it suits me. Most of us were orphans or runaways plucked from squalor by traveling Floendahl monks, who crisscross the Three Kingdoms selling their gadgets to anyone who will buy. And there are lots of buyers, from peasants, farmers and craftspeople to merchants, royalty and governments. *Magic for the Masses*, as the sales patter goes, is serious business.

Beside me Snout alerts, then sinks to her belly, wags her tail and whines. That can only mean one person, I think, and it's not a big surprise. It takes a full minute for him to appear, though, such is the perfection of Snout's snout.

I'm down on a knee, scratching the top of Snout's head, which she can't get enough of, when enormous Brother Isanor Janx rounds the corner and trundles towards me like a cave bear scenting dinner. Now I'm a big guy, with muscles honed by years surviving a Tester's life. But Janx, a former Tester himself, dwarfs me. "Egon!" he booms up the corridor. "Egon Brodie! Glad I caught you."

Yeah, right. Since I don't know yet where I'm going, there was never any chance I wasn't going to be 'caught' by Janx. He just loves to sound all jovial and casual.

"Brother Janx," I say neutrally, with a nod.

I guess I don't really have too much against him, if I think about it. He has been a good section leader, and I take his orders without too much complaint. But still, my relationship with him is pretty contradictory.

10

On the one hand, he made me a Tester. He showed me the ropes at the Abbey after he recruited me at 16 out of a flatlander jail, guilty of stealing a chicken for food. He offered me a way forward, gave me a purpose, saw to it that I was educated, and generally helped me clean up my act. I don't know why he bothered, but I guess I owe him for that.

On the other hand, he made me a Tester. The training was grueling, with brutal field exercises in rough camps and frequent brushes with death, all of which he presided over with relentlessly cheerful energy. Downright jolly, in fact, as if he liked nothing better than to torture us. It's what we used to call him behind his back, Jolly Janx, until we came up with an even better nickname. As trainees, we pitted ourselves against opponents both natural and unnatural, and whatever else was out there that a magical device might, I say might, overcome. Not all the trainees survived.

So anyway, here comes Janx, who always seems to have some last minute instructions for us Testers just before our missions begin, instructions that are guaranteed to complicate already complicated jobs. It is why we now call him Jinx, although still behind his back.

He stoops down to rub a now delirious Snout behind her ears, then straightens up and begins. "I just came from Abbot Tenebrus, and I can tell you that he is not happy," he says, perversely grinning. "And when he is not happy, I am not happy," he says, still grinning. "And you know what, Egon? When I am not happy, you are the unhappiest of us all. You see how that works?" he asks, breaking out his brightest and most irritating smirk yet.

For some reason Snout sounds a low warning growl, but I'm not paying attention.

"Wait," I say, surprised. "You were with the actual Abbot?" Which I quickly realize sounds like: Why the hell would Abbot Tenebrus see the likes of you? Yet another reason I'm the longest living Tester who still hasn't moved higher in the organization.

The sneer on his face is classic Janx. It's still his standard grin but then something goes up or down until it transmits an opinion of you so low that you feel it down to your boots. "Ah, what I mean to say, sir," I stutter, "is, well, no, I'm not quite seeing how it works. Can you tell me again why we are all so unhappy?"

"Oh yes," Janx says, definitely not grinning now. "I'll make it plain as day for you, Brodie. You, me and our leader are all unhappy because it seems Monkworks didn't sell enough devices last year. And what with manufacturing costs, a standing militia, a surplus of Testers (he looks at me meaningfully, I think), not to mention the tribute we pay to the Kingdoms to keep the peace, Floendahl Abbey needs some device prototypes to hit really big and really soon, to refill the treasury. Is that clear enough for you, Brodie?"

Now it should not be possible to have a monopoly on magical devices in the Three Kingdoms and ever be short of money. But for once I manage to keep the thought to myself. Still, I'm unwilling to accept responsibility for prototype success. "But sir," I say in protest, "I only test the damn devices. If they don't work they don't work, and it's not on me."

Snout alerts again, but again I ignore her.

Janx looks me up and down, not much liking what he sees. "Oh, but it is," he says. "It's most definitely on you because this time we are doing things a little differently."

Snout is outright growling now and I hear a sneeze behind me. I turn around and there stands a slight, brown-robed monk about my age and shorter, with a shaved head and a runny nose, using his cassock sleeve to wipe it. What Snout was trying to tell me. "It's the dog hair," the monk says to no one who asks.

Who is this asshat?

I turn back to Janx. "Is he here for you?" I ask.

"Nope," he says, and the grin is back, "he's here for you. Let me introduce Brother Caelum Venarius, a Monkworks engineer, maybe the best Monkworks engineer, and he's going out there with you."

I have never met him before but I know the name immediately, although the Testers I know don't call him by it. When they talk about him they call him *Big Foot*, I don't know why. All I actually know about him is that he's supposedly some kind of boy genius device designer who is high up at Monkworks. Oh, and that I've trashed dozens of his prototypes in my field reports over the years. This is really not happening, period.

"No way, sir," I blurt to Janx. "I work alone. I can't take him. People and things are trying to kill me out there. He'll only get in my way."

"You can and you will take him, Brodie," says Janx, setting his voice on serious.

"But why?" I practically whine.

"Because those *Floe* prototypes in your pack are potential treasury toppers to the Abbey," says Janx, "but only if they come back cleared for manufacturing. That's where Brother Venarius comes in. If a prototype doesn't work in the field, then the good brother here is going to fix it in the field. That comes straight from the Abbot. So you come back with four fully saleable Monkworks devices or don't come back at all." He pauses before finishing: "But make sure Brother Venarius gets back. Him we can't afford to lose."

Damage done, Jinx starts to trundle away, but pauses to make one last comment: "By the way," he says, "your first test site is Aurelia in Nir." Then he's gone.

I'll learn more about my itinerary at our first camp tonight but for now, as unhappy as Jinx predicted, I turn to Brother Venarius.

"Let me be as clear as I can be," I say. "Do what I say out there, when I say it, or you are going to die. Got it?"

He sneezes again, wipes his nose with his sleeve, and says, "Got it." I start to reach for my pack but then he surprises me by adding: "But there's just one thing." I turn back to face him.

"No one," he says intently, "under our three moons knows more about *Floe*, more about how to make our devices work, than I do. So yes, it's up to you to make sure that we survive, but it's up to me to make sure the Abbey does. I get the last say when it comes to the mission."

I have to hand it to him. I pushed, but he's no pushover. If he's as good as he claims, he might not be a complete asshat after all.

TWO: GUTS, MUSCLE AND STEEL

Venarius and I buckle up and follow Snout up the tunnel's last incline before we exit. There are other exits out of the Abbey, and I've used them all at one time or another. I pick this one today because it sets me on an easterly course for the Kingdom of Nir, purely routine, not at all suspecting that there would be consequences.

Magically warded, whatever is waiting for us out there doesn't know exactly where the tunnel exit is. They only know that Testers are often spotted in the woods below the eastern flank of the Abbey. There they watch and wait for an opportunity to waylay us and steal our *Floe* merchandise, which pound for pound is the most valuable loot in the Three Kingdoms.

My pack hangs over my left shoulder to rest comfortably at my right hip. My short sword hangs from my left, a magical Monkworks device that is imbued with extraordinary cutting power. There's a knife in a boot sheath and a hand ax on my belt, both magically enhanced. I wear an emerald threat ring on the fourth finger of my right hand, an enchanted gift from the Gryphons, a race of half lion\half eagle mythic creatures who possess an ancient magic some say is the far more powerful progenitor of *Floe*.

In addition, a Monkworks medallion hangs around my neck that offers temporary body protection in combat against edged weapons, hammers, claws, fangs, and probably some stuff I don't know about yet. I say temporary, though, because repeated blows can wear down its effectiveness until it has time to recharge itself. As far as Monkworks devices go, this one is still a work in progress.

My final and most invaluable piece of gear is the combat vest that only Monkworks Testers wear. Its multiple pockets hold many dozens of devices that Testers have found useful over the years, as they fought to stay alive on their missions. Any Tester worth his field pay knows the location of every device in every pocket, and can reach them without conscious thought. It has magical properties as well including, but not limited to, warming and cooling me as required, and completely blending in – to the point of invisibility – with the clothes I am wearing at the moment.

Snout carries a pack too, with food and water, booties, a woven coat, some herbs and bandages and whatnot for travel emergencies, and a mat. There's a protective medallion hanging from her collar too, along with some additional Monkworks stuff.

Venarius is wearing a medallion, also, but I see no weapon of any kind. His pack looks identical to mine, although I wonder what he has in it. For the first time I notice that his right boot is bulkier than his left. I point to it. "Birth defect," he says, "but don't worry, I won't hold you back." I hope he's right.

We move out along the corridor a few feet further before I get it: That's why they call him 'Big Foot.' I shake my head. Doesn't that fucking blow. I'm relieved at least that while I was trashing his work for all those years I never called him that. Given half a chance, people suck.

We get to the tunnel's great bronze exit gate, feel its magical buzz, and pause. "Ok, Brother Venarius," I say, "here's the plan." He sneezes and wipes. He looks a little nervous, too. He would look a lot more nervous if he had any idea what is about to happen. I have to say, though, that having done this exit routine out of the Abbey literally hundreds of times before, I have grown to enjoy it.

"The path we're on leads straight out of the tunnel and into the woods," I continue, "where everyone and everything that wants us will be waiting. That's why we won't go there." Venarius is focusing hard. "Just before we start, I'll launch a distraction and we'll follow it out. But where the path goes straight we'll go hard right and up the cliff. Be right on my ass. Don't stop for anything. Here we go."

I reach into my vest and pull out a coin-like device with a runner engraved on both sides. I throw it through the tunnel entrance and run after it, Snout at my side and Venarius on my heels. I see the coin hit the ground and basically explode into a running replica of a Monkworks Tester in full mission gear. It races straight up the tree-lined trail hurling smokers and noisemakers, and disappears around the first bend. Bedlam erupts.

We turn sharply right, moving quickly, obscured by smoke, and after twenty strides I see what I am looking for: little more than a goat path that winds up the cliff and out of sight. We hear our decoy off through the trees to the left, the shouts and growls of pursuers, and the occasional clang of steel on steel.

I reach into the vest again and pull out a tiny Monkworks squirt bottle. "For the bottoms of your boots," I whisper in Venarius' ear, "and then the palms of your hands." I squirt each in turn. Then I do the same for Snout's four paws and my boots and hands. "It will help us stick to the cliff," I explain to the monk.

And so it does. We follow the path higher and higher, our hands and boots and paws gripping anything the cliffside offers. Venarius has no problems climbing on that bulky boot, I'm relieved to see, and Snout is a surefooted shepherd born to the mountains.

Floendahl Abbey towers above us to start, but gradually the trail curves up and away until we emerge from its shadow into early morning sunlight. We stand atop a sharp ridgeline hundreds of feet above the Abbey towers and further east. Even from this height, though, the Abbey looks huge. From our vantage point its multiple structures blend together into the unified image of a mysterious and monumental mountain fortress reaching for the sky.

I always find the Abbey complex hard to describe because it's just so strikingly eccentric. Sure, its buildings are made with materials I've seen throughout the Three Kingdoms; mostly iron and glass, with some copper, bronze, and wood ornamentation and detailing. But each structure is uniquely original, as if designed by a mad geometrist – or magician - and totally unlike anything I've ever seen in my travels.

Dead center within the protective Abbey walls, and built directly over the mysterious *Floe* source, is the Monkworks manufactory itself. It is wide at its base, ridiculously tall, and narrow on top. It's basically an iron-and-glass tower, but it looks as though it took many detours on the way to reaching its final height. Each of its many floors doesn't quite sit squarely on the one below. Some are more rounded; others are more square. Many feature balconies and ledges. All use heavily decorated metalwork to encase their columns, supports, entranceways, windowsills and magical globes of light.

Its most extraordinary feature though, I think, is its central core of glass through which balls of light travel at regular intervals from the bottom to the top of the structure, and then out into the sky, in a never ceasing effervescence of multicolored sparkles. The whole journey of light repeats every few minutes. I told you the place is eccentric.

Clustered around Monkworks are 11 other fantastical, not-quite-as-tall buildings. There is an administration building; an armory; a granary; a food hall; a storehouse; the Abbot's magnificent mansion; a blacksmith/stable combination; and three barracks housing staff, troops, and assorted low levels like Testers. There is also an incredible cathedral, honest-to-gods shaped like a leaping Gryphon, that actually holds services for local townsfolk, which is kind of funny since Floendahl monks worship no god but *Floe.*

The grounds are enclosed on three sides by an intimidating iron wall topped with crenellations and arrays of bristling spikes. The wall is pierced by a massive bronze entrance gate in the form of an elaborate 'M,' some say for Monkworks, others for Magic itself. In this age of peace in the Three Kingdoms, no one I know can remember the last time the raised gate was closed.

There are archery towers rising up from atop the wall in regular intervals, giving our archers an unobstructed view of a theoretical adversary's approach. On top of their copper roofs sit imposing iron Gryphons – 22 in all - who, legend has it, come alive to fight if ever the Abbey is in dire need. Yeah, right.

The fourth side of the complex, opposite the front 'M' entrance gate, is a sheer cliff of white granite that rises up above where we stand and to our left, and ends the ridgeline trail we're on. Residences for the most elite monks of the Abbey have been carved by magic into this granite wall, and are reachable by bronze and glass bubbles that ride up and down the cliff on steel rails. Some of the clear glass facades of these "perches," as they are so casually known, are beautifully lit from within right now, as the morning sun still struggles to ascend past the mountaintops.

"You live there?" I ask Brother Venarius, pointing to the granite power-cliff of 'perches.'

He nods to a line of dawn-streaked windows almost level with the heights we stand on. "There," he says. "Mine is top row on the left."

I point far below to the shadowy floor of the complex. "My 'perch' is way down there on the right," I say. "Barracks Number Three."

Brother Venarius shows no reaction, but I'm pretty sure he thinks I'm the asshat now.

The Abbey's final touch is a powerful cascade of spring water streaming out of a hole in the cliff face that is surrounded by a copper escutcheon of flying Gryphons. The torrent tumbles down to an immense and beautiful, copper and stone fountain that sends huge sprays of water back up into the air in graceful arcs. The spring is the water source for the Abbey, and the fountain conceals channels leading to underground storage. The channels can be diverted to fill the moat surrounding the outer walls at a moment's notice.

What is even more spectacular, if you ask me, is the natural setting. The Abbey's front 'M' gate faces the literal crossroads of the world, where the trade routes connecting the Three Kingdoms meet on the edge of a vast plain some six thousand feet above sea level. This highland mesa is in turn dwarfed by the enormous Infinity Mountains surrounding it, whose peaks jostle the horizon in all directions.

The world famous intersection is formed by three cobblestone-paved highways which wind through narrow breaks in the mountains to meet in front of the Abbey. In the west, our left, is the road from the woodland Kingdom of Enduron. In the north, laid out straight ahead of us, is the road from the snowbound Kingdom of Rusk. And to the east, on our right, is the road from the desert Kingdom of Nir. Together, these thoroughfares form the only land route connecting the three sovereign kingdoms of the world.

A significant town, really a city now, called Floendahl Heights to distinguish it from the Abbey, has grown up around the crossroads. It services the needs of traders, travelers, pilgrims and troops journeying through the mountains, and also provides additional housing for the Abbey's workers. Its spectacular recent growth from humble village to thriving metropolis, mirroring the sales growth of the Abbey's magical devices, is the source of irritation and envy in some parts of the Kingdoms. I love it.

"I never tire of this view," sighs Venarius, no doubt referencing his fucking 'perch' and taking a shot back at me. The asshat is back on his head.

"Will we rest here, Brodie?" he asks, and it is tempting after the climb, but I know we aren't on safe ground yet. "Not yet, Brother Venarius. We're exposed up here. We need to keep going until we get down into the woods." The thought is right, but it turns out we aren't quick enough.

We set out towards the sun across a narrow iron bridge on the high trail towards Nir, shadowing the cobblestoned trade route which at this hour is just a vague and mist-shrouded line far below us. The spring air is frosty. I wonder as I walk if I owe this guy anything in terms of deference, since he's a big deal at the Abbey and all. But then I realize that Jinx wouldn't have paired us up if he was expecting me to be anything but my usual rebellious? immature? surly? self. Fuck it.

We don't get more than another couple of miles along the ridgeline when Snout goes rigid, her tail goes up, and the hair rises off her neck. I stop and look to where she's pointing, but see nothing. Then my threat ring starts to pulse: Three quick hits, a pause, and repeat. Worse, its emerald green stone is flashing black. "Fuck," I say, and Venarius turns towards me.

"We've been noticed," I say. The Gryphon ring senses occult threats from magical or alchemical sources nearly as well as Snout's nose, but in addition can identify and quantify. "There are three of them," I tell Venarius, "and they are the wrongest kind of unnatural."

"What do you mean, Brodie?" the monk questions, frowning.

"Constructs," I tell him, "kymera from the flesh farmers of Immobilin Keep in Rusk."

What I know about kymera, or '*Ky*' as they are often called, is that they are biological mix-and-matches grown by alchemical breeders to possess specialized abilities according to the requirements of their customers. These *Ky* breeders use potions and elixirs to produce mixed body-part monstrosities that are barely sentient, but who nevertheless can perform their assigned tasks exceptionally well.

"What kind are these?" Venarius asks grimly, implying his own base of knowledge.

"I don't know yet," I say, "but judging by how excited my threat ring is, they are predators and we are definitely the intended prey."

"What the fuck," Venarius is saying but I'm already running.

"C'mon," I yell, over my shoulder, "they're closing in and we have to try to make the trees."

Venarius, Snout and I tear ass down the trail towards the distant tree line, Venarius limping but nevertheless keeping up. But then the first construct appears, maybe two hundred strides in front of us, bounding up onto the ridgeline from the scree slope below, trying to block us. We slam to a halt. Now I can see that this particular construct is a shrieker, an enormous wolf/cave bear/other hybrid built for tracking and murder, and named for the godsawful wail it breaks out to stun its prey just before it makes its final deadly leap.

"What the hell is that thing?" cries Venarius.

"A shrieker," I tell him. "An assassin. Thing is, it's built to be impervious to *Floe* magic, at least directly, and our protective medallions won't work against it either."

Venarius looks stunned. "Then what do we do?" he chokes out.

Oh man, can't have the engineer panicking on me now. I pull myself up into my finest steely-eyed pose, trying to shore up his vanishing confidence. "As Brother Janx would say in these situations, we're going old school," I declare, in what I hope is my grittiest, chest thumping voice. "We give 'em guts, muscle and steel."

Venarius looks so stunningly unconvinced I almost laugh. "Wonderful," he says.

The shrieker is gathering speed towards us and I'm grasping wildly for a useful idea. But another part of my brain is thinking that this is really freaking odd. Shriekers are hired muscle, created to kill by *Ky* bioalchemists in godsforsaken and ice-locked Immobilin Keep, way up in the mountains of faraway Rusk. What the hell are they doing here? As far as I know, no shrieker has ever been seen near the Abbey or gone after Testers before. And constructs don't come cheap - only wealthy individuals or governments can afford them. So why come after us? And who's paying the *Ky* breeders, or are they be doing it themselves for their own reasons?

And hell, how did they even get onto us?

I'm beginning to realize that this is no random encounter. For some reason, there are big forces at play here, using some rarified assets to get whatever it is they want. Just fucking great.

I decide about then that maybe later would be a good time to puzzle it out, because things are getting tense. A shrieker is formidable, and three of them together are terror inducing. Like standard cave bears, they have long arms for hooking prey with 4-inch, knife-sharp claws. Thus locked in place, a victim's last image is of a gaping wolf-like snout full of yellowed spikes arching towards their face.

Although they are not particularly smart, shriekers can form a rudimentary plan, work somewhat together, and move fast. As a pack they surround and annihilate prey, and they are in the process of doing that to us. I know this one in front is only showing itself to get our attention, so the other two can make stealthier approaches to our flank and rear. Surround and annihilate. We are so screwed.

Just then, the second shrieker vaults onto the track some two hundred paces behind us, cutting off any hope of retreat. The third must be climbing up the steep grade directly below us on our flank, I realize, and I don't wait for confirmation.

"Brother Venarius," I bark, "get down." I reach into my Tester's vest for a handful of marble-sized steel ripplers, and I throw them underhanded on an angle along and just beneath the very edge of the trail. They explode on contact with the slope, and then fragment into smaller balls which keep rolling along the same vector, which in turn explode/fragment/explode until the momentum of my initial throw runs out. *Floe* magic may not directly harm a *Ky* creature, of course, but I'm counting on the concussions to cause the loose scree of the slope to slide down and scrape the bastard off the mountainside.

It seems to work. Above the sounds of the explosions there rises the signature shriek of the construct, but instead of signaling an attack it fades and then abruptly cuts off. One down, but no time to celebrate though, because just then the other two shriekers launch their attacks.

I have no good ideas for taking on two shriekers charging from opposite directions. Snout is snarling, baring impressive fangs, and generally looking ferocious. Too bad it's a fraud. She is a scout dog with impressive skills, but also the sweetest companion you could ever have. Actual fighting, she apparently feels, is beneath her.

That's when Venarius surprises me again. "I'll get the one behind us, Brodie," he shouts, "and you get the one in front." I have to hand it to him again. If he does what he says, he is definitely not a total asshat.

I turn towards my attacker and see that he is only one hundred strides away now, and closing incredibly fast. I decide to disrupt his timing by charging right at him, pulling my magically enhanced sword as I run. Unfortunately it is just an ordinary blade against this alchemical beast, but it will have to be enough.

I glance over my shoulder to see a fireball from Cael race towards his attacker but the construct runs right through the flames, unaffected. I told you so, dumbass, but oddly I see that Venarius is actually laughing. What the hell?

I turn back to my own *Ky* monster, and we are so close now that I can see he is literally foaming at the mouth. He opens his slavering jaws to emit his scream and I make my move. I reach into my vest for what appears to be a rock, and throw it ahead of me. It erupts into a stone ramp that we use in the field to build bridges or fix washed out roadways. It is made from *Floe* magic so it can't actually stop him. But I think it may confuse him just long enough to cover my actions. Up the magic incline I race and launch myself as high and far as I can.

The shrieker is caught by surprise. He is trying to slow as the apparently solid stone obstacle erupts into his path. He rears up on his hind legs, and his arms go up and out . I fly high off the ramp and descend on him like a bolt of lightning. My sword slams through the top of his skull with a sickening crunch and he is gone before his arms can close around me. A wail dies in his throat.

I roll away and jump up, hoping I can help Venarius before it is too late. I needn't have worried. Damn if the monk hasn't recovered nicely from his fire-throwing rookie mistake. Now he's gone and somehow iced down the section of trail between him and the monster, so that when the speeding shrieker hits it his legs go every which way and he starts sliding forward on his hindquarters at no apparent loss of speed, completely out of control.

Just before the thing collides with him, Venarius does something I don't see that rolls the ground in front of him into a wave. The surging earth slams into the sliding shrieker and, shrieking away, it flies off the edge of the ridge and into the mountain air. Once again, fading wail and abrupt cut off. Suddenly, the fight is over.

"That was cold, Brother Venarius," I say, grinning, impressed. But then I can't help but notice that the fingers of his right hand are actually frosty, and although he looks happy he also looks completely exhausted.

"You were a little over the top yourself," he says, smiling and panting.

My mind is suddenly exploding with new questions, like, what exactly did he just do? I saw him ice the trail, ripple the ground, and shoot fireballs, all without seeing a Monkworks device. How did he do that? Did he channel *Floe* directly? Did he just *do* magic? What the hell? Nobody *does* magic anymore, do they? Who is this guy?

None of this makes sense. Not him, and not the constructs coming after us. What in gods names is going on here?

I leave it for now though as Snout comes out from around a rock she's been hiding behind. Damn if Venarius doesn't get down on one knee and scratch behind her ears, and without so much as a sniffle. "You were magnificent," he lies, as Snout grins and wags her tail.

THREE: WE LAUGH, OR SOMETHING LIKE IT

We reorganize ourselves as ice melts behind us and, it seems, between us. The rock incline I'd conjured is vaporizing in the breeze. Even the dead shrieker dissolves away, so everything appears eerily as it was before the attack. We continue our trek along the ridgeline, eager to get in among the trees and set up camp.

"I've recently discovered, Brother Venarius," I say, "that 'Brother Venarius' is a mouthful to say in combat. Have you got something shorter?"

He smiles, a little ruefully. "As you can imagine," he says, "I've accumulated a long list of nicknames related to my club foot. But I used to have a friend who called me Cael, on account of my first name being Caelum, and I liked that. Will that work?"

"That'll work fine, Cael," I say. "Call me Egon. You said you *used* to have a friend?"

"Brother Bernum. Cecil Bernum. CB to me. He died inside Monkworks," Cael says. "Abbot Tenebrus found him. Unexplained death."

And here I though it's only outside the Abbey that's dangerous.

"I'm sorry, Cael," I say. He nods and we walk on.

"So listen," I say to him after a bit. "None of what just happened makes any sense to me."

"Same, Egon." Cael says.

"And not to make matters worse," I say, "but it occurs to me that, although we launched two of them off the side of the mountain, we don't actually know that the shriekers are dead. They may still be hunting us."

"Well that's scary," says the monk, frowning.

"You said back there that you have heard of constructs, of *Ky*, before," I say. "What do you know about them and the whole flesh farming thing?"

"Well, I don't know them from first-hand experience like you do," Cael says, "like their ability to evade the effects of *Floe* magic. But I can give sort of the political overview I learned in the Abbey."

"Fair enough," I say.

"Well, as you know, kymera, *Ky* for short, are the product of life force manipulation by the breeders of the Kingdom of Rusk," Cael says. "Ky breeders are alchemically enhanced humans and the ruling class in the kingdom, and only they can sit on the High Council in Rusk's capital city of Immobilin Keep. They actually call themselves The Breedership, if you can believe that. The council's overriding mission is to safeguard and expand the major product Rusk's economy depends upon: the sale of quasi-living constructs grown to match the specifications demanded by their customers. To that end, they have created an underclass of enhanced humans called alphas, who serve The Breedership as internal enforcers and as handlers of construct teams working in the Kingdoms under contract."

"Is what the *Ky* breeders do magic?" I ask.

"Some say yes, some say no," Cael says. "The *Ky* breeders use mysterious chemicals on pre-birth flesh to rearrange the natural progression of growth in hideous fashion. That sounds like some combination of magic and alchemy, but the Floendahl monks just think they're butchers and fakers. They say there is no magic in their secret solutions, just craven experimentation."

"How much of the breeders' business involves predatory monsters like the shriekers, and how much is more routinely commercial?" I ask.

"Killing and intimidation is a big part of their business," Cael says, "maybe the biggest. But the *Ky* breeders sell scads of purpose-built constructs for farming, transportation, mining, construction, infrastructure and who knows what all, throughout the Three Kingdoms. At least, they used to."

"What do you mean?" I ask.

"They are not selling nearly as many as they once did," Cael says, "because much of what they do can be more easily and cheaply performed by Monkworks magical devices."

"So we're competitors," I say.

"Very much so," Cael says, and frowns. "I see what you're getting at, but..."

"Yeah," I acknowledge, "an attack on us seems too small and local to address the much bigger problem they appear to have with the Abbey."

"Again," Cael says, "it makes no sense."

"Well tell me this," I say. "Why is *Floe* magic winning this competition with *Ky* bioalchemy?"

"They say *Floe Goes*, and it's true," Cael says. "*Floe* is the Three Kingdom's most versatile energy source. It is almost sentient in the way it seems to anticipate what you need it to do. Once upon a time it only could be manipulated by gifted magicians, but today and for the last 30 years we've been able to channel its power into producing a growing number of problem-solving devices that are relatively affordable, abundant, and easy for everyone to use. *Ky* breeding, on the other hand, is time consuming, expensive, grotesquely unethical, and limited by the ability to grow or otherwise source pre-born flesh."

I chew this over. I mean, I get the whole competition thing. But why did the constructs attack us in particular? It sure didn't seem haphazard; it felt like a well-planned ambush. I mean, shriekers just aren't used for attacks against random travelers on seldom used pathways.

"The breeders or their constructs have never gone after a Tester before, so why now?" I muse out loud.

"To steal the prototypes?" Cael proposes.

"Maybe," I say. "But would they even know what to do with them if they did steal them? Know how to operate them? Fix them? If they are impervious to *Floe* magic, would they even be able to operate a *Floe* device? I don't know. And anyway, shriekers don't strike me as purpose-built for thievery. More like purpose-built for crapping my pants."

Cael laughs. "And you're right," he says. "The Abbey sells devices to Rusk civilians, but I've never known the *Ky* breeder-class, alphas or constructs to use them. Now I can guess why."

"Well, I suppose someone could be paying them to steal the prototypes," I continue, sort of contradicting my own point about the shriekers' abilities. "Someone who knows their value and who wants them now, before anyone else can get them."

"Well sure, it's possible, I suppose," Cael says. "But, either way, attacking us is a dangerous play. Is the need so great that they are willing to risk war with Floendahl Abbey? I can't imagine why."

Maybe he has a point. "Ok, Cael, let's say that's true. So what if the goal was to destroy the prototypes rather than steal them?" I ask. "Maybe to hurt the Abbey financially?"

"Well that would be more in line with shrieker capabilities, I guess," Cael says. "But remember, there are more back at the Abbey. Destroying them would cause only an annoying delay."

I stop and turn to him. "Well, if it's not the prototypes they're after," I say, "and Testers are worth a bint a bushel so it's not me, then the only thing left is you, Cael."

"Me?" he asks, stopping too. "Why?"

"On account of what I saw back there with the shrieker," I say.

He looks at me, and at first I think he is going to deny it. Then he shrugs and owns up to it. "Well ok, yes, it's true," he admits, rubbing his nose with his sleeve again. "I channel *Floe* directly, imprint my will on it. So yes, I'm not only an engineer, I'm also a *Floe* magician."

"What does that mean exactly?" I ask, resuming our march.

"Well," he says, "in olden times, *Floe* magicians were plentiful, and they channeled *Floe* using objects like wands or crystals. Today the magic is device-based rather than object-based, and as that transition took place the number of actual *Floe* magicians declined for whatever reason. Now there are only two: the Abbot and me. Somehow, we don't need objects or devices."

"So you can do with your mind alone whatever a *Floe* device can do?" I ask.

Cael hesitates. "I think so," he finally says. "Maybe even more, but I don't really know."

"How can you not know?" I ask.

Cael looks a bit embarrassed. "Remember my fireball against the shrieker?" he asks.

"Yes," I say, "and I remember that as the shrieker is running right through it you are laughing."

Cael smiles. "That's because up until then I had never tried to conjure one before and I was thrilled that I could," he says.

"So what kind of magician are you?" I ask, sounding pretty dismissive, even to my own ears.

"I don't really know," says Cael sheepishly. "At Monkworks, all I really do is channel *Floe* into the devices our engineers design and manufacture. Whole trays of them at a time. That's basically all the Abbot and I do with our talent. I have way more fun as an engineer."

"So the ice and the ground wave?" I ask. "You never did those things before either?"

"Nope," he says, "and I must say, I clearly don't have the stamina of a device, because I am beat to shit."

I laugh. "Well good for you," I say. "You should be tired after what you pulled off. Still, and no offense, but are you enough of a threat to someone to merit an attack like today's?"

He starts to shake his head but then stops. "You know," he says, "maybe it's right there in front of me. Because here's the thing: Only *Floe* magicians like the Abbot and me can channel *Floe* solutions into the manufactured Monkworks devices."

"You mean if you and the Abbot are eliminated, device production stops?" I ask.

"Yes, for now, at least until another *Floe* magician emerges from somewhere," he says.

"So that sounds like a pretty strong motive," I say, "to someone with something against Monkworks devices."

"But killing me out here is not the same as also killing the Abbot in Floendahl Abbey," says Cael. "All eliminating me does is put him on his guard. He is impossible to get to inside Abbey walls, so device production will continue."

"Still," I say, "I'd check on his current health if I were you, as well as warn him about what just happened to us, in case he has any new instructions."

"Yeah," says Cael, "I was waiting until we camped for the night but you're right. Let's stop for a couple of minutes and I'll do it now."

"Good, but don't take long," I say, glancing around uneasily.

Cael sits on a nearby boulder, and I stay standing to watch the trail. He pulls an ordinary-looking notebook and stylus from his robes and starts writing. A few moments later he replaces the notebook and stands up. "I'm done," he says.

We resume our march. "What did the Abbot say?" I ask.

"His health is fine, he's shocked we were attacked by the *Ky* and will protest, he is happy we are safe, and he will be on his guard," Cael recites. "What you'd expect."

"Why didn't he say 'turn around and come back?'" I ask. "I'd say our travel plan is a bust."

Cael doesn't reply and I look over at him. "Well?" I ask.

Then doesn't he go and surprise me again, because now he is honest-to-gods blushing.

"Cael?" I ask.

"Well, I wasn't going to talk about it now," he says, "but I guess this attack changes some things."

"Talk about what?" I demand.

"My mission," he says.

"Gadget repair?" I ask.

"No, my other mission," he says.

"Whoa," I say to this multi-layered monk. "Explain."

"Back in the tunnel, Brother Janx said the Abbey is trying to raise revenue," Cael says, "and that's true, as far as it goes. But he didn't know it isn't about flagging sales."

"Then what?" I ask.

"Well, Egon, five years ago Abbot Tenebrus created a device that was designed to detect new sources of *Floe*," Cael says. "The device found one, but couldn't do more than point in its general direction. So the Abbot sent Brother Janx on a special mission to locate it. He followed the device's signal along this exact ridgeline, east out into the flatlands, and then far into the desert to the very edge of Nir. There, he was able to pinpoint the location of a second source of *Floe*."

"So why is a second source important?" I ask, still not getting it.

34

"The demand for Monkworks magical devices is increasing every year," he explains, "and we can't keep up with it, Egon. A second source of *Floe* will allow us to build a new manufactory and double our output."

"OK," I say, "makes sense. But how does this all lead to money problems for the Abbey?"

"The Abbot told me that since the discovery we have been secretly stockpiling construction gear, building material and manufacturing equipment in the desert, with the aim of building a complete new Abbey complex over the source," Cael says. "That's enormously expensive."

"I get it," I say.

"The plan now," he continues, "is that before the Kingdoms or The Breedership of Rusk can react, we will have a second Monkworks facility close to up and running at the opposite end of the world."

"Why the secrecy?" I ask, feeling a little lost.

"Because, Egon, everyone and everything in the Three Kingdoms wants what we have, doesn't want anyone else to get it, and will destroy us to get the first or prevent the second," Cael says grimly. "We sell the world's most treasured products, but it makes everyone jealous and suspicious of our every move. We are always on the defensive. Always allaying fears of favoritism towards one Kingdom or one powerful merchant over another. Paying huge taxes which are nothing more than bribes to keep governments' mollified.

"It's the Abbot's great vision," Cael continues, "that having two Monkworks facilities so far apart, yet supporting each other, enlarging each other, fortifying each other, will make us exponentially less vulnerable. Harder to attack. With more leverage to negotiate world politics. Neither the Kingdoms, the *Ky* alchemists, the other clergy, or the wealthy merchants will be able to touch us for a long time to come."

"So where do you fit in, Cael?" I ask.

"The Abbot is sending me out there to run the new manufactory," he reveals. "He said just now that the mission is too important to cancel and that he still believes, even though someone is clearly on to us, that this is the safest and most inconspicuous way for us to travel, as far as the rest of the Kingdoms is concerned. He doesn't want us to attract attention to our desert activities, under any circumstances."

"You're ok with that?" I ask. "I mean, your ass is really on the line out here."

"Abbott Tenebrus is a great man," Cael says, "and I owe everything to him."

"And you agree with everything he says?" I ask, skeptically.

"Well, no," he says, "not always. I mean, we are the only two magicians at the Abbey, and we can get in each other's way sometimes. I'm the junior partner, of course, but still, we can't help but to be rivals in some sense. We both try to keep tension at a low simmer, working on separate projects and the like, as much as possible."

Something clicks into place. "So that's the real reason he won't cancel your mission," I say. "He wants you to have your own base of operations, as soon and as far away as possible, so that his position at Floendahl Abbey remains unchallenged."

"You might be right," Cael says, a little sadly.

"What do you think about that, Cael?" I ask.

"I trust the Abbot," he says simply, "so I'm all in. And, after today, I can see why Janx picked you for this job, even though he didn't like the plan. He believes in you, and so do I. Will you stick it out with me?"

Well, shit. "Janx actually said he believed in me?" I ask, to give myself some time.

"To me and the Abbot," he says.

Well shit again. Weird. "So I'm not here to test prototypes," I say.

"Oh, we need to test them alright. I've planned four stops on our way to the new *Floe* site," he says. "I want to use the tests to make friends with the rich and powerful in Nir, the kingdom that still technically owns the land the source sits on. Also, I designed the prototypes specifically to help me manage the new Monkworks, so I need them to work. Plus, last but not least, they have huge sales potential, I think, so I hope they'll become the first devices mass produced by our new facility."

It is a lot to take in. "So, since only a *Floe* magician can do the job, stopping you stops the new Monkworks. That sounds like another great reason why someone might be trying to kill you," I say.

"It could be, I guess, if they know about it," Cael says, and swallows. "I'm betting you make me unstoppable."

"I wouldn't take that bet," I say. "I'm just a Tester, and those shriekers back there are manufactured in mass quantities. So there are plenty more where they came from, and who knows what other kinds besides. Getting you safely to the far side of nowhere with those things on our asses is going to be next to impossible."

"So what?" he says, brightening. "I'm a *Floe* magician, for gods' sakes. I do the impossible every day."

I laugh. He has a point.

"Look," he says, "what I need is for you to figure this thing out. You've already worked out that there seem to be three possible reasons for today's attack: The prototypes are financially important to the Abbey; I am one of only two *Floe* magicians who keep Monkworks manufacturing from stopping; and I am to be the head of a new Monkworks facility. I need to know which it is, if it is just one, and who's behind it. And I need your help defending the prototypes and saving my life."

Gods, this is crazy. But I don't actually know how to turn the guy down, and it's not like I'm in a position to quit anyway. Testers don't get sick days, after all, and they certainly don't get consulted on policy.

"Alright," I say, casually throwing myself into a swirling cauldron of oh fuck. "I guess we'll just have to take it one step at a time."

"Thanks, Egon," Cael says. "I really appreciate it."

I nod. "Do you have any thoughts about who might want to stop a new Monkworks manufactory?" I ask.

He shrugs. "I guess all those people we were trying to outflank in the first place," he says.

"So the Kingdoms, the clergy, the merchants, and the bioalchemists," I say. "In other words, everybody."

We laugh, or something like it.

FOUR: AND THE SPERM HE RODE IN ON

We finally come down off the ridge and into the tree line. I lead us off trail towards a small, shadowy hill that I know to be a Testers Haven. Havens are scattered around the Kingdoms and there aren't enough of them, but when you reach one you can rest and recover in relative safety.

This Haven is warded in useful ways. For instance, passersby aren't able to see the hill from the trail unless they wear a Tester's combat vest. The path I make to the hill is actually closing in behind us, shifting undergrowth to leave no sign of our passage. Plus, anyone wandering too close to the hill will find the vegetation increasingly difficult to work through.

We reach the top of the rise, and I'm eager to settle onto the flat summit under its sole tree, a truly ancient rowan laden with ripe fruit. The wards make us completely invisible to the outside world, and none of our noise or scents can escape. Overhead, immense branches interlock to prevent an aerial approach, and underneath is pure bedrock.

But beyond all else protecting us are the Guardians, a quartet of immense, magical and mythical Gryphons that ceaselessly patrol the Haven's compass points, allowing nothing uninvited to intrude. They possess an ancient earth-based magic that is much older than *Floe*. Some say *Floe* is descended from Guardian magic, which is why the Gryphon is such a prominent symbol at Floendahl Abbey, and presumably why Guardians are so protective of those connected to it. Half lion and half eagle, they are beautiful and majestic creatures, their perfect naturalness making clear the fact that they were first before evolution split the non-magical species in half.

I drop my pack to the ground and take off Snout's. Cael sits on a rock and removes his modified boot and the wrappings underneath. He starts rubbing some Monkworks cream I recognize onto his damaged foot, with evident relief. "Is it giving you trouble?" I ask.

"It's had an eventful day, Egon," he says smiling.

"That makes two of us," I say, inanely. I walk over to the rowan tree for the bonus feature I really enjoy at Testers Havens: the armory. This magical tree's grape-like fruit clusters - some white, some red, and some orange – are not fruit at all yet always replenish. They are actually bunches of Monkworks munitions, the kind we don't generally sell to the public. There are devices like ripplers and other explosives, noisemakers, stink bombs, incendiaries, fuses, tripwire mechanisms, and a new projectile weapon. I load up with today's attack in mind, pulling the ones I want off the tree and loading them into my combat vest.

Meanwhile, Cael does something I don't quite see, and a large, carpeted tent with two cushioned cots springs into existence, outside of which are two rustic camp chairs, a small table, a doggy bed, and a lit fire. I do a double take.

"My Monkworks shelter devices are a lot rougher than this," I say, jealous.

"Wait until you see the newest models," Cael says, enthusiastically.

Then he does some magical razzle dazzle to produce dinner, and afterwards it's time for the evening's main event. Tester tradition calls for a thorough review of the mission at the first safe camp out of the Abbey. That usually entails examining the prototypes, and reading detailed   instructions about how the devices work and where I will be testing them. But this time the guy who writes the instructions is sitting across the campfire from me.

I pull a compact box out of my pack that contains the four prototypes, and hand it over to him. "Why don't you brief me in, Cael," I say, and push back into my charmed camp chair to listen as leg supports automatically whisper out from underneath to receive my tired limbs. I pull out my worn Tester notebook to record my impressions. Snout snores on her magical bed.

Cael holds the box up. "I truly believe these four devices will change the world, Egon," he begins, quite sincerely. "They are all Finder devices, but unlike any we have ever made before."

"I'm familiar with Finders," I break in. "Last year I tested *Flock Finder*, which allow farmers, ranchers, shepherds and the like to always find their livestock for roundup. Before that it was *Flavor Finder*, to help travelers find ethnic restaurants in strange, new cities."

Cael smiles. "Some of my earlier work," he says. "These Finders are *Fact*, *Freight*, *Family*, and *Friend & Foe*. Truly next generation."

I smirk. "What's with all the F's?" I ask. "I mean, why not also *Fuck Finder* for lonely pilgrims looking for an evening's comfort?"

Cael laughs. "Marketing says the F's are catchy," he says. "I'm just the magician."

He reaches into the box. "Check this one out," he says, and takes out a soft, red leather drawstring bag. In it is a chunk of solid gold cast into the 'M' symbol for the Monkworks manufactory, and it hangs from a gold chain.

41

"This is *Fact Finder,*" says Cael, "a device that finds the truth by detecting lies. They must be either spoken to you or written to you by the liar. I haven't yet made it work if there are intermediaries involved."

"Hmmm," I say, and make an entry into my notebook.

"Yeah," says Cael drily, "I'll work on that."

I nod. "I don't want to hear any more about this one," I say. Cael stares at me. The 'M' softly buzzes and glows.

"It was a test," I say.

"Funny, Egon," Cael says, not laughing. "So then, the mechanics are simple enough, as you can see. For spoken lies, the 'M' medal can be worn around the neck, or under your clothes if you are being discrete. As it just demonstrated, the medal gives your choice of a slight vibration or hum when it hears a lie, along with a slight glow."

"And lies in writing?" I ask.

"Again you use the 'M' medal," Cael says. "Just run it over the writing in any kind of document, like an order or a letter, that is personally written by the liar. The medal will signal the detection of any lies it passes over."

"So tell me," I say, "How is this possible?"

Cael smiles now, very proudly. What a nerd. "It's something I discovered about the elemental nature of *Floe,*" he says, "and really about Truth, too. Think of it like this: *Floe* only knows how to be itself, a forward-moving force. It cannot vary, it can only follow its path. We take advantage of its force, but we can't stop it. Truth is the same way, or wants to be. But as powerful as it is, we all know that it can be twisted and turned. And that's what *Floe* can detect: that little hitch when Truth expects to go one way but ends up somewhere else."

"Interesting," I say, not revealing my own amazement. "And you think this has more potential then *Flock Finder*?" Oh, that was a good one.

Cael sputters, annoyed. "Of course it does," he says, with his compelling earnestness. "Just think what it means. The real criminals will be caught. Dishonest rulers will reveal themselves for what they are. Sellers and buyers can detect who is swindling whom. Women can uncover the con man, and men the reverse. There's no telling the good it will do."

"Good needs all the help it can get," I say.

We're off to a great start. This guy is taking *Floe* devices to a whole new place, beyond practical applications and into thought itself. Of course, it wouldn't do for a Tester to get all gushy about a prototype in front of an engineer, so I'll just keep these thoughts to myself.

Next, Cael pulls out a highly polished black box containing a black velvet drawstring bag. Inside is an intricately carved ivory statue of a mermaid, about the size of a major chess piece, with a design etched into the bottom of its base. "This is *Freight Finder*," he says. He grips it in his fist and presses the design into his pack, like he's using a wax seal. A mermaid design appears imprinted on it.

Cael holds the statue up. "It works like a woodblock used for printing and it never needs ink," he says. "Just press it into something and it leaves its mark until eventually fading away. Each design is unique to the owner of the device. With it you can keep track of everything, instantly."

"Show me," I say, secretly intrigued.

Cael takes the top and bottom of the black box in each hand and twists. It instantly transforms into an upright surface about shoulder width and half that in height, resting on a solid black base, which he places on the table between us. He presses an indentation on the base, and a map-like image of our clearing appears on the dark polished surface, as if viewed from high up. He keeps pressing, and the image changes each time to cover a larger area, from the surrounding forest to the entire Three Kingdoms and encircling seas. He presses one more time and the view is back to the clearing, with a glowing dot where his pack is.

But now there is the most extraordinary apparition above the dot: a window in the device surface with a clear, incredibly lifelike view of the pack as it sits in the clearing between Cael and me. I move the pack with my hand and the hand and pack movements are mirrored on the display. Cael stands up and moves the pack across the clearing. I watch him do it in the surface window. I am floored.

"I see," I manage.

And there's more. Next to the dot it says 'Carrier,' and then Cael's full name. Underneath that it says, 'Manifest,' and then lists a complete inventory of his pack, which turns out to be the usual plus some tools and devices I don't recognize. Then he takes an item out of the pack and comes back to the fire. On the display manifest a line has been drawn through the item, signifying its absence.

I maintain a dignified silence as befits a professional Tester, but really, wow.

Cael holds up a hand. "I see I have to explain to your skeptical ass how this changes the world," he says. "I designed this with some random merchant in mind who owns a fleet of ships, thus the mermaid. At any one time, some ships are docked in foreign ports taking on cargo, some are on the open seas, and some are about to come home. When they arrive, their goods are unloaded and shipped by caravan or lorry or what-have-you to buyers all over the place. If you use this device to stamp what you ship, you can track your goods around the world. And you can see your sailing ship plowing safely across a great ocean with your cargo inside. No more worrying if and when your goods arrive, or where they are anywhere along the way. You can even see who's stealing from you as changes to inventory are flagged."

"I agree it has some potential," I acknowledge, all too calmly for Cael. "By the way, I noticed you only stamped your pack, yet the display lists all of its contents."

"Exactly," Cael says. "An agent can stamp a crate containing a thousand porcelain dinner plates from China, without having to stamp each one individually. The device knows."

"I have to hand it to you, Cael," I say, "your designs have really improved." Oops, that was a mistake.

He looks at me hard then, and for a long moment. "You're the guy," he says finally, pointing at me accusingly. "It's you, Egon. That Tester who always fails my prototypes."

"Yup," I say, grinning, "that's me."

"What an asshat," he exclaims with conviction, and suddenly I'm laughing so hard that he's laughing too.

"Hey," I say, shrugging, "it's my job."

"Well, you take it quite seriously," he grumbles.

Still smiling, I say, "Knowing Janx, he must have loved matching up the two of us for this mission."

"Hilarious," Cael mutters.

After a moment we get back to the business at hand. "I bet you had more than ship owners in mind for this," I say.

"Oh sure, Egon," he says. "Lots of people will be interested in this. Anyone who buys and sells goods can track the process with this device. Or a manager of a trading post, who wants to keep track of inventory to know when to reorder or to track theft. A princess can keep track of her jewels. I can keep track of building materials and crews as I construct Monkworks II. Hell, a general can follow troop movements as they happen over a wide battlefield."

He pauses for a moment, suddenly grinning. "Or you know," he says, malevolently, "I'm thinking now that the Abbey can use it to keep track of its Testers. Your vest would look great with a nice asshat stamp on it."

"You really hold a grudge," I say.

He smiles and nods, looking vindicated. What a dweeb. But still, I like his new stuff a lot.

The fire is cheerful as both darkness and temperature descend. I'm not expecting trouble within the Haven tonight, but I don't think either of us feels completely at ease. I catch a glimpse of a Guardian every now and then, and I'm grateful to. It means that, for one night at least, we're not completely on our own. It makes me realize, though, that we are going to need help if we are to have any hope of completing the mission. Or missions. I keep the thought to myself, but pull out another pad. Cael stirs.

"Let's keep going," he says, and draws the next prototype from the box. It appears to be a deck of faceless cards made of gold, with two posts embedded in it. A gold chain made of a pair of entwined snakes, one of yellow and the other of rose, is curled around one of the posts. Another chain, made of many fine twisted strands of gold, all of them yellow except for one in rose and one in white, encircles the second post. The double snake chain post is engraved with the word, 'Parents,' and the twisted gold chain post is engraved with the word, 'Children.'

"This device is *Family Finder*," Cael says. "It finds lost children and missing parents. As a byproduct, it confirms paternity and lineage."

Cael places the device on the table. He presses on the post labeled 'Parents.' The gold 'cards' of the deck beneath the posts fan out and snap together to form a map of the Three Kingdoms. That was slick.

"So, for example," he continues, "this device will help a mother who loses her child in a crowded market square, or a merchant whose heir has been kidnapped, or remorseful parents who want to reach out to the infant they abandoned long ago. Conversely, it will allow children to locate parents that they are separated from or have been abandoned by."

I have no snide comment. If this works, it's obviously huge.

He presses the 'Parents' post a second time, and the double snake chain wrapped around it seems to come alive. First, it unwinds from the post and wraps its tail around Cael's wrist. Then the double-heads end of yellow and rose undulates across the gold map, back past Floendahl Abbey, down through a pass and out of the Infinity Mountains, lengthening as it goes. Then it circles itself around a city in the woodlands.

"I've never met my parents," Cael says, "but this device is telling me now that both are alive and together in Kinor, the capital city of the Kingdom of Enduron. If they were in separate cities then the snake heads would have separated to identify both locations, yellow gold for my father and rose gold for my mother. If one was dead, then only one snake head would have unwound from my wrist.

"If I want to meet them I can travel there," he continues, "and this Three Kingdoms map will change to a detailed Kinor map. Another press on the post and the snakes chain will locate them precisely, and when we encounter each other the chain will split in two and clasp themselves around whatever limb that presents itself belonging to each parent."

"Do you plan on meeting them?" I ask, admittedly a question outside of testing parameters.

"I wouldn't be welcome at the palace," he says.

"The palace?" I exclaim.

"Oh, I've looked into this before," Cael says wearily. "Everyone without them is curious about their parents, right? Well, it turns out I'm the firstborn son of Enduron's Queen Miran and King Leander. But my deformity came as a shock and a disappointment to them, according to my wet nurse. I was shipped off to the Abbey, along with the nurse, before I was one month old. And before, it should be said, I manifested any talent. I was not considered royal material, apparently."

I sense that Cael feels the same hole inside that I do. "The Abbot sure got the better of that deal, Cael," I say, and surprise myself by meaning it. "You were a fucking hero today, worthy of any court in the Three Kingdoms."

"Thanks, Egon," he says, "but it's an old wound. I've moved on." Yeah, sure, I think. I know I haven't.

"Doesn't that make you an heir to the throne?" I ask.

"Only if I want to pursue it," he says. "But I like what I do and have no need to be royalty."

Jeesh, here's a guy that can turn down a kingship. That's got to mean something. And it makes me wonder about my own situation. This device is suddenly an opportunity I can't pass up.

"In my case, Cael," I say, "my mother died when I was 12, but I never knew my father. Mom was great, better than great, but she wouldn't talk about him. No matter how many times I brought it up, she just said there was nothing to be gained by looking back. After she passed I tried to just accept that this is the end to it, and I will never learn anything about him. But now I'm thinking I should try this thing. Hell, I could be royalty, too."

Cael smiles. "Be my guest, Prince Egon," he says, "but be prepared for disappointment." Instead, I get a mystery.

I press the 'Parent' post and everything reverts back to the original state. I press again, and the map reforms. I press a third time and the snakes chain reanimates and wraps its tails around my wrist. The yellow gold head glides back the way we marched today and circles, of all the places in the world, the Abbey. Floendahl Abbey. My fucking Abbey, where I have lived for years.

"Well shit," I say, shocked. "Can this even be true?"

"It seems clear, Egon, that someone in the Abbey is your father, your living father," says Cael softly. "Maybe even someone you know."

Someone I know? Someone who maybe knows me for a son and has said nothing all these years? Weird. "Can we change to an Abbey map?" I ask.

"I'm sorry, Egon. Not until you arc back there, where the two of you share the same location," he says.

"You'll have to work on that," I say, Tester instincts flaring while being totally beside the point.

Cael ignores me and I fall silent, trying to grasp the implications. Am I a reject too, like Cael, or does my father not know that I exist? Or does he know who I am, but just not care to make himself known? It wouldn't take a fucking genius to know that I have spent my whole life wondering who he is. No matter what, if he knows he at least should have said something. Damn.

I hear a low rumble and feel Snout's snout slide up between my ribcage and arm, and then she's staring into my eyes. I rub her head and feel an angry black cloud lifting. "Thanks, girl, and you're right," I whisper. "Fuck Dad, and the sperm he rode in on."

And then I laugh. "You know, Cael, I'm not sure we are doing the world any favors with these prototypes."

"I hear you, Egon," he says, "but they'll sell, and that's what it's all about."

"What's with the other chain?" I ask.

"That proves paternity," he says, "and identifies the firstborn of each gender. I can't demo that yet," he says with a smile. "You?" he asks.

"Nope, me neither," I say.

Once again we just sit awhile, trying to enjoy what surely is the calm before the storm.

It is full dark by now, but some pale light filters through the leafy overhang from the two moons that are up. It's downright cold now, too, but the *Floe*-conjured fire keeps us comfortable. I realize, at some point, that Snout is restless, pacing then sitting, pacing then sitting. I look around. The Gryphons are nowhere to be seen. Then, suddenly, my ring starts to pulsate. It turns to black, and I count nine pulses before a pause. Then it turns to red and there is one pulse. Oh shit. Wasn't expecting this.

I sit forward. "The shriekers are back," I tell Cael, calmly as I can. "Maybe the two from today, plus seven more. And there's an alpha with them now."

"Nine? Nine fucking shriekers?" he sputters, and stands up. "And with a fucking alpha?"

"I guess I should have realized that the *Ky* who attacked us would have a pack leader around," I say.

"Shouldn't we be freaking out, Egon?" Cael asks.

"Not just yet," I say, as coolly as I can muster. "They can't know where we are exactly, because of the wards. They can't see us, hear us, or smell us. They just know we were on the trail into the tree line, and then we weren't anymore. They're trying to puzzle it out."

"I still feel like we should be doing something," he says.

"They'll be time for that, Cael," I say, "if it becomes necessary. For now, the Guardians are on top of it, so I suggest we try to finish the briefing."

Reluctantly, Cael sits back down. "I guess," he says, monumentally unconvinced. "I'm not used to this, Egon. I've never used magic in combat before. Hell, I've never even been in a fight before. I don't really know what I'm doing out here."

"You're doing fine," I say. "Just trust in your abilities, Cael, because you have an armload. Look at today: You found a great solution under a lot of pressure. No one can do better than that."

He seems mollified for now, and reaches for the prototypes box. The briefing continues.

Cael pulls out a burgundy leather pouch and removes a heavy, highly polished silver cube no bigger than a signet ring. It has a small hole drilled into one side. "This is *Friend & Foe Finder*," he says, placing it on the table, hole side up. He presses a finger down on it until I can see light leaking from underneath. He removes his finger and before us, projected right into the air, appears a silvery representation of the clearing we are in, the hill we climbed to get in here, and some of the surrounding area along the high trail.

"This looks amazing," I say.

Cael, Snout and I are very recognizable solid green shapes next to the silvery tent and fire. There are four more less distinct shapes patrolling around us on the hill, also green, the Guardians. Down along the high trail are several indistinct bodies in dark gray with bright red outlines, plus one all in intense black with a bright red outline. They are moving along the trail and probing the woods to either side.

"Tell me how to interpret this, Cael" I say.

"So this is very interesting," Cael says. "On the display you are seeing my 'friends' and 'foes' in the immediate area, based upon true intention not pretense. There is no hiding possible. The solid green shapes are on my side, and look, I can identify each of you."

He touches my shape in the air, and 'Egon Brodie' and 'Floendahl Abbey' appear momentarily next to it in silver letters, then disappear.

"Now look at these red-outlined shapes," he continues. "They are my opposition, but they would normally be solid red on the display if they were ordinary human opponents. Instead, what we are seeing here with red outlining is my *Floe* device having to deal with the weirdness of *Ky* breeding. These are fundamentally altered creatures, even the human alpha. *Ky* alchemy can't hide intent, but it can suppress identity apparently, so it dampens shape and we can see only the outline of hostility. And here, watch this." He presses on one of the dark gray shapes and no name or nationality appear. "So, what we are seeing are two types of nonidentifiable kymerical creatures," Cael says, "the many shriekers in dark gray with red outlines, and the one handler in utter black with a red outline."

"What about people who have no particular feeling towards you, one way or the other?" I ask.

"Anyone neutral towards me around here would have shown up in white and remain anonymous."

Snout is back on his feet and pacing, and my ring continues to pulsate, but nothing else has changed. Cael sees me checking.

"We've still got time," I say.

He's edgy.

"It's pretty damn impressive, Cael," I say. "Can you widen the display area so we can see any enemies down the trail?"

"Just one magnification from here, out to about 500 strides," he says. He puts his finger back over the hole in the silver cube and there's a pulse of light. When he removes his finger the silvery display has changed to show a wider area around our hill. I can see the high trail in front and behind us, but it doesn't show the trade road far below us. "We now see all nine shriekers plus the alpha," he says, "spread out all along the high trail that's visible."

"So personal features are only recognizable if someone is close?" I ask.

"Yes, so far," he says.

"And this is only as far out as we can see?" I ask, my Tester Notebook poised.

"Watch for future upgrades," Cael says, testily.

"Hmmm," I say, and conspicuously make a note.

"Asshat," Cael growls, and I grin.

Cael rolls his eyes. "Think about what it can do, Tester," he says. "Imagine a king in a troubled kingdom who calls a meeting of all his advisors. Or a captain of a ship with a fractious crew, on a voyage lasting way too long. Or a merchant walking into a meeting with his investors, who may be questioning his stewardship of their money. Or an elderly patriarch of a family gathered to discuss the leadership of the clan. Or even me, for that matter, calling my first meeting of everybody at the new Monkworks facility. For each of us, and for untold others in uncertain circumstances, knowing truly who to count on and who to distrust could make all the difference in the world."

"Go on" I say.

"Imagine a politician speaking to a crowd, or a lawyer facing a jury," he says. "With this device you can tell as you are talking whether you are convincing people or losing them. You gain the ability to alter your approach or pour on more of it in the actual moment. Or how about a protection detail trying to keep someone safe in a crowd. This device can show them where the hostiles are located and identify them by name and origin. Or consider anyone in an organization who suspects someone is leaking secrets to competitors or worse, to foreign governments. This device will point out the malcontented."

"Sounds…goodish?" I say, with some reservations. "Maybe a bit diabolical in the wrong hands?"

"Maybe," Cael admits, "but nearly anything in the wrong hands can be diabolical."

He has a point. I move on.

"So is that it?" I ask brusquely, putting my notebook away. "Is that all you have for me, engineer?"

"Yes, Tester," he says like it tastes bad, "that's ...all."

"I suppose it will have to do," I say airily, and he makes a non-magical gesture with his finger.

"Ok, ok," I say, laughing. "So how are we going to test all of this?"

"The plan is to go to four different cities in Nir," Cael says, "each one with a problem one of these prototypes can solve. Each city is further away from the Abbey than the last, with the last one close to where I need to go to complete ..."

That's as far as he gets, because our time suddenly runs out. One of the Guardians draws up in front of me, and I stand to press my ring to his eagle's forehead. "He says the constructs are pushing closer, simply through blind persistence," I tell Cael, "and there may be fighting soon. It's time for us to go."

"But how, Egon?" he asks. "Aren't we sort of surrounded?"

"C'mon, I'll show you," I say.

I turn again to the Guardian, and press my ring to his forehead. It nods its otherworldly eagle's head up and down, then lowers itself onto its lion haunches.

"Grab your pack and climb aboard, Cael," I say. "Sit at the base of his neck." I shrug on Snout's pack and my own, and we follow Cael up the huge Gryphon's furred back and between his black feathered wings.

The wind picks up, and we are hearing cries, keening, and angry roars now. Our campsite furniture is dissolving away. Overhead, the great boughs shift apart and our prodigious steed begins his leap. "He is protecting us so we don't fall," I shout to Cael. "He's a decent flyer, but with both of us aboard he doesn't have the strength to get us all the way to Aurelia. He'll be able to give us a good head start, though."

All Cael can do is nod.

And then off we go, leaping towards the moons.

FIVE: NO HICKEYS!

It's cold as we fly, and scary – protection notwithstanding – and there are snowy mountaintops both higher and lower than we are. We follow a scar through the Infinity Mountains that's been carved by the Arcano River over eons. Above us, all three moons are out now in their various phases, and the countless stars bunch and scatter in mysterious patterns. The trade route to Nir is far below, clinging to the river's course. We can see the fires from travelers' camps all up and down the roadway.

After several hours we start a steep descent though the dark sky towards a still darker segment of road, the canyon walls narrowing around us. We land on a deserted stretch of cobblestone, one overnight camp a ways behind us and another a ways ahead. No one notices our arrival. I thank the Guardian and it flies off. Cael conjures a small fire to warm us up, and we both sit down with our backs to boulders, still a couple of hours before dawn.

I figure the Gryphon has put us two days ahead of the shriekers, but even though we've completely broken contact I have no doubt that they will be able to track us here eventually. They are known to never give up. They'll chase Cael like the sun chases the moons, until the alpha calls them off or we kill them all. I think about that for a while, and consider our new circumstances.

"You know," I say, since I can see that Cael is as awake as I am, "when we came out of the Abbey and climbed to that ridgeline, it should have been safer for us. No one uses the high trail much anymore, since this trade route was built and patrolled. Of course, you saw how that worked out." Cael smirks.

"So clearly I don't have a great track record predicting events on this mission," I say, "but I can't seem to stop myself from trying."

"Please do," Cael says.

"Well, now that we're down here," I say, "I think our situation changes. We're more in public view, on the trade road. We were attacked by alchemical constructs on the ridgeline, but anything so outrageous like that down here immediately draws attention from Abbey and Nir military patrols. Plus, we have a good head start, thanks to the Guardian, so while I have no doubt the shriekers are up on the high trail tracking us at this very moment, it still will take a while for them to catch up. So, I'm hoping our unnatural enemies ease off for now."

"Sounds good," Cael says. "So we're safe for the moment?"

"Unfortunately, no," I say. "There are still plenty of strictly human dangers to contend with, possibly including whoever is behind yesterday's attack, plus others who we don't know about yet, and the usual ragtag thuggery who may attack us for whatever we carry."

"How big a threat does all that represent?" Cael asks.

"I don't know," I say, "but let's start with this: How do I kill you?"

"What?" Cael sputters.

"I'm trying to answer your question by figuring out how vulnerable you are," I say.

"Ok, I get it," says Cael. "We know I can be killed by *Ky* constructs, because neither my magic nor my medallion will protect me. I am also vulnerable to an attack with a *Ky* weapon, one that is grown like a construct, say from living bone or carapace. Beyond that I can be killed by an intense and sustained conventional attack that overwhelms my medallion, or poison, or a natural occurrence like a landslide, that buries me."

"So then, pretty much everything," I say.

Cael chuckles. "Pretty much," he says, "although if none of that gets me I'll live for a long time."

"I wouldn't buy the rocking chair just yet," I say, and we laugh uneasily.

A breeze has come up and I tighten my cloak around me.

"I don't know much about these *Ky* construct weapons you mentioned," I say.

"We have a few at the Abbey," Cael says, "a sword, some crossbow bolts, and a couple of daggers, locked away for obvious reasons."

"They can't be common," I say.

"They're not," Cael says, "I guess because they're hard to make, not to mention there has never been a need."

"Still," I say, "a Ky crossbow bolt is probably the most difficult thing out there to protect you from."

"There's not much we can do about it," says Cael.

"Ok, well let me give that some thought," I say. "But for now, let's try to get a couple hours of sleep while it's still dark." Cael starts to ask more but then nods. I shift and struggle to wrest what comfort I can from my granite backrest. Eventually, I fall into a restless sleep, troubled by construct weapons.

I awake when Snout alerts with a whine. It's lightening around us in the canyon, and far above I can see the blue and pink sky of dawn from a sun we won't actually get to see down here until after mid-morning. My ring stays quiet. I nudge Cael.

He looks around and stretches. "So, what's the plan for today?" he asks.

"You're about to find out," I say with a grin, "and it's going to cost you some gold."

We both hear the sound of hoofbeats, from what sounds like a fairly good-sized party.

"Up in the Haven last night," I say, "I realized we were going to need help, so I sent a message on a pad I have."

The horses sound as if they're almost upon us now.

"Prepare yourself, Cael," I say. "We're about to be helped, mercenary style."

A strikingly beautiful woman, with glossy black hair like Gryphon's wings, bursts around the nearest bend, all leather, straps and skin, riding a huge white horse and leading a band of close to a dozen other riders. They're all wearing oddly elegant white sashes over otherwise rough and tumble ruffianwear. We are quickly surrounded.

"That's Mika Marianis, ex-Tester," I say to Cael, as she slides off her horse and runs towards me, her steel capped shoes sparking the cobblestones, and her smile lighting me up inside. I open my arms to catch her, and with all the momentum she is able to muster she kicks me in the balls.

My protection kicks in, no pun intended, so no damage done, but all that energy has to go somewhere. I fly up and back several feet and land hard on my ass on the cobblestones. When I can focus again, Mika is standing over me, and she and her compatriots are laughing.

I reach a hand out for some help up and, when she grabs it, I yank down hard and simultaneously scissor-kick her legs out from under her. She falls backward into my arms. I lean in and begin sucking on her irresistible neck, while wrapping my arms and legs around her as tight as I can. She writhes and bucks, screaming "No hickeys!" at the top of her lungs. I ruthlessly ignore her.

When I finally stop munching she says, "Did you really do it, Egon?"

I look at the glistening marks on her otherwise pristine skin and say, "They're absolute beauties, Mika."

"You bastard," she howls, laughing.

"Well, you deserve it," I say. "Will you ever get tired of testing my protection?" I ask, still on the cobblestones, still holding her close.

"Nah," she says, "I enjoy it too much. Not to mention you left me alone out here for four weeks."

"Yeah, sorry, I know how much you miss me," I ill-advisedly say.

"Expect more attacks, numbnuts," she says, elbowing me.

"You know, speaking of that," I say, "it's strange how your medallion allows me to slide inside your guard and devour your neck, while my medallion completely blocks your kick."

"Yeah, I noticed, Egon," she says. "Next time, I'll move in real slow and just start gnawing."

"Ewww," I say, concerned for my stuff. "I'm going to need some new device against that."

"I don't know, you may not want protection," Mika says, her tongue wetting her lips, "at least not right away, and certainly not that kind. Now let me up."

Oh man, that's my Mika.

Snout is sniffing among the horses, everyone is dismounting, and Cael is standing around uncomfortably, when Mika and I finally untangle. We dust ourselves off and Cael comes over. "Mika Marianis, this is Brother Caelum Venarius," I say. "Cael for short."

"Nice to meet you, Mika," Cael says. "So tell me, is this how Testers say hello to each other when they meet up out in the field, you know, like a secret handshake or something?"

"Why, yes it is," Mika says, adjusting her short sword, her protective medallion swinging on a chain around her neck. "It has been, ever since we tested the medallion prototypes. We knew we had a good one when it could handle that kick."

I can tell Cael doesn't know whether to believe her or not.

"So, not to cut the chitchat short," Mika continues, "but you must be the monk we have to deliver to Aurelia. I assume you know we get paid for our work?"

Cael reaches a hand out towards her and it's holding a sack that's too big and too heavy-looking to be something he just hauls around in his robes. I think I know what it is, and he just fucking *made* it.

"Will this do?" he asks.

Mika pulls open the drawstring and gold gleams out. "Very nicely," she says. She turns towards her group of mercs. "Neenah," she yells. "You too, Brik."

Two of her crew disengage from the others and saunter over. They have rings through everything, tats everywhere, plaited hair, weapons anywhere they can plausibly hang, and gold-toothed smiles. Both are over six feet, Brik considerably over. "Neenah and Brik," Mika says, "this is Cael. You already know hickey man."

We all laugh and Neenah says, "How you been, Egon?"

"Good to see you guys," I say. "You're both looking as charmingly lethal as ever."

We horse around some more, and Mika heaves the gold to Brik. "We've got a paying customer," she says. "Divvy it up when we're done here." Brik grunts and swallows the bag in a massive hand. "The five of us need to have a talk before we get started," she adds.

We sit together on boulders as Snout curls up at my feet. "We've got about six days on horseback to reach Aurelia," Mika says. "People we don't know may be coming after us, and some *Ky* constructs and an alpha above us are waiting for a chance to pounce. That about the size of it?"

"As far as we know, yes," I say. "We don't know why this is happening. Best guess is they are either after our prototypes for their potential value, or they're after Cael because he's a top engineer at Monkworks. In either case, I'm thinking Cael and I need to blend in, move fast, and be ready for anything."

"Neenah, thoughts?" asks Mika.

63

"We've got the Nir Sultan's warrant to patrol this section of road, right up into Aurelia," Neenah says. "These white sashes give us some authority to issue orders and move through traffic jams and the like, and I think we use them to hide Egon and Cael in plain sight."

"How so?" ask Mika.

"All we have to do is give them their very own sashes, ditch Cael's robes, disguise Egon's vest, and add some badly needed barbarian style," Neenah continues, grinning. "Then they blend right in with the rest of us savages. For all the world, we continue to look like the Sultan's road monitors doing our duty."

"I like it," I say. "Maybe you can also throw some chain mail on Cael to protect his torso. What do you think, Mika?"

"We can do that, and I also like the plan," she says. "Plus, Neenah and Brik, I want you two a mile out in front of the group as we ride, and ask the SenSen twins to watch our back door. I'll send your relief in four hours."

"Here," I say, reaching into my vest. I hand Mika four devices. "Each of the scouts can carry one of these. Squeeze it if you see something and my ring flashes." Mika nods assent.

We all stand up, and Mika yells, "Mount up." Cael and I don some scruffy thug duds, plus some light body armor for Cael, and throw our official white sashes over everything. Then we hustle to catch up to the departing desperadoes.

"I love your new topknot," Mika purrs, when I ease my mount in next to hers. "I want to learn all about your sexy barbarian self tonight."

The barbarian shivers.

SIX: AMBUSH

And then we're off, Neenah and Brik in front, two other mercs trailing. We alternate the horses between a walk and a trot, and soon we are encountering other travelers, many of them guarded by mercs like Mika's. We also pass a few groups of the scumbags Mika's mercs protect against, us and them eyeing each other warily.

On our left are those travelers heading in the opposite direction, back towards the Abbey and points beyond. Further to our left is the Arcano River, an unnavigable torrent whose banks hold the canyon's only vegetation. Its water is used to carry away human waste and is undrinkable. We carry our own or drink from the springs and streams coursing out of or down the canyon walls.

To our right is slower moving traffic heading in our direction, with the slowest on foot next to the granite. A Tester I know comes by heading back towards the Abbey, and we stop for a few minutes to trade shop talk. I tell him shriekers have been seen on the high trail and he tells me there are small groups of black-armored soldiers on the trade road that he hasn't seen before. Once, our group moves over to let a faster moving Nir military patrol pass us without incident.

We see many travelers using Monkworks devices. They are used to ignite fires that need no fuel; corral kids in disposable play pens filled with toys; and quench thirsts with water bags that refill themselves multiple times. It seems like there is hardly a human problem that Monkworks doesn't have a solution for, if you have the money.

We ride through the deserted campsite of a large group ahead of us, a temporary town of Monkworks tents dissolving into ghostly vapors. My horse shies away from a near disbursed Monkworks outhouse designed for groups, apparently unconvinced the four-holer has dematerialized enough. To our left are three bathing tubs so insubstantial that I can see right through them to the river beyond.

Snout spots two Monkworks dogs, caught frozen by their built-in duration allowances, in the act of fighting over a knotted rope. She races over to join in the fun and jumps right through them. She sniffs and whines for a minute before rejoining me.

I also see some of the displacements caused by the growing popularity of Monkworks devices. Two carts are parked in a shallow divot in the canyon wall, one selling water to refill travelers' containers, and one offering repairs for everything from shoes to wagon axles. Two men, presumably the owners, are sitting at a table playing cards in lieu of servicing customers, as people who used to need them trudge by. I have to say though, in the case of canyon water carts, that I never trusted where the water came from.

There are *Ky* constructs on the road as well, of a more everyday variety. We pass a team of bioalchemical 'oxen' pulling a heavily laden industrial cart that have overly muscled humanoid tops set on four elephantine legs, useful for both hauling and loading and unloading.

Cael rides over now, and he asks about Mika. "So you met when she was a Tester?" he asks. "Oddly, no," I say. "It was after she left. We met in a mercenary pub in Aurelia almost three years ago, where she was recruiting for her posse. She works mostly on this route between Aurelia and the Abbey now, and some of it is even legit."

Cael laughs. "How often do you get to see her?" he asks.

"Not as often as I'd like," I say, "but more often than you'd think. I've been a Tester long enough to have an occasional say about the places I get sent."

"I like her a lot," says Cael, in that open way he has.

I smile. "Me too," I say.

By late morning, we finally catch our first glimpse of the sun. It only has a few short hours above us before it completes its traverse between one granite wall and the other. The bottom of a deep canyon is a gloomy, claustrophobic place to me.

About noon we work our way through a crowd to where the river crosses over from the left to the right side of the road. A Monkworks bridge sitting across the rushing water is blocked in both directions by four guards armed with pikes and wearing black chainmail with red surcoats displaying a wolf-like insignia in black. The same insignia is painted on the doors of a red carriage on the other side of the bridge from us. Parts of the washed out original stone bridge lie in a jumble against both banks.

"Those wolf fucks," says Mika, on the horse next to me.

"What's going on?" I ask.

"This kind of thing happens all the time," Mika seethes. "See that guy in the carriage? Cunning bastards like him use Monkworks devices to throw up a bridge across obstacles like this, before road crews can come in to make repairs. But instead of letting regular folk use it, until it fades out, they charge a toll to let people pass. This road is blocked up because of all the people who can't afford to pay. I'm going to enjoy breaking this party up."

Before she can move, though, three things happen at once: the red carriage pulls away in a big rush, the driver cracking a whip above six huge horses; the bridge guards look back to the fleeing carriage, then face forward, their pikes pointing aggressively; and then my ring flashes once, and again. It's the scouts, raising the alarm, front and back. "Ambush," I shout.

Mika's head whips around. "Attack coming in, ahead and behind," I yell.

Mika starts giving orders. "Stay to the right and keep moving," she barks at the nearest group of civilians. Then she starts splitting her crew to the front and back. "Take out those bridge guards," I hear her shout.

Just then, Neenah and Brik come galloping in, along with the SenSen twins from behind us. They converge on Mika, gesturing wildly. "Egon," she yells. "50 riders in back of us, 25 in front."

"Let's fight the 25," I shout back. "Get across the bridge and Cael and I will take it out." She rounds up her posse and they shoot across.

"Cael," I yell, and he's right beside me. "We go across too, and you destroy the bridge with some of your trusty new razzle dazzle." He nods, grinning that grin again. I throw smokers, and we race over to the other side. Travelers are fleeing towards safety. Mika has set up three archers on foot facing back the way we came, across the soon-to-be-bridgeless roaring river. The other eight of her people are dismounted, most holding pikes, including the four taken from the now dead bridge guards. The horses are tethered to what looks like the old stone bridge's guardrail.

Cael goes to work behind me, although rather than blow the magical bridge up he just sort of dissolves it into a mist. "Hold here," I tell Cael and he nods. I run to the front and quickly use devices to put up magical, shoulder height, stone barriers in front of us. I place them so that they run flush to the canyon wall on the left, but leave a gap a few feet across by the river, now on the right. Then I throw explosive devices at the canyon walls to bring down some boulders and debris, to slow the attackers and help funnel them towards the opening I've allowed them.

I glance back across the river and my smoke still obscures the far bank. Even if they have Monkworks bridge devices, I know now that Cael can knock them down. I hold out hope that the attack from that direction is neutralized. I turn back around, and the 25 horsemen we are expecting are in sight, black chain mail with black wolves on their red surcoats: The wolf fucks.

They charge straight at us, no hesitation. When they get close enough I pull another rippler out and fling it as hard as I can to the left above their heads. A line of explosions burst along the granite wall, and stone and steel shards start to rain down upon the attackers. They swerve into one another, and the horses are having trouble picking their way through the rubble. Their advance is in disarray, and I hear someone give the order to dismount.

A few of the wolf fucks are down in the road, but most come charging towards the gap on foot. "Pikes right," Mika shouts, "and the rest of you behind them."

I fling another rippler, this time right at the attackers' feet, doing devastating damage, as Mika's mercs form a line that covers the breach. They kneel and jam the heels of their pikes into the ground behind them to take the force of the charge. "Egon, with me," Mika yells, and I follow her onto our horses. We wheel and charge back into the fight.

The wolf fucks hit our pike line and there is chaos. At least two of the attackers are impaled on pikes through their chain mail and are screaming, as those behind them continue to push forward. Part of our line gets pushed back and Mika and I hit that hole on the run, slashing with our swords, as our horses lash out with their hooves at the dismounted soldiers. We both take hits but our medallions are holding for the moment.

69

Meanwhile, the pikemen see our charge and they come out of their crouches with a roar. Between their long, lethal pikes and our murderous swords, we demolish what's left of the attackers. A few of them turn and flee, but most are dead. The few wounded but still alive aren't for long at the hands of Mika's pack, who begin picking over the battlefield. "Leave us one alive," Mika shouts.

We hear explosions behind us and swing around as one. Everything on the other side of the river is still covered in smoke, and we can here shouts and curses and cries. Our three archers are pumping their shafts untargeted into the mayhem. It's when crossbow bolts start coming back at them that Cael starts conjuring fireballs and explosives. Now, a rout is on, and soon the sounds of battle fade to random moans and low cries for help.

"Casualties?" Mika calls to her crew. All of her band are unharmed, except for one of the archers who stood with Cael. He has taken a crossbow bolt as he was in the act of drawing back his own bow. It hit him under his elbow and traveled up the bone, partially exiting out of his shoulder. He is down and twisting in the road, blood spraying everywhere. Cael races over to him and kneels. Then there's a shimmer around the two of them, and godsdamn but all of a sudden Cael is helping the stricken archer to sit up. The bolt is out and the blood is stopped. The two of them are actually smiling and talking.

Mika and I look at each other, open mouthed. "And here I am thinking he is just a payday," Mika says, when she gets it together enough to speak.

"He is one for surprises," I reply, shaking my head.

She looks at me. "You should tell me more about that sometime," she says. "Sometime soon."

Just then Brik calls us over to a wolf fuck soldier who is propped up against the canyon wall. "He's on his way out," says Brik, "so talk fast."

Mika kneels down, reaching for her water bag, and the soldier opens his eyes. She helps him drink and asks, "Who do you ride for? Who is the wolf?"

The man closes his eyes and it looks like either he is refusing to speak or he's dead. Mika leans close and touches the man's neck. He opens his eyes one last time then and whispers, "Wolffang," and dies.

"What the fuck," says Mika.

"Who the fuck," I add. I turn to look for Cael, but he's still off helping the archer. "What say we discuss this later," I say. "Right now we need to get moving."

Mika nods, and sets about organizing her crew. I head over to Cael, who looks to me as I approach.

"You seem to have a taste for combat, Cael," I say and he grins. "Not to mention surgery."

"Who knew?" he says and we laugh. "Take a look at this," Cael says, pointing to the crossbow bolt on the ground.

I look, and it has none of the uniformity of a standard issue military bolt. It's bone white and somehow organic looking, as if it grew in a field. Then I get it. "*Ky*," I say, "a construct weapon. Alchemical. Probably meant for you."

He nods, then turns back to the wounded man on the ground next to him. "Egon, this is Noony Bencher," Cael says. "Everyone calls him 'Fletch,' because repairing damaged arrow fletching is his side job among the mercs."

"You're looking surprisingly well, Fletch," I say, "for a man who should be dead."

"Cael, here, put me right somehow," he says. "And it's true, that is a *Ky* bolt," he says.

"You've seen them before?" I ask.

"Never around these parts," Fletch says. "They're more common up Rusk way, I assume because bone can be easier to find than wood."

"You think that's carved from bone?" I ask.

He picks it up using his unwounded arm, and examines the shaft and looks closely. "It's odd," he finally says. "It doesn't look like it has been worked or shaped by tools at all. It almost looks like it grew this way."

"Egon and I think this is grown by *Ky* breeders," says Cael, "just like they grow constructs."

"Well that's pretty creepy," Fletch says. "Does it do any more damage that a normal bolt?"

"The big thing is that it evades our medallions," Cael says, "but its damaging effects are the usual kind. You'll be fine before long."

"Thanks, again, Cael," Fletch says.

Cael nods and smiles, and pats him on his good shoulder.

"Well," I say, "if you're feeling steady for the moment, Fletch, I could use some help from the miracle monk," I say.

"I'll stop back later, Fletch," Cael tells him and stands up.

"We've got to get moving as fast as possible," I explain to Cael, "but I need your help to do a few things first."

"Great, let's hear it," he says.

"First, can you check on any other wounded among the travelers?" I ask. "And then we need the road cleared of debris in both directions, so we can get it back open for everyone."

"Sure, Egon, I'm on it," he says, "but I've spent a lot of my power so give me Snout in case I need the devices he carries to treat anyone."

Oh my gods, in all the chaos I forgot about Snout. What an asshat I am. I look around, increasingly frantic, and don't see him right away. I don't see him right away because he is ten feet above us in a safe little niche in the canyon wall, wagging his tail and chewing on what appears to be a broken wagon wheel spoke.

"You comfortable?" I yell up, and now her tail is scouring the granite wall shiny. "Come on down here, killer dog," I say, "and give Cael some help." She starts working her way down and I head off towards the bridgeless crossing.

Travelers are already lined up on both banks of the river, completely ignoring the carnage, as I arrive. I toss three devices in quick succession: Ramp Up, Roadway, and Ramp Down. If I had needed more length I could have thrown multiple 'Roadway' devices, but they weren't necessary here. Everyone starts moving then, and I move with the flow back towards Mika. My stone barriers have faded, and Mika and company have pulled bodies to the side of the road. They've thrown a tarp over the dead, good enough until the wolf fucks can retrieve their own.

"Cael should be done shortly," I tell her. "He's checking on civilian casualties and clearing up the road."

"I've sent Neenah and Brik out front again," Mika says, "and the SenSen twins are holding here until we depart, and then they'll follow at a distance."

"Where are the twins?" I ask, and Mika points to where Weedom Sen and Marta Sen are sitting with their backs to the canyon wall, amid the debris.

I walk over to the legendary SenSens. "Weedom, Marta, good to see you again," I say.

They smile shyly and say hello. Mika says they both have crushes on me, which I guess explains their uneasiness when I'm around. I get a kick out of that since first, they're nowhere close to being teenagers anymore and, second, because I've seen them work their deadly pikes. It's not they who need ever to feel uneasy around anyone.

"Thanks for the early warning back there," I say.

"Anytime," Marta manages, and they both giggle. I smile and take my leave.

Cael is back up front and clearing boulders off the road with a sweep of his magical hand. "I'm not sure how Testers got along without you all these years, Cael," I say. He blushes again.

Mika and crew are mounted up, and she's holding the reins of my horse. I see Fletch has Cael's horse.

I mount up. "You and your people did good back there, Mika," I say. "Thanks."

"You did good too, my big barbarian stud," she says, laughing delightedly.

In all the action I had forgotten my ridiculous mercenary disguise.

"And I am just getting started, dark temptress," I lamely attempt.

She laughs again. "Oh yes, oh yes, oh yes," she cries breathlessly, and then wheels away to the front of her cutthroat troop.

She is one in a million.

SEVEN: THERE'S NO SEX LIKE MONK SEX

And so the afternoon passes. I see Cael talking with Fletch, and Mika and Neenah are gesturing back and forth about something, tactics I guess. I'm back to fretting.

Less than 12 hours ago we severed contact with our enemy, flew a full two days ride ahead of them, yet get ambushed by human forces who could only be directed to us by the alpha with the shriekers, but who should have been too far away to know our new location yet.

But wait, is that true? Did the soldiers actually need the handler's information to ambush us? Not necessarily, I realize. Not if they were prepositioned on the trade road and waiting for us, ahead and behind, just like the constructs were waiting for us on the high trail. Meaning whoever is after us was prepared to attack us no matter which route to Nir I chose to take. They didn't know for sure, because the decision was mine, and I didn't know for sure until the last minute, when I picked which Abbey tunnel exit to use, and then decided to climb the cliff to the high trail.

So all the wolf fucks actually needed to know to ambush us was that we were now on the trade road in the canyon. Maybe they had watchers on the road to locate us, and when they did, they set up the bridge scene, which they figured both halves of their forces would have time to converge upon. Their timing was only a little off, or else the smaller group of wolf fucks would have arrived sooner to hold the bridge with the four guards. Then we would have been crushed against the river by the larger group coming up from our rear.

Snout is waiting for me on a boulder ahead, and my horse and I pause as first her front and then her back paws step delicately onto the saddle and she curls up in front of me. "You must be knackered after that fight," I say and, I swear to gods, she snorts.

We ride on together, her sort of snoozing and me continuing to pick at the puzzle. It looks like two different groups were set up to attack us before we even left the Abbey, one directed by a *Ky* alpha and the other by someone named Wolffang, who for some reason doesn't care about publicly attacking us. We end up walking into both ambushes, but the bridge attack can't be a response to the failed high trail attack because of the short timing. Logistically, it had to be set up before we arrived on the trade route.

Are the two sets of attackers working together or independently? Again, neither group could know which route I would take out of the Abbey, because I didn't choose it until the last minute. Yet the constructs only set up on the high trail, and the wolf fucks only set up on the trade road. That seems to mean that they were coordinating with each other, covering both routes without wasting resources. And that, I realize, just takes this thing to a whole other level.

If these two groups are coordinating, it means someone is directing it all; someone with the power to move both military and alchemical chess pieces across the board. Could it be Wolffang, whoever he is? He clearly has the power to direct human military personnel. But he would have to be a *Ky* breeder to direct an alpha. Is that who he is?

Or maybe it's the *Ky* alpha who coordinated both sets of our attackers, working under orders from a breeder? He pays or coerces Wolffang into covering the trade road, while he covers the ridge, because surely a shrieker attack on the trade road is too public. An attack on the trade road by a company of wolf fucks is pretty attention grabbing too, I admit, but a magic versus alchemical fight here would be unheard of. Regardless, it's plausible the alpha is calling the shots. Another open question.

Or, is there someone higher than both Wolffang and the alpha who directs them both, someone who is after Cael or the prototypes or both? And, of course, the ultimate question is whether this whole thing is an Immobilin Keep plot with an as yet unknown purpose, or is someone paying Rusk to do this?

All this is making my head hurt.

I realize suddenly that there is a piece of this thing that I can resolve, and that is who the fuck Wolffang is. Cael can find out from the Abbot. I catch up to Mika and suggest we rest the horses. "I think you, me and Cael should talk for a few minutes," I say.

Mika nods, and sends riders forward and back to alert Neenah, Brik and the SenSen twins, and everyone else dismounts. The horses are watered and tethered, and the mercs find places to flop. I wave over Cael and the three of us head into the shade near a cliff overhang. I bring them up to date on my thinking.

"So you think someone knew when we and the prototypes left the Abbey, and the shriekers and the wolf fucks were prepositioned to intercept us along either possible route," Cael summarizes.

"Yes," I say.

"But how did they know when we were on our way and where to intercept us?" he asks.

"I knew for several days that I was going on a prototypes mission," I say, "but I didn't know you were coming until we were in the tunnel. When did you learn you were going?

"The Abbot told me a couple of weeks in advance," Cael says.

"So that is as close as we can get to an answer, right now," I say. "Somewhere in that stretch of two weeks, word leaks that you and the prototypes are leaving the Abbey. Then the ambush plan is set in motion."

"They had to know we were heading towards Nir, rather than Enduron or Rusk," Cael says, "otherwise they would have had to set up ambushes in those directions as well."

"Maybe they did set them up," I say, "but I think you're right. Having to arrange so many ambushes would have made their plan impractical."

"Well," Cael says, "I made no secret of my trip. I had the Abbey diplomats arranging our testing itinerary for days."

"So that's how they knew, then," I say.

"How can you be sure the shriekers and the wolf fucks were working together?" Mika asks.

"I can't yet, although I bet they were," I say. "But I think Cael can get us closer to an answer."

"How so?" Cael asks.

"Contact the Abbot and ask him to find out who Wolffang is. Describe the carriage and the wolf crest. Between him and your diplomats, someone at the Abbey has to know."

"I need to check in with the Abbot, anyway." Cael says. "Maybe he sees some pattern we don't."

"Sounds good," Mika says. "Just leave me out of the discussion. I'm ex-Tester and he definitely won't approve of my involvement."

Cael and I look at her but she says nothing more.

"For now, then," I pick back up, "about all we can do is ride out the afternoon and find a defensible camp for the night."

Mika springs up and starts rousing her ruffians. Before long we're riding out as the late afternoon shadows begin to creep up the canyon walls.

We make camp in a hollow cut out of the granite wall by time. Mika sets a sentry rotation and I use a device to erect a stone barrier between us and the road. I throw another device over the barrier and towards the road, which will alert the sentry to any approaches.

Some of Mika's posse members are using Monkworks devices to raise tents, while others set up a picket line the old fashioned way to secure the horses for the night. Real food is soon cooking on fake fires, and we start to settle in.

Cael calls me over to a tent he's conjured, its flap open to reveal one carpeted room with a luxurious bed and a bottle of wine chilling on ice, and another with a huge steaming tub for bathing. "Thanks, Cael," I say, without missing a beat, "but I'm with Mika now."

"Asshat," he says, grinning, "this *is* for Mika, you and Mika."

"But believe me it was a tough choice," I tell him grinning. "I'm told there's no sex like monk sex."

"And I'm a magician in bed," he says, laughing. "But it is clear to me, after that embarrassing hickey incident this morning, that Mika has captured your heart. So yes, really. All this," he flourishes, "is for the two of you."

I'm honest-to-gods touched.

"For me, you say?" Mika asks, strolling past us into the tent.

"Don't forget me," I say following her inside.

"Thanks, Cael," she says while closing the flap. She yanks off her tunic and heads for the bath. "Let's get this party started," she says.

If you happen to be recovering from say, a deadly ambush, you want to begin by drinking wine in a magical steaming tub with the companion of your dreams. I want it to never end, except I want the rest of the evening to never end more.

Later, we're clean, robed, and on the bed, drinking more wine. "Do you have it?" she asks.

I reach over to the pocket of my breeches and pull out a small Monkworks vial.

"Oh my gods," Mika says, "I was two weeks in the saddle without this."

She turns on her stomach, lays across my lap, and pulls up her robe. "Can you do a girl a favor?" she enquires.

"I'll give it my best shot," I croak out, uncorking the magical Monkworks remedy for bruised skin. Whatever it's made of feels like cool, creamy silk, and it glides onto her tender skin like it was blown on by a soft breeze.

"Hmmmmm," she sighs, and I begin a slow rhythm of brief capture and slippery escape. "You seem to enjoy your work, sir," she murmurs, relaxing under my hands.

"I do," I say, "and it's the worst part of being away from you."

"You mean because you miss doing this so much?" she asks, dreamily.

"Well, no," I say. "It's because I know how much you miss me doing it."

"Oh, not to worry," she says, without a pause. "Rump rubbers are easy to find where I travel. I like to keep them stationed a day's ride apart."

Oh, she's good. "Sounds like I may have had to share you tonight," I say. "Maybe get assigned to just one cheek."

She sighs. "Now that is an interesting thought," she says, languidly, "but I'm afraid I'm just an old fashioned one guy/two cheeks sort of girl."

"Well, that's a relief," I say, continuing my never ending quest to cure saddle soreness in the most seductive way possible.

"Does this robe make my ass look fat?" Mika asks.

"No, but your ass is making this other thing look huge," I say.

She shifts on my lap. "Oh my, you *are* a barbarian," she practically growls, and I begin to maraud.

EIGHT: HAVE A MAGICAL DAY

Next morning, we are jolted out of bed by a series of rapid explosions, and Mika and I scramble for our swords. I grab my vest as we race out of the tent, where we see the camp has similarly erupted. We follow the racing crowd to a small gap indented into the walls of the granite canyon, and we can see smoke pouring out of it along with flashes of flame.

We race to the front of the crowd of mercenaries and see Cael, maniacally gesturing, as fireballs and concussives streak off his fingertips and explode against the stone. As he spins towards us I see he has that gleeful grin from the construct fight plastered on his face. He has definitely found a new hobby.

But then Cael sees us all gaping at him, swords and pikes drawn and, there he goes again, he blushes. "Just practicing," he mumbles, sheepishly. "Sorry." Well damn if just then the rest of us don't start hollering and cheering wildly. Back comes his grin and then he's screaming at us: "Did you see that shit? Magic is SO epic."

The excitement over, everyone scatters to their morning chores. Mika and I head to our fire to see about breakfast, as our luxurious tent vaporizes behind us. After a while, Cael comes over and he's all business again, saying he has heard from the Abbot.

"Abbot Tenebrus says he will contact Immobilin Keep and the *Ky* breeders there to personally protest, and to ferret out what they are up to," Cael says. "And he congratulates us both on staying safe."

"So it's definitely Rusk?" I ask.

"He says Wolffang is *Lord* Wolffang, Rusk's all-human ambassador to the royal court in Aurelia. The Abbot doesn't know why Rusk would be involved in an attack on us, or if someone is paying them, but says that we may just be victims of transactions between individuals rather than government-level policy."

"Regardless," I say, "this just makes me more suspicious that the *Ky* Breedership on the High Council and Wolffang are coordinating together."

"So what does this add up to?" Mika asks.

"A high level conspiracy, I guess," I say, "regardless of whether it's a governmental action or something initiated by rogue individuals."

"So what you're suggesting," Cael says, "is that someone in Immobilin Keep or someone paying them wants me or the prototypes, and finds out when we leave the Abbey and which direction we are heading. That mysterious someone then makes arrangements to cover both our possible paths, using Wolffang out of Nir to cover the trade route, and shriekers from wherever to cover the high trail."

"Yes," I say. "I think that sounds right."

"But who would have the juice to order something like this?" Mika asks. "To openly attack Abbey officials in public who are performing their authorized duties, using both alchemical and military assets?"

"I don't get it either, " I say. "There must be someone big behind the scenes giving the orders, someone who can brand our attackers as renegades and deny responsibility, if it comes to that."

"Fucking rat's nest," Mika says.

"Did the Abbot say anything else, Cael?" I ask.

"Just one odd thing." Cael says. "He suggests we stay away from Tester Havens for the rest of the mission."

"What? Why?" I ask, surprised.

"I think because of how close the shriekers came to actually locating us inside the Haven," Cael says. "He feels they all may be compromised somehow."

I think about that. "Interesting," I say. "Did he order us to stay away?" I ask.

"No," Cael says. "It just sounded like he was offering helpful advice."

"None of this adds up to me," Mika says, uneasily. She turns to Cael. "And I don't make a habit of questioning my paying customers."

"But?" Cael asks.

"But," Mika says, "you are no ordinary Monkworks engineer. Before I and my crew get in any deeper with you, I want to know who the hell you really are, and why these people and things are so intent on attacking you."

Cael looks over at me and then back to Mika. "I'll tell you what I can," he says.

"Start with miraculous cures," says Mika.

Cael chuckles. "Oh that," he says, and sighs. "I am a *Floe* magician, which means I don't need devices to channel *Floe* magic. It seems I am able to do some amazing things with it, like healing Fletch, although I didn't know that until I just did it."

"Why kill you for that?" Mika asks.

"Not sure, but maybe because only the Abbot and I are magicians, and only the two of us can channel *Floe* into the devices we produce. Without us, Monkworks stops manufacturing."

"So why are you out here, at risk?" she asks.

"I'm also on a second mission," Cael says, "a diplomatic mission, I guess I can call it, that comes direct from the Abbot. It is very important to the Abbey, and it has the potential to shake up the Three Kingdoms power structure."

"I see," says Mika. "So that's another possible motive for all this."

"That's right," Cael says.

"So the prototypes are just a smokescreen?" Mika asks.

"Not at all," Cael says. "Egon and I really are on a mission to test, repair and certify four valuable prototypes for the Abbey," he says.

"Wait, repair?" she asks. "You mean repair in the field, instead of sending defective devices back to the Abbey to be fixed?"

"That's right," Cael affirms.

"You can do that? Just fix devices, wherever?" she asks, incredulous.

"Fix them, build them, whatever," says Cael.

"You really *are* a magician," she says, and we laugh. "Ok, but why change the normal process?"

"Abbot Tenebrus has high hopes for these prototypes," Cael says, "and he is moving up the production timelines to start their revenue streams as soon as possible."

Mika thinks about all this for a bit. "So I think I get the picture," she says, finally. "There are reasons to go after you, and reasons to go after the prototypes. In either case, your secret gets out to someone before you leave the Abbey and you are trying to figure out who. That the size of it?"

"That's about it," Cael says. "and I'm sorry we didn't discuss this sooner. I can only say that I feel like I can trust you, and that you and your people deserve to know whatever I can tell you. But listen, there's a lot that we just don't know yet, and some stuff I can't talk about, so if you want to pull out, I understand."

Mika pauses a couple of beats. "Your gold is good to Aurelia," she says eventually, looking troubled. "After that we have to talk again." She walks away to organize our departure.

Cael looks at me. "I appreciate your keeping the mission secrets to yourself," he says.

I shrug. "They're your secrets to tell," I say. "Mika understands that. But I think if we want her help beyond Aurelia, you are going to have to tell her more."

"You're probably right," he says.

About mid-morning, Snout alerts. She is roaming out in front of us, heading towards a blind curve, and goes rigid. There's no one on the road around us at the moment, but we have no visibility to the front. My ring is silent, the horses seem calm, and Neenah and Brik have been through here ahead of us. So why am I jumpy? Mika leads us forward.

I catch up to Snout and together we round the corner to find a heavily-laden cart with a broken axle. A man stands beside it, awkwardly trying to hold a small, 'M' labeled device box and an unraveling scroll. "What the fucking fuck?" he yells in exasperation. A woman sits on a boulder in the shade, looking annoyed. Both of their horses are head down, waiting patiently in harness. The scene looks rehearsed.

I brace for another ambush and Mika puts a hand on her sword. Fletch strings his bow and starts scanning in both directions. Cael, seemingly unaware, leads his horse over to the cursing cart man. "Watch that device," I hiss at Cael, but I don't think he hears me.

"Can I give you a hand with that?" Cael asks.

"Fucking Monkworks directions," the man barks in reply, brandishing the scroll, words tumbling out in a sputtering rush. "The fucking monks write one sentence of directions. One godsdamned sentence." He waves the scroll. "I thought all monks had to do all day was write, but I am completely and utterly wrong. Because the rest of this is just stupid fucking pictures."

"Well maybe I…" Cael starts but cart man keeps going.

"Listen to this shit," he grouses, and starts to read from the scroll with seething sarcasm: "'All of us at Monkworks Roadside Assistance thank you for entrusting the maintenance of your carriagewagoncartcoachbuggy-gigorother to us.'" He waves the scroll. "That's their one sentence of instruction. You must be fucking kidding me. Because let me tell you, all of us here on the fucking roadside don't thank Monkworks Roadside NoAssistance for its uselessridiculousinsincerestupidcompletefucking-wasteoftime directions."

Mika keeps us slow-walking by. The woman on the boulder is shaking her head from side to side.

"What's in the box?" Cael asks patiently, and cart man thrusts it up to him so spasmodically that I stand in my stirrups and half draw my sword. Oblivious, Cael takes the box and pulls from it a miniature wagon wheel.

"You won't do any better than the last guy," cursing cart man says, still fuming about the directions. "First you have to scroll through pictures for your type of rig, then you have to scroll through the kind of repair you need, and when you finally get to where you're supposed to be, the pictures are fucking indecipherable, something that looks like pushing while pulling or twisting while whatevering. And I've got all this shit to deliver," he says and finally peters out.

My ring is still quiet.

I see Cael squeeze the device's hubcap and it depresses with a click. He holds both sides of the wheel and pulls, and it snaps into a rectangle. Then he holds both ends and twists.

The carriage lurches. The horses' heads jerk up. Snout jumps back. A heavy load of raw oak barrel staves shifts back into position. The wheel begins to straighten, pulling the cart level, and the ends of the broken axle rise off the ground and visibly knit back together.

I am past the cart now, and ahead I see Mika visibly relax.

"Well what the fucking fuck?" cart man says.

"Have a magical day," says Cael, and the woman chokes out a laugh.

NINE: HOW DO WE KILL AN ALPHA?

We continue on by as cursing cart man and his companion fall in some ways behind us. I try to relax, too, by attempting to identify what is making me so uneasy. Cael catches up to me and I congratulate him on his outstanding customer service.

"Your satisfaction is guaranteed here at Monkworks Roadside Assistance," he drones, and we laugh.

Then we ride on in companionable silence until I bring up what I finally realize is bothering me. "We need to give some thought to the next attack," I say to Cael, "because there is going to be one, and it will be the worst yet."

"What are you thinking, Egon?" asks Cael.

"I'm thinking about the alpha we saw at the Haven."

"I see what you mean," Cael says. "This is a major commitment by someone, and the alpha is not going away."

"They attacked us with two shriekers and then it becomes nine plus the alpha," I say. "Next comes 75 horsemen who are connected to the *Ky* breeders of Immobilin Keep through their ambassador to Nir. It doesn't seem like they are giving up, whoever they are. In fact, I think they will order the handler on scene to escalate."

"You're now convinced that they would dare an alchemical attack against magic on the trade route?" Cael asks.

"I think it's better for them than attacking us in Aurelia," I say, "which might cause some sort of international incident. And I don't think they have a choice, given how determined they seem to be. If I were them I'd try to isolate us out here, then attack using both constructs and the wolf fucks again."

"Maybe Mika and company will have some ideas about where we can be isolated on the road ahead," Cael says.

"Let's bring it up at lunch," I say. "Meanwhile, let's talk about alphas."

"Ok," he says, "what about them?"

"You talked about their crossbow bolts and other alchemical weapons," I say. "What else do they have that can hurt us? Start with how they control their packs of constructs."

"I don't actually know much, Egon," says Cael. "Just the scuttlebutt and speculations I've heard in passing in the Abbey. But what I gather is that the alpha may use scent to communicate with and control the constructs. My understanding is that it's a very sophisticated system, almost telepathic in its effectiveness, and no one knows how to disrupt it. A controlled pack is exceptionally dangerous."

"Interesting," I say. "What else do they have?"

"They have bodies altered for immense strength and speed, and their five senses are inhumanly acute," Cael continues. "All alphas are proficient with sword, dagger, and crossbow and, because the *Ky* breeders are alchemists, their alphas are all equipped with chemical-based personal weapons including hand-held explosives and incendiaries. And, as you informed me, they cannot be harmed directly by *Floe* magic, but because they are altered to resist magic they can't use *Floe* devices either, including weapons and defensive medallions."

"At least some good news there," I say. "So how can we protect ourselves from one?"

"The only defense is a physical barrier," Cael says, "one of sufficient strength to weather alpha alchemical attacks."

"But we may be on the move when they attack," I say, "rather than behind prepared fortifications."

"Nevertheless," Cael says, "when the attack starts we need to get behind something solid or we are all dead."

"So if the alpha had attacked us together with the three shriekers on the high trail," I muse, "we would have died."

"Afraid so," Cael confirms.

"Ok, that's a problem to work on. Now what about the shriekers?" I ask.

"A shrieker is made alchemically, using rarefied potions and elixirs," Cael says. "It's a serious physical threat. Its teeth and fangs can hurt us all, including me. Again, my magic can't hurt it directly and medallions are no good. Plus there are other kinds of constructs with gods know what abilities out there. The good news, if there is good news, is that none of them are particularly smart as individuals."

"Like those we fooled on the ridgeline," I say.

"Exactly," says Cael.

"So let's talk about offense now," I say. "How do we kill an alpha? Do they have a weakness?"

"Alphas, and constructs as well, are vulnerable to physical attack," Cael says, "or to an indirect magical attack that has a physical effect, like a landslide. But it will be next to impossible for any of us to get close."

"Can a non-magical arrow kill them?" I ask.

"It would have to hit the right place," Cael says, "but yeah, it's possible."

I get an idea. "So tell me this," I say. "I know we can't make some sort of magic arrow because *Floe* won't hurt them. But what if we magically enhance our bows to be stronger, easier to draw, and somehow way more accurate, but leave the arrows as they are. Would that work?" I ask.

"Well, yeah," Cael says. "I think it might."

"Good. Now one other thing," I say. "Is there some existing Monkworks device, or one that we can modify or quickly create, that somehow gets us around this magic prohibition, for either offense or defense?"

"Nothing comes to mind," Cael says. "I'll think about it."

"Ok, so here's what we've got," I say. "We can anticipate an attack before Aurelia in an isolated spot on the road. The attack probably will include humans, constructs and an alpha. Yes?"

"It's plausible," says Cael.

"You are most effective against humans," I continue. "You are also effective in indirect attacks against *Ky* opponents, as well as rapid defensive arrangements like your icing move and wavy earth. Correct?"

"Sounds right," says Cael.

"Then as for the rest of us unmagical types, we are highly vulnerable and must first stay alive; then we must use devices and non-magical weapons to kill humans, alphas and constructs. Correct?"

"It all almost sounds feasible when you say it," says Cael. "Let's run it by Mika when we stop."

TEN: WE NEED MORE MERCS

A while later we settle in for lunch in a narrow grassy strip beside a bend in the boisterous river. Mika organizes the crew and then seats herself on the grass with Cael and me. "'Have a magical day,'" she says to Cael. "Seriously?"

"I took my turn in Marketing at the Abbey, just like everyone else," he says defensively.

"They never tried me in Marketing," I say, and Mika laughs.

"You'd be like, 'Have a magical day, asshat,'" she says.

Cael laughs. "Have a magical day or you will die," he mimics, recalling my perhaps too dramatic tunnel instructions of what, only two days ago? Mika howls.

"You have him down perfectly," she says.

"If you two are done besmirching my character, this is a working lunch," I say, trying to rein them in.

"Be-whatting?" asks Mika.

"It means highlighting," says Cael. "Egon wants us to stop highlighting his character."

"Asshats," I mock grumble, "the both of you." They laugh.

"So anyway," I say, when they wind down, "marketing genius here and I spent the morning ride trying to figure out what we're facing ahead, and what to do about it."

"What's it look like," says Mika, suddenly all business.

"It's not good," I say, and give her a quick summary.

"Fletch," she yells, and the archer comes over. "Send a couple of bodies out to replace Neenah and Brik, and tell them to join me here. You join us too." Mika turns back to us. "I want them to hear this."

We use the break to eat something, and when everyone is assembled I repeat the summary.

"OK," says Mika the organizer, "let's take it in order. Nina, Brik, where on the road between here and Aurelia can we be isolated and attacked?"

"Somewhere between two bridges," says Neenah. "We pass the first bridge and official-looking wolf fucks behind us stop traffic because of a fake landslide or something. Same with the bridge ahead. And if the stopped travelers hear explosions and the like, they'll just think it's part of the fix."

"That's good, Nina," Mika says.

"Here's something else to consider," says Brik. "The narrower the canyon the better for us because we're outnumbered. So they'll hit us where the canyon widens and they can flank us."

"Ok," says Mika, "another piece of the puzzle."

"There's another thing," says Neenah. "If the alpha and the shriekers are going to fight us directly, they need to come down off the high trail to do it." Mika and I nod. "The only place to do that before the Nir & Far Inn is Pagan's Notch."

"I think that's right," Mika says. "Tell us about it."

"The Notch is the name of the general area where there is a break in the ridgeline and the high trail dips to within only several hundred feet of the trade road," Neenah says. "A spring flows across the high trail up there and runs down the canyon side until it meets up with the trade route, where a culvert carries it under the road to join the river. Anyone hardy enough can follow the spring up or down between the high trail and the road, if they have a reason to."

"On top of that," Brik says, leaning in, "near where the spring meets the river the canyon widens considerably. It's the only really wide spot in the road I can think of until we get out of the canyon and into the foothills at the Inn.

"And here's the clincher," Neenah says. "There are bridges around there, too, both before and after you get to the Notch, which can be blocked to isolate us."

"That sounds like the place." Mika says, then reconsiders. "But could they attack us at the Inn instead? They would have access from the high trail, plus it sits on a big open plateau for them to use to outmaneuver us."

"Pretty public," Brik says. "No real way to isolate us there."

Mika nods. "Ok, I'm sold." she says. "So let's concentrate on the Notch. Tell us more about it."

"Well, as we ride into the area the canyon wall swings out to the right away from the road," says Brik, "while the river swings way out left in a deep crescent bend until it comes back close to the road near the culvert. Inside that river bend is a big grassy meadow that sees a lot of campers. You can't quite see the spring from the meadow, as I remember, because the road curves."

"I remember the meadow," says Mika, suddenly energized, "and it's not terrible for us. Not at all. The meadow is way more deep than wide because of how the river runs. If we're set up in it facing the road, with the canyon wall beyond that, we'll have fast moving water both behind us and on each flank. We may be able to defend that, if we can protect the front."

"It gives the archers room to work, too," says Fletch.

"So we're all agreed?" I ask. "This is the most likely ambush spot?"

Everyone nods. "As long as we're right that they want to keep it as quiet as possible," Cael says.

"Agreed," Mika says. "I want to get to your role in this fight, Cael. But before we do, Egon, paint us a picture about how the ambush unfolds."

I pause a moment before answering, trying to raise a clear picture in my mind of both the place and our pursuers. "I think they will go ahead and let us set up camp in the meadow before they attack. They actually want us in a fixed location rather than on the move, not only because this is the wide spot they want us in but also because they have to coordinate riders coming in from two directions, as well as their own descent from the high trail. Their lack of coordination cost them at the stone bridge skirmish."

"Good point," Mika say.

"So then those 50 wolf fucks Cael and Fletch drove off yesterday will close the road at the bridge behind us," I continue, "and others will do the same in front of us. Suddenly we'll notice there is no traffic on the road."

"Where's the alpha?" Cael asks.

98

"I think he and the constructs will come down from the Notch between the time the roads get closed and the time we arrive at the meadow. They will position themselves ahead of us on the road, to be ready to attack us whether we come straight on or decide to camp."

"How does their attack develop?" Mika asks.

"I see us settling in for the night, and it's getting gloomy in the canyon as the sun goes down," I continue. "The alpha is fine with the lowering visibility because he and his shriekers have no problem operating in the dark. Suddenly, Snout alerts, and then my ring buzzes and turns black and red. I think the shriekers come first, because they're fast and freaky. I expect they'll come in a rush from the road ahead to the left of our position. They'll try to overwhelm us."

"What comes next?" asks Mika.

"Then," I say, "while we are engaging the shriekers, I expect the wolf fucks will hit us to take advantage of the disarray the monsters may cause. And after them I think there will be some kind of dedicated team of constructs and humans whose sole mission will be to take out Cael."

"We can't let them have our marketing genius," Mika says, and Cael grimaces out a smile.

"So now we get to the alpha," I say. "I have the least feel for what he may do. Does he direct the troops from a safe distance, or does he go in with the shriekers? Does he concentrate on Cael or on the rest of us? But no matter what, if he chooses a hands on approach he's vulnerable to ordinary weapons or to some natural occurrence that either Cael or a device can create, so going after any of us could be dangerous for him."

"So best guess," Mika says.

I look at her, trying to reason it through. "You know, I think his main concern, maybe his only concern, will be killing Cael, maybe secondarily taking the prototypes. He's under pressure. The bosses want results. So if I had to guess, I'd say he leads the dedicated group of assassins."

"That sounds right," says Mika.

"Oh goodie," says Cael, and we laugh.

"So ok, Cael," says Mika, "Now it's your turn. Where do you see yourself in all of this?"

"From the time Egon's ring signals the start of the attack, I figure I will have one to two minutes to build our natural defenses," Cael says. "I will run out to the road and hit the canyon wall with explosions, which will knock debris into the cobblestones to hinder the attack. Then I will turn towards our camp and push up earth into an embankment across the meadow, so attackers will have to run down the incline my earthmoving has created and then confront an earthen wall looming over them. Basically, they will be fighting up from a ditch. Egon, Mika and her crew can shelter behind this barrier or come out to fight on its raised lip. When I'm done, I'll jump up behind the embankment with the rest of you."

"Wait," says Brik. "Mika tells us you are a magician and have certain powers. Are you sure you can do all this?"

"Am I sure?" asks Cael. "Honestly, no, but I've sort of done the earth moving thing before, up on the ridge with Egon, although on a much smaller scale. So I feel like I can, the same as I felt when I healed Fletch." Brik looks skeptical. I see Cael catch it. "You know, you're right," Cael says. "We have to know for sure."

He stands up and walks away from us and from the relaxing mercs. He stands in the road and faces a vacant part of the grassy strip. Both arms come up from the sides and he seems to push. A

20-stride section of ground is pushed down somehow and then glides away from him towards the river, slanting down at an angle, pushing soil up in front to form a high embankment.

All of us are standing now, and Mika lets out a whoop and a whistle. Mercs start to clap. Cael looks embarrassed. He walks around the embankment and is lost from sight for a minute. Then the embankment rolls back in the opposite direction, to leave the meadow looking almost untouched. We can see Cael again as he lowers his arms.

"Show off," yells Brik, as Cael heads back towards us.

He sits back down looking none the worse for wear. "I think that was worth knowing," he says. "Good call, Brik."

We go back to our discussion. "Tell me, Cael," Neenah says, "why not build the embankment as soon as we reach the meadow?"

"I've been giving that some thought," Cael says, nodding. "I think we could be watched so, first, I want them to make their plans not knowing about the embankment. I want it to be a nasty surprise. Secondly, I think if I build it early it could precipitate an early attack, maybe before the camp is fully prepared."

"Makes sense," says Neenah. "Will the shriekers be able to jump the barrier?"

"Unfortunately, yes," says Cael. "It will blunt their attacks, but I don't think I have the power to build an embankment tall enough to completely hold the shriekers out. From what I've seen of them, the best I can hope to do is just slow them down somewhat, and possibly make them targets for our archers as they come over the top."

"Will there be gaps in the embankment?" asks Brik.

"Yes," says Cael. "One each near the riverbanks on our flanks, or I risk flooding us out as I move the dirt around."

"Alright, so now you've jumped back behind the barrier with us, Cael," says Mika. "What's next?"

"The wolf fuck riders are next," Cael says. "It will be hard for me to manage riders coming in from both sides simultaneously, so I think we should plant devices on the road after we cross the first bridge and after the last of the travelers pass us."

"Good thought," I say. "Explosives, I presume?"

"Yes, anything we can think of that will hinder or kill them," Cael says. "I hope we can reduce or maybe even eliminate what they have coming at us from that direction. We don't know how many they'll be from the other direction, ahead on the road, but I will be able to throw all the whiz bang magic I have at them until I tire. After that, we'll have to fight them with devices and steel."

"There's one other thing we'll need from you at the beginning of the fight, Cael," I say, "and that's light. Hopefully, out in front of the barrier so we can stay a bit in shadow."

"Not a problem," says Cael.

Mika turns to me. "How about you, Egon," she asks . "What do you plan for yourself?"

"With your permission, Mika," I say, "I will borrow Fletch here and together we will protect Cael from the assassin crew and kill the alpha."

"That's a pretty tall order," Mika says, "since neither of you has protection from an alpha attack."

"True, but after what Cael just described of our defenses, I realize that we have a really potent advantage," I say. "The alpha will have to come to us to get to Cael. That's key. That means we don't ever have to show ourselves. We fight from behind Cael's embankment, concentrate on blocking up the gaps on the flanks, and have a reserve in the center for anything that comes over the top. Our archers cover everything within our perimeter and along the top of the embankment, throwing support wherever it's needed."

"That is good thinking, Egon," Brik says, "but how does it help you protect Cael and kill the warlock?"

"It comes down to this," I say. "Cael is able to stay behind the barrier within our perimeter while the alpha has to fight his way inside. That protects Cael from the *Ky's* construct weapons like crossbow bolts, and it lets us prepare for the assassin team's attack. Remember, the handler and his pack are vulnerable to our non-magical weapons, and Fletch will be wielding an enhanced bow that can kill anything they throw at us."

"An enhanced bow?" asks Mika.

"It's Egon's thought," Fletch says, "but I'll work with Cael to figure it out. Essentially, the idea is to use magic bows, since we can't use magic arrows effectively against the alpha or the constructs. All of us archers will have them."

"What improvements will you make?" Mika asks.

"I want to improve targeting, make drawing easier and impacts harder, and increase our firing speed," says Fletch.

"That's all possible, Cael?" asks Mika.

"Definitely," Cael says.

"One more thing regarding the assassin team," says Fletch. "I think Cael needs to be wearing armor for if and when they get inside the perimeter. It's the only thing that might deflect a bolt."

103

"Good idea," says Egon.

"Ok with me," says Cael. "I'll sit in a hole if you want me to."
We laugh.

"OK then," says Mika, "so that leaves the rest of us. I see
myself with the archers in the center, where I can see everybody as
conditions shift. I may be able to move people around, and I can
fill in with pike and sword as needed. Neenah, Brik, how do you
see things?"

Neenah starts out. "It sounds like our main job, meaning the
mercs, is to mind the gaps, beat back the shriekers coming over the
top, and kill any wolf fucks that get through. Is that about it?"

"Sounds right," Mika says. "Can you do it?"

"Sure we can do it," Neenah says, "depending on the
depending on."

"What does that mean?" Mika asks.

"We don't know the numbers against us," Neenah says, "or
how hard these shriekers will be to kill, or how easy it will be for
them to get over the embankment. Things are a bit up in the air,
wouldn't you say?"

"OK," says Mika, "let's say 50 soldiers and 10 shriekers, 10
very hard-to-kill shriekers, who will be able to get over the wall
with a brief hesitation at the top. With me and the archers in
support and Cael, Egon and Fletch offering some level of
additional backup."

Brik stirs. "With you fighting with the archers, Mika," says
Brik, "and Fletch otherwise assigned, that leaves three pikemen
each at the gaps, one in the center to protect the archers, and three
archers plus you for whatever comes over the top or past the
flanks. If we are to have any chance at all, either we have to

104

reduce the number of the enemy reaching us, or we need more mercs."

"I will seed the embankment gaps and the road in front of our position with devices to confuse, slow and kill the human attackers," I say.

"That will help," Brik says, "but it's not enough. The shriekers are the main threat, and we don't know their numbers for sure."

That silences us. Finally, Mika looks up. "Speega Somes is working out of the Inn," she says.

"Slick Speega from your crew?" I ask.

"She's got her own crew now," Mika says. "All women. All archers. They sell protection packages to the merchant caravans out of Nir who pass by the Inn."

"They bill themselves as the KILLER spARROWS," Neenah says, "with an emphasis on the *ARROWS*."

"You're kidding," Cael says, amused.

"Speega can flat out fight," says Mika. "She will help us if she's not out on a job, but I don't see how we can mobilize her and her crew in time."

"My pad," Cael says. "The one I use to contact the Abbot."

"What about it?" asks Mika.

"I think I can modify it so you can contact her without her needing a corresponding pad," Cael says. "But it can only work if she is carrying some kind of *Floe* device with her, to provide power."

"She usually wears a protective medallion," Mika says.

"That will work," Cael says, reaching into his pack. There's a flash, and then he is handing the pad with its stylus to Mika, some smoke curling around the edges.

"Just write 'SPEEGA SOMES' on any page," he says. Mika does, and suddenly the edges of the page begin to glow.

"Ok, good," Cael says. "That means the pad is now linked to Speega through your knowledge of her. Now we need to get her attention."

"What do I do?" Mika asks.

"Write this," Cael says: "'SPEEGA, THIS IS MIKA. NEED HELP. GET TO PEN AND PAPER WEARING YOUR MEDALLION AND REPLY. BE ALONE.'"

"But how does she get this message," says Mika, as she writes.

"She and only she will be able to see it on reflective surfaces, like marble or glass, as she goes about her business," says Cael. "She may not notice it right away."

"So what do we do know?" asks Neenah.

"Let's wait a few minutes," Cael says. "If we get nothing back we can move out while we wait for her reply."

They didn't have to wait long. Words started appearing on the pad: "I'M HERE. IS IT REALLY YOU, MIKA?"

Mika picks up the pen: "IT'S ME."

"PROVE IT."

"I TOLD YOU SPARROWS WAS DUMB."

"LAUGHING. IT TICKLES THE OLD MERCHANT TYPES. SO WHAT'S UP?"

"NEED YOU AND CREW. AS MANY AS POSSIBLE. MEET NOON TOMORROW MEADOW BELOW THE NOTCH ON TRADE ROUTE. I HAVE GOLD. CAN YOU DO IT?"

"FOR HOW LONG?"

"CAN LEAVE THE NEXT DAY."

"WHAT'S THE JOB?"

"PROTECTION. GUARANTEED FIGHT. NEED ARCHERS AND MANY ARROWS. PIKEMEN TOO."

"SOUNDS EPIC. ARCHERS EASY. WILL SEE ABOUT PIKEMEN."

"BE DISCRETE. LORD WOLFFANG AND HIS WOLF FUCKS THE ENEMY. PLUS *KY* TYPES."

"HOLY SHIT!"

"YOU IN?"

"WOULDN'T MISS IT. SEE YOU NOON TOMORROW."

"I OWE YOU."

"So there are our reinforcements," says Mika, looking a little stunned. She looks at Cael. "You weren't kidding when you said you could fix things in the field. That was amazing."

Damn if he doesn't do it again. "You're blushing," says Mika, grinning.

"Isn't it time we were on the road?" asks Cael.

And off we go, into gods know what.

ELEVEN: YOU ARE EVERYTHING

Cael comes up next to me as we ride, wondering if I still have some of the *Flock Finder* devices I was testing last year. "Well sure," I say, "It's not like I clean out the vest between missions."

"Yeah, right," he says. "You mean it's not like you don't keep leftover prototypes in your vest to sell, like all the other thieving Testers."

I laugh, and hand over some small cylinders. "I've got *Flavor Finders*, too, if you need them," I say. "Cheap too."

"Yeah, give them over too," he says. "I think I can use these to modify the bows to improve accuracy. I can make them 'find' a kill zone if it's anywhere close to where the archer is aiming prerelease. Your pilfered devices should give me enough for us and the spARROWS, too."

Later, we pass a huge wagon with high wooden sides and a wooden roof, pulled by four horses, accompanied by two guards on horseback, and driven by a *Floe* monk. There are big red letters painted on the side panel that read:

DON'T THINK TWICES
BUY MONKWORKS MAGICAL DEVICES

"Marketing worked overtime coming up with that," Cael says, smirking.

In every other available space on the wagon's exterior surfaces are drawings that depict the uses the devices can be put to. There are shelters and meals, auto-refill water bags, hands-free horseshoe replacements, wheeled transportation repair kits, and various children's activities. The wagon is full of dozens and dozens of different solutions for humans on the road, all in tiny containers that each fit in a pocket.

"Checking up on me are you, Brother Venarius?" asks the grizzled driver with a twinkle in his eye.

"You caught me," says Cael, walking his horse over to the wagon. I keep walking but when I look back they seem to be having a good time, shooting the monkish shit.

We stop for a break at midafternoon and I see Cael again, this time huddled up with Fletch, working on a pile of bows. Maybe things are starting to come together a bit. The one factor that is still nagging at me, though, is the big one: Are my assumptions about where and when the *Ky* will strike all wrong? I decide to try to confirm it.

I hold my ring and concentrate on the Gryphon who flew us from the Tester's Haven. Images of people I know swirl across the face of the emerald. Then it settles on the Guardian, and I feel us connect. It's weird how such an intimate form of communication can also be non-intrusive. I have to project my message to the Gryphon to be understood; what I'm thinking at the time remains private. Neither of us can read each other's mind.

Now the thing about Gryphons is that they only guard, it's all they do. Period. They will only fight to protect a Haven, so I can't ask them to aid us offensively. But I have something else in mind. I ask for my favor and get his agreement, all of it non-verbal but as solid as carved words on a stone tablet.

We make camp at twilight, new fake tents going up and magical fires igniting. The SenSens have been relieved and are cooking dinner. Neenah and Brik come in too, and sit with the twins. Mika is circulating among her crew and Cael is still locked up with Fletch. I decide to sit with the scouts.

"How was the day?" I ask, sitting down.

"Pretty routine for us," says Neenah, "except for some flaming asshat who couldn't figure out the Monkworks directions for fixing his busted cart."

"I tried to help," says Brik, "but it was all those stupid fucking pictures it takes a magician to figure out, so I wished him good luck and moved on. He wasn't happy."

Amused, I turn to the twins. "Weedon? Marta? See anything on our back trail?" I ask.

They're still acting shy but Marta finally says that they saw a black and red wolf fuck skulking about. "He stayed back, mostly," adds Weedon, "but, like, every once in a while he gets careless and lets himself be seen."

Marta stirs an iron pot. "There's another fight coming for sure," she says. "They're just waiting for something."

"We think Pagan's Notch might be the place," Brik says.

"Yeah, could be you're right," says Weedon, surprising me. "It widens out for them there."

Marta serves herself some stew and then we all do the same, camp cook protocol. The sound of the rushing river water is ever present, and a half moon is already visible. The steep canyon walls make it seem an especially long way away. I'll be glad to get out of this canyon and off of this road.

We chew over the usual camp shit for a while. Marta and Weedon start to relax. They are ex-palace guards from Aurelia who got the urge for travel and adventure. Neenah and Brik are ex-Testers from before my time, who new Janx back then and still call him Jolly Janx.

"Everybody in this outfit is ex something," Neenah says. "Ex-military, ex-wives, ex-husbands, ex-cons, ex-everything. Mika hasn't named us yet but it will have to have an ex in it."

"You mean like The Exceptionals?" asks Weedon.

"Oh, I like that, sis," says Marta.

"How about The Xcentrics," Neenah says, crossing her fingers. And then we're all chiming in:

"The Sad Excuses."

"The Exhausted."

"The Early Exits."

"The Extinguishers."

Then Weedon says, "But I still like The Exceptionals," and we laugh and call it the winner.

Back in my once again miraculous tent, I am pouring some wine when Mika comes in. "Egon, you'll never guess who I saw going into you'll never guess whose tent," she says.

"Ok, I give up," I say. "Spill."

"Fletch going into Cael's tent," she whispers, as if revealing the keys to immortality.

"They're working on bows," I say. Mika snorts.

"Well I say they've been 'strung pretty tight' since Cael saved Fletch at the bridge," she says.

"I haven't noticed anything," I say.

"You wouldn't," she says, in that special voice that women reserve for remarkably dense men.

I give her a glass of wine. "Well then, here's to Cael and Fletch, whatever they're up to."

We sip. Mika says, "I've been thinking about you today."

"And yet you're still here," I say lamely, feeling unprepared for whatever's coming.

Mika ignores me. "I've been thinking about why you're still a Monkworks Tester, when you should be running the place," she says.

"I like being a Tester," I protest. "I'm more now than I ever thought I would be."

She sighs. "Did you see how my people listened to you today?" she asks. "They are hard people. Smart people. Fucking murderous people. And they listen to you. They are betting their lives on you and are willing to do it. Why? Because they respect you. They think you are a man of courage. And more than anything they think your plan is a winner. That you are a winner. For gods sakes, Egon, you are so much more that a Tester."

Now some people, maybe most people, would be unbelievably gratified to have an amazing partner say such wonderful things about their potential. But I am comfortable with who and what I am; comfortable in some deep and defining sense, as if it's equilibrium I seek above all else. But Mika is on to me. She comes after me like a badger.

"You are scared to be depended upon, Egon," she says. "It terrifies you. You think you're not worthy. Or that other people are smarter. So you stay in your sheath where you're safe. But I'll tell you something: You betray your true self over and over again, by settling for less than who you really are. I'm with you because you are great. Cael trusts his life to you, because you are great. My cutthroats stay together despite all that's happened and all that's about to, because they think that with you we'll get through anything."

I think about it for a while. It feels so big I'm not sure what to do with it. "What about you?" I finally ask. "I'm sure you had a big future at Monkworks. Why did you give it up?"

She ponders the question for a minute, and sips some more wine. "Not the same thing," she says. "I left the Testers because I wouldn't work for them anymore."

"What do you mean," I ask, suddenly feeling like this was a moment there was no going back from.

"I am an ambitious person, Egon, and I expect to do well at whatever I try," she says. "So I expected to go up the ladder at Monkworks until I was running a division or something. But somehow I caught the eye of Abbot Tenebrus. He made it known that, if I wanted to advance, I would have to sleep with him."

"What the fuck?" I growl.

"You got it," Mika says.

"What did you do?" I ask.

"I told Jinx," she said. "I don't know what he did or said but he shut the Abbot down somehow. A few days later I was promoted to Section Leader, but I had already made up my mind to quit."

"Godsdamnit," I say.

Mika looks at me hard. "People like Tenebrus rule the world if we let them," she says. "Let's not let them, Egon. We both need to be more."

And that was it for me. The moment I realized that I had to come out of my turtle shell because I had things to do. "You're right," I said, and pulled her close. I kissed her. "I may amount to something, Mika, if you say so," I whisper. "But to me, you already are everything."

Outside, the moons go down, couples pair off, and friends laugh by a glowing fire. For just tonight, the world leaves us in peace.

TWELVE: COURAGE IS A DECISION

I wake with an urgency it takes me a moment to place. Mika's out already although it's still nearly dark, and the camp is beginning to stir. Then, what's had me tossing and turning all night comes back with a rush. I'm up and out of the tent like an exploding ember. Mika is sitting by our fire sharpening her short sword, and Snout is worrying a stick at her feet. I race over to them still putting on my shirt. "We have to talk with Cael and Fletch," I say breathlessly. "It's life or death." Mika bounces up, pointing to where the two are eating breakfast. They see us coming and I see them recognize the look on my face, which is telling them that they're finished eating.

"What's wrong," says Cael, as Mika and I sit down.

"Two big things I totally missed," I say. "I am an asshat."

I see Cael start to smirk and then think better of it. "OK, let's hear it," he says, "one at a time."

"First, it's the strategy of fighting at ground level from behind the embankment," I say. "It gives the alpha free rein to wreak havoc before he makes his move inside for Cael. He can bombard the flank gaps with his alchemical weapons without consequence before he sends his shriekers and wolf fucks, for instance. Or maybe he's strong enough to throw his nasty stuff up over the barrier at us. Or maybe he just pounds the shit out of the barrier until it crumbles."

116

"So do we change the strategy or suppress the alpha," Mika says, seeing right to the heart of the matter.

"Unless you guys think the strategy is wrong, I think we disrupt the alpha," I say.

"How?" asks Cael.

"With something you are about to invent," I tell him. "Something that will smack him down hard every time he opens up on us, until he stops."

"You have something in mind for me to invent, I hope," says Cael, wryly.

"Sort of," I say, gathering myself. "The only weapons that will work against the alpha are non-magical, and at a distance, so I'm thinking natural projectiles of some sort, like stones, placed to fire automatically over the embankment. We fill canisters with stones, figure out how to aim them, and use my explosive devices to power them. That would give us a rapid fire, wide field weapon."

"Is that feasible, Cael?" asks Mika.

"Probably," says Cael, calculating. "I can use the same Finder modification we're using on the bows to aim this weapon at Ky chemical signatures. I just have to isolate the alpha for targeting, likely by following the alchemical weapons he throws back to the source. That way every time he hits us we hit back immediately, and maybe catch him before he moves location. I can link the canisters to your ring, Egon. One push will aim and fire one weapon. But what about sourcing the actual canisters? Any ideas?"

We think for a bit. "Tie-out stakes," Mika finally says. "We each carry one in our saddle bags, and Speega's people will have more. They are hollow iron rods that are sharp on one end so we can drive them into the ground with rocks. We tie our horses to them when we're traveling alone, away from a picket line."

117

"That could do it," Cael says. "I'm thinking I can bind four or five of these stakes together into one unit, connect to it a modified finder device, and then add a rippler so each individual stake of the unit fires in rapid sequence. Sounds like we have enough stakes to make three or four multi-fire weapons."

"Outfuckingstanding," I say. "Is this engineer Cael doing all this, or magician Cael?"

Cael grins. "A bit of both," he says.

"Since you're on such a roll," I say, "do you think you can position each unit high up the canyon wall across the river behind our position? Like your perch back at the Abbey?"

"I'll make it happen," Cael says. "Now, tell us what your other earthshaking, breakfast ending problem is, Egon, because frankly, that first one was a yawn."

We laugh. "What an asshat," I say.

"Well?" Cael says.

"It's our protective medallions," I say. "I know they won't work for the alpha and his constructs. But what if the all-too-human wolf fucks have scrounged some up since we beat them at the bridge? They're still rare in the Three Kingdoms, but even a few could do us damage."

Cael nods and thinks for a moment. He looks up suddenly. "I can just blow them up," he says with relief. "If ours are off, I will be able to isolate theirs and overpower them. We'll hear theirs exploding and then we just reactivate our own stuff."

"Well, you are mister fixall today, Cael," Mika says. "Maybe tomorrow you can arrange world peace."

Cael smiles. "I'll work on it," he says. "Fletch, what say we scrounge up some stakes?" They get up and get scrounging.

"You're the only person I know who wakes up with impossible problems and then has the solutions before breakfast," Mika says. "Neat trick."

"It's easy when you know a magician," I say.

Just then my ring buzzes once and the eagle face of a Gryphon swims into view in the stone. I stare at the image and think hard, and then I link with this awesome, ancient creature. He shows me the images he's seen as he flew from the Haven to the Inn, looking for our enemies. I thank him for this favor and he is gone.

Mika is staring at me because of my sudden trance, and I tell her I have news from the Gryphon.

"What is it?" she asks.

"The alpha and at least 15 fucking shriekers are camped on the high trail at Pagan's Notch," I tell her. "The Gryphon can't be absolutely sure of the construct number, because he says they are partially shielded from even his magic. He also says at least 30 wolf fucks are on the road behind us, with another 50 camped between the Inn and the Notch on the trade road. Lord Wolffang's carriage is at the Inn."

"Oh my gods," say Mika. "It's all happening, just the way you laid it out."

I shake my head, slumping. "There are 15 shriekers now. I don't see how we hold them back," I say.

"Maybe Cael can come up with something," Mika says.

"We're overtaxing him now, I'm afraid," I say.

"Then let's you and me figure it out right now," she says. "The real problem is we have too few people covering too much ground. We have to funnel them more efficiently somehow, keep our fighting to a narrow space."

I smile at the way she can always define the issue. Then I sit up as the start of an idea hits me. "If the embankment is tall enough it forces most or all of the shriekers to the gaps instead of coming over the top," I say, "where we maybe have a chance of handling them."

"But Cael says he can't do that," Mika points out.

"I know," I say. "He'll be at max load with what we already have him doing. But what if we put something on top of his embankment that gives it the deterrence power we need?"

"Like what," Mika asks.

At first I draw a blank but then it hits me. I laugh, thinking about where the solution is coming from. "Staves," I say. "Big, solid oak staves for wine barrels, each taller than I am. It's what the cursing cart man has in the back of his cart."

"Holy shit," Mika says, getting it. "We sharpen them up, and jam them every which way we can at the top of the embankment. Tie them together and really dig them in."

"Can you send people back to get them right now?" I ask. "The cart should be right behind us."

"Oh, this will be fun," Mika laughs. "I'll just go ahead and send Neenah and Brik."

Hah," I say. "Give them enough gold to buy the cargo, the cart and the horses too. Leave them some tent devices. Tell Neenah and Brik they can't take no for an answer, and we need them back here fast with the goods."

"We just have to hope cursing cart man is still ahead of the trailing wolf fucks," she says. "Let me get them moving."

Mika takes off, new scouts go out to replace the night crew, and Neenah and Brik race off in a shower of flying sparks from horseshoes hitting cobblestones.

Cael gets the kinks worked out of his plan for our new projectile weapon before camp breaks. He will collect more tie-out stakes from Speega's people when we meet up at the Notch this afternoon, and be ready for a rapid assembly of as many units as possible.

I hear Mika talking battle plans with her crew: at least three pikemen each at the gaps on our flanks near the river, depending on what Speega is able to add; two more pikemen in the center, in front of our archer position, in case shriekers or crossbowmen still manage to get over the top of the embankment; and then the line of our archers, commanding a full view of our defensive positions, bolstered by as many of Speega's KILLER spARROWS as she is able to bring. Mika plans to stand with the archers to manage the flow of the battle, and add her pike and sword as needed. Then behind the archers will stand Cael, Fletch and me, looking to take on the alpha and his assassination team, and until then adding what we can to the fight.

I feel like I've done all I can do for now. I join the other riders and saddle up.

Mika leads us out at an easy pace. She says she expects we'll reach the Notch before midafternoon and, mindful of hostile watchers, that it's plausible that a group might stop early there in such a beautiful spot to camp.

We are an hour into our march when Neenah and Brik come riding in with the couple on the cart behind them. Cursing cart man doesn't fully stop before he starts ranting, possibly to Cael, but just as possibly to the whole camp. "I don't care how much fucking gold you hold under my nose," he shouts. "You can't buy my fucking cargo. Like I told these two, it's already spoken for and I'm a man of my word."

Cael eases his horse over to the cart and nods to the woman. "Hello, ma'am," he says. "And good to see you again, sir. I see the cart is doing fine."

"You're the one that helped us and I appreciate it," cart man says, "not like them other two. But be that as it may, you can't have these staves."

"Ok, ok I get it," says Cael, "but what if we just borrow them for a few hours. We'll pay you the same."

"Borrow them? Borrow them for what now?" he asks suspiciously.

Cael is smooth. Did I mention Cael is smooth before now? Oh, he's an operator. "We're picking up a bunch of new horses over to the Notch," he says, "and these staves are going to help us corral them for a few hours while we brand them and get them on the picket line."

"What the fucking fuck?" cursing cart man says. "I don't see how that's ever going to work. Not to mention I can't have them damaged at all."

"No damage at all," agrees Cael. "I'll give you the gold, you can camp right here for the night, and first thing tomorrow morning, I'll be back with your load in tip top shape."

"Oh no," says cart man. "There is no fucking way I am letting these staves out of my sight until I reach Aurelia, gold or no gold."

"But you'll be bored sticking around with us" Cael protests, "and this is a crude bunch I'm riding with that your missus doesn't need to be hearing."

"She hears plenty already," says cart man, with surprising self-awareness. "I've told you my terms. Take it or leave it."

Cael gracefully folds, accepting the cursing cart man's conditions. Maybe he's thinking he can divert the guy somewhere on the road between here and the Notch?

Afterwards, Mika, Cael and I ride together, figuring out how to make the staves idea work, as cart man and his wife follow along. We come up with a feasible, three part plan that we just hope we'll have time to execute. As soon as we get to the Notch, Mika will put her crew to work sharpening both ends of the staves. Next they will lash eight or ten staves together in the middle, and then open them up so some of the ends can dig into the ground, while others point up, out, and every which way.

Then it will be up to Cael to embed these 'porcupines' into position on top when he makes the embankment. We estimate this will add something close to the height of a man to our barrier, impeding the ability of shriekers to jump it. At the very least, fighting their way through the thicket of staves will make the beasts easier targets for our archers.

Mika moves off to hand out tasks, and Cael and I ride in silence for a while. Then Cael says: "So Egon, I'm scared I will fuck up today. That I will run out of power. Or freeze when everyone is depending on me."

I've wrestled with the same thoughts in many dire situations over the years, and if I am being honest I have to admit I'm wrestling with them now. But, because I've had the practice, I've learned a thing or two about it. "That doubt that you feel," I say, "that frantic tumbling of worries in your brain, those are just the devils that courage is meant to combat."

"But do I have the courage?" Cael asks.

"Courage is a decision, Cael," I say, "one I've seen you make before. Maybe you'll amaze yourself today by the great things you'll do. But you won't amaze me. I already know what you can do." Cael looks like he's about to, so I head him off. "Just don't blush," I say. He does anyway.

"Thanks, Egon," he says. He reaches out his hand and we shake. "No matter how it goes today, it's been an honor to know you," he says.

I guess that it's because he's just so close to the surface and genuine, but he gets to me. "You know," I say, "I never thought I'd be friends with a 'perch' asshat, but friends we are. Good hunting today, Cael."

About then the river switches sides of the road again, now on our left, and we cross it on a stone bridge. Mika comes over and says, "This is it, the last bridge before the Notch. If we're right, they'll close the road behind us soon, and have probably stopped traffic already on the other side of the Notch. We should wait a bit to make sure all civilians get clear, but then you can start planting your devices."

"And so it begins," I say, and she nods.

Then she looks at me hard. "Take care of yourself today, Egon," she says. "I don't really have a ready supply of random rump rubbers."
I smile. "Having seen your rump, I find that hard to believe," I say, and draw a small smile in return. "Please keep it in the condition I left it in, Mika."

She taps her heart twice with her fist. "I love you, Egon," she says, for the first time. I clasp her hand.

"I love you, too," I say.

THIRTEEN: THE BATTLE OF PAGAN'S NOTCH

Then I'm dropping back down the road, pulling at my vest for devices that I hope will decimate the wolf fucks following us. The first thing I decide is that I want to disrupt the fucks' timing. I guess their lead scouts will ride right down the center of the road, so I place devices to the side so they'll ride safely by, primed to activate when the horses hooves of the main body disturb the debris.

The devices are a combination of irritators: stink bombs, noisemakers and spark-offs. I expect that when these start to go off they will freak out the horses, and the wolf fucks will be forced to dismount. That will cause their commander to order a double time march so they can still arrive at the Notch on schedule, which will make it easier for them to pile headlong into my next trap.

I continue to place disrupters at random, in case they get any ideas of remounting, until I see what I'm looking for on the canyon wall to my right. It's a jumble of good-sized boulders that have collected over time in rockslides from up above, but which haven't quite reached the road surface. I place a concussive device in their midst to encourage them, run out of the way and, pow, the pile hits the cobblestones.

I get what I want, which is a barrier of rock across about a third of the road, not enough to make them suspicious or to delay them, but enough to bunch them up as they veer towards the gap. I sow a line of ripplers under rocks for a hundred feet back in the direction from which they will march. I come back to the boulders and hide a trippler there, which is an explosive that detonates upon disturbance. I anticipate the trippler explosion to set off the ripplers, right among the slowed down and bunched up wolf fucks. The results will not be pretty. Then I head back towards Mika's gang, planting random trippler and rippler devices as I go. All of the explosive devices will disintegrate within 12 hours if unexploded. I see no other travelers. Things are feeling very real.

I join up with the crew as they are pulling into the meadow at the Notch, and there I see a welcome sight. Speega has arrived with eight other women, and damn if they're not all dressed in matching brown leather outfits, with yellow hats that resemble beaks. They each hold bows and multiple quivers of arrows, and there are more quivers hanging from their picketed horses. In addition, Speega brought four dangerous looking men, each carrying several pikes along with a glut of personal weaponry. Neenah is already rummaging through all the newly arrived saddlebags, looking for more iron tie-out stakes for the canister tubes. With all the new horses, I'm thinking we'll score enough to make a couple more weapons than I was expecting. I head off to see Cael.

"Hey Cael," I say, when I find him and Fletch amidst a pile of iron stakes. "If we end up with six canisters, we can have four ready for the alpha as planned, then maybe two more with a fixed aim, over the heads of our pikemen at the gaps on our flanks."

"Sounds diabolical, as usual," says Cael, grinning. "I'll set it up. And when I'm done I'll modify the bows of Speega's spARROWS."

I head over to Speega to say hello. "Hello, Slick, it's really good to see you," I say.

"I'll be damned, Egon," she says. "I can't believe Mika is still putting up with you."

126

"I can't either," I say and we laugh. "Did Mika fill you in on what we've got going here?"

She spits. "I must say, Egon, you sure can attract more that your fair share of trouble. You think we can handle this?"

"Now that you're here," I say, "we can't miss." I leave her looking indescribably unconvinced. It's a talent of mine.

I see Cael over with cursing cart man and his wife, and he's showing them the features of a spectacular new tent he's conjured for them near the river, a tent more sumptuous and substantial than the one Mika and I shared. The walls look suspiciously sturdy to my eye, like they are meant to stop, oh say, explosive projectiles? Leave it to Cael; he thinks of everything.

The man has his hands on his hips, and looks to be talking belligerently to a placating Cael. The wife is pulling on the man's elbow, as if she's sold on the tent idea and wants a little rest and relaxation. Finally they go in together and close the unusually firm flap.

As soon as that happens, Cael signals Mika, and eight of her crew start unloading the staves. I go over to Cael and ask him how cursing cart man will react to the sounds of wood chopping when he hears the sharpening begin. "I 'improved' their wine somewhat," he says, somewhat guiltily. "I don't expect them up anytime soon." Hey, what would you do if the world hung in the balance?

Shadows are creeping up the walls of the canyon beyond the river, when Cael does some move and blows six evenly spaced holes out of the granite. Then he does something else and a Monkworks bridge appears across the flow. The cart man's cart goes flying by me over the bridge, driven by the SenSen twins, six improvised iron canister weapons tied down in the back. The SenSen's use the bench of the cart to give them the height they need to reach the holes, one Sen in the bed passing canisters one at a time to the Sen on the bench, who then stuffs them into the holes and cements them in with packed stones and dirt. The whole time, there is no reaction from the nearby armored tent. Cael mixes a potent potion.

Back up near the road, there are many dozens of oak stave 'porcupines' spread out from bank to bank, across what will be our front line barrier. Any watchers will laugh at what is currently a flimsy looking barricade.

Scout is sleeping in the road. My ring remains quiet. A bend in the road blocks my view of where the spring comes down from the Notch, but it's close enough that Scout or the ring would have noticed if the alpha or the shriekers had climbed down from the upper trail. So either they've been down since before I got here, or they haven't made their move yet.

I see Cael has come back from positioning the new projectile weapons and is working on the bows of Speega's archers. I go out to the road directly in front of our position and seed it with explosives, stink bombs, noisemakers, and Tester decoys like I used back at the Abbey. Then I string ripplers from the canyon wall near the road, linked to my ring to detonate.

Back inside our perimeter, preparations are beginning to slow. People are grouping around their eventual battle positions. Our little army has nearly doubled to 27, and I can only hope it will be enough. Now we have six pikemen apiece plugging the gaps on our flanks against the river, bolstered by Speega's recruits and two SpARROWS with pike experience who agreed to help out there. Two more pikemen will take a central position of protection in front of the archers. Nine archers plus Mika will hold a spread out line behind the two central pikemen, looking to support the gaps and take out anything coming over the top. Behind this line comes Cael, me and Fletch. I'll be filling in as needed while guarding Cael, who will throw destruction at the wolf fucks and provide light. Fletch will be trying to get a shot at the alpha when he makes his expected move against Cael.

About then we start hearing distant explosions to our right, from the road portion I seeded. Snout raises her head but doesn't stand.

Light is fading in the canyon. Cael is poised to jump out front and build the embankment. Mika is set to yell 'medallions off.' Distant explosions continue from back down the road. My ring stays quiet.

Brik walks behind the archers' position with an armful of pikes, driving one upright into the ground every few feet in case the archers are in danger of being overrun by shriekers and need to defend themselves.

Snout stands up.

Archers push arrows into the ground in front of them for fast access. Their bows are lumpy with modifications Cael and Fletch have made to improve targeting, ease of draw and impact. Each hold three arrows in their bow hands as well, and there are stacks of quivered arrows behind them. I hear Mika reminding Speega about the crossbowmen who may carry bolts that can defy medallions.

Suddenly, Snout lets out an angry howl I've never heard from her before. Everything starts happening at once. My ring turns black and I don't bother counting the buzzes. "Now," I yell and Mika shouts, "Medallions off." Cael, in chest armor, sprints for the center of the road, passing Snout, who is sprinting back to me. The battle of Pagan's Notch is about to explode.

Out front, the *Floe* magician clenches both fists and there are explosions up and down the road. Some wolf fucks did have medallions after all, I think. Mika yells, "Medallions on," and those few that have them reactivate. I pull Snout's medallion out of my pocket, activate it, and put it around her neck. She races back towards the cart man's tent, no doubt feeling her job in the current battle is done. Then I flip open the stone on my ring to reveal a rectangular surface of seven glowing marks: a grouping of four and two for the canister weapons, and a seventh mark for the ripplers on the canyon wall to the front.

Cael yells from the center of the road, "Keep back," and pushes out with his hands. The ground between him and us undulates up into a wave, picking up the oak stave 'porcupines' in its path. The whole thing is over our heads and nearly bank to bank in an instant, staves rolled up and embedded like broken teeth along the top.

I run up the slope for a view of the road. I see Cael stagger and recover. Everyone is taking their positions. Cael seems to swell and starts pumping explosives and fire up and down the road and high on the canyon wall, bringing down tons of debris onto the cobblestones. Some of my seeded explosives go off from Cael's actions, but I know there are plenty to go around. Then Cael somehow shoves some fallen boulders into semicircular obstacle courses around the entrances to our flank gaps, in order to slow the attack. Our pikemen hug the inside slope of the embankment, shielding themselves from the alpha's anticipated alchemical assault until it's time to take position against the shrieker onslaught.

"Nice moves," I yell, as Cael maneuvers through the boulders back to our side of the barrier, but he looks too wasted to reply.

As I run back down the embankment to my position I hear my seeded explosives on the road in front of the barrier going off, along with noisemakers and the rest, signaling our enemy is on top of us. I use the seventh mark on the ring to fire off the ripplers, but I can't see their impact.

The embankment in front of us shudders from one end to the other as the alpha opens up with alchemical explosives. Ominously, he's already blown two new gaps in our bristling barricade of oak staves before I can even trigger my first canister. I press down on the ring and the weapon ignites with a series of five rippler-induced explosions from out of the granite wall behind us. Stone projectiles sizzle overhead towards the left. "Eat rocks," I growl to the alpha.

Brik raises his arm from the right gap, to let me know the shriekers are coming. I grab a pike from the archers' stash and run through them to join the SenSen twins, who are holding the center in front of the archers and watching the new gaps in the staves.

Overhead, the sky flares as Cael throws up fireballs, some of which slowly drift down to light the chaotic scene, and others which plummet to earth and explode among our enemies. The noise is deafening.

Suddenly the flank gaps are hit in rapid succession with fireballs and explosives from the alpha, demonstrating his superhuman speed. It signals the start of the shrieker attack, and I trigger a second canister blast at the *Ky* handler. The pikemen sheltering against the embankment jump up into position in each gap to confront the shrieker assault.

Then, all of a sudden, there are two shriekers on top of the embankment, each filling a break in the line of 'porcupines.' I hear Mika say, "Now," and bowstrings start twanging behind me.

Up on the barrier, the two shriekers are backlit by Cael's lights, and seemingly held there in place as their thrashing bodies are pin cushioned by streaking arrows. Some hit so hard they explode out the other side, powered by the modified magical bows, until finally the constructs fall backwards off the embankment. Two down, 13 to go, I think. Behind me the archers cheer.

On our left and right flanks the pikemen are engaged. They work from a crouch, the ones in front with the back of their weapons jammed into the ground behind them. Shriekers are flinging themselves at the iron-headed shafts and swinging out with their claw-tipped arms. Arrows fly over the lowered pikemen and into the beasts pushed high by their frenzied efforts. I catch a glimpse of Brik bent low, fending off a shrieker at close quarters who is snapping with his jaws and swatting with his lethal arms, fighting for an opening. Suddenly, a second construct jumps high over the first. Neenah, at Brik's shoulder, rises up to meet the attack, thrusting up violently with her pike, pushing with all her might to keep the beast from falling onto Brik.

Then, the alpha fires again at the embankment in front of me, opening several more breaks in the 'porcupines.' The *Ky* handler is smart enough to move around, because when I fire off my third canister, the projectiles are now aimed to the right.

Out at the flanks there are wolf fucks now mixed in with the shriekers, and their combined weight appears to be pushing the pikemen back. Up on the embankment, shriekers and soldiers appear in multiple gaps. They are inviting targets for an instant but the action on our flanks is so hot that the archers suddenly have too many targets at once.

Two shriekers bound down the embankment towards us. The SenSen twins confront the first one and I square off with the second. I found out later it came from Fletch, but an arrow hits my beast right in his mouth as he opens it to shriek, and he goes down. I turn towards the SenSens to see Weedom swatted aside by the beast as Marta goes in screaming with a desperation thrust of her pike. Her iron tip slams into the shrieker's midsection, but it's flailing arm catches Marta high on her shoulder. She goes flying in a spray of blood as my pike takes the beast under its raised arm. I grind it back into the embankment and keep grinding until its final shudder.

Our flanks are buckling, our pikemen pushed back far enough to make it safe for me to blow the two canisters aimed over the riverbank gaps. I hit both marks on my ring and it is instant carnage. Shriekers and wolf fucks are down or staggering around in circles. Those pikemen of ours who are still able-bodied push forward and retake lost ground.

The embankment jolts again from a massive and sustained barrage from the alpha. This time, he concentrates his fire in the center, and makes a wide and deep breech. They're coming for Cael, I think, but the alpha has made a mistake. He's been firing for so long from one position that I manage to fire the last canister before he stops. Mika, Cael and Fletch come up beside me in preparation for the assault and, with pressure off our flanks for the moment, some of the pikemen run towards us to lend support.

Four shriekers bound through the new opening first, followed by a handful of wolf fucks with their deadly crossbows. The shriekers peel off left and right to engage the converging pikemen. The crossbowmen drop to the ground at the top of the embankment and start firing. Our archers fire back and I hear a snap followed by a curse as a *Ky* construct bolt splinters on Cael's chest armor. Our archers blanket the top of the barrier with arrows from their murderously enhanced bows, and Cael finishes the human assailants with one of his own magical bolts.

Then comes the main event as the alpha's breach, still backlit by Cael's continuous firelight, is filled by an enormous shape I hoped I would never see again. It is a godsforsaken fyrboren, shielded somehow from the Gryphon's flyover, impervious to *Floe* magic, and by far the worst construct I know of. Years ago, on a Tester training mission, Jinx and I had watched helplessly as one attacked and utterly destroyed a caravan of travelers on the trade road ahead of us. In the time it took for Jinx and I and the other trainees to run to the scene, the humans, horses and cargo wagons were ablaze, and the fyrboren was gone.

It's basically a boar, or used to be, before the *Ky* flesh farmers started their hideous experimentation on the breed with alchemical potions. What they produced was a beast so large it barely still resembled the original animal, with enormous curved tusks murderously sharpened at their tips, gleaming white armored skin where the fur used to be, and demonic red eyes. But the worst thing of all is the fire.

"Scatter," I scream as the fyrboren's eyes lock onto us, and it opens his hideously fanged mouth. I dive to the side, taking Mika with me. It belches out a stream of yellow fire that would have cooked all of us if we hadn't moved. Nevertheless, there are sudden screams behind me, so I know some of us have been hit.

Then Cael, like he always seems to, steps up with something that gives us a chance. He blasts a hole in the ground at the feet of the alchemically-twisted boar, and it tips down into it headfirst, temporarily disabling his deadly fire. It's but the tiniest wisp of a reprieve, as the creature immediately begins to climb back out, but it's just enough time to put us on the attack.

As the boar lurches down, we can see that its huge form has been blocking the alpha from view in the breech on top of the embankment. My last canister shot must have hit him because he is a mess, cape shredded, head bleeding, one arm gone at the elbow. He holds his construct sword in the other and, still freakishly fast, streaks down the barrier past the struggling fyrboren and directly at Cael.

He doesn't get there. An angry arrow from Fletch's enhanced bow explodes through the head of the bastard, and he topples backwards. Unbelievable shot. Yay, Fletch.

But now the fyrboren is scrambling up out of the hole and I yell, "Its underbelly, Cael. Raise him up." Cael does that rippling thing with the ground again and makes the earth push the fucker back and up, flames shooting harmlessly from its mouth towards the sky. Mika and I charge with our pikes leveled and skewer the brute through its unarmored belly on seven feet of iron each. We dodge back as the fyrboren writhes, arrows now pounding it, too. Finally it shudders, then breathes its last.

I look around and realize the fighting has stopped. The converging pikemen and remaining archers have combined to overcome the charge of the last shriekers. It's mostly silent now, and everyone is just sort of stuck in place, not quite believing they are still alive. Then Cael moves off to see about our wounded. Mika sends two archers to the top of the embankment to watch the road. "Kill anything that moves," I hear her instruct them. The other exhausted warriors are beginning to drop to the ground where they stand, too spent to look for anyplace better. Some are pouring water from their bags all over their heads.

Mika and I turn towards each other and clench together fiercely. "What the fucking fuck," I hear from back towards the cart man's tent. I can feel Mika laughing against me. Or maybe she's crying. At a moment like this, it's all the same.

FOURTEEN: THIS MEANS WAR

Mika and I end our embrace and start to take in the carnage. She follows me, as images begin to flash in my head, and I move towards the last place I saw the SenSen's. I hear Mika gasp and then she's running past me towards a body on the ground. Two bodies. Mika is moaning, "No, no, no, no," as she drops down beside them.

The blood tells the tale … a puddle of it to the right, where Weedon first landed, stunned and bleeding out, thrown by an inhuman monstrosity … but still she moves somehow, leaving a trail of her remaining blood across the bruised meadow grass to where Marta lays on her back … her shoulder and throat torn apart … but her good arm stretched out to find and grasp Weedom's hand with the last of her dying strength. Twinned in death as they had been in life. The Exceptionals, I think. My shy friends. And for a time after that, I lose it.

Mika brings me back with a gentle hand nestling into mine. We continue our inspection and find Speega next, alive but sobbing over two of her SpARROWS who fell when the fyrboren burst through the breach breathing his yellow death. We drop to our knees on either side of her, and we each cover a hand. Speega grasps us hard, and for a time her sobbing is uncontrollable. "I'm so, so sorry, Speega," says Mika. "Without them, without you, all of us would be dead." Speega just nods, and after a time we move on, feeling helpless and, to be honest, guilty.

136

We see Cael next, kneeling over Neenah, who is straining in pain, gasping in huge lungful's of air, and holding on with all her might to the massive, scarred hand of Brik. She has been raked across the middle by a shrieker's deadly claws. Cael's hands are full of her blood, as he gently presses into her with healing magic. Mika takes Neenah's free hand, and I put a hand on Brik's hunched shoulder.

Neenah's tortured breathing eases a bit, and her straining body begins to relax. "He's got nice hands, Brik," she manages to gasp out at one point. "You may have competition." And once more, in waning fireball light, Cael blushes.

The pikemen at the flank gaps were decimated by the shriekers' continuous attacks. All four of Speega's pikemen received what would normally be mortal wounds, but Cael is able to save two of them. Two more of Mika's people are dead, but the two SpARROWS who volunteered at the last minute to fill the gaps at the flanks are alive. The rest are banged up to varying degrees, and await Cael's care.

From our total complement of 27 before the battle, we lost an irreplaceable eight. I feel guilty for getting Mika, and through her, Speega, involved in my troubles. But more than that, I'm feeling anger - red hot burning anger - at whoever is doing this, at Jinx for picking me, and yes, unfair as it may be, at Cael for bringing this catastrophe down on my head. I know it is an unworthy thought, but still I have to struggle to focus my anger where it truly belongs: the hellspawn of Immobilin Keep and whoever's paying for them.

I make a vow to make them all pay.

I hear Mika setting up a watch schedule, and I go to help Fletch wrap bodies in blankets in preparation for burial in the morning. The carcasses of the fyrboren and shriekers inside our perimeter have already misted away. No one bothers to check on what's outside the perimeter. "You did good tonight, Fletch," I say as we labor. "That was an unbelievable shot you made on the fast-moving alpha."

"Killing him isn't enough," Fletch says, angrily. "There's a lot more killing needed to settle this score."

"You'll get your chance, I'm afraid, if you stick around."

"Oh, I'll stick," he says, with finality.

When we finish our sad work I head back towards the river and throw a shelter disc to erect an ordinary, two-cot, Monkworks tent. I pull the cots together and start taking off my boots. Mika comes in, strain and pain and anger on her face, and she gets ready to turn in. We lay in our cots for a while, holding hands, listening to the camp settle down. Sometimes there really are no words.

Next morning, everyone is up early, the day for burying our dead. Cael magically carves eight graves into a rise overlooking the river, and we gather to lay our comrades to rest. Brik speaks first for his two pikemen-in-arms, who died holding back the shrieker onslaught with their courage. He speaks plainly and warmly of their years together, their adventures, and how he'll miss them. He places a pike with the body in each grave.

Speega stands up next and clears her throat. "I lost four of mine last night," she says, "and I would have lost more but for Cael. Two were from my crew, sisters in every way but birth. Two others were from a larger group of brother and sister warriors who I've come to know and trust in my years out here. All were valued colleagues, all were known for their valor and dependability." She wipes an eye.

"We sell protection," Speega continues, "but last night it cost us dearly. We can say, though, that because of these dead, and all of you, it cost the godsforsaken bastards who attacked us so much more. Together, we sent a force three times our size back to the steaming hell it crawled out of.

"Some may say that I was reckless to lead my comrades onto this killing ground, without a moment's hesitation, and they wouldn't be wrong. But if they are truthful, they also know why we did it. Why I did it. They know that we were answering the call of a mate who needed our help. This is our code. This is how we live and die. I would do it all over again. And I think all of you, living and dead, would do it too." Mika's face is covered in tears.

"So to the dead," Speega concludes, "I say that it has been my great honor to know you. And to the living, I say that I am proud and humbled to fight beside you. You will all live forever in my heart."

Speega sits down, and there is loud sobbing everywhere. I look at Mika and know that she, like me, is pierced by guilt for bringing Speega's people into this mess. I am grateful for the archer's attempt to absolve us.

After she gathers herself, Mika stands up. "Yes," she begins, "you all answered the call last night, and no one has ever done it better. You met abomination with skill and courage that are beyond compare. You stood here and beat back those *Ky* freaks, and their evil allies, with unmatchable ferocity. I am forever grateful to you, the living. My heart is broken by you, the dead."

Mika pauses, then moves over to the graves of the sisters.

"You all know the SenSen twins," she continues, "either by working with them in my crew, or through their fearsome reputation as warriors without equal. I've been awed by their fearsome side, like everyone else. But I've also been blessed to get to know a gentler side. Weedom and Marta were, above all else, devoted sisters who loved each other fiercely, and who refused to die unless it was in each other's arms. They were the two sweetest souls you could ever hope to meet in all of this godsforsaken world."

Mika is crying openly now. Everyone is.

"The SenSen twins were exceptional in every way," she continues, "and their memory will always stand as the very definition of exceptional. Weedom and Marta , I mourn your passing. I shall forever mourn. Rest, now, in peace."

Mika sits back down next to me. I feel the need to take the blame for this battle and these deaths, and I begin to stand up. But Cael puts a hand on my shoulder from behind, and walks past me to the front, his limp more noticeable today. I settle back down as he turns to face the mourners.

"Ultimately," Cael begins, "it was my desperate call for help that all of you answered. I am responsible for the pain and death here today. I am sorry." He pauses, seeming to look at everyone individually before continuing. "Saying 'thank you,'" he goes on then, "and handing you gold, is completely inadequate for expressing how much I owe you.

"But there is more that needs to be said to you about what happened here last night. You all know that I am a *Floe* magician from Floendahl Abbey. For reasons I don't understand, forces from Immobilin Keep in Rusk are trying to kill me, and those who stand with me. I don't know if this is official policy or the actions of a few, powerful renegades. I don't even know if it's Rusk alone that's doing this, or if someone is paying them, but it really doesn't matter. Because make no mistake: This attack on us is nothing short of an undeclared act of war. The battle you fought and won last night is part of something that's larger than all of us; a battle to determine whether humanity continues to lead the Three Kingdoms, assisted peacefully by a benevolent magic; or instead, whether an evil and rapacious regime of alchemists rises up to rule us all, assisted by soulless humans who are traitors to their kind.

"Those are the stakes. Your future is what you fought for last night. And these dead did not die in vain, but rather to safeguard our entire way of life. I promise you that one day soon I will come back to this burial ground to give you the answers to the questions we all have. And I also promise you that those responsible for this will pay."

Unlike the tears following the two previous speakers, everybody is talking to everybody else as Cael sits back down. I am shaken. I've been too busy trying to pin down shadowy details to see that no matter the specifics, Cael is right. Immobilin Keep's breeders, along with their alchemical and human military assets, plus a possible shadowy paymaster, have attacked a highly placed representative of its magical competitor and, unless somehow contained, this means war. Exact combatants to be named later. Holy shit.

The group is breaking up now, some feeling pride and comfort from Cael's and the others' remarks; and others saying things like, 'I didn't sign up for no war.' All of us stop for breakfast except Cael and Fletch. First, Cael moves earth to cover the graves and places an unbroken 'porcupine' on the mound as a temporary marker, until something more suitable can be arranged. Then, I see he and Fletch head around the embankment to, I assume, survey the battleground beyond our perimeter and up and down the road.

Mika and I sit by ourselves, porridge in a pot over a low fire. "I feel that there are big changes coming to the Three Kingdoms," Mika says. "Maybe big hardships."

"I hear you," I say. "Cael said some sobering things."

"We can't go on the same way," she says.

"What do you mean?" I ask, alarmed.

"I need you close to me now, Egon," she says. "We can't continue to be separated all the time. We need to face whatever is coming together."

141

I look at her, and come to a realization. "This whole time," I say, "from the moment I left the Abbey on this mission, I've been feeling uneasy. And each time I try to confront the issue, I end up going deeper and deeper into this puzzle surrounding Cael. But now, I realize that deep down below everything else, what's really been bothering me is the puzzle surrounding you, Mika."

"How do you mean?" she asks.

"These times we share together, our adventures, in and out of danger, are the most wonderful and most precious parts of my life. So I don't want to change it."

Mika takes my hand.

"But I realize now that there are bigger adventures to have, and more important things to do, if only it's always with you. I have no idea how to make that happen. At least, I had no idea until a minute ago. Now I think it's really very simple. It's like courage. It's just a decision. So I decide now: We need to see this thing through to the end, Mika, but from here on out nothing will ever separate us again."

Of course, love is the definition of unforeseen consequences. So we don't think twice about our quick agreement to end our Tester and mercenary leader eras for whatever come next, just as soon as this last mission is over. 'Just as soon as...' may be the most unattainable goal in the world. But at least for a while, and maybe forever, we see nothing but each other.

Cael and Fletch come back with the news that any dead shriekers have faded away. Presumably, all the shriekers are dead but, like the last time, we have no proof. They also report that there are dozens and dozens of dead wolf fucks as far as two miles away, victims of my traps, plus Cael's medallion sabotage and fireballs. They saw no other construct weapons, which says something to me about how on-the-fly these attacks on us have been. And I think about how ill-used the unmagical soldiers were in this fight, just thrown away like stale ale.

Cael and Fletch bring back one more thing: the personal effects of the highest ranking wolf fuck body they find: a Captain Thoron Rask. There is a sword with TR engraved on the hilt; there are riding gloves similarly engraved; and there is a signed order from Lord Wolffang to the commander of his House Guards, Captain Rask, directing him on orders of the High Council – the so called 'Breedership' - to report to an alpha named Ansgar in Aurelia for further instructions.

"So this is it," I say. "It was no renegade operation. The leaders of Rusk are calling the shots, officially, whether they are being paid to or not."

"And the alpha is calling the shots locally," Mika says, "placed in charge of both the constructs and the wolf fucks."

"And look at the date," Cael adds. "That's two days before we leave the Abbey."

"So now we have a clear idea about how the three attacks were put in motion," I say. "The High Council gets word you're leaving the Abbey, Cael. They order this alpha, Ansgar, to attack us with his pack of constructs and use Lord Wolffang's troops in support."

"Immobilin Keep is officially making war-like moves," Cael says.

"A lot to discuss with the Abbot," I say.

"You bet," says Cael. "I told him about the attack, and the attackers, last night. I told him I wanted to discuss it further but would have too much to do for the next couple of days to get into it. That's where things stand."

I nod. As it seems so often with this situation, I don't know what to do with what we are learning. I decide to get back to the pressing matters at hand for now. I borrow the cart man's cart once again and, with Brik, Fletch and two of the healthier pikemen, I haul enemy bodies to the trench that formed when Cael pushed up his embankment. It takes most of the rest of the day.

When we're done, Cael stands within our perimeter and pushes with his hands. A wave of earth thrusts the embankment, and what's left of its 400 oak barrel staves, back the way it came. It covers over the mass grave, and fills in the gouge its creation made in the meadow. Then Cael does another push motion and moves the rock debris off the road. It's almost as if nothing happened. Almost.

We prepare to camp in the meadow for one more night. Cael, Fletch, Mika and I sit together for dinner. I ask Cael how drained he feels from all his magical exertions. "It's weird," he says, "but I feel much better than I expected. I used to think I had limited power as a magician, but it turns out my magic works like a muscle: the more I use it the stronger it gets. Someday I may be powerful."

He's perfectly serious, but the rest of us laugh. "I can't even picture that," says Mika.

Cael shrugs.

"I haven't heard the cart man all day, Cael," I say. "What magic did you work on him this time?"

"No magic, Egon," he says, smugly. "I simply settled the matter with cutthroat negotiations."

"Do tell," says Mika.

"Well," Cael says, warming to his story, "it turns out that the two of them have a carpentry shop and hate their biggest

144

customer: cart man's skinflint uncle, who owns the winery that was getting the oak staves. I find out that they are desperate for another source of revenue, so ..." he coughs, "...I knew I really had them ... 'over a barrel.'"

None of us laugh.

"What is wrong with you people?" he gripes. "A wine barrel. Staves. I know that was funny."

Then we fake laugh. "Asshats," he says. Then we laugh for real.

"So ok, Cael, you steely eyed bargainer, how did you take advantage of their dire circumstances?" asks Fletch.

"I offered them a contract to supply the Abbey's carpentry needs, guaranteeing them only twice the money their shop currently makes," he says proudly.

"Wait," says Mika. "You're paying them twice what they're making now? That's your killer deal?"

"Well, yeah," Cael says, surprised that we don't seem impressed. "We did put them through a lot, you know. A real lot. And the Abbey will spend the money anyway. Right, Egon?"

"Absolutely," I say in full support. "Personally, I am willing to pay any price to never hear 'what the fucking fuck' from him ever again." We all laugh, and maybe start to shake off a little of the insanity.

We pull out early next morning, and traffic on the road has resumed. We hear people talking about the danger of avalanches and assume the wolf fuck cover story is intact.

When we stop for lunch, Cael comes over to talk to me. "We're less than two days from Aurelia, and I've never had a chance to brief you on our first prototype test," he says. "How much do you know about the Sultan of Nir?"

"Not a thing," I answer, not being one to follow the doings of royalty.

"Well, wait until you hear this," he says, and I settle in to listen.

PART 2: *THE PROTOTYPES*

ONE: I HOPE YOU KNOW WHAT YOU'RE DOING

"Well, right now," Cael says, "there is a very public succession battle going on that will determine who sits on the Nir throne when the old Sultan, Anseem Hawarri, passes away. In their system, the next ruler of Nir is the first born son of the present sultan, unless there are unusual circumstances, like he has no son. Then, different rules apply, but, hell, I'm getting off topic."

Cael drinks some water and starts up again. "The Sultan had two children, a boy and a girl, with his first wife, who died in childbirth having the girl. He has no children with his second wife, the present Sultana Cadiah Hawarri. Follow me so far?"

"Like a royal lap dog," I say.

"Well here's the thing," Cael continues, ignoring my lack of enthusiasm. "This succession was considered obvious and straightforward until recently, when a woman emerged claiming she gave birth to the Sultan's male child when they were engaged to be married before his first marriage. She produced a trove of love letters between them as proof and – get ready – she presented her supposed son to the court. Adding plausibility to the story, it is said that this middle aged man looks a lot like the Sultan did at that age."

"Ok, I get it," I say. "It sounds like there couldn't be a better test for *Family Finder*."

'Precisely," says Cael. "The Sultan denies knowing the woman and having the illegitimate son, but the palace, indeed the Kingdom, has divided on the issue. Everyone is trying to decide who to support depending on where they think their best interests lie. The Sultan wants an end to it, so his true son can begin his reign on firm footing."

"So how did you get involved?" I ask.

"I asked the Abbey's diplomatic people to reach out to the Sultan," Cael says. "My message simply was that although the Abbey can't take sides, we do have a tool that can settle the matter one way or another. Eventually, the King let us know that he is interested, and so I added a visit to Aurelia to our itinerary. The king is expecting us in the near future. We are to contact the palace when we arrive."

"What's my role?" I ask.

"The usual," Cael says. "You conduct the test."

"What about you?" I ask.

"I try to build goodwill without revealing anything about the second *Floe* site," Cael says.

"We seem to be moving into a new phase of our mission," I say. "Or maybe I should say we're finally starting the mission we embarked upon. I just don't know whether that's good or bad."

"What do you mean?" asks Cael.

"Well," I say, "it seems like all our old enemies are still out there, and we are about to conduct a test that's sure to anger one side of Nir's hierarchy or the other."

"Do you have thoughts?" Cael asks.

"First we need a group to accompany us into the city, to protect you," I say. "After, I'm not sure what we'll need."

"It can't be a large group in the city," Cael says. "We're still trying to not draw attention to ourselves."

"That ship has sailed, as far as I'm concerned," I say, "but either way I think we have to solidify our arrangements with Mika, and also Neenah and Brik, for the duration of the mission. It will mean telling them what we know, including your true mission, and paying them a bunch of gold."

"Agreed," says Cael. "What else?"

"Second," I say, "I think that, when you discuss this last battle with the Abbot, you should press him about what's going on. We can prove the Rusk High Council is behind the attacks now, but we still don't know if someone is paying them to do it. Tenebrus has had time to make inquiries. We need to learn what we're dealing with."

"You're right," Cael says. "I'll do it tonight at the Inn."

We continue our trek, and the rest of the day is uneventful. We've walked out of the canyon now, and the mountains are turning into foothills when we arrive at the famous, vast and haphazard Nir & Far Inn. It sports a huge magic sign from Monkworks that alternates lighting up 'Nir' in red with 'Far' in blue. The word 'Nir' starts out small and gets big, as if it's coming towards you. The word 'Far' does the opposite, starting big and getting small. Then the words evaporate and the cycle starts all over again.

Whole wings have been added over time to the original stone block structure, with no regard for style cohesion or guest navigation. Still, it's a welcome sight after a long week on a bloody road. I'm longing for a peaceful night's rest with Mika.

We are riding towards the stables when suddenly a red coach races around a corner and hurtles past us. The black wolf crest on the door is plain to see, and Cael isn't having it. He twists a hand and the front left wheel explodes, the whole carriage lurches, the driver grabs a bench brace to stay aboard, and the coach skids to a halt on the gravel lane.

Mika pulls open the coach door a second later, and hauls out the frightened little head wolf fuck himself, Lord Wolffang. "Let me go," he screams in a high, imperious voice, as his driver scurries off. "I am the Rusk Ambassador to Nir, and you are assaulting me."

Mika has a hand on his throat, and is in his face. "You call this assault, you cowardly little fuck?" she spits. "Tell us why you attacked us or you will learn what an assault actually means."

"Attack you?" he shouts back. "You have decimated my House Guard with no provocation. I will see you hanged."

Inn guards and Nir militiamen start converging on us from all sides, summoned, no doubt, by the scampering coach driver. "Arrest these people," Wolffang shouts. Then Mika is yelling over him that she is a White Sash, warranted by the Sultan of Nir, and the man she holds is a murderer. It's a tense moment, and everyone's hands are near their weapons.

Enter fucking Jinx. A head taller than anyone else, he pushes through the crowd in his monk's robes, trailing a dozen Testers and Tester trainees in his wake. "Let's all calm down here," he orders with his commanding voice. "There's been a simple misunderstanding." He flicks something at the wolf fucks coach and it starts to repair itself. "Egon, Mika, Cael, the Ambassador has the right to travel these roads unimpeded. Lord Wolffang, your coach is repaired now, and the Abbey sees no reason you should be delayed any longer."

The rest of us stand there trying to read the shades of meaning that seem suddenly to be obscuring the basic point.

Wolffang looks at Janx for a long moment, obviously calculating, before turning on his heel and reentering his coach. The driver, back in his seat, flicks his whip and they are off.

Now a lot has happened in the last few days, and I'm not the same reclusive Tester I was. I turn on Janx. "That slimeball tried to kill all of us," I say, low and seething, "and did kill some of us. You don't get to stand us down."

"What I get to do, Egon," Janx says quietly and patiently, "is save my people from a world of shit they don't understand. Now come on. This joint has a world class pub and, if you buy me an ale, I'll try to explain. You have some explaining to do too, I think."

I've got to give it to him. He's a wily bastard. Maybe it comes down to a simple benefit-of-the-doubt thing. But for whatever reason Cael, Mika and I calm down enough to follow him into the Inn, Snout at my feet, trailing the rest of our bedraggled party.

The Entrance Gallery is made of cool and gleaming marble blocks. It is a long and narrow corridor leading to a far wall made entirely of stained glass. It's a mosaic scene of a magnificent golden city against a desert landscape, and it is back lit by the evening sun. As we walk towards it we pass intricately carved stone columns supporting a triple height arched ceiling. Behind the columns on either side of us are passageways to who knows where, spaced at regular intervals. At the top of the side walls near the ceiling is more stained glass, so the entire space is filled with multi-hued light.

Passing and crisscrossing us are all the colors and looks of the Three Kingdoms: the turbans and layers of light cloth of Nir; the earth tones and fine leathers of Enduron; and the shaggy animal skins and wooly, dark grays and blacks of Rusk. Everyone excited to be heading for, or leaving behind, Aurelia. Interspersed among the travelers are uniformed Nir & Far Inn workers carrying bags and running errands. All the noises from all the bustling humanity reverberates off the marble in an undulating burble.

As we get closer to the stained glass wall, I can see a row of tables with clerks sitting behind them, apparently sorting out room arrangements. Fletch, and the rest of Mika's crew, peel off from us now to see about their lodging, and Speega takes her SpARROWS to the rooms they already keep here. Not sure what happened to the trainees, but maybe the other Testers took them to back to their high trail camp.

Janx leads Cael, Mika and me to the right, and through to one of those mysterious passageways lining the walls. The corridor ends in a massive pair of leaded glass doors under a sign reading, 'The Iron Oak Ale House,' and featuring the image of what I assume is the namesake tree spreading out wide above the lettering.

Through the doors is a landing high above the ale house floor. My first impression is of hundreds of raucous people spread out over a vast patchwork of separate sections. Each section is cordoned off by wrought iron railings and requires a step up or a step down to get to. It could have been as haphazardly arranged as the Inn itself, but for its centralizing feature: an absolutely massive, dead, peel-barked tree trunk rising up from the floor to the ceiling. The Iron Oak, no doubt. The trunk is silver gray and gleaming, and from its top spring massive limbs in a roughly wagon wheel arrangement that extend all the way out to the large room's walls. Damn if the ancient tree isn't holding the place up.

We walk down the stairs and eventually find a table to sit at. Someone brings us ale, and Mika slips her hand into mind. I'm almost ready to let my anger slip away. But not quite. The ale is just the right temperature, and it tastes so good, that for a moment I don't want to begin the conversation. Cael jumps in first. "So why are you here, Brother Janx?" he asks.

Janx puts down his tankard and sighs before beginning. "Well, that's a tale whose telling will take more than one of these," he says, his big body bunching towards us. "But first, if you will indulge me, I have only a scant understanding of what took place at the Notch. Can somebody fill me in?"

Mika takes him through it: the anticipation of a big battle and its location; the preparations; Speega and the SpARROWS; the magic bows; Cael's earth moving; the staves; the cylinder weapons; Wolffang's troops; the shrickers; the alpha and his weapons; the targeting of Cael; the fyrboren; the dead captain's orders proving all three attacks were coordinated by the same *Ky* alpha who was acting on behalf of Rusk's High Council; the fact that the high road and bridge ambushes were set in motion before Cael and Egon left the Abbey; our victory and our eight dead.

"This is an evil, evil business," Janx says when she's done. "Short of sending an army, the *Ky* bastards expended every possible resource to kill you, Cael. And they risked every possible diplomatic sanction as well. I just don't understand why they would do it. It is an unbelievable act of treachery."

We talk battle details for a while - the fight with the fyrboren, Neenah's horrific wound, the composite crossbow bolts – before Cael brings us back to the business at hand. "So, Brother Janx," Cael says, "you were about to tell us of your presence here and your intercession with Wolffang."

"Yes, of course," Janx says. "Let me just say that I am glad you are all safe. You went through an incredible ordeal, and I don't think anyone could have done better."

He stops and nods at each of us in turn, before stopping at Mika. "I also want to say that it is good to see you again, Mika. I miss you at the Abbey, and I am glad you are doing well."

"Likewise," Mika says.

155

"And to you, Egon," he says, looking at me, "I feel I owe an apology. I thought it was harebrained of the Abbot – you'll forgive the aspersion, Brother Venarius - to send Monkworks Number Two out of the Abbey without a full escort, but I was overruled. So then I felt I had to send my best with Cael, Egon, and that is you. I just didn't think it through, and I put you in great danger. I should have found another way, and I'm sorry."

Wait, this is Jinx? Jolly Janx, the sadistic Tester trainer? That Janx? To borrow a phrase: 'What the fucking fuck?'

Mika breaks the silence, to pile on. "The fact is, Brother Janx," she says, "that none of us would be here except for Egon puzzling out what was coming next and preparing us for it. So regarding my own skin, I'd say you made a grand selection." Janx and Cael laugh. I still can't think of something to say.

"I've been trying to straighten you out, Egon, since I pulled you out of that jail," says Janx. "But I can see now that whatever I thought I was doing is long done. You are a fine young man, and you did most of it your damn self, and that's the truth of it."

Under the table, Mika squeezes my hand. I squeeze hers back.

Finally, I clear my throat. "Do you know what we call you, behind your back, Brother Janx?" I ask.

"Jolly Janx?" he asks. "Jinx?"

"Mostly it's 'Jinx' now," I say, "since we all sort of expect you to bring calamity down upon us. So no apology due on that score. And I appreciate what you've tried to do and be for me for all these years. Nevertheless, you are a hard man to like, Brother Janx. I also have to say, though, that you are a hard man to dislike, so I find myself always bouncing back and forth between the two. Like how you butted in at the stables before, compared to now with your complimentary words." I shrug. "I guess what I'm trying to say is that no matter which way I'm leaning at any given moment, I have never lost my basic trust in you."

Everyone's quiet for a bit, and I wonder if I should have just accepted the compliments and moved on. Finally, though, Janx says, "Fair enough, Egon," and raises his tankard. "Let's drink to trust." And so we do.

The house is completely packed now with travelers looking to let loose. One section is for ax throwers gambling over their throws into mythological creature-shaped targets. Another is for card-players seated at tables who are mostly silent accept for the occasional shout and groan. A third section is packed with those gambling on fights among small, fire-breathing creatures produced by throwing Monkworks dragon coins into a pit. They battle each other to the death, then they all evaporate. It's a bit bloodthirsty, admittedly, but no harm to anyone. This place is fun, I think, and I make a promise to come back with Mika under less fraught circumstances.

Janx takes a swallow of ale and starts up again. "Now before I finally get started on my explanations," he says, "I want to take a moment to talk to you, Brother Venarius."

Cael leans in towards him.

"You're the future of the Abbey," Janx says, "and someday you will be in charge. So no matter how vital you think what you are doing out here is, the most important thing is getting back safe. We are all depending on you."

Cael chooses not to get into it with him. "I appreciate that, Brother Janx," he says, "and I can't tell you how appealing getting back safe sounds to me." He smiles. "So now," he continues, moving on, "tell us your tale before the ale runs out."

We laugh, and Janx continues. "Anyway," he says, "two days ago I'm contacted by a Guardian, the same Guardian you asked to do you a favor, Egon. He shows me what he showed you: a godsdamned *Ky* alpha, a bunch of shriekers, and about a company of Lord Wolffang's troops coming at you from two directions. So I went to Abbot Tenebrus. That's when he informed me of the first two attacks on you. After that, it was clear to see what was going on, and I convinced him a potential massacre was unfolding."

"What did he do?" I ask.

"He sent two companies of Abbey militia down the trade road after you," Janx says, "with orders to defend you guys if necessary, but only if necessary, and otherwise not engage with anyone except in self-defense. And he fired off a warning to Immobilin Keep."

"So what did you do then, Brother Janx?" Mika asks.

"I had a training mission on the schedule," Janx says, "so with the Abbot's blessing I moved it up and double-timed the trainees along the high trail day and night, hoping I could reach you in time to help. The Guardian kept me abreast of potential danger on the high trail ahead of us, and then showed me the aftermath of the Pagan's Notch battle. I decided to continue anyway, thinking I might catch up to you here at the Inn."

"What happened to the Abbey militia?" Cael asks.

"The Abbot called them home when he heard from you that the battle was over," Janx says.

"Makes sense," says Cael.

"Not to me," says Janx. "He should have sent a military escort with you right from the beginning."

"He didn't want to focus attention on our mission," Cael says.

"Don't you think that, after Pagan's Notch, it's time to rethink that strategy?" Janx asks.

"I think the Abbot knows what he's doing," Cael says, stiffening up. I'm reminded that Cael outranks Janx in Abbey hierarchy, and has no obligation to listen to him.

"So when you solve the Sultan's very public succession problem in a very public way in the next couple of days?" Janx persists. "Will that keep the focus off your mission?"

"Everyone's attention will be on the prototype, and not on my ultimate mission," says Cael.

Janx jolts, and leans in. "Your ultimate mission," he says, his voice soft, his eyes intense. "And what might that be?"

I would come to find out what a chance this was for things to go in a whole other direction. But, it wasn't to be.

"It's a diplomatic mission straight from the Abbot," Cael says. "It's not my place to discuss it."

Janx looks at him and shakes his head. "I hope you know what you're doing, Brother Venarius," he says.

"I believe the Abbot does," says Cael.

If Cael doesn't mention the second *Floe* site to the man who discovered it, I can only assume he has his reasons. Anyway, it remains his secret to tell.

"So let's go back to Lord Wolf Fuck and my hand on his throat," says Mika. "Why did you let him ride away?"

Janx shrugs. "Think about it. He's an official representative of Rusk in Nir. Attacking him risks an immediate war between those two kingdoms, pulls the Abbey in, and leaves all of you liable to be hanged."

"So then why did he back off?" asks Mika.

"You, for one thing." Janx says. "That white sash business was inspired. It unbalanced him. It gave you authority. Then I come along invoking the name of the Abbey, and he decided to cut his losses."

"So he just gets away with it?" I demand.

"I'd have to know a whole lot more about what's going on before I answer that question, Egon," Janx says. "But I know how hierarchies work when someone fails to do the job they are assigned. This guy fucked up royally, along with the alpha, and he'll be called to answer for it."

"Do you have any idea what this whole thing is about?" Mika asks.

"Well, Mika, I only know what I see," says Janx. "What it amounts to is that the alchemists and the military of Rusk have joined forces to attack the Abbey. How that gets sorted without a war breaking out, I don't know."

"Did you know that the Abbot warned us about further use of Tester Havens?" I ask.

"What? No," says Janx, surprised. "When was this and what reason did he give?"

"It was after the first wolf-fuck attack on us at the bridge," I say. "He said he thought the Havens may be compromised, because of how close the shriekers came to finding us there that first night out."

"Well, that's really odd," says Janx. "He's said nothing to me. In fact, I'll be stopping with the trainees at the one you used, before we go back to the Abbey."

"When do you go back?" I ask him.

"It will be a few days yet. I plan to stick around on the high trail with my people, in case there is any more trouble. You know how to reach me, Egon," he says, standing, and holding up his ring.

I nod. "Thanks for coming after us, Brother Janx," I say.

"Sorry I was late," he says, and moves off through barroom crowd.

TWO: DISAPPOINT ME AND YOU DIE

After Janx leaves, a barmaid comes over with a fresh round of ale, and says it's compliments of a gentleman over there who wants a word with us. We look to where she's pointing, and there's a tall, middle aged, richly dressed man leaning against a column watching us. When he sees us notice him he straightens up and briskly walks over. "A minute of your time?" he asks.

We point to the chair Janx has just vacated and he sits down. "I come from the palace," he says, and that gets our attention. "My name is Encos Var, Minister to Sultan Anseem Hawarri, who has tasked me to speak with you." Cael makes introductions, and Var starts asking about our satisfaction with the Inn, so I take a moment to discreetly rummage through the pack at my feet for the 'M' medal of *Fact Finder*. I don't know this guy, so let's see if what he's about to say is true.

I find it and clasp it in my closed fist, and Cael is saying he hasn't had the time to brief Mika and me on our visit with the Sultan and Sultana. He says that if it's important for what Minister Var has to say, he will do so now.

"I don't think that will be necessary for this," Var replies. "The Sultan merely wishes me to welcome you to Nir. He has asked me to offer my services as a guide to our court politics, as well as to bring you up to date on the current state of affairs. Would that be acceptable?"

Hmmm, Mr. Charm. At least the medal stays quiet.

"Please proceed," says Cael, sounding so official.

"I guess the first thing I should bring up," says Var, "is that the Court –indeed, all of the Three Kingdoms – is aware of your unfortunate hardships on your journey from the Abbey. The Sultan, along with his Most Exalted Sultana Cadiah Hawarri, offer their heartfelt regrets and good wishes."

"Thank you," says Cael. "What has been the overall reaction in the Kingdoms?"

"Everyone is trying to walk back from the brink," Var says. "The High Council of Rusk in Immobilin Keep has recalled Lord Wolffang, claiming to be completely unaware of his actions. I believe your encounter with him at the stables coincided with his receiving the news."

"You saw that?" Mika asks.

"Oh yes, I've been here waiting for you since last night. I was figuring out how to intervene myself when your impressively large and decisive colleague beat me to it." The medal stays quiet.

"Meanwhile," he continues, "Rusk says that there is no evidence linking it to the reported attacks on Abbey representatives, and categorically denies any involvement."

"Lying bastards," says Mika.

"Be that as it may," Var says, "that's their position and, without new developments, I don't think they'll budge."

Cael reaches into his pack for the orders he took off of Wolffang's dead captain. He puts it on the table in front of Var. "This is an order we took off of a dead captain of Lord Wolffang's House Guard after the battle of Pagan's Notch. It was issued just before I left the Abbey on my mission. In it, Wolffang says he is acting on orders from the High Council and directs the captain to

163

put his troops at the disposal of the *Ky* alpha who eventually attacked us. Would you say this qualifies as a 'new development?'"

"Could Wolffang be lying about the High Council's involvement?" Var asks.

I bring my fist up from underneath the table and open it, revealing the *Fact Finder* 'M' medal. I run it over the written order and it remains silent. "He's not," I say, "and we can prove it." I leave the medal out on the table. Let the minister make of it what he will.

Var eyes the medal and then goes back to studying the document. "What will you do with this?" he asks.

"Inform my Abbot of it, for starters," Cael says.

"When?" Var asks.

"This evening," Cael says.

"As you must inform your Abbot," Var says, "so I must inform my Sultan. It is my hope that communications about it ends there, for now, although who knows where this will lead? It is a very dangerous document, I think."

"Don't you think it utterly refutes the notion that Rusk had no official involvement in these attacks?" Cael asks.

"I do," Var says. "I just don't know if that's a good thing or a bad thing, if our goal is to avoid outright war."

"But what about simple justice?" Mika asks.

"I want justice for you," Var says. "I just want peace more."

The Monkworks lie finder remains silent. Regardless of where we stand on matters it is useful to know he's not trying to deceive us.

"So how do you suggest we proceed from here?" I ask.

"I suggest you do nothing more with the order than what we've discussed here," Var says, "so that we can see how the situation progresses. Maybe your Abbot will agree with that, we shall see. In any case, I think you should relax for a couple of days here at the Inn, recover from your ordeal, and watch for developments. You are in Nir territory, I have posted guards, and I think you will be safe for now, at least. After that, I will escort you to the palace."

"We'll discuss this among ourselves and keep you posted," Cael says.

"Very well," Var says.

"So tell us," Cael says, "what do we be face at the palace?"

"Of course," Var says, "let's get on to that. May I suggest, though, because I know you have just come off the road, that we order dinner while we are talking? They have a famous saffron lamb stew with Allavian rice that I think you will like."

We all agree, and Var signals our barmaid and says a few quiet words. Then he begins his introduction to Nir life at court. "I'm afraid you are facing quite a spectacle at the palace. It has been the talk of the Kingdom for months now, ever since this woman, Azedeh Azad, came forward claiming her supposed son, Ali Hawarri, of all the surnames, is the rightful heir to the throne. Add to that the drama on the trade road, and this showdown with your device has become a 'can't miss' event."

"What if we find that Ali is the rightful heir?" Cael asks.

165

"There will be bedlam, of course," says Var, "followed by some intense negotiations. One way or the other, I expect the Crown Prince, Adib Hawarri, will sit on the throne."

"Will the event remain peaceful?" I ask.

Var shrugs. "We'll be prepared for anything," he says.

Their barmaid comes back, this time with a tray containing separate pots of seasoned lamb, rice, vegetables and fragrant sauce, as well as bread, eating bowls and utensils.

"This is what I do with this," says Var, breaking off their conversation to concentrate on their delicately scented dinner. He dishes rice into a bowl, then vegetables and meat, and then ladles on the sauce overall. Then he pulls off a hunk of bread for dipping and scooping. "Please enjoy," he says, waiting for us to fill our bowls in similar fashion.

All is silent eating for a moment, until Mika says: "Oh my."

"It's good, no?" asks Var.

"It's heaven," says Mika, and I have to agree.

"So tell us about this famous Inn, Minister Var," says Mika, between bites.

"Well, let's see," he says. "It is over 700 years old, the recipe for this stew is over 500 years old, and you may be 100 years old before you find your rooms tonight."

We laugh. "So navigation is as bad as it looks from the outside?" I ask.

"If anything, it's worse," Var says. "But it's not all bad, because hidden along these meandering corridors are wonderful shops where you can buy everything from clothes and jewelry to haircuts and wagon wheels."

"I know what I'm doing tomorrow," says Mika.

"Go for it," I say. "We need to tell the others, too."

We finish the stew, and then some sort of delicious lemon cake, before Cael resumes our earlier conversation. "There are three things I hope you can arrange for us at the palace, Minister Var," Cael says.

"If they are within my power," says Var. "Please, what do you need?"

"First," says Cael, "a private audience with the Sultan and the Crown Prince, just before the public event."

"What do you have in mind?" asks Var.

"I wish to demonstrate our paternity and lineage tool, which we call *Family Finder*, in private first," says Cael, "as a courtesy, so that they will know what to expect in public."

"Yes, I think they will appreciate that," says Var. "What else?"

"Next," says Cael, "we will have to demonstrate the accuracy of our device to all present at the public gathering, before we use it on something as important as succession."

"Of course," says Var. "What do you propose?"

"I'm thinking," says Cael, "that you select five nobles, well known, from across the political spectrum and above reproach, to help us with our demonstration. We ask that their children hide in any part of the city they choose, with an escort of course, and we let the parents watch as *Family Finder* finds them."

"That is possible, I think, yes," says Var.

"Then I would like to do the reverse." Cael says. "Five other nobles can hide themselves in the city, and have their children watch as *Family Finder* find them."

"Yes, I see,'" says Var. "I will just have to explain the demonstration clearly to the nobles, so there are no surprise public revelations."

Cael chuckles. "For sure," he says.

"Was there something else?" Var asks.

"Yes, one more thing," says Cael. "We'll need a big table to accommodate the *Family Finder* tool and the participants in the big reveal, including: the Sultan, the Crown Prince, and the Crown Prince's sister; Azedeh Azad and Ali Hawarri; Egon, and I; and anyone else you think protocol demands."

"Mika will not be joining you?" Var asks.

Cael smiles, and looks at Mika. "This is one of those things related to not having had time to discuss things previously," he says. "I am hopeful that while Egon and I are running the test, Mika will be running our security."

Mika nods.

"That will require coordination with our own security services," Var says.

"Of course," Mika says.

"Then so be it," says Var. "That is all for now?"

"Yes," says Cael.

"Very well," says Var. "I will do my best to make these things happen." He raises his tankard of ale. "Here's to our success," he toasts, and we all toast with him. He stands up, suggesting we meet for lunch tomorrow to plan our arrival at the palace. We agree, and he says goodnight and departs.

"That was interesting," Mika says.

"And," I say, grabbing the 'M' medal again, "truthful."

"So you think we can trust him?" Cael asks.

"So far, so good," I say, shrugging.

"Well, I for one can't handle any more intrigue this evening," Mika says. "Let's call it a night."

We head back up the stairs and out the glass doors to the Entrance Gallery. The sun has gone down behind the stained glass wall, which nevertheless retains its arresting beauty, and the few clerks left behind desks are a lot less busy. Before we can approach one, someone in an Inn uniform comes over and says our suites have been arranged for by the royal palace, and we should follow him. I lose track of how we get to our rooms, but it involves two sets of stairs and many turns. Eventually, we arrive at the end of a long corridor, where a guard in Nir military uniform nods to us. "Have a good evening," he says. Our Inn guide directs Cael to the door on the left, and Mika and me to the right. Matching corner suites, courtesy of the charming Encos Var.

Before we enter, the guide says, "We have a suite for Snout as well, if she'll come with me, with toys, treats, groomers, and other dogs to play with."

"By all means," I say, and thank him for his courtesy with gold. Snout pads off peacefully in his wake. We say goodnight to Cael, who I very much hope sends for Fletch.

169

"Breakfast will be sent up when you call for it," the Nir guard says. "Just notify whoever is here."

We thank him and go inside. Mika does a twirl, taking in the view of foothills, the moonslight, a bed so lofty with pillows and comforters that we will have to jump up to get into it, flowers, and chilling wine on a table against the wall.

"For a barbarian," she says, with a sly grin, "you take me to the nicest places."

"Perhaps you can help me with this topknot," I suggest.

"Follow me," she says, pulling me towards the bath.

I go meekly.

Later, washed and refreshed, I am on my back among mountains of fluff on the bed. Mika comes out of the bath wearing a towel wrapped around her head like a turban, and nothing else. She arranges herself at the bottom of the bed and I can no longer see her, just her turban, so far have I sunk into the mattress. Still, she soon makes me acutely aware of the location of her mouth and lips, by the clever use of which she rivets my attention for long, slow, incandescent minutes. I watch her turban move, mostly up and down, sometimes circularly, sometimes still. I cannot possibly be more attentive.

But then, she pauses.

"Don't stop," I moan.

She uses her fingers to play me like a flute, then blows warm air along my quivering length. "I don't think you understand the situation, warrior scum," she purrs.

"Wha?" I manage to gasp out. "What situation?"

I feel Mika move back up to the top of the bed and then she straddles me. "The situation," she says, flinging off her turban and slipping me inside her, "is that I am a powerful desert princess, and you are my helpless captive." She begins a slow, steady churn. "Disappoint me," she says, "and you die."

What can I say? I do my best to rise to the challenge.

THREE: CAEL IS ABOUT TO DIE

Next morning, after more revelry and a delicious breakfast, Mika and I decide clothes shopping and personal grooming are our top priorities. "We owe it to the mission," I say. As a precaution, I transfer the four prototypes to my vest from my pack, which I will be leaving in the room.

We knock next door, and Cael and Fletch approve of our plan. With our guard showing us the way, the four of us end up on a floor with a wide corridor and dozens of shops on either side. We all agree to go off on our own, but to meet at the far end of the corridor before lunch. I'm looking for palace-worthy clothes and a barber, while Mika goes off on her own errands. At one point, I see her through a window wearing a pale green robe and holding a bright red drink while being escorted by two smartly-robed and exotic-looking women into the mysterious interior of a scented shop. I see our guard ahead, presumably shadowing Cael.

My first stop is a barbershop, where my hair and beard are trimmed. Then I look for an expensive men's clothing shop. I'm stumped as to how to find one with a sense of humor, where I can explain without being judged why I must always wear a vest and that it will change color depending on what I am wearing. Then I figure, what the hell, they all must be used to eccentricity, given the wealth they cater to.

That, in fact, turns out to be true. I buy three outfits from three different shops, all assuring me that I am now completely royalty-worthy, and that the palace will be paying the bill. Gods almighty.

Additionally, they all pointedly urge me to have the vest washed thoroughly before approaching the palace. I have to think on it. You don't want to jump in to something like that. Maybe Cael has a magical solution. Maybe there is a device I don't know about yet.

Eventually, the four of us meet up again, laden with packages and sporting new looks. Mika's skin is glowing, and her lustrous black hair falls away from her face and across her shoulders in rivulets, like a raven river. "Wow," I say, taking her in. "You really are a desert princess."

She takes my arm. "Wait for show and tell later, Egon, when I model everything I bought," she says. "You won't leave me alone for four weeks ever again."

"Can Not Wait," I say, with feeling.

I ask our guard to guide us to our lunch with Encos Var. He moves off, with us following behind and laughing and chatting about the morning's paid-for adventures. We do the usual maze-like maneuvers, but at some point the narrow corridor we are in ends at a beautiful outdoor courtyard, still surrounded by hotel walls, ringed with vendor carts, and decorated with huge pots of blooming flowers.

The guard leads us through the happy throngs of shoppers, slowing down to allow us to browse. Cael and Fletch move a ways in front of us, as Mika and I get distracted by a table of ladies' flimsy nightclothes. Then we run into Neenah and Brik, on their own shopping spree, and we compare notes. I glance up towards Cael and Fletch to make sure we're not holding them up, just in time to catch fast movement coming in from their left. I take off running.

"Cael," I scream, but neither he, Fletch nor the guard react like they hear me. I surge forward, and indignant shoppers are spinning out of my way. Cael is about to die, I can see it all unfolding, and I'm too far away to stop it.

The three of them are still walking forward, their backs to the attacker. He is a small, wiry-looking cleric with a shaved head and light purple robe, raising a long, bone-colored dagger above his head. A *Ky* dagger. I run forward, still shouting, as the man extends his reach to maximum height, preparing to launch his deadly downward arc.

Suddenly, I flash on those new projectile devices I took from the Haven's rowan tree armory, and as quick as thought one is in my hand. The device is simply a handgrip, with a short, metal tube that fits between the fingers of my clenched fist. I swing it up and around from my vest pocket and, as its trajectory changes, the objects and people in its path are briefly silhouetted in radiant silver.

Cael, Fletch and the guard are turning towards the danger now, too late to react to the blade that is plunging down towards the *Floe* magician. My device settles on the would-be assassin and, when he lights up in a sparkling nimbus, I squeeze. Simultaneously there is a harsh sizzle and strong jolt to my hand. The attacker lurches violently against the courtyard's back wall, drops the dagger, and goes down.

The happy day in the courtyard is complete bedlam now as I put the spent device back in my vest. Mika moves up beside me and grips my bicep, her short sword drawn. Neenah and Brik appear on either side of us, their blades out as well. I see the guard waving his arm at us frantically, as he talks to an Inn employee, who then runs off. The four of us remember to snatch up our purchases before working through the agitated crowd to join the others. The three of them are at an exit to the courtyard when we catch up. Before I follow them through the door I pick up the dagger from next to the obviously dead knife-wielder, and toss it into one of my shopping sacks. Another reason why clothing merchants to the faking-it wealthy need a working sense of humor.

174

We do the maze thing again, and we eventually go through a door and out to the stables. Encos Var waves us over to his big coach, which conspicuously has no horses and no place for any, but does have a driver. "Ah," says Cael, "the M12, a special order we filled for the Sultan."

"The M12?" I ask.

"The M is for Monkworks," Cael says, seemingly unflustered, "and the 12 is for the number of horses we've replaced using *Floe*. It's an armored horseless carriage."

Why don't I ever get the good stuff to test.

The six of us pile in and are moving before we properly sit down. There are a dozen horsemen in front and behind us, and there is a bowman on the coach's roof. We swerve around the stables and onto the hotel lane that will take us out to the trade route. The ride is unbelievably smooth.

"Where are we going?" asks Cael.

"To a palace hideaway where I can protect you better," says Var. "I am abjectly embarrassed by this security breakdown. I apologize to each of you."

"The guard couldn't have done anything," I say. "It happened too fast in a crowded space."

"The fault is entirely mine," says Var, "for underestimating the threat inside the Inn. Unfortunately, the guard will pay the price. I fear he is already dead."

There is shocked silence inside the coach for a moment.

"But why?" Cael finally asks.

Var shakes his head. "It is the unyielding code of the Palace Guard," he says. "They know that mistakes cannot be tolerated because the stakes are so high. Even, apparently, if the real mistake is someone else's. It is not something I can stop. The most I can do is take care of the family."

After that, we ride on in dejected silence through rolling foothills that are becoming lower, dryer and browner as we proceed. Where once there was only the trade route, now there are other roads frequently intersecting it. After about an hour we take one of them to the left, and wind our way up one of the dehydrated hills. The palace hideaway turns out to be a walled compound built on a low cliff overlooking a desert plateau. In the distance, behind us, we can still make out the peaks of the Infinity Mountains.

We drive through an elaborate and sentried gate, and godsdamn if it doesn't begin to snow. Our horseless coach is suddenly a great open-air sled pulled by horses, and we are covered in blankets against the abruptly chill air. There are several buildings inside the wall, most connected by covered walkways, and they are all built on an alpine theme. They feature great vertical wooden beams supporting steeply sloping slate roofs, all frosted with snow, and bejeweled with hanging icicles. There are decorated snowmen about, and children are throwing snowballs. Actual children? Could be, I suppose.

"This week is Winter Wonderland at the compound," says Var. "I'm looking forward to next week, Tropical Breezes."

"This came out great," exclaims Cael. Maybe admiring his own work?

"The Sultan and his family love it," says Var. "His particular favorite is 'Oasis Dream.'"

"I'll be sure to let the Abbot know," Cael says. "He was also involved with this project."

176

Also involved? What a show off.

We pull up under a portico in front of the largest chalet, a wonder in giant, leaded glass windows, lit from within by warm yellow light. Fake Monkworks reindeer are grazing on the front lawn, poking their faces into the snow, presumably trying to reach the magic grass below. We hop out of the sleigh and onto a moving staircase that takes us gradually up to the chalet's raised main floor.

We follow Var through big wood-plank doors and into a grand vestibule, whose ceiling rises the entire three stories of the structure. A long chain holds a huge wooden chandelier above our heads, lit by two dozen Monkworks torches. There is a large sitting room to our left with ceilings crossed with massive beams, and to our front is a carved stone fireplace blazing away without visible smoke. On our right is a glass bubble on a glowing vertical tract, which I assume transports people to the upper floors.

Var turns to us. "Welcome to the ever-changing and completely delightful Lake House," he says, "the occasional getaway home for the royal family. You will be safe here for tonight and tomorrow night, and then we can proceed to the palace in Aurelia. Meanwhile, Snout is on her way to us by luxury coach, along with the things you left behind in your rooms, due to our hasty exit."

"Thank you, Minister Var, for your wonderful hospitality," Cael says. "You have thought of everything."

"It's the least I can do, under the circumstances," Var says.

"I brought my enemies to you," Cael says, "so it is for me to apologize to you for this burden."

Var shrugs. "Let us say no more of it, then," he says. "We will show you to your rooms so you can freshen up, and then I suggest we reconvene down here to enjoy a delayed lunch. Is that acceptable?"

We all sound our agreement, and he leaves us to make the arrangements.

"We have a lot to figure out while we rest here," I say, "because so far we are just bouncing from one crisis to another. We have to get out in front of this mess."

"Agreed," says Cael, "although I fear it won't be easy."

"And you call yourself a magician," says Fletch.

"I feel like a trainee," Cael says, and we laugh.

"I think I should pay my people and release them for now," says Mika. "Same with Speega and her spARROWS. We can always ask them to rejoin us when we have need."

We all agree with that, and Mika asks Brik – who appears to always handle merc money matters – to make arrangements with Var to send the word back to the Inn, along with a suitable amount of gold.

A Lake House housekeeper comes for us then, and we follow her into the glass bubble. She presses something and we smoothly glide up two flights to the sitting room of a suite. There are three doors open to separate bedrooms. Cael and Fletch go left, Neenah and Brik go right, and Mika and I go straight ahead into an enormous room. It seems to run the entire length of the chalet.

On our left are a row of three glass double doors leading out to a long balcony overlooking an interior garden open to the sky. Everything is blooming, yet everything is dusted with snow. I don't know whether to admire it or make a note about a device glitch. To the right is a wall of frosted window panes which, at this height in the house, frame a spectacular view of the snow-covered compound and the scorched desert plateau beyond. The room's furnishings are even more luxurious than those at the Inn. Our morning's purchases are neatly arranged on an oaken bench.

Mika is out on the balcony on an inspection tour, and I come over and hug her from behind. "I know what you're thinking," I say, "and all I can say is don't get used to this."

She covers my arms with hers. "Too late, my prince," she says. "You have already accustomed me to a life of pampered excess."

"In that case, your highness, I guess all I can do is escort you to an exquisite lunch," I say.

"Do you think it is permitted for a princess to wear a sword while dining?" she asks, her hand on its pommel.

"Perhaps if the fish is overcooked," I crack.

She ignores me, and sighs. "It's just so hard to know how royalty should act."

I gallantly dive into that opening. "In my experience," I say, "a princess must always act to please her beloved prince."

"I see," she says haughtily. "It's clear you have much to learn as well. Shall we go?"

And we do.

The others are in the sitting area when we come out, and together we manage the bubble. On the main floor, we follow the irresistible aroma of cooking past double doors open to a huge kitchen, and into a cheery sunroom set for a feast. The room is warmed by a dazzling fireplace. Outside, the snow has increased in intensity, but inside we are deliciously cozy. Var rises from his chair at the sumptuously arranged table, and gestures for us to join him.

The food is wonderful, endless, and varied. Var tries to keep the mood light, telling intriguing, and sometimes hilarious, stories about the royal court in Aurelia. Like the time the Sultan wanted

Oasis Dream, while his much younger Sultana insisted upon Jungle Safari. 'But I'm the Sultan,' the Sultan cried. 'Well, dearest Sultan," the Sultana says, "if you ever want to slake your thirst at my oasis again, you'll take me to the jungle.'

"And jungle it was," says Var, as we all laugh.

Together, we work towards our own small oasis of relaxation before, all too soon, it's time to reengage with the business at hand. As the final plates are being cleared and there is a lull in the otherwise lively conversation, Var clears his throat. "I have had some word from the Inn," he says.

"What is it," says Cael.

"It's about your attacker," Var says. "He was a Nir cleric and a member of the Swin Jin Ree, a secretive cult opposed to your magic devices and funded by the *Ky* breeders of Immobilin Keep."

"So this was no isolated attack by a fanatic," Cael says. "He was encouraged or sent to assassinate me by the *Ky*."

"It appears to be the case," says Var. "He arrived at the Inn just this morning, from Aurelia. He must have traveled through the night after receiving his orders. And as you know, he was carrying a rare *Ky* blade."

"He worked fast," says Mika. "I suppose Wolffang could have reported seeing us if he was headed to Aurelia after our encounter. He could have arrived there by midnight."

"This is insane," Cael mutters, and he is right. This is the fourth attempt on his life since we left the abbey. Sooner or later they will get him if we don't change the dynamic.

"We have the rest of today and tomorrow to put our heads together and figure out a better strategy," I say.

"Use your suite sitting area to meet privately," Var suggests.

I nod. "Once again, thanks for your hospitality."

He nods, puts down his napkin and stands. "And now I must attend to other duties," he says.

Cael holds up a hand. "I think you should hear this too, Minister Var," he says. "I spoke to Abbot Tenebrus last night, but with all the craziness I haven't had a chance to share the conversation."

Var settles back down.

"I gave him a full report about the Notch," Cael says, "including the alpha, the Wolffang troops, the shriekers, and the fyrboren. I also told him about the orders we found on Wolffang's dead captain, the confrontation we had with him at the Inn, and the news that he has been recalled to Rusk."

"What did he say?" I ask.

"He said that he is being stonewalled by Immobilin Keep. And now, given my report last night proving official coordination among the *Ky* Breedership, the alpha, and the military to attack Abbey officials, he has no choice but to act decisively. So he will immediately recall our ambassadors from Rusk, and he will begin to mobilize the Abbey for war."

Var looks stricken. "How so?" he asks.

"He said he will strengthen our patrols in all directions on the trade route," Cael says. "He will close the trade route to Rusk to military or construct traffic of any kind. Plus, he will recall any available troops to the Abbey from around the Three Kingdoms, to reinforce our garrison. Oh, and he will increase the stockpiling of food, weapons, and devices of the more destructive kind."

"This is very serious," Var says. "Is there more?"

"The Abbot told me he is going to reach out to Nir and Enduron," Cael says, "to buttress our alliances and to consider a joint strategy. And lastly, he will call for the leaders of Nir, Enduron and Rusk to meet him for a last chance peace conference, to be held at Floendahl Heights in four weeks' time."

"These are breathtaking developments," Var says. "Things are moving faster than I expected."

"He is smoking them out," Mika says. "When this goes public they won't be able to stonewall anymore."

"Did he change his stance on ending this mission?" I ask.

"He has formally requested that Nir provide me with an escort while I am in their Kingdom on Abbey business, and they've agreed," Cael says. "Additionally, he is issuing a starker warning today, which will say that any further attacks by agents of Rusk on Abbey officials will be considered an act of war with immediate consequences."

"Will a warning like that work?" asks Fletch skeptically.

"We can hope so," I say, "but we have to assume it won't until it's proven otherwise."

"Agreed," says Mika.

A Nir military officer enters the sunroom then and whispers something to Var. "I fear I really must leave you now," Var says, standing back up. "I am summoned to Aurelia for consultations with the Sultan. I will return in time to brief you on the plans for the big succession event."

We all stand up then as Var leaves. Then Snout comes bounding into the room, fresh from her luxury suite at the Inn. She briefly bumps her butt into my knee, then heads for her one true love, table scraps. There still are a few, so I feed her some bits to keep her from jumping up on top of the table and embarrassing the shit out of me. Then, we head back upstairs to begin our planning.

FOUR: I'VE BEEN VERY BAD

The six of us gather in the suite's sitting room, and I use my Guardian ring to shield our conversation. I open things up: "In two days we will reach Aurelia and that will conclude our business arrangement," I say. "So the first order of business today is for me to ask each of the four of you to sign back up to help Cael and me finish the rest of the mission. There will be gold, of course, but beyond that we will share what information we can with you today to help you make a decision."

Brik gets right down to it. "Why are you continuing to test these devices, Cael," he asks, "when you're being hunted relentlessly and the Kingdoms are heading towards war?"

"I'm afraid the urgency has only increased," says Cael. "If there is war, the Abbey will need the income from the prototypes. Plus, we've already agreed to the tests, which are aimed at cementing ties with important segments of Nir society. Now, with war looming, it is more important than ever that I don't disappoint them."

"So explain that part," Fletch says, "about the tests cementing ties with Nir."

Cael looks at me for a moment, trying to come to a decision about what he should say. Finally, he seems to make up his mind. "Nir will be an important ally in case there is war," he begins, "but there is another reason the Abbey needs Nir's support, and it is the true purpose of my mission."

I have to hand it to him. Cael really knows how to get people to pay attention.

"My ultimate assignment," he says, "is to establish a second Monkworks manufactory over a new source of *Floe* that's currently within Nir territory. I need to build strong relationships with the Nir hierarchy, so that when the time comes and I ask, they will grant us the land. It's the same as Floendahl Abbey, which is situated on sovereign land granted jointly by the Three Kingdoms. To cultivate the relationships I need, I worked with the Abbey's diplomatic corps to schedule the prototype tests in ways that would be useful to Nir power players."

"So that's why you're heading into Aurelia," says Neenah.

"Exactly," says Cael. "My first stop is to employ a prototype to try to be of use to the Sultan and the ruling class. Then, we go out into the deep desert to the prison city of Gume, which is run by Nir's powerful military. After that, we go to the coast to Portus Sironika, to meet with the leaders of the Seafaring Merchants Guild, a major force in Nir's economy. And then we test the last prototype in the holy city of Jakarina, where we will try to earn the support of the clergy. When the tests are done, I will head further up the coast to the site of the new *Floe* source."

"So I gather the *Ky* breeders don't want to see a second Monkworks location," Mika says. "That's why they are hunting you?"

Cael laughs. "Take your pick," he says. "The new site, the prototypes, the fact that I'm a *Floe* magician; they are all reasons someone might want to kill me. So let me be candid: This will be a dangerous undertaking and if you choose to come with me your lives will be at risk."

"What will you need from us, Egon?" asks Brik.

"I need you to protect Cael during the tests," I say.

"What about between tests?" Neenah asks. "Are you talking about more ambushes on the road? Because I don't think that will work for me."

I nod to Neenah. "You are absolutely right. We need to change our tactics, or Cael and anyone with him will eventually get beaten. So no, I'm not asking anyone here for a repeat. I would like to propose something different."

"We're all ears," says Brik.

"I want to use the Guardians, if they'll agree," I say. "There is a Tester Haven in the desert between Aurelius and Gume, and a second on the coast between Portus Sironika and Jakarina. I haven't had the chance to discuss this yet with you, Cael, but, depending on the outcome of this meeting, I intend to ask the Gryphons to allow Cael sanctuary between the tests, and to fly him in and back for each testing event. Meanwhile, the rest of us will ride between cities with a Nir military escort. I can't say we won't draw an attack before they realize Cael is gone. But I think everyone here will be a lot safer than we have been so far. What do you think?"

There's silence for a few beats while everyone absorbs the implications.

"You think the Guardians will participate?" asks Neenah.

"I think they might, for the same reason they flew Cael and me out of the first Haven: They are angry about the attack on the Haven by the *Ky*."

"But you're saying we could still be attacked on the road?" Neenah asks.

"Can't rule it out," I say. "But, we are going to be in the desert instead of a canyon, with fewer places for enemies to hide in ambush, and we will have the military. I also hope to enlist the Guardians for surveillance."

"I should tell all of you up front that I'm in this thing to the end, regardless," Mika says. "But I have to say I like the plan. If the Guardians come in with us, I think we should go along with it."

Neenah and Brik look at each other for a moment and then Neenah says, "Ok, we're with you, Mika."

"I'm in if Cael is on board," says Fletch.

"I like the plan, too," Cael says. "I'm pretty much willing to do anything to reduce further risk to you all."

"So this is great," I say, smiling. "I can see the mission working out now."

"And I'm grateful to you all," Cael says. "The only other thing I would ask is to not mention the new Monkworks site to anyone outside this immediate group."

Just then, we hear the bubble coming up. Its door opens and two Lake House palace workers enter the sitting area to deposit trays containing six colorfully wrapped squares. They leave, and Cael passes out one to each of us.

"Just think of the best meal you've ever had in your life, and then open your package," he says.

I think of elk from Enduron and, you guessed it, that's what's sizzling hot inside my square, along with all the fixings. The others find their own special feasts. Cael looks at me, grinning. "All those times you trashed my devices?" he says. "I learned to really enjoy not giving you anything to test that I thought you might like."

"What a vindictive asshat," I say ruefully.

He just smiles.

After dinner we decide to call it a day. We each grab snacks and carafes of sweet wine from the remains of dinner, and then head into our respective rooms.

Mika looks through our packages and packs that have been delivered from the Inn, then heads towards the bath. I sit on the four-poster bed to take off my boots, and immediately the headboard glows with what appears to be a menu. I move closer. It says:

CHOOSE YOUR ADVENTURE

Full Moons Romance
Pirate Intrigue
Fun In The Sun
Snowed Inn
Secret Rendezvous
Dungeon Indulgences
Mellow Bordello
Girls Night Out
Bachelor Party
Lords & Ladies
Midnight Sail
Home Alone
Working Weekend

I press on Pirate Intrigue, and the room is transformed into a lavish Captain's Quarters, with a floor to ceiling view of gently rolling seas lit by three moons. I am now shirtless, wearing red pantaloons, a blue bandanna around my head, and a gold ring in my ear. A parrot swings on a hanging perch, and I feel the floor smoothly roll. "It's mutiny, Captain, mutiny," the parrot squawks out. "Punish them. Punish them."

Mika comes out of the bath then, naked, her black hair now flaming red, and her hands bound in front of her with what appear to be chains. "Something is happening," she says.

She looks around at the changed room, the moonlit sea, then sees me, earringed and pantalooned, as I move towards her out of the shadows. "Oh my," she says.

"It's mutiny, Captain," the parrot squawks again. "Punish them. Punish them."

I grip Mika's chained wrists and pull her towards the driftwood Captain's Bed. "Nice try, Flame," I say, "but the ship is still mine." I lift her up and lay her down amongst the furs. Then I raise her wrists up over her head and hook the chains to a super convenient knob on the headboard.

"Oh Captain," Flame cries, "what are you going to do to me?"

I settle at the bottom of the bed and start to move up between her legs, my lips brushing her thighs. "No more than you deserve, Flame," I say. "Forty lashes."

"Forty lashes," the parrot squawks. "Forty lashes."

One of my arms slides up the outside of her left hip, and my fingertips reach her breast. The other hand snakes around her right hip, and comes to rest just above the slightest wisp of hair.

"Just the forty lashes then, Captain?" Flame asks. "I know I've been very bad."

I don't answer, just begin her punishment.

There is a long silence, then a gasp, and then a sigh. "Oh dear gods, Captain, was that just one lash?" Flame asks, panting slightly.

Slowly, I start all over again.

"Well, in that case," Flame whispers, "carry on."

FIVE: BALANCE MUST BE MAINTAINED

Next morning it's still snowing as we gather in the sunroom for a late breakfast. Neenah says that she and Lord Brik waltzed the night away in a clifftop castle. Fletch says that he taught Cael how to swim in a crystal clear ocean. Mika says that through tireless effort her heroic pirate Captain put down a mutiny aboard ship. The rest of us concentrate on eating without making eye contact.

When we're done eating Mika says to the group, "Let's get back upstairs and figure out our next moves."

We take the bubble up to the sitting room, and once again I use my ring to block our conversation. "So now we have to focus on getting Cael, and us, safely through the Aurelia event," I say, "which will be public and possibly divisive."

"How do we coordinate with the Nir security and military people?" Mika asks.

"Yeah," I say. "Good question. "Var should have more information when he gets back. Let's figure out our own moves first, then work with them when we get the chance."

"What are your thoughts so far, Neenah?" asks Mika.

"Well, the main thing is that without Cael with us, our between-city travel has become a secondary issue. If we are sure Cael is secure with the Guardians, then I think we should concentrate here on close-in body protection during the event, and the security of his entrance and exit site. The problem is that we know very little about the palace or how the threats may develop. Also, we may be separated within the building without good communications."

"Ok, good thoughts, Neenah," Mika says. "Let's take it one at a time. Are we all agreed that we can wait to talk to the military escort people before we get into the between-city travel issues?"

Everyone nods.

"Then let's talk about the Guardians," Mika continues. "The Abbot doesn't think the Havens are safe anymore, because of the close call against the shriekers. What do we think about that?"

"I've concluded that it was just the Abbot being overcautious about my safety," Cael says. "I don't have any reservations about trusting them."

"Nor do I," I say. "Their magic is older than *Floe*, and they are impervious to it and anything the *Ky* alchemists can do. Nor can they be killed by ordinary weapons. Traditionally, they have favored *Floe* practitioners over the *Ky* alchemists for reasons lost to the ages, and that favoritism is even more pronounced now after the Haven attack. So I believe they can and will safeguard Cael, and if we are all in agreement, I will contact them when we take a break and try to secure their cooperation."

Everyone nods, but Mika holds up a hand. "Just one thing bothers me," she says. "I don't like the thought of Cael being alone off and on for two or three weeks. It would be unbearable for me. I think Fletch should go with him. Would you be ok with that, Fletch?"

"It's no secret that Cael and I are involved, so I'm fine with it," Fletch says, "if that's where everybody wants me."

"It's good with me," says Cael, and the two of them fist bump. "Thanks for suggesting it, Mika, because it would have been a little creepy out there alone."

"I'm in favor of it, too," I say, "as long as the Guardians can handle the flight distances involved with the extra weight. If we are all in agreement on that, then I'll run it by them."

Again, everyone nods.

"Ok, then," says Mika. "Let's talk about close-in protection. Brik?"

"It seems like there will be two kinds of threats to Cael," Brik says. "Those that have been coming after him will continue to come after him, and those new enemies that may arise with the test. They each present challenges."

"How so?" Mika asks.

"Well, let's start with those who fear the tests or who oppose the results. They will more than likely be Nir citizens and, politically, I don't think we want to get involved in a fight with them. I think we have to stay away from any civil unrest, leave that to the Nir authorities, and just concentrate on Cael's immediate perimeter."

"That sounds right to me," I say, "and we may even be able to use *Friend & Foe Finder* to help the Nir authorities to anticipate where their internal trouble will come from."

"Good idea, Egon," Cael says. "And speaking of the prototypes, do you think they will be safer with me from here on out, given my isolation with the Guardians?"

"You're probably right, Cael," I say, and hand them over.

"Ok," says Mika, "what about the threats coming from our known enemies, the breeders?"

"It's hard to imagine a full scale attack - with alphas, fyrboren, shriekers and Rusk troops – inside a sovereign Nir city," I say. "I could see small scale attacks as a more likely threat, say with construct weapons, poison, strangling, explosions that might cause a floor or a ceiling to cave in, or other physical 'accidents' that circumvent Cael's medallion. And they could occur anywhere along Cael's route, as far as we know now, from the time he touches down to the time he takes off."

"So then here's how we position ourselves," Mika says. "I see Egon, Neenah, Brik and me covering Cael close in at the compass points at all times when he's on site. I see Fletch as our point man, leading us from place to place inside the palace, being the first inside any destination to assess the layout, and then positioning himself and his bow inside the testing site to best cover Cael. Sound right?"

We each nod. "Well then," I say, "I think we've done all we can do for now, given the information we have. So if this is a good time for a break I'll excuse myself for a few minutes and check in with the Guardians." Everyone nods and gets up to stretch and I go into our bedroom, which is no longer the Captain's Quarters and now looks out again over a winter wonderland. Figuring out what to wear could become a big problem in a Monkworks world.

I sit on our balcony and concentrate on my Guardian ring. The same Gryphon as before swims into my consciousness, and I think to him our mission to protect Cael against Immobilin Keep, his need of the Havens, four flights to and from the test cities, and the addition of Fletch. I ask that Cael and Fletch be flown to a Haven tonight, in preparation for his flight to Aurelia tomorrow night. And I ask the Guardians to consider giving Cael a ring to allow direct communication, at least until the flights are finished. Finally, I request Guardian overflights on the caravan roads we will use between cities, to spot any potential trouble.

I pause for a response, and almost immediately sense the presence of other minds. Somehow I understand that the first Gryphon is communicating my requests to other Guardians and, most importantly, that there seems to be no resistance. 'AGREED' reverberates in my mind, and then, cryptically, 'BALANCE MUST BE MAINTAINED.' What the hell? Then, the connection is ended.

There are relieved smiles and fist bumps when I relay the good news to the others. I leave out the end, because I'm still trying to figure it out. Then Mika calls for us to refocus on the questions at hand. "We're making progress, but we're not quite done," she says. "We should talk about communications inside the palace."

"I've been giving that some thought," Cael says.

"Look out, people," Mika says, "the magician awakens."

We laugh, and Cael says, "No, no, just a simple tweak."

"A little something you cooked up, right?" says Mika.

"Well, yeah," says Cael, "It's about the wrist bracers you all wear, and somehow combining them with the communications pads that I use to contact the Abbot."

"What are you thinking?" I ask.

"That I use the pad magic on a personal item from each of you, which puts you in instant communications with each other. Your bracers will each act like a convenient scroll, so the messages between you keep updating in sequence. Just look down at your wrist to see what's what."

"How would we operate it?" I ask.

"You can use a stylus to write on it, as though it were a pad. But I can also add preset messages like 'Help,' or

'Acknowledged,' which you just press to instantly transmit. I can include all of your names as well, in case you need to personalize a message."

"I love it," says Mika.

"Can you produce them before you leave tonight?" I ask.

"Of course," says Cael, as if it's no big deal. "Everything already exists. Just give me your bracers."

So we do that, and he heads off to his room to get to work. The rest of us decide to go outside and horse around in the snow before lunch, and that's where Var finds us, as he arrives back from Aurelia in his horseless coach turned horse-drawn sled. We gather again in the sunroom, including Cael, who has finished his 'simple modification' to our bracers. Var has two people with him, whom he introduces as Colonel Seetim Fareen, the Sultan's military attaché, and Fizo Ali, Chief of the Palace Guard. "Let us have lunch," Var says, "and then we get down to business."

We sit, and as lunch is served Var brings us up to date on Three Kingdoms politics since he left us yesterday. "The Abbot has done what he said he would do," Var says. "He has recalled his ambassador from Immobilin Keep, while the *Ky* breeders continue to claim 'rogue elements' and to promise a full investigation. Enduron and Nir are considering sending military delegations to Floendahl Abbey to develop a joint strategy against the Northerners, and everyone, including the Keep's breeders, have agreed to meet for peace talks. The trade road from Rusk to Floendahl Heights is now closed to Rusk military traffic and constructs, as promised, and the Three Kingdoms are each recalling all available military personnel to their respective home bases. The tension continues to heighten."

"Where is Nir in all of this," Cael asks.

"We have not broken off diplomatic relations with Rusk yet," Var says, "and are serving as a conduit for messages between the Keep and the Abbey. Our military is standing by for mobilization, we have fully manned our border outposts, and have ramped up military manufacturing and food stockpiling. And, of particular interest to you, we have warned the Keep that violence against our citizens or guests will be considered an act of war."

"We appreciate that," Cael says.

Lake House staff begin cleaning off the table, and Var rises and suggests we follow him into a more secure chamber. We walk through the house to a windowless room with a large table and thickly upholstered leather chairs. There are two maps on the wall, one of the palace and one of Nir.

"Let us start with palace arrangements for the testing event," Var says. "The two of you, Cael and Egon, will conduct a private demonstration of your device for the Sultan and Crown Prince, after their evening meal. You will coordinate with Chief Ali here about where to station your guards in the reception room during the audience."

"Fine," says Mika, and nods at the chief.
"Following the private demonstration," Var continues, "we will all proceed to the Great Hall, where we will join the Sultana and Princess Hawarri at a large table, as requested, for the public demonstration. Ten nobles and their children have been selected and briefed for the two pre-tests, after which we will again test the Sultan's relationship to the Crown Prince. Following this, the pretenders, Azedeh Azad and Ali Hawarri, will enter the hall and sit at the table for their test. If things go according to plan, the evening will conclude with their arrest."

Var turns to Chief Ali and Colonel Fareen. "And now, I will leave all of you to coordinate both security at the palace, which is Chief Ali's primary concern, as well as ongoing security in between the remaining test sites, which Colonel Fareen will supervise. If any issues arise that require my presence, please send someone for me. Good day for now."

Both officials prove to be completely professional and accommodating. They immediately grasp the value of separating Cael from the group and using the Guardians for protection. We arrange separate arrival and departure locations for Cael, Fletch and the Gryphon, to throw off any watchers at the palace. We go into the details of sweeping corridors for hostiles and devices, securing a potentially angry crowd, and screening for Rusk breeders, alphas and constructs, citizens or hostile clergy. And we discuss the group's transportation escort and our route out of the city on the caravan road.

We wrap things up then but, before they leave, Cael hands newly modified bracers to Ali and Fareen so all of us can stay in touch. They promise to wear theirs. Then Cael and Fletch go off to their rooms to gather their things for the upcoming night flight with the Gryphon. What could be done is done. We now have but to wait.

SIX: THE PROBLEM, IN A WORD, IS MAGIC

Cael and Fletch lift off from the roof of Lake House without incident, and fly under triple moons to the Haven between Aurelia and Gume. Cael immediately sends all of us a preset message, 'Cael arrives,' to successfully test our newly enhanced bracers. "See you tomorrow night," Mika writes with the stylus. Before lunch the next day, Neenah, Brik, Mika, Snout and I pile into a sled-then-coach for the ride to the palace, proceeded fore and aft by a company of Nir mounted soldiers.

Foothills turn to desert as the day wears on; cypress, sycamore and eucalyptus trees giving way to date palm trees and thorny shrubs. The city comes into view in late afternoon, the weakening sun slanting off the gold domed mosques of the Jakarines, all topped with statues of the Jakarine Falcon that symbolizes their god. I've taken this journey many times before, in far less comfort, but always eager in anticipation.

Aurelia is a wonderful city, definitely my favorite. It does not dwell in harmony with the desert that surrounds it, so much as stands in utter defiance of it. Built around a central oasis, the city is full of orange groves, blooming flowers and elaborate gardens. Its pink stone buildings house universities, libraries, mosques and medical centers. Its people are friendly, hardworking and generous to strangers. Its governmental policies have made the population safe, prosperous and educated. There is art, music, dance, and performances to suit every taste, and every cuisine is represented in its myriad restaurants and cafes. In short, it is a complete delight to visit.

The city began as a small trading post, and grew as the needs of the local mines grew. When the world discovered the beauty of dazzelite, the unique gem extracted from nearby foothills, the small outpost grew exponentially into perhaps the most beautiful city in the Three Kingdoms. Exports of dazzelite, together with jasmine extract used throughout the Kingdoms by perfume manufacturers, are the foundational elements in Aurelia's booming economy.

We drive through a main gate without stopping and head for Oanhe Palace. I've never been there before, but I know it is built on the lake in the center of the city. It is said that the Arcano River, the one we followed in the mountains, long since vanished underground, is the source of the lake and the rest of the oasis as it rises close to the surface once more. The lake and the surrounding canals, fountains, irrigation systems, drinking water, and waste removal are all supported by Monkworks devices that pump water from underground, and keep it circulating as needed.

As if all of that isn't amazing enough, there is a famous canal that winds through the city, and children float down it in round, pink, cuplike boats. Around them waterspouts erupt, seemingly at random. Occasionally one will erupt right under a boat and launch its giggling and screaming occupants high into the air on a column of water, before gently returning them to the canal surface. The whole time, Monkworks magic keeps the children as perfectly safe as if they were in their mothers' arms.

Our coach arrives at a side entrance to the towering glass and stone home to the royals of Nir, and Encos Var is there to greet us. He escorts us to a bubble that takes us high into the tower. We unload into a vestibule, where a guard takes Snout to the palace's royal doggy playground, of all things. Colonel Fareen and Chief Ali are waiting for us, both wearing their new bracers. We are directed to a balcony where, within a few minutes, Cael and Fletch arrive. We surround Cael, and gold-robed guards surround us, as Var and Fareen show us to an anteroom with comfortable seating and a side table filled with food and drink. "The Sultan has just sat down to dinner with his family," Var says, "after which he will see you. In the meantime, please relax and enjoy some of the delicacies of Nir."

We savor flavors of dates, cinnamon, saffron and lamb. Cael hands me *Family Finder* and *Friend & Foe Finder*.

"I expect high marks for these tonight, Tester," he says.

"Then they better not be your usual work," I respond tartly.

He laughs. "Still sore about *Best Meal Ever?*" he asks.

"I have a right to be," I say.

"Well, don't take it too hard," he says. "Early Testers complained of leaky packages and stomach distress."

My turn to laugh. "So you see," I say, "it wasn't just me who had problems with your prototypes."

"It's the price all great innovators pay," he says breezily, "when dealing with the unimaginative." At which point Var signals us that it is time to go. I see Chief Ali directing Fletch to move forward ahead of us. The rest of us form a box around Cael: Mica and I on either side and to the front; Neenah and Brik watching from the back. Once again, palace guards encircle all of us.

"When we get inside," Var says, "Brother Venarius and Tester Brodie should proceed to greet the Sultan, while the rest of you please follow Colonel Fareen's directions to your security positions."

Mika winks at me and in we go. Me and royalty is not something I ever thought would mix, but here I am. Var goes first, followed by Cael and me. The room is a small mirrored dining room with a wall of windows looking out on a garden. The scent of jasmine pervades the room. Guards and servers hover. Mika,

Neenah, and Brik take up positions along different walls, and I hear Chief Ali tell Fletch that he will take him to a hidden position in the rafters above the Great Hall.

Two men in elaborate robes and turbans sit at a stone and glass table; one older and bearded, one younger and clearly related, both looking relaxed, interested and completely in charge. There is a large gemstone in the center of each man's turban made of dazzelite, and I find the gem's shapeshifting effects mesmerizing. Looking into a dazzelite stone is to look in sequence at all the moods of the natural world: swirling or scudding or cyclonic clouds; fiery or softly romantic sunrises and sunsets; riveting lightning displays across black skies; and more. Each scene appears and disappears at random, in a sequence and pace unique to each stone. To say these two turban ornaments were worth a fortune understates their value on a stupendous scale.

As we get close, Var stops and bends down on one knee. "My sovereign," he says, "and my most esteemed Crown Prince, it is my privilege to present the representatives from Floendahl Abbey, here to confirm the royal succession and unmask the pretender."

"It is a pleasure to see you, as always, my most valued Minister Var," says the older man. "Please proceed."

Var stands up and beckons Cael and I forward. "Sultan Anseem Hawarri, Lord of the Desert and Sovereign of Nir, and Crown Prince Adib Hawarri, Rightful Successor to the Throne of Nir, I present Brother Caelum Venarius, *Floe* High Magician, Engineer and Creator of the Succession Device; and Monkworks Tester Egon Brodie, who will conduct the demonstration."

Cael and I move forward, then stop to take a knee. "Sultan Hawarri, I honor you," Cael says. The older man nods. "Crown Prince Hawarri, I honor you," Cael says to the younger man, and he nods. I repeat the process and Var signals us to rise. "Please sit for a moment with us," the Sultan says, "before we turn to the matter at hand."

I sit down across from the Crown Prince, while Cael sits facing the Sultan. It turns out the sovereign has more on his mind tonight than paternity. "The attacks on you and your party have distressed me greatly," he says, "and I thank the Falcon that you have survived." He nods to both of us, as I sense deeper waters approaching. "I condemn this violence, of course, " he continues, "and the instability that now rages in its wake. But I also am trying to understand the causes of these provocative actions by the *Ky* breeders of Rusk. My conclusions trouble me, and I would do my Kingdom a disservice if I didn't take this opportunity to share them with a leader of Floendahl Abbey."

"Of course, Sultan Hawarri," Cael says.

"The problem, in a word, is magic," the Sultan says. "Magic is out of balance, and ultimately that is the cause of the crisis in the Three Kingdoms."

Cael looks alarmed. "How so, your majesty?" he asks.

"Let me say first, Brother Venarius, that I do not fault you or the Abbot," the Sultan says. "I merely point out that Monkworks - with its ubiquitous *Floe* devices - has completely outcompeted and upstaged the alchemists of Immobilin Keep when it comes to expanding the influence of the arcane among the general masses of the Kingdoms.

"My kingdom greatly profits from your skill with devices, as do the other Kingdoms," the Sultan continues. "Your devices are everywhere, servicing humanity in many different areas of life. But there are prices to be paid. The breeders, for instance, see your ascendance as a sign of their weakness, of the possible obsolescence of their constructs, and they are aggrieved.

"Then, all over the Three Kingdoms, ordinary workers are displaced by devices that take their jobs, often by devices that they, themselves, cannot afford," continues the Sultan. "Merchants and manufacturers routinely lose whole lines of revenue because of things you've created. The clergy, both here and abroad, fear your secular influence will transcend their religious messaging. And rulers like me worry that the power calculations of old are shifting in unforeseen or unfavorable ways."

He pauses. "I know this is a lot to trouble you with right now," the Sultan concludes. "But this is an opportunity to speak to you of troubling things and I do not wish to squander it. I invite your thoughts on these matters."

Up until now, Cael has been sitting stiff backed and formal in his chair, his hands in his lap. Now, he leans forward and places his hands on the edge of the table. I notice he's now wearing a newly gifted Guardian ring on his right hand, and it reminds me of what the Guardian recently said to me about the need for balance to be maintained.

"I can't speak for the Abbot, as you no doubt know," Cael says. "Nor do I think from the perspective of a leader of a people. I am a magician and engineer, and as such I am a goal-oriented problem solver, a dog scenting a bone. So I rarely look up and around to assess a wider field."

And then he does that Cael thing, where he just doesn't get how disarming and appealing his simple honesty can be.

"But I have eyes to see and a brain to think," he says, "and I'm very much afraid there is truth in what you say."

The Sultan smiles for the first time. "You may be disheartened to learn that your Abbot completely disagrees with me, Brother Venarius," he says, "for we have had a similar communication. I won't tell him that you have a more open mind."

Cael smiles back. "Maybe more open but certainly more confused," he says. "I need time to think about what you've said, before I know what to do about it."

"Well spoken, young man," the Sultan says. "All I can ask is that you give it your attention."

I've got to hand it to him. It doesn't matter who Cael is talking to, from lowly Tester to all-powerful Sultan, he only does it one way: thoughtfully, honestly, respectfully and sincerely. He is as genuine a person as I have ever met, asshat or not. I think the Sultan gets that to.

"And now," the Sultan says, "shall we see if the Crown Prince is actually my son?"

That's my cue, and I pull *Family Finder* out of my vest and move the gold device across the table towards the Crown Prince. "When you press on the 'Parents' post once," I explain, "a map of the palace will appear." He presses, and the thin gold cards under the post spread out on the table and click together. "Press again," I say, "and the yellow gold snake will flow to your father, while the rose one will locate your mother on the map."

He presses again and the snakes chain animates. Its tail end moves to wrap itself around the Crown Prince's wrist, which clearly delights him. Then the gold portion elongates, circles the map, and glides unerringly to the Sultan, where it wraps itself around his wrist. The rose gold snake is still, signifying that the Crown Prince's mother has passed.

"That proves that the Sultan is, indeed, your father," I say to the Crown Prince. The Sultan and the Crown Prince nod. "Now let's prove that you are the Sultan's firstborn son," I say, as the snake rewinds on the post. I move the *Family Finder* device over to the Sultan. "This chain on the second post is made from many strands of gold, your highness," I say, "each one representing a potential offspring. Most are yellow gold, but one is rose gold, representing the first born daughter, and one is white gold, representing the first born son. Push the 'Children' post when you are ready."

The Sultan pushes it, and immediately one end of the chain wraps around his wrist. The rose gold strand extends across the map and circles a room adjacent to ours. The white gold strand slides across to the Crown Prince and wraps itself around his wrist. "This is telling us, Sultan, that the Crown Prince is your first-born son, while your first-born daughter is in the room next to us, and you have no other children."

The Sultan and the Crown Prince smile and nod. "Very good," the Sultan says.

"Now tonight," I say, "I will first demonstrate the validity of this device to the audience, using Nir nobles with well-known progeny. After that, with our credentials established, so to speak, we can retest royal succession for the public to see, and then test the claimant."

"I am very pleased," the Sultan says, and stands up. Cael and I stand up too. "We will leave you now for a few minutes, and then rejoin you in the Great Hall, which I'm sure is full to bursting by now." He and the Crown Prince leave by a side door as the rest of us bow our heads, and then we turn to a smiling Var. "Things are going very well, indeed," he says. "Shall we head down to the main event?"

Once again we box Cael and follow Var to a bubble, descending all the way back down to the ground floor. "Right now," says Var, "there are jugglers, troubadours, storytellers and the like keeping the crowd entertained. We'll go in amidst all that excitement and take our places while we wait for the Sultan's party."

I check my bracer but there is nothing from Fletch, Ali or Fareen. I look at Mika, and she looks alert now that we're on the move again. We head in to a large circular hall, surrounded by guards, where all eyes are on an acrobat act in the center. It's a raucous crowd, everyone standing except for some in seats tiered off three walls. We move along the perimeter past numerous gold-robed guards, to one end of the hall. There, a large wood and stone table is set up in a shallow alcove, which allows it to be seen from all directions but gives it some protection on three sides. There's a door on the wall behind it, where I expect the Sultan's party will enter and exit. The ceiling is many stories high and spanned with rafters and circled by a walkway. I can't see him, but I expect Fletch is up there somewhere by now. Neenah, Brik and Mika move into positions around us.

Acrobats fly about the central area. People are cheering.

Suddenly I'm not liking things. The ruling family will be in here in a few minutes, and we have brought our enemies right to them. Everyone, including me, seems to think that no one would dare an overt public attack in Aurelia, let alone in the Oanhe Palace, but do we really have a handle on the level of animosity or desperation or whatever it is? "Stay alert," I write on my bracer. One by one, everyone presses their Acknowledged button.

Var positions Cael and I on the same side of the table that the Sultan's party will occupy, with our backs to the wall and our faces to the crowd. Mika is behind me, and Neenah and Brik stand to either side between the table and the crowd. Suddenly my ring buzzes three times and flashes red. Not good. I write on my bracer: "Three *Ky* just entered the hall. Chief Ali, Colonel Fareen, are they expected?"

Ali: "Expecting only one. New ambassador. A breeder. Will look to identify the others and isolate."

Egon: "Consider abort. Suggest tell Sultan."

Ali: "Event too important."

I see Fareen walk into the hall looking at his bracer, and then he comes towards us. He agrees with Ali. "Ali's guards will put a blanket over them," he says, and strides off.

207

I pull *Friend & Foe Finder* from my vest, and I ask Cael to cover the hole on the silver cube so the device recognizes those friendly and hostile to him, not me. After a couple of seconds the Great Hall is represented in the air before me as a silver outline. I see Cael and the rest of our group, plus Var, all of us clearly recognizable and green on the display. It is filled with mostly the white shapes of neutrals, since Cael is not well known to Nirians, but there are some scattered reds as well. I spot the breeder right away along with the two alphas accompanying him, in this sea of mostly white; two intensely dark shapes outlined in bright red, standing together with a completely transparent shape outlined in red. It's as though the breeder can hide everything from *Floe* but his animosity. My bracer scrolls.

Ali: "Starting to isolate."

Looking straight through the display to the real hall, I see a Gold Robe enter the hall from another side door and approach the *Ky* breeder/ambassador.

Ali: "Ambassador invited to join the Sultan. It's a ruse."

The ambassador whispers something to an alpha next to him, and exits the hall with the Gold Robe. The acrobats are driving the crowd into a frenzy, as a second and third Gold Robe slide to either side of the remaining two alphas. One alpha starts to physically react to something that is said, and suddenly both Gold Robes are pressing blades to each alpha's throat. Other Gold Robes move in quickly and the whole group flows as one from the hall. My ring stops blinking red. Impressive moves, I think.

Jugglers continue to juggle and someone is breathing fire, so hardly anyone sees the disturbance.

I look back to the display and briefly spot a flicker of red high on the hall's outline, but it disappears. Strange, I think, but then remember back at the Haven when the device failed to see what was going on down on the trade road. It has trouble seeing heights and depths, I recall. "Fletch, there may be a hostile your location. Find, ID, kill."

Fletch: "Acknowledged."

Ali: "Sending guards as well. Mind your arrows."

Fletch: "Acknowledged."

Meanwhile, Cael is touching the remaining hostile red shapes on the display, one by one, to identify. There are fourteen in all. Eight are from Nir, including clergy, merchants or others who may just feel negatively towards *Floe* devices in general, although the two clergy bother me. I put their names out on the bracer, and tell Ali and Fareen that I can point out their locations. But it's the other six who turn out to be a much more concerning problem, because they are all from Rusk and they all have a military prefix in front of their names, ranging from 'Pfc.' to 'Capt.' So, Rusk military in civilian robes, all fairly close to us but spread across the width of the hall. I put it out on the bracer.

Egon: "See me for locations."

Then there are two loud gongs, the acrobats collect their things and disappear, and someone I can't see announces the arrival of the Sultan. Everyone stands as the door opens behind me, the crowd hushes and bows, and the Sultan, the Crown Prince, Sultana Cadiah Hawarri, and Princess Faraah Hawarri, enter the hall and take their seats. Everyone straightens and soft music issues from somewhere.

Then a court minister in flowing green robes and white turban moves out to the center of the hall to address the crowd. He turns out to be the evening's host and guide to the succession event, and we proceed into the credibility-building demonstrations. I have *Family Finder* set up by now, and the well-known nobles use it to find their hidden children, including first born, and the children find their parents. There are no errors and no embarrassments.

Green Robe takes the crowd through every step, and at each conclusion the crowd cheers approvingly.

Ali and Fareen arrive and I show him the six red shapes of the Rusk military hostiles, as well as the two suspicious clergy and the other red-coded Nir citizens. They go off to direct a Gold Robe response, as Green Robe announces the succession test. Again, I take the Crown Prince and the Sultan through the procedures, and Green Robe narrates. The device repeats its earlier findings, also identifying Princess Faraah as the Sultan's daughter, and the crowd begins a long cheer.

Meanwhile Gold Robes, three to a man, are slicing through the standing crowd towards the eight possible hostiles, including the six Rusk soldiers and the two local clergy. Again there are some physical reactions that the guards quickly suppress. All eight are escorted from the hall before the cheering stops. I have to admit that the Nirian security authorities are running a tight operation. 'Well done,' I write on the bracer.

Then Green Robe is back up to announce the evening's big confrontation, with the Sultan and Crown Prince facing off against the pretenders, Ali Hawarri, and his mother, Azedeh Azad. Two chairs are placed across the table from Cael and me. Neenah and Brik move to either side of them, and I see that they are scanning the lofty ceiling. I ask Fletch for an update but he says he's seen nothing yet. Ali and Fareen are back and standing behind the Crown Prince and the Sultan.

Doors open opposite us in the hall and I see two figures begin to enter. Suddenly, my ring is flashing and pulsing: black/pulse then red/pulse. One construct and one alpha. I can see them on the *Friend & Foe* display as well, with their gray and black shapes and bright red outlines. What the fuck? A construct impersonating a human?

I am instantly on the bracer.

210

Egon: "Alert. Pretender is human-looking *Ky*. Mother is alpha. Suggest keep them back NOW."

I turn towards Ali, who whispers in the Sultan's ear and then moves off with Fareen. Two Gold Robes take their places. Mika comes around to the front of the table to stand between Cael and the crowd.

The mother/son pretenders from Immobilin Keep have now reached the center of the hall. He has a resemblance to the Hawarri royals, no doubt, but he also has a facial tic that sporadically jerks his lips to the right. Maybe his construction didn't quite take. The woman with him is tall and powerful-looking, with a haughty lift to her head. Just then, perimeter doors slam open and the two are quickly surrounded by Gold Robes, this time with bared swords and aggressively pointed pikes. The crowd makes a collective huff and pulls back from the center.

The son stops, but the mother keeps walking, right up to the point of a pike. She stares straight at the Sultan. "This is your justice, lover?" she shouts. "This is your fairness? I demand the test I was promised."

The Sultan rises. "You are not the simple mother you claim," he roars. "You are a *Ky* alpha from Immobilin Keep." There are gasps from the crowd.

"I never claimed otherwise, lover," she shouts back, "but *my* parentage is not the point of today's event. Will you acknowledge your true first-born son today, or will you renounce him untested?"

The crowd goes silent.

"Seize them," the Sultan commands, "and bring them forward." Bad move.

The crowd goes crazy.

211

I catch another flash of red, high on the *Friend & Foe* display, and tell Fletch on the bracer that his hostile is making a move.

Fletch: "Acknowledged. Searching."

The pretenders are pushed into the chairs across the table from Cael and me, Gold Robe hands on their shoulders. The crowd pushes in. Mika, Neenah and Brik are on high alert. The construct is sweating and the tic is getting worse. I move *Family Finder* over in front of him, and tell him to press the 'Parents' post. It takes his shaking hand three times to succeed. A golden map of the Three Kingdoms flicks out and snaps into place. I have him press 'Parents' again, and the snakes respond by wrapping themselves around his wrist. Then the rose gold snake separates from the yellow gold, and each flows across the map as though searching, before retreating back around the post, tail end still connected to the construct's wrist.

"As the whole hall now sees," booms the Sultan, still standing, "this is a *Ky,* an inhuman construct, and not my son. He is an empty shell with no parents."

The crowd begins to cheer, but chaos ends the celebration.

"This is a fraud," screams the powerful alpha. She erupts from her chair, throwing off restraining hands with her alchemical strength, and jumps lightening quick onto the table in front of Cael. In her upraised hand now is a wickedly curved construct dagger. Before either Cael or I can react, Mika, standing to the right in front of the table, pivots left and cuts with her short sword, taking off the alpha's leg below the knee. She screeches, and lurches down hard onto her stump, one hand pressing the tabletop to right herself, and the other still thrusting the dagger towards Cael. Which is when Mika's devastating back cut takes off her head. There is no blood. The corpse evaporates before the head can hit the floor.

Meanwhile, the construct is howling like a shrieker – despite his Hawarri appearance - and has swatted away his Gold Robe captors. He rips a pike from one of them, and starts flailing about with fatal abandon.

Mika moves in front of Cael for protection when, inconceivably, a bone-white construct bolt slams into her chest. I scream "Mika," and jump across the table to get to her. But Cael is there first yelling, "I got her. Watch our backs." I look up into the rafters in time to see a crouching man with a crossbow taking aim. I move to block him from Cael and Mika when his head erupts from what must be Fletch's arrow, and he topples into thin air. I look back to the pretender and he is foaming at the mouth while shrieking, stabbing and clubbing. I pull out a projectile device, get his silvery outline, and shoot him dead.

And then I'm with Mika. I have one arm cradling her head and my other hand is holding her rigid hand. Her body is straining and convulsing, and she is gasping for air. Blood pulses from her mouth. Cael has her laid out on her side on the table. Her blood flows everywhere. He has one hand around the bolt in front, and the other around it in back. His eyes are wild and he is drenched in sweat. Neenah and Brik are across from me, both holding Mika's other arm, and they are crying. I look from one to the other, fear cascading over me. "No, no, no," I moan, as Mika's eyes start to roll back in her head. Gold Robes surround us protectively.

"Come on, you piece of shit," Cael screams, and his bloody hands are shaking. I watch then as, unbelievably, the construct shaft begins to slide out of Mika's body, back the way it entered. The point recedes into her back and the exit wound is healing as it goes. Then out her chest it glides, the entry wound closing as the deadly shaft drops to the tabletop. Mika gasps in big lungful's of air, and I feel her hand squeezing mine tightly. She is looking at me now, and I know she is coming back.

"Cael," I begin to say, my gratitude overwhelming me, but he is up then and running over to help the injured Gold Robes who fought the construct pretender. I look back down to Mika, and she is trying to say something. I lean over until my ear is next to her lips. "Did I scare you, studly?" she asks in a whisper, and godsdamn it if I don't laugh out loud. She's smiling. "I love you, Mika," I say.

Neenah and Brik are wiping tears from their eyes as Fletch arrives from his cat and mouse struggle with the crossbowman, who lays on the Great Hall floor about 20 strides away.

He kneels down next to Mika. "I'm so, so sorry," he says, looking completely stricken.

She lets go of my hand to place hers on Fletch's wrist. "You can't take a shot you don't have," she says and, miraculously, starts to sit up. I help her get upright.

"I just couldn't find him up there among all the rafters," Fletch says. "I got him too late."

"You got him when you could, Fletch," Mika says, with conviction. "Cael's fine and I will be too. It's all good."

"Thanks, Mika," he says. "I'll do better next time."

"Go help Cael now," Mika says, patting his wrist.

We start to look around ourselves for the first time in what seems like hours but was only minutes. The alpha and her son have completely faded away, not leaving a trace. There are several Gold Robes on the floor, some with cloths over their faces, and others being attended to by palace physicians. I see Cael and Fletch helping Chief Ali to sit up, blood all over his tunic, and realize he must have been gravely wounded in the battle with the construct pretender. The Sultan and his family are long gone, and the crowd has disappeared. I can't yet wrap my head around the repercussions of all this.

Colonel Fareen comes into the hall through the door behind us. "The Sultan would like to see you and Cael when your duties here are done," he says, "and I will take your companions to a comfortable place to rest and refresh themselves while they wait." Then he moves off towards Cael and Fletch, who are finishing up their work.

In short order thereafter the wounded and dead Gold Robes are moved into the palace proper, as is the dead crossbowman. Mika is now able to stand and walk, so the group of us follow Colonel Fareen out of the hall and into a bubble. He takes us high up in the palace to a room with comfortable seating, soft Monkworks lighting, a sideboard laden with food and drink, as well as access to bath facilities. I kiss Mika and, together with Cael, go with the Fareen to see the Sultan.

This time the Sultan is alone, in what appears to be his study. There are open doors to a balcony, and I can see the outline of an apparatus there for viewing objects in the sky. Two crescent moons are visible in a bed of stars, and a desert breeze brings that scent of jasmine to us again. The Sultan comes around from an ancient wooden desk as we enter, and, with a complete absence of ceremony, waves us over to a seating area of plush leathers and cushions. Var is already sitting there.

"My family is safe, thank the Falcon" the Sultan says, apparently believing that this would or should be the first thing on our minds.

"I am relieved," says Cael the diplomat, as I try to nod empathetically with images of Mika's spasming body still foremost in my thoughts.

"I am pleased that those in your party are also well," the Sultan continues, "including your Mika, who I am told is miraculously healing after suffering a grievous wound."

"Thank you, your highness," I say. "Without Cael's intervention, I would have lost her tonight."

"Without Cael, if I may use the informal," the Sultan says, "we also would have lost Chief Ali and several guards. You have remarkable abilities, young man, and I am grateful you used them to heal my people."

"I am the reason for this tragedy," says Cael, "so I am owed no gratitude."

"That's one interpretation of tonight's events," the Sultan says, "but not the one I'm going with."

"What do you mean?" asks Cael, obviously confused.

The Sultan looks at Var, who leans forward in his chair. "An attack on a Monkworks official," Var says, "in our palace by foreign powers, is an outrageous violation of international protocol that eventually will be smoothed over and will do nothing to heal our country, which has fractured over the succession issue. But an attack on the Sultan, the Crown Prince and the royal family is an act of war which will immediately unite all Nirians behind the Falcon-blessed throne. So this our position moving forward."

"You are declaring war against Rusk?" I ask.

"We are *threatening* war," the Sultan clarifies. "We have recalled our ambassador, severed diplomatic relations, expelled their ambassador and the Keep's two alphas from the event tonight, and we are fully mobilizing our army. In addition, we have asked Floendahl Abbey and Enduron to condemn this attack and join the Kingdom of Nir in a united front against the aggressor. While I have committed to attending the peace conference at the Abbey in less than four weeks, I will also send advisors - immediately and very publicly - to Enduron and the Abbey to discuss joint military operations."

216

"What are you expecting from us?" Cael asks.

"I am asking you and your party for a favor," the Sultan says, "for which I will owe you. You are obviously free to discuss your candid assessment of tonight's attack among yourselves and with the Abbot. But as you continue your testing mission and meet with various Nirian officials, I ask that you maintain our position that the attack was against the royal family. This will be of great help to me as I work to unite my Kingdom once again."

"Could you not just send us home, your highness, to avoid any need for us to corroborate your position?" I ask. "Besides, we bring violence to the places we visit."

"We considered that before you arrived here," the Sultan says, "and decided that you should proceed. Why? Well, look at what has happened here objectively. Tonight's succession event was a huge success, in terms of its original intent. Plus, we will be able to capitalize on the attack to unite our country and put Immobilin Keep on the defensive. And on top of those very important accomplishments, your journey from the Abbey to the far reaches of Nir is exposing a rot, a threat, an enormous intent, that none of us in the Kingdoms knew existed before. Continuing your mission is a statement of strength by both you and me, and may well bring whatever evil underlies all this out into the open so we can destroy it."

I know what I'm feeling about being the tethered goat in this narrative of stalking predators, but Cael seems undeterred, clearly sensing the opportunity to further ingratiate himself with the Nir ruler. "Very well," he says. "I will discuss this with our group, but I think what you are asking is reasonable and that we should agree to it."

"Very good, Brother Venarius, I thank you," the Sultan says, becoming more formal again, as he apparently wishes to conclude our discussion. "It has been my pleasure to meet you, and you as well, Tester Brodie. Please consult with Minister Var on plans for continuing your journey in Nir." With that, he stands up, causing us to rise as well, and starts to exit through a side door. He stops and comes back, taking something out of his robes. It is a communications pad with the Falcon sigil embossed on the cover. He hands it to Cael. "Let us be in touch if there is a need," he says, and then walks out. Var motions us to sit back down.

"So," he says, "a couple of updates. We had no choice but to release and expel the Keep's ambassador and the two alphas with him, in the interest of having our own diplomats returned safely. However, we did learn something from the Rusk military personnel we took into custody. They were all carrying Monkworks disruption devices like flashbangs, smoke bombs, and stinkers."

"A diversion," I say. "Stampede the crowd."

Yes," Var says, "we think to provide cover for the designated assassin in the rafters, and to allow the mother and son pretenders to escape. The plan was disrupted when your device identified them, so the alpha posing as the pretender's mother went for the kill herself."

"And the two alphas with the ambassador?" Cael asks. "What were they doing here?"

"The ambassador said that they were here to investigate the death of the alpha at the Notch," Var says. "All three deny any knowledge of the attack tonight or on the trade road."

"Your assessment of that?" Cael asks.

"Who knows," says Var, shrugging. "But let's address the future. We will see you, Brother Venarius, and your companion off with the Guardian momentarily, for your trip back to the Haven. Tester Brodie, a company of mounted Nir rangers will escort your party by coach through the desert, where you will join Brother

Venarius at the Haven for a day of rest. From there, you will proceed to the prison city of Gume. Questions?"

We have none, so he leads us back to where our group is waiting. Chief Ali is there when we arrive, and thanks Cael effusively for saving his life. "If there is anything I can ever do for you," he says, "you only have to ask."

Mika is looking much better, and I go over to hug her. Fletch and Cael hug too, and then we all follow Var again, this time into a bubble and up even higher in the palace. He takes us to a new room and then out onto a balcony where a Guardian is waiting. I give Cael the two prototypes back, and then he and Fletch climb on the Gryphon and are gone.

"Now if you will follow me one more time," says Var, "we have prepared sleeping quarters for you for tonight."

He takes us to wonderful rooms on the same level, complete with balconies and a gorgeous view of the moonslit city. I don't have it in me to appreciate it, though. Var takes his leave saying, "Your coach and escort will be ready to leave at dawn." I cling to Mika all night.

SEVEN: HE IS A PIG

We leave the city after a peaceful sleep, a happy Snout reuniting with us as we depart the palace. Mika is sore but her energy is returning. I keep revisiting the moment I thought Cael couldn't save her. I keep re-feeling the gut churning dread of loss I felt in that moment, and the horror and helplessness of living in a magic world when magic fails. I held Mika all night, and would be holding her still if she hadn't told me to grow a pair and get moving.

So here the five of us are, in a luxury coach drawn by six horses in the old fashioned way and escorted by a company of Nir's elite troops. The city is still asleep when we drive out of the east gate and into the desert. We are following the main caravan route leading from Aurelia through the desert and eventually to Nir's east coast. The surface of the road is hard packed and smooth, and the air in the coach's interior is magically cooled. I haven't heard from the Guardians, which means Cael and Fletch are safe and the road ahead is clear of threats. There are travelers on the road with us, and they move over for our uniformed escort. A promising start to the rest of our mission.

"How are you feeling," Neenah asks Mika, as the sandy and shrubby countryside rolls by.

"Not dead. Still sore," says Mika.

"About the best you could hope for, given the hit you took," says Brik.

"If it wasn't for Cael…" she says, shuddering, and trails off.

"He'll make a good Abbot someday," Neenah says.

"Yeah," says Brik, "it's been awhile."

Mika snorts. "I forgot you two knew the old Abbot back in the day, before this current asshat," she says. "He died just after I got recruited, so I don't remember much about him."

"Brik and I liked him well enough," Neenah says. "He made sure that all new recruits were treated well, got an education, and were offered options for working for the Abbey or for moving back into the outside world."

"I remember he used to hold a Tester's Day once a year," Brik says, "where the whole Abbey came out to honor us with speeches and awards. Plus there was food and drink, games and contests, acrobats and magic shows. It was an amazing thing for a street kid like me."

"All that was over by the time I got there," I say.

"Me too," says Mika, "but I can remember people talking about it."

"Things changed when Tenebrus took over," Brik says. "We left right after that, maybe 10 years ago, because we just didn't want to risk our lives for someone like him."

"What do you mean?" I ask.

"He is a pig, first and foremost," says Neenah, with feeling. She looks at Mika.

"Egon knows about Tenebrus and me," Mika says, and takes my hand.

Neenah nods. "He used to travel around the Three Kingdoms a lot," she continues, "selling big devices and device systems to rulers and merchants, and servicing ones that needed updates or repairs. And everywhere he went we'd hear stories back at the Abbey about pregnant women, abused young men, disgruntled husbands, abandoned babies and what have you. More than once the old Abbot sent Janx and others out to smooth over his brewing scandals."

"He was as bad inside the Abbey, as well," says Brik, "with males and females alike. The word was that he had invented a seduction device that reduced a person's defenses, something which is illegal in all three Kingdoms."

"And the old Abbot tolerated this?" I ask.

"Yes and no," says Neenah. "On the one hand, he was one of only two *Floe* magicians at the time, one of only three when Cael came along, and therefore too valuable to expel. On the other hand, various monitoring and containment strategies were tried until, finally, we heard that he was headed towards formal disciplinary action. Then, the old Abbot died, and the disciplinary thing evaporated."

"I never quite bought that whole situation," Brik says. "The old Abbot is bringing his heir apparent up on charges, and the old Abbot suddenly dies of natural causes, even though *Floe* magicians can last for centuries."

"You're suggesting that Tenebrus actually killed the old Abbot?" I ask, incredulously.

"I'll never prove it," Brik says, "but I'll never stop believing it either. And there have been other mysterious deaths around Tenebrus as well. Like one of Cael's friends, maybe his only friend at the time, Brother Bernum, who I knew was one of the young men mentioned in the formal complaint against Tenebrus."

"Did Cael know?" I ask.

"I doubt it," says Brik. "I only knew because Bernum started talking to me about becoming a Tester. He confided that he wanted to get away from the Abbey because he no longer felt safe in it, now that the case against Tenebrus had collapsed. I sent him to Janx, but I heard nothing more about it, and then he was found dead inside Monkworks and by Tenebrus."

"'Unexplained death,' Cael called it," I say.

"That's one name for it," says Neenah.

We ride on in silence for a while, digesting the indigestible. I notice we've been passing groups of soldiers all day, heading in the opposite direction towards Aurelia. One group of merchants we passed had a giant Monkworks sunscreen shaped like a cloud floating above their heads and following them without any need of support. Some individuals had personal floating sunscreens as well.

After I while I say, "It's interesting that I hear none of this talk about sexual predation now at the Abbey. People complain that he's arrogant, cold, and uncaring, but that's as far as it goes."

"I wonder if Janx has something to do with it," Mika says. "He kept the Abbot away from me back then, and I think that somehow he has reined the fuckhead in."

"I always thought there was more to Janx than met the eye," Brik says.

"What does this all mean for our mission?" I ask.

"Nothing," Mika says. "We're in this to get Cael set up in his own facility and out from under Tenebrus."

Neenah and Brik each nod. "Sounds right to me," I say. "I'm glad you guys are with me." The four of us bump fists. Snout barks.

We reach our overnight camp in late afternoon, a small oasis watered by a natural spring. We settle into a grove of date palms, our escort encircling us. We set up our Monkworks tents, camp furniture, fire, bathhouse and outhouse in short order. We eat Monkworks camp food that isn't half bad, although not *Best Meal Ever*. And just after a spectacular triple moonrise, we head into our respective tents.

"Stop hovering, Egon," Mika says, when we're alone. "Everything is fine."

"Easy for you to say," I say, sitting down beside her on the camp bed, "when I'm the one trying desperately to recover."

"You? Recover from what?" Mika demands, outraged.

"No *Best Meal Ever*, no sleigh rides in the desert, no pirate sex on tropical seas," I say mournfully. "I'm having a hard time dealing with all this."

"You," Mika says, "are an asshat."

"Ok, ok, you are absolutely right," I say. "That's why I plan to make this evening completely about you."

"Oh, really," she says, suspiciously.

"Yes, Mika," I say, "and I've got just the thing. I found it in the Monkworks employee gift shop before I left the Abbey. I was saving it for your birthday, but I think after what you've been through maybe now's the time."

"What is it?" Mika asks, softening up and a little curious.

"It's supposed to soothe and relax," I say, "and the guy behind the counter told me it's what every woman deserves." I reach for my vest on the chair.

"What the fucking fuck?" Mika says, back to suspicious again.

I pull a nondescript tube out of a paper wrap. It's about the size of my pinky. "The same guy said it activates by body heat," I say, and hold it against her bare thigh.

I feel a slight hum then as it starts up, and it slowly thickens and elongates to about the length of my hand. One end is softly rounded, and the other end is flat, like it could be stood up.

Mika looks at me. "Do you know what this is, Egon?" she asks, amused.

"No, just what the advertising says," I say. "But it comes with directions."

She giggles.

I reach back into my pack and pull out the scroll. I unroll it and begin reading. "All of us at Monkworks Intimate Rewards" I read, "thank you for entrusting us with the intensely pleasurable experiences you have longed for and so richly deserve." I look up from the scroll. "That's all it says," I say, looking confused. "The rest is just weird pictures."

"You'll figure it out," Mika says, settling down into the pillows and loosening her robe.

I go back to the scroll and start looking at the pictures from different angles, working to catch a glimpse of something I recognize. "I think it will ease the tenderness you're feeling from the wound," I finally say, and move the device up between her breasts. It grows warm, and the hum increases a little. After a bit I ask, "Are you feeling anything, Mika?"

She looks at me without speaking, and puts both her hands around mine and the device. She begins a slow push down her body, her eyes never leaving mine. I use my other hand to spread out the scroll, trying to find some visual purchase as her hands descend. And suddenly I see it. I look from the directions to her hands and back up to her eyes. "Oh," I say. "Silly me. I can take it from here." I reposition my hands into the first visual's starting position. Mika releases me and lays back. "Prepare yourself," I say, "for the intensely pleasurable experience you've longed for…" I move to the second position. "…and so richly deserve." She sighs, although I'm not entirely sure that it was about the pleasure.

By the time Mika shudders to a landing, I am deeply curious about the scroll's last section. It is all about new devices offering "realms of forbidden pleasure you've never even dreamed about." I'll have to see what they have at the next Haven's rowan tree. Either that or I will have to wait until I can ask Augie back at the gift shop.

Mika turns on her side and pushes her back into me. I curl up around her and murmur, "You never think about me, about *my* needs."

But she's already asleep. I grin, and order lights out.

EIGHT: TENEBRUS USED NIR

We're up and out by dawn again, and just after midday we arrive at the oasis which envelops a Tester Haven. The captain of our escort can't see anything, but I assure him it's there, just past a screen of date palms and tamarin. Snout and the four of us push through the foliage to find Cael and Fletch playing cards in the game room of a mansion, a Rowan tree growing incongruously in its center. There are butlers standing by with trays of food and drink, and musicians are playing from a raised dais off to the side.

"Come join us," shouts Cael with a friendly wave. By the time we walk across the clearing, the table has expanded and there are five more chairs including one for Snout, who jumps up to sit with the rest of us.

Two butlers arrive with nine squares of *Best Meal Ever*, and we sit down to a feast. Others march past us carrying stacks of meals. "For your escort," Cael says.

"How was the trip?" Fletch asks.

I say, "Enlightening," at the same time Mika says, "Intensely pleasurable."

Everyone looks back and forth between Mika and me, but we give nothing away.

"Well," says Cael, "that's great to hear. Tell us about it?"

"You have some explaining to do first," I say, gesturing to our surroundings. "Your powers seem to be growing."

He shrugs. "What good is being a sought-after magician if you can't enjoy it?" he says.

Mika snorts. "Sought-after, indeed," she says, laughing.

"Finally," says Cael, shaking his head and rolling his eyes. "Someone with a sense of humor."

I don't even look up. I just dig in and manage to avoid describing to Cael and Fletch our complete dissection of the Abbot's character, or the high marks Mika bestowed on the Monkworks intimacy enhancer.

When we finish eating, Cael asks what we thought about the humanoid construct.

"It seems to be a work in progress," I say. "Like it had nervous system problems that haven't been resolved yet."

"Yeah," says Cael. "I noticed the tic and the shaking, too. But what if they're easy to create? Someday, Immobilin Keep could field an army of them to impersonate humans at all levels of the Kingdoms."

I yawn. "We'll need a device for that, magician," I say.

Cael shakes his head.

Mika gets us refocused. "Tell us about the prison test, Cael," she says.

"Very well," he says. "As you know, we are heading for the city of Gume and the Gume Joint Military Detention Facility. All of Nir's military personnel who commit serious crimes are confined there, although there are some special- case civilians as well. No one has ever escaped and lived past their run into the desert. Despite its relatively enlightened policies, the prison is plagued by the highest levels of brutality and prisoner deaths in the Kingdoms."

"Why have you chosen to go there, Cael?" Neenah asks.

"I am going there to impress the facility's commandant, General Antin Miza. After his stint at the prison, he is slated to become Quartermaster General for Nir's armed forces, controlling all future purchases of Monkworks devices for the military."

"I get it," says Neenah.

"You guys will meet up with Fletch and me at the prison's guest quarters tomorrow evening," Cael continues. "General Miza will brief us about the next day's activities, which I believe are two-fold. First, he is conducting a Disposition Hearing for a number of prisoners who for one reason or another may incur a change of sentence. Secondly, he will be examining three people on his staff whom he suspects of smuggling, instigation of prisoner fighting for the purpose of gambling, and sexual predation. In both hearings, he wants to employ *Fact Finder* to assist him."

"And our duties?" Mika asks. "Same as Aurelia?"

"Pretty much," Cael says. "Egon will work the *Fact Finder* device and you guys will have our backs."

"What are the threats?" Brik asks.

"Hard to imagine the *Ky* getting to me in there," Cael says.

"Unless they pay someone on the inside," Neenah says. "Like one of those bent staffers you mentioned."

"Good point, Neenah," says Mika. "We need to learn more from the General tomorrow night about how and where that examination will be conducted."

"Have you been in contact with the Abbot, Cael?" I ask.

"Yes," Cael says, suddenly appearing troubled. "I told him about the attack at Aurelia, the successful succession results, and the Sultan's moves to unify his kingdom under the threat of war from the north. Oddly, he already knew about our using Guardians to keep me off the caravan road, and he wasn't happy. Same comments about the Havens being compromised. And here was a stunner: He mentioned you by name, Mika. He said you were an ex-Tester who left under suspicious circumstances and can't be trusted."

"That vile piece of shit," Mika said, reaching her limit. "I left because I refused to sleep with him, Cael."

Cael looks stunned.

"Brik and I go back 30 years at the Abbey, Cael," Neenah says softly. "And it's only been in recent years that the Abbot's reputation as a serial sexual predator has been toned down. I know you look up to him, so I'm sorry to speak against him. But he has some serious flaws."

"Not to pile on, Cael, but this stuff about the Havens being compromised is complete rubbish," I say. "He's giving you bad advice that, if you listen to it, could get you killed."

Cael looks around the table at us four Tester veterans. "So you guys have had reservations about him right from the start?" he asks.

We all nod.

"Then why are you still here with me," Cael asks, "on a mission from the Abbot?"

"We believe in *you*," Mika says as Cael, you guessed it, blushes. "And now that we know about it, we want you to be the Abbot at your own Monkworks far away from Floendahl Abbey."

"I don't know what to say," Cael says, "about you all…the Abbot… about any of this. I guess I'm beginning to see the world a little differently now."

"In that case," says Brik, "it's time to see what you stocked in that liquor cabinet over there. I say some day drinking is definitely in order."

So that's what we did. A rare, relaxing afternoon among friends in a magic mansion, surrounded by earthly and unearthly guards.

At one point, I throw a Monkworks cube on the ground, expecting a bucket of ice, and get nothing. I do it a couple more times before Cael comes over. "Let me see that," he says. I hand it to him and he examines it. Then he scoffs and says, "This expired over a year ago, Egon. Don't you ever check the dates?"

"That's just Marketing bullshit," I say. "I can't believe you've fallen for it. I still have good stuff in my vest from my first mission."

"And yet," says Cael, and throws the cube to the ground, again without result.

"A faulty device," I say. "It must be one of yours."

"Faulty, my ass," Cael says. "This is just more evidence that Testers can't follow directions."

"No one can follow Monkworks directions," I say.

"We had to go with pictures because Testers can't read," Cael retorts.

"Boys, boys, boys," Mika says, coming between us and grasping our arms. "You guys should have a duel, settle things here and now."

"I'll kick his ass," Cael says.

"Prove it," I say. "Set it up, Mika."

So we all gather under the Rowan tree, Cael and I next to each other. "Ok, guys, here are the rules," says Mika. "This is a simple best of three contest. I name an object and you two create it, one by magic and one by device. Fastest creation wins. The rest of us are the judges." There are catcalls then and cheering. Maybe even some betting.

"What's the prize?" Cael asks.

"Bragging rights," says Mika. "You win and your prototypes were always great and Egon is lower than dirt." More cheering and catcalls. "You lose, and Egon was only half as hard on your devices as he should have been, and you are pond scum." More cheers and catcalls.

"Are the contestants ready?" Mika asks.

We nod.

"First round," she calls. "Standard bridge."

Now you may be thinking that I have no chance to beat Cael since he needs no devices. But I know I have the edge, because he has to think to build, and I don't. Plus, I'm good at what I do. Maybe the best ever. So, in a move that would have stunned Janx and the other instructors back home, I grab all three devices required to build a bridge at once, in the right sequence, in one hand: up ramp, road bed, down ramp. I throw them on the ground and, as I let them go, I see Cael's bridge already standing. Even has lights.

"You asshat," I say, as everybody cheers and he dances around with his arms over his head.

"Lift a glass to Cael," Mika shouts, and we all take a drink. It is time for drastic action.

"Second round," calls Mika, "Standard…"

I drop a stinker, and a cloud of sulfurous reek envelopes us.

"…bathhouse," Mika finishes, and my device flies. Cael is thrown for just long enough and my bathhouse rises first.

"Hey," Cael protests, "that's cheating."

"Judges," cries Mika. "What say you?"

"Nothing in the rules against it," says Neenah, coughing, eyes streaming and waving a hand in front of her face. The others, except for Fletch, agree, so I'm still in the game. I throw another device and the stink cloud vanishes.

"Let's drink to Egon," Mika cries, and so they all do.

"This is it," Mika says, "the final and deciding round." There is hooting and hollering, and I definitely see gold changing hands.

"For all the bragging rights," Mika proclaims, "now and for all time, build a standard…"

I'm looking right into the eyes of Snout, who is furiously wagging her tail. I nod my head and flick my eyes at Cael, and she jumps right up on Cael and starts licking his face. Cael, meanwhile, has launched a hornet the size of my fist and it is bearing down on my face.

"…canoe," finishes Mika. I flinch but my device is out fast. I know Cael flinches too.

"Judges," shouts Mika, "I see a tie. What say you?"

"A tie. A tie," they all say, as Snout stops licking and the hornet disappears.

"So what does this mean," Cael asks, exasperated.

"It means," says Brik, "that the feud continues and will never end."

"Oh for gods sakes," says Cael. "I need a drink."

"Here you go," I say, handing him a magic brew. "I have to say, you did better than I expected."

"Asshat," he says. And we laugh.

We spend the rest of the day exploring Cael's mansion, and enjoy a peaceful night in the fully equipped guest bedrooms. Before we leave the next morning, I restock my vest from the Haven's Rowan tree armory, but find no supply of Intimate Rewards creations. Then, it's an uneventful, daylong trip to Gume.

We arrive as the sun is setting behind us. Despite the prison's grim reputation, the city itself is lovely. It is mostly low stone construction with the occasional gold-domed and multistory Jakarine mosque. As we mount the last rise before the city we hear competing Umams calling the faithful to prayer. There are date palms, eucalyptus and orange trees everywhere, and vines filled with blooming red and yellow flowers drape the buildings.

Our escort leads us around the city's central water source and through to the eastern outskirts, where we ascend a bluff to the prison complex. It is a square, windowless, stone fort-like structure with guard towers and a central gate. We stop at a brick building outside the walls and off to the side of the entrance, which turns out to be the guest quarters. Our escort posts double guards, and the rest leave us to find their own accommodations for the evening.

The four of us elect to wait outside for Cael and Fletch, who arrive just after sunset on a Gryphon. Cael puts his ring to the majestic creature's forehead, and communicates his thanks, before it flies off. Together we go into our quarters and settle our things in three separate bedrooms. An adjutant arrives then, to invite us next store to a commissary for a light dinner. "The General will arrive back at your quarters in one hour for your briefing," he informs us, and departs. We are the only guests in the dining room, and we eat fast and head back.

General Antin Miza arrives shortly thereafter with four uniformed escorts, who take up positions on either side of the door. He is tall and lean with a commanding presence. He has a long scar on one side of his face, but what I notice most about him is his brisk intelligence. He goes directly to the round table in the common area and gestures for us to sit with him. Four of us join him there while Neenah, Brik and Snout spread out around the room. I see Miza take note of this, but he doesn't comment. "I trust these accommodations meet your needs?" he asks, by way of introduction.

"Yes they do," says Cael. "Thanks for your hospitality, General Miza."

"Thank you for coming all this way," says Miza, "and under such great duress. If my information is correct then you, Commander Marianis, slew the alpha attacking our Sultan," calling Mika by her formal title as leader of her White Sash mercenary band. "And you, Tester Brodie, dispatched the

235

construct pretender. Nir is indebted to you both, and to all of you," he says, gesturing to the others.

Cael can't do his usual 'aw shucks' about his bringing the violence with him because the official narrative is that the Sultan was the target and we saved him. The General makes a reply unnecessary by not waiting for one.

"On a personal note," he continues, "it is not common knowledge that Chief of the Palace Guard Fizo Ali is my half-brother. So, Brother Venarius, on behalf of my family, thank you for saving his life."

Cael doesn't blush but I know he wants to. "Chief Ali is a brave man," Cael says, "and he runs an incredibly professional organization. He is the real reason that attack was disrupted."

General Miza nods approvingly. "A modest response," he says. "Forgive my impoliteness but you have none of the arrogance of the other *Floe* magician."

Maybe on an earlier day Cael would have bristled at a slight to the Abbot. But by now he is realizing that he needs to repair Abbey relationships on this mission, as well as Monkworks devices.

"I take it that you have had a difficult encounter with Abbot Tenebrus?" Cael asks neutrally.

"Several," Miza says. "Back in the day I was assigned to captain the Abbot's escort on some of his official trips here. He did not comport himself like a head of state – or even a gentleman - should, and I was glad to move on to other duties. I must confess I was wary of having another encounter with a *Floe* magician, but my need of your truth tool takes precedence."

"I guess all I can say at this point," Cael says, "is that I hope I can be of service in your current situation."

"Then let us talk about tomorrow," Miza says. "First, in our Disposition Hearing, we will use your device to test the veracity of ten inmates who either want their sentences reduced or seek to avoid an increase. It is the last case that I think you will find most interesting, both because it concerns an ex-Tester, and because he has an interesting story to tell about your Abbot Tenebrus."

Miza has our full attention now. "Care to elaborate, General?" Cael asks.

"I think not," he says. "I didn't want to spring such a connection on you without some notice, but I think it best if we let the hearing unfold as it will, before we discuss it further. Is that acceptable?"

"As you wish," says Cael.

"Then moving on," Miza says, "we will also question three of my staff separately in connection with allegations of serious misconduct which, if true, will cause a wider investigation and shake this institution to its roots. It is vital that I ferret out the truth, because how I proceed afterwards may have major repercussions. At least for my successor."

"You are leaving here?" asks Cael.

"I leave in two days for a mutual defense strategy conference at your Floendahl Abbey," he says. "Enduron will be represented there as well. Then I will return to Aurelia to take up my new assignment to vastly increase our stockpiles of war materiel."

"About the war," Cael says, "we've been out of touch for the past two days. Is the situation worse?"

Miza shrugs. "Nir is girding for war with our northern neighbor," he says, "and rattling sabers loudly. Our Kingdom is uniting behind the Sultan and Crown Prince in the process. All talk

237

of a contested succession has ended. So the news is both bad and good."

I clear my throat. "If I may, General Miza?" I ask.

"By all means, Tester Brodie," he says.

"The rest of us are here to provide security for Brother Venarius on his mission. What should we expect inside, and how can we best coordinate with your staff?"

Miza nods. "Captain Motan," he says, "please come forward." One of his four escorts approaches the table, comes to rigid attention, and salutes.

"Sir," Motan says.

"At ease, Captain," Miza says, returning the salute.

Miza shifts back to us. "I will return to my duties at the prison now," he says, "but I have asked Captain Motan to stay behind and work out the best uses for our combined resources." With that he stands, as do we. "I will collect you here two hours after sunrise, and we will proceed. Good evening to you all." He turns swiftly and is gone with his other three aides.

Motan turns out to be courteous and professional, and we wrap things up in half an hour. He leaves, and the six of us speculate for a while about the ex-Tester we are soon to meet. Neenah and Brik in particular are wondering if they know him. But, solving nothing, we turn in for a quiet evening's rest.

Next morning, General Miza escorts the six of us plus Snout through the steel-gated entrance, where we confront a second stone structure nested inside the larger outer edifice. There is a five stride no-man's-land between the walls to our right and left, heavily patrolled, and presumably stretching fully around the prison. A few narrow, steel-grated windows have been cut through the walls of this interior building.

We go through the second entrance gate and down a narrow stone corridor, then proceed to an open space in the center of the prison. Noise, heat and human smell assail us. Stacked on the building's four interior walls are three tiers of prisoner cells and walkways. Each cell is a stone box on three sides, plus floor and ceiling. The side facing the central courtyard is fronted floor to ceiling with steel bars. Many of the cells hold maybe five or six prisoners each. The prison ceiling is partially open to the sky, with more steel grating covering it, and I can see guards up there too.

The General steers us across the open space and through a locked and guarded, steel and wood door to a corridor of other doors I assume lead to offices and hearing rooms. He guides us through one such door and onto a balcony of sorts, which looks down into a room furnished with a long rectangular table and several chairs. There are steel rings sticking up from the floor in some places, presumably to receive prisoner chains. Currently, no one is in the room, except for several guards.

General Miza takes the middle chair at a long table at the front of the balcony, and his staff take the chairs to his right. We take the chairs to his left, and I sit closest to him in order to conduct the test. I take out *Fact Finder* and place it on the table in front of the General, and explain how it works. I suggest he start his interrogation of each prisoner with simple questions for which there are well verified answers, in order to establish the reliability of the device.

It works flawlessly. Nine chained prisoners are ushered in. Nine are ushered out. All of them lie. All of them refuse to name names. And all of them will have years added to their sentences, for smuggling, fighting, attacking a guard, throwing feces and more. But what all of us are waiting for is prisoner number 10.

Caton Welty is immense, grizzled, and scarred. He is escorted in by four guards, manacles at wrists and ankles. His prisoner clothing is ripped and filthy, but he holds himself upright and retains what dignity he can despite the shuffling his manacles induce. He scans us with unflinching eyes, as he sits at the prisoner table and his chains are bolted to the floor.

An aid to the General takes Welty through a series of contextual questions. We learn that he is 10 years into a 30-year sentence at hard labor for running a smuggling operation out of the Nir & Far Inn. He is convicted of selling illegally obtained Monkworks devices to travelers, including weaponry. He is also convicted of trafficking an illegal Monkworks device used for coercing sex from unwilling partners. The purpose of today's hearing is a routine 10-year review for prisoners serving lengthy sentences. But things get far from routine very quickly.

Aide: "Is there any reason your sentence should be reviewed today?"

Welty: "Yes. I am innocent of the charges."

Aide: "You were given a fair trial and convicted."

Welty: "I was convicted for sure, but my trial was not fair."

Fact Finder remains silent during this exchange. Welty's voice is strong and matter-of-fact.

Aide: "The evidence was overwhelming. You were found with illegally obtained goods, and witnesses confirmed that you were the seller."

Welty: "No one testified about how I obtained the Monkworks devices, which were outside of what I carried as part of my Tester job. Additionally, none of the witnesses were Nirian, or from anywhere else but Floendahl Abbey."

Aide: "Under Nirian law, it was not necessary to show where the goods were obtained. It was only necessary to show possession. As for the witnesses, their national origin is not relevant."

Welty: "I maintain that the goods were planted in my room by elements from the Abbey. This was never investigated because the Abbey refused to allow its officials to be questioned."

Aide: "Prosecutors were satisfied that no further investigation was warranted."

Welty: "Nor did Nir investigate the complaint I lodged with the Abbey against Ichanor Tenebrus, who soon thereafter became Abbot under mysterious circumstances."

Aide: "Again, there was no legal imperative to investigate. Nor is the death of an elderly head of state by natural causes in any way mysterious."

Welty: "It is well documented that *Floe* magicians live unusually long lives. The Abbot was not elderly by *Floe* magician standards at the time of his death."

Still *Fact Finder* remains silent, and General Miza stirs. He nods towards the aide, apparently signaling he is through and Miza is taking over the questioning.

Miza: "Prisoner Welty, please tell this hearing in your own words what you believe happened in your case."

Welty: "After years of stopping there, I was friendly with some of the Inn staff, including a bartender, a room service maid, and a stable hand. They knew I worked for the Abbey and shared with me disturbing stories about Tenebrus' activities. They said he tried, and often succeeded, in coercing sex from seemingly unwilling staff and guests. They said he had a Monkworks device for this, and he was heard trying to sell copies of it. And they said his room

241

was stocked with Monkworks devices, including weapons, and that all sorts of people came and went at all hours of the day and night. Based on these assertions, I reported Tenebrus to my section leader."

Miza: "Who was this section leader?"

Welty: "Brother Ven Mirrin."

Neenah and Brik startle, and Fact Finder stays silent. Welty is telling the truth.

Miza: "Ok, what happens next?"

Welty: "Shortly thereafter, I am arrested and charged by Nirian authorities. While in jail I learn that the old Abbot has died, Tenebrus is the new Abbot, and Mirrin has been promoted to his Chief of Staff. Then I go to a hearing where the evidence against me is revealed, and I am offered the choice of facing a trial in Nir or being extradited to the Abbey. I refuse extradition because I now fear for my life in an Abbey run by Tenebrus."

Miza: "And you say you or your lawyer raised your concerns to the presiding judge and prosecutors?"

Welty: "We did, and got similar answers to what you heard here today. I never again saw or heard from my three friends at the Inn. And the so-called witnesses against me were all Abbey staff I had never heard of who testified by affidavit instead of in person, and who couldn't be cross-examined by my lawyer, supposedly for diplomatic reasons."

Miza asks his aide where these witness transcripts are now, and is told they are no longer in the file. He turns back to the prisoner.

Miza: "Did you ever sell for personal gain any Monkworks devices in your possession during your time as a Tester?"

An abrupt segue, I realize, meant to trip Welty up.

Welty: "Yes. I think it's safe to say that we Testers all sold our mission leftovers if we could, for pocket money. But never illegals, and never weaponry."

Miza: "If the hearing finds in your favor, what remedy are you anticipating?"

Welty: "Exoneration, compensation, and legal status to stay in Nir. In the alternative, a new trial where I am free to fully investigate the charges and witnesses against me, as well as an accounting of the witnesses on my behalf who never showed up at trial."

Miza: "Thank you for you testimony. You will hear our decision within 24 hours. Guards?"

Welty is dismissed and the hearing room clears. Personally, I'm stunned, and I know Cael must be staggered.

"That Mirrin is another pig," says Neenah, unbidden.

"You know him?" Miza asks.

"Back in the day, before he became Chief of Staff, he was Tenebrus' running buddy. They were always together, through all of the scandals."

"I see," says Miza.

After lunch in the guest house we head back inside for the afternoon session. Miza is without staff this time, for which he gives no explanation. I wonder if he is concerned that one or more of his aides is involved in the activities under investigation. He doesn't waste time on preliminaries as the first suspected staff member is brought before him.

Miza: "What do you know about the smuggling of Monkworks devices into this facility for the purpose of sale or trade to the inmates?"

Staff 1: "I have no knowledge of this, sir."

Fact Finder buzzes and glows.

Miza: "Dismissed."

A second man enters.

Miza: "Your colleague says you are involved in the smuggling of Monkworks devices into the facility for sale or trade to the inmates. Is this true?"

Staff #2: "Untrue, sir."

Fact Finder buzzes and glows.

Miza: "I know for certain that you are lying. Admit you are involved or you will lose your one and only chance to save yourself from prison."

Staff #2: "I have no knowledge of this, sir."

Fact Finder buzzes and glows.

Miza: "Dismissed."

The last staff member is escorted in.

Miza: "Both of your colleagues accuse you of being the ringleader of an operation that smuggles Monkworks devices into the facility for sale or trade to the inmates. Is this true?"

Staff #3: "No sir, I have no knowledge of this."

Miza holds up a buzzing and glowing *Fact Finder* by its chain, where Staff #3 can see it.

Miza: "What is your title?"

Staff #3: "Guard Supervisor."

Fact Finder is silent.

Miza: "Are you married?"

Staff #3: "Yes."

Fact Finder is silent.

Miza: "Have you ever cheated on your wife?"

Staff #3: "Of course not, sir."

Fact Finder buzzes and glows.

Miza: "Oops. And you were doing so well. Now listen closely before you answer my next question. This device knows when you lie and it will put you in prison, maybe even this prison, if you don't answer me truthfully. Are you involved in a smuggling operation bringing Monkworks devices into this facility for sale or trade to the inmates?"

Staff #3, squirming and sweating now: "Are you offering me full immunity from all charges?"

Miza: "I am."

Staff #3: "Then yes, I am involved. And so are the two guards you questioned. And others."

Fact Finder is silent.

Turns out five staffers and one of Miza's aides are involved in smuggling, sexual coercion, gambling over inmate fights, and other offenses. Unbeknownst to me, inmates have access to personal accounts that are often kept filled by family and friends, which made the smuggling worthwhile. And in lieu of money, the conspirators took sex, work on their homes during outside-the-prison details, and even contract violence against designated individuals.

Of most interest to Cael and I is that the source of the smuggled devices is the traveling Monkworks cart driver that Cael chatted with way back in the canyon. Every three months he dropped off a new package of devices for meals, cooling, medicine, wine and more, in return for an under-the-counter cash payment.

"This trip has been a real eye opener," Cael says grimly.

After the hearing room is cleared, we sit around the table on the balcony with Miza, who has even dismissed his guards.

"Thank you for your assistance," says Miza, "in what was a difficult day for all of us. For my part, I have arrested my corrupt staffers and already shipped them to Aurelia for trial, where I can keep my eye on it. My successor will have a clean slate. I have also decided, as a result of the Welty hearing, to forego my trip to the Abbey for strategic consultations, where word of what transpired here will surely arrive quickly. There would be awkward questions that I don't wish to answer at this time. Who knows, there might even be danger. Instead, I will beg off, truthfully citing my need to assume my new duties as war threatens. A suitable replacement will be sent in my absence."

"What happens to Welty?" I ask.

"Ah, now," the General says, "that is the question, and the answer is less than straightforward."

"How so?" asks Cael.

"It is clear to me that a corrupt Abbot Tenebrus used Nir reprehensibly to falsely convict and imprison Welty, in order to avoid facing allegations that might well have prevented him from becoming the head of the Abbey. But I don't have the authority to simply exonerate prisoners, let alone compensate them, or give them legal status in Nir. And leaving Welty's case to my successor to handle, who will not have access to your *Fact Finder* device, may delay his disposition indefinitely. But I have a suggestion."

"What is it?" asks Cael.

"I propose," says Miza, "that I use the authority I do have to parole Welty into your custody, Brother Venarius. As a high official of the Abbey, you will vouch for the released prisoner's behavior while on Nirian soil. We will leave issues of exoneration and so forth to a later date, although I can promise him I will work to make it happen."

"There is no way he agrees to put himself in my hands," Cael says, "given his history with the Abbot."

I realize Cael is absolutely right, and I'm flailing about for some alternative, when Brik steps up.

"Maybe Neenah and I can talk to him," Brik says. "We're of the same generation at the Abbey, and he may listen to us grunts more than he would the big shots."

"What would you say to him?" I ask.

"I'll just tell him who Cael is as a person," Brik says, "and what he's discovered on this trip, and what we're doing out here. And then I'll remind him of the alternative. What does he have to lose?"

And that's how it goes down, although not before Cael cautions Brik and Neenah to keep the whole second site thing out of the discussion for now. In any case it works, and Welty is released into

Cael's custody. General Miza hands him his long-since-pilfered Testers vest and short sword, then wishes us all luck. Cael and Fletch fly back to the Haven, and the rest of us leave Gume the next morning for a two day ride to Portus Sironika on the coast.

NINE: THIS HARBOR IS A SMUGGLERS' HAVEN

Caton Welty turns out to be a pleasurable travel companion, telling us tales from his adventurous life as our coach rolls through the desert. He tells us he served on sailing ships of one sort or another from the time he was 14 until, at 20, he and his entire crew were thrown in jail in Enduron until his ship captain could come up with the money to pay harbor duties. There he was recruited by a traveling monk to train to become a Tester.

"Did you know Brother Janx?" I ask him.

"Oh sure," Caton says. "We hung out quite a bit before he became a Section Leader. Not too much after. Our thing together was to explore the tunnels under the Abbey."

"Why?" I ask. "Aren't they just ways to enter and exit the Abbey less publicly?"

"Well," he says, "that and a whole lot more. We used to meet our girlfriends down there for one thing. Had separate little rooms fitted out."

"Wait, Janx had girlfriends?" I ask, completely skeptical. "As in, any, let alone more than one?"

"Oh yes he did," Caton says. "Women always liked him and he liked them back. And why not? The *Floe* hierarchy had nothing against it."

I ponder this for a bit, trying to reconcile this new information with the bear-like overseer who so often made my life miserable. Then I get drawn back into Caton's revelatory narrative.

"There was one corridor that I will never forget," he says. "Seemed blocked, but if you persisted you came to a cavern decked out like a private club with music and soft lighting, only with magic, so it was beyond wild. For instance, the walls and ceilings were alive with completely lifelike moving images of beautiful nude people doing the most imaginative things to one another. But if you got very close to a wall, like we did when we were sneaking around, it was just ordinary stone."

"Who went there?" Neenah asks.

"A lot of the elites," Caton says, "including Tenebrus and Mirren. Plus there seemed to be visiting dignitaries from the Kingdoms, and half naked young men and women from gods know where serving drinks or just mingling. Couples, threesomes, and foursomes kept disappearing down a corridor in the back. Some others were openly smoking opium, in a section partially obscured by magic curtains that appeared to be made of writhing snakes."

"Nothing surprises me anymore about the Abbey," says Mika, "but at least Cael isn't here to hear this. He's been dealt quite a few eye-opening blows on this mission."

"What else is down there in the tunnels?" I ask.

"There was a lot of that kind of illicit activity going on," Caton says, "but the most interesting corridor to me was one we found that confirmed something I had heard in my sailing days. It was said that there was a hidden port where the unclimbable mountains behind Floendahl Abbey met the Great Southern Sea. Turned out to be true."

"What do you mean?" I ask.

"Janx and I found a guarded corridor," Caton says, "and because of the heavy security we couldn't resist exploring it. We used distractors, smokers and stinkers and got past them. The corridor was long, took us forever. I remember passing mounds of stacked Monkworks crates along the walls. We finally started feeling a fresh breeze and came to an opening to the outside. Sure enough, down a carefully graded switchback trail there was a little keyhole of a harbor where ships were loading and unloading."

"They were shipping Monkworks devices?" I ask.

"Seemed like that to me. Maybe influence peddling and bribes around the Kingdoms? Maybe just good old smuggling. I don't know. Plus, they were offloading fine wine, exotic foods, furnishings and, unbelievably, young people for purposes I could only guess."

"Did you report this?" Neenah asks.

"Janx did," Caton says. "To the old Abbot."

"What happened?" Mika asks.

"All I know for sure," Caton says, "is that shortly thereafter the harbor corridor was sealed off and the club shut down. My assumption was that Tenebrus was too valuable to lose, but he had been told to keep his activities out of the Abbey."

"Well holy shit," Brik says.

"This all went on under our noses," Neenah says.

"Yeah," says Brik, "and me not once getting a club invite."

Neenah slams his shoulder. "Pig," she says.

It is past sundown, when we've settled into our oasis camp for the night, that Cael and Fletch fly in unexpectedly.

"I've news," Cael says, and joins us by the fire. "I contacted the Abbot after we arrived at the Haven. I told him I was encountering people, credible people, who accused him of corruption and worse. At first he was quite angry, and denied everything. He even said Caton, here, is a madman and a criminal who lies to cover for his own crimes."

"He used Caton's name?" I ask.

"Yes," Cael says. "He apparently already knew or guessed from our itinerary that we met up with Caton at the prison."

"He always seems to know our moves," Mika says. I look at her hard.

"It gets worse," Cael says. "I told him these allegations required an investigation by the Abbey Governing Board's Judicial Tribunal, and he flew into a rage. Way beyond anything I had ever heard from him before. He said he was done being judged by 'insects,' that was the word he used. He said he and I were gods, we should be treated that way, and we needed to act for the good of magic."

"For the good of magic?" Mika asks, "What the fuck does that mean?"

"I took it as a statement of pure superiority," says Cael. "That there are magicians and magic, and then everyone and everything else. The Sultan was right: Magic *is* out of balance. And now I know the reason."

"Tenebrus," says Caton.

Just then, my ring signals me, and the others hear it. Faces swirl in the stone until settling.

"It's Janx," I say.

I feel us connect, and he is radiating worry. He communicates that the Abbot is bringing corruption charges against Cael and all of us, and is demanding that the authorities in Nir find and extradite us per their treaty. He asks if I know of any reason for this action, and I communicate what Cael just told us. He is shocked by only one thing, Caton Welty's name. Caton is supposed to be dead ten years on, he communicates. Died trying to escape Nir custody, according to Ven Mirren. Bastard.

I look up at the group, who are all staring at me. I take off my ring, and hand it to Caton.

"Just look at the stone and think of Janx."

Caton hunches over the stone and reaches out to his old friend. I tell the others about the charges and extradition request. Cael reaches for his pack and pulls out the communications pad embroidered with a falcon sigil. A moment later he looks up.

"The Sultan told the Abbot that it aggrieves him to say that we are out in the desert and unreachable," Cael says. "That he will certainly look into the matter if we come back through Aurelia."

I laugh. "Did I hear that right?" I ask. "The Sultan just told Tenebrus in cordial diplomatic niceties where to shove his extradition request?"

"That's about it," Cael says, "so for now nothing's changed. What it means for the longer term is unclear, although it doesn't sound like we can go back to Floendahl Abbey any time soon."

"I'm fine with that," I say, and Mika squeezes my hand.

"Here's what I don't get," Mika says. "The Abbot has been insisting we continue this mission all along, despite everything. Now he wants us stopped. What's changed?"

Cael snorts. "You're right, Mika, it's a big turnaround. I was thinking that it's because he gets nasty when angry, but this is more. I'm thinking now that it's because we're learning too much, I'm learning too much, about things he went to a lot of trouble to keep secret. Not only am I a magician with the power to replace him at Monkworks, but I now have knowledge of his transgressions."

"Suddenly you've gone from vague threat to an existential one," I say.

Cael nods. "We need the second source now more than ever," he says, "so we have the magical and economic power to push back against him."

"We're with you all the way," I say, and the rest of us mouth agreement.

And yes he does … he blushes. What a revolutionary.

"There's just one thing, Cael," I say. "Something that Mika said before about Tenebrus knowing our moves."

"What are you thinking, Egon?" he asks.

"The communications pad you use with him," I say. "Could he be tracking us with it?"

The color drains from Cael's face. He reaches into his pack and pulls it out. "He gave it to me for this mission," he says. Then he sort of concentrates on it for a minute, and abruptly flings it into the fire. "There's a tracker in it," he says. "Of course there is. How could I be so stupid?"

"Not your fault, Cael," I say. "You had no reason to suspect him before now."

Cael does not appear convinced by my words. Then he takes out the Sultan's pad and examines it. "This one's clear," he says.

Then Caton comes back to us. There are tears on his grizzled face, and his scarred hand shakes as he hands me back my ring.

"Thanks, Egon," he says, and wipes his eyes with his hands. "Janx thought I was dead, that was the story they told him. He was the one who broke the news to my wife in Floendahl Heights back then. He's been looking after her and my son ever since. He says they are well."

"Will Janx tell them you're alive now?" Neenah asks.

"He asked to," Caton says, "but I told him I didn't know."

"Why not?" Neenah asks gently.

"They must have entirely new lives by now," Caton says. "It's been 10 years. I've never even seen my son, my wife gave birth after my arrest. I am afraid to just barge in on them now."

"It's true that your wife may be with someone else now," Neenah says. "But she will want to know you're alive if your marriage meant anything. And as for your son, that's a bond that nothing can break. You need to let him know he has a father. After that, you can decide together what is the best thing you can do for them."

I can tell Neenah's words strike home. Caton sits there thinking for a while, until finally he says, "I think you're right, Neenah." So he borrows my ring again to ask Janx to let them know.

After that, we sit around the fire talking things over but, oddly, without much in the way of anxiety. I guess it was because, after all we have been through together, this Abbey news felt like just some more administrative bullshit. Caton has a question, though.

255

"Why go on testing devices for the Abbey," he asks, "when it's clear the Abbot wants to shut down your mission?"

We all look to Cael, who barely hesitates before nodding.

"We're continuing to do the tests now," Cael says, "because it's on the way, we're expected, and we are making friends with the movers and shakers of Nir. But our true motivation is that after the tests we are headed a little farther up the coast to a second source of *Floe*, with which I will be able to establish a second Monkworks and, in effect, a second home for any of us who wants it."

"Holy shit," Caton says, and we laugh. "But how do you know it's there?" he asks.

"Janx found it, "Cael says, "about five years ago, testing a new device."

"Holy shit," he says again.

Cael and Fletch stand up then. "Gods willing, my friends, we'll see you tomorrow night at the Seafaring Merchants Guild Hall." And with that, they're back to the sky.

We leave early next morning, and travel through an oddly beautiful landscape of soaring stone towers and arches, sandblasted over eons into grotesque shapes. By late afternoon we're out of that, and the desert gives way to gently rolling hills, stands of trees, and rows of farmers' crops. Then we begin to smell the ocean: salt tang, rotting seaweed and shellfish, and sweet unknowable scents on cool ocean breezes.

The city of Portus Sironika is small, low, mostly wood and glass, and painted in wind-muted blues and grays and greens. There are no mosques, turrets or date palms; in fact it looks nothing like what we've seen of the rest of Nir. All of its buildings fit on the slopes of the natural amphitheater formed by the hills surrounding its picturesque harbor, affording great views of the water from almost anywhere. In the distance at first, then drawing closer, are the many masts of tall ships. We clatter over cobblestones through busy streets until, as the sun starts to go down, we arrive at a stately, three-story building in a row of stately three-story buildings that sit together like hedges facing an open plaza, and then wharfs, ships and a large bay beyond.

I signal to the captain of our escort, and ask him to deploy his troopers in front of the building, and also behind it if there's a street back there. I also alert him to the fact that members of the Abbey claiming some type of authority may try to approach us, and I ask that his troops intervene. He is fine with both requests.

He takes off and I nod to the group. "Let's go see what we're facing," Mika says, and five of us humans follow scout dog Snout up brick steps, through a wide plank door, and into a large vestibule. All around us the walls are covered in seafaring artefacts and art. There is a huge glass box in front of us filled with sand, water and colorful fish. To our right, a circular staircase winds its way up to the next level. A man with bushy gray hair, a captain's hat, and mutton chop sideburns, is coming down the stairs with a big smile on his face and an outstretched hand.

"Bayton Nayby," the man says as he shakes my hand, "Master of the Seafaring Merchants Guild."

I introduce him to everybody, and he makes a point of making friends with Snout. I like him already.

"Follow me," he says. He heads back up the winding staircase to the top floor, which is basically one large room with windows floor to ceiling along its bay-facing wall. Several arrangements of low tables and cushiony chairs are lined up to take advantage of the view. On the opposite wall from where we enter is a map of the seas and harbors surrounding the Three Kingdoms, and moveable representations marking the locations of the ships presumably owned by Guild members. Old school, I think. Wait until they see *Freight Finder*.

Mika asks Bayton if there is access to the roof from here, and he points to a doorway. Mika explains Cael and Fletch's mode of transportation, which amuses him, and she asks Neenah and Brik to wait on the roof for them to arrive. They barely leave when they are back with the twosome. I make introductions, and then Bayton leads us over to chairs by the windows. Neenah, Brik, Caton, Fletch and Mika hang back, and I hear Mika deploying them defensively. Someone brings refreshments for Cael, me, and the others, as the Guild Master briefs us about tonight's event.

"It is membership renewal time for about a third of our members," he explains, "and tonight's get-together is part of the process of getting them to sign back up. We charge a great deal of money to be a member of our Guild, so it's no simple decision for even our wealthiest merchants. But members get a lot from us in return.

"We use consensus to establish rules of order for the shipment of goods throughout the Kingdoms," he continues, "and then we enforce those rules with speed and impartiality. No member gets an unfair leg up, and none gets bullied about. We mediate disputes between members, and we intercede when authorities clash with one of us. We advocate for policy positions favorable to our merchants with all levels of government throughout the Three Kingdoms. Plus, because of the size and professionalism of our membership, we have tremendous leverage when it comes to negotiating for reasonable harbor fees, lower tariffs, sufficient and well maintained dock space, adequate warehousing at fair prices, and the like."

"Impressive," says Cael. "How can we help?"

Bayton smiles. "I'll be honest," he says. "I want you to prove your device does what you say it can, and then I want you to sell it to me, exclusively, so no individual merchant or competing guilds can own one of their own. That way, I have another tool for attracting and keeping members."

Cael smiles. "I appreciate your candor," he says, "so I will lay my cards out on the table as well. *Freight Finder* is going to be too big to corner. Everyone from army generals to hat shop owners will want one, virtually anybody who has anything to keep track of."

Disappointment is written on Bayton's face. I wonder if our evening is about to end abruptly.

"But," Cael says, raising a finger, "that doesn't mean I can't help you."

"How so?" Bayton asks, with renewed hope.

"I will create sales categories for this device," Cael says, "in your case, seafaring merchants. I will design each device to work only within its intended category so, for instance, a general can't use a hat shop owner's device to track his soldiers. And I will give you exclusive use of the seafaring merchants device for, say, one year."

"Four years," says Bayton instantly.

"Best I will do is two years," Cael says. "And it will cost you a great deal of gold. Even after your exclusivity expires, few other seafaring individuals or groups will be able to afford it, so this will be a useful recruiting and retention tool for years to come."

Bayton smiles. "You're a shrewd young man, Cael," he says. "You're offering less than what I want but enough to make it useful. If the device works, it's a deal."

They shake hands, and Cael asks if he received the two mermaid stampers he sent to him.

"Yes," says the Guild Master, "and we stamped the cargoes of two ships that are now out at sea. We made sure the crate packing was the most haphazard we could manage."

Good," Cael says grinning. "Then it will be a fair test. What happens now?"

"Now we sit back, relax, have a drink, and wait for our members to arrive. It's real informal around here. They'll show up, maybe 15 merchants or so representing hundreds of ships. I'll introduce you all around, and we'll drink some more. Then I'll call the meeting to order, we'll gather around you at a seating area like this, and you'll do your, er, magic. Sound good?"

"Perfect," says Cael.

"There's just one thing," I say, catching the attention of Cael and Bayton. "I'm wondering if either of you would mind if we move the seating arrangement to the center of the room, for security reasons, so we're not so viewable from the outside?" My ring and Snout have been quiet on this leg of the trip, but why take chances?

"I'll do you one better," the Guild Master says, and signals to have shutters closed on all the windows facing the now darkened bay. He signals someone else and suddenly several people are moving all the seating arrangements away from the windows and into the center.

"Thanks very much for accommodating us," says Cael. "Unfortunately, I have been a magnet for violence on this trip, as you probably know."

"Glad to oblige," Bayton says. "Now sit, sit."

So the three of us sit and sip drinks, Snout at my feet.

"I'm wondering, Guild Master," asks Cael, "what you can tell me of a harbor on the coastline where the Great Southern Sea meets the mountains behind the Abbey?"

Bayton looks at Cael appraisingly. "Not much, actually," he says. "It's not the kind of anchorage our members frequent."

"Why not?" Cael asks.

Bayton looks a little uncomfortable, not sure where this conversation is going or where Cael stands on the matter.

"Our members adhere to strict rules," he finally says. "Our cargoes are certified and inspected, our itineraries posted for public inspection."

"You're saying this harbor is a smugglers' haven," Cael says.

"In a word, yes," says Bayton.

"Do you know when this activity started?" Cael asks. "And do you know if it is still operating?"

The Guild Master thinks for a bit before answering. "I can't say for sure when it started, but it was running 25 years ago when I came to work here. I think it stopped or quieted down for a while, more than a decade ago, but it started right back up. Black market Monkworks devices are a hard thing to keep secret."

"Why doesn't someone stop it?" Cael asks.

"No one wants to take on the Abbey," he says, "and everyone likes the devices. It really only undercuts the Abbey, because no one else can sell Monkworks devices legally, so there is no incentive for others to stop it."

"So we're stealing from ourselves for personal gain," Cael says. "That's pathetic."

"You're a *Floe* magician, yet you're saying you knew nothing about this?" Bayton asks.

Cael looks at him thoughtfully. "You know, it's funny you should ask. I mean, why *don't* I know about this, and all the other questionable things I've learned on this trip? I mean, I always felt isolated growing up in the Abbey; I used to think it was because I was an orphan, or because of my twisted foot. But now I'm beginning to think that the network of people who knows what's going on at the Abbey just didn't want to take a chance on trusting me. I'm a magician, I'm from outside, I have no family roots within the Abbey like they all seem to. It was just easier to keep me uninformed and at arm's length, and just let me quietly do my job. So, to answer your question, I didn't know about this until recently, and if I ever get the power I will shut it down."

We're quiet for a minute, me contemplating a lonely, hobbled child with immense power but completely unable to break through the wall of avoidance that was placed around him. People suck if given half the chance. Or, I amended, a lot of them do.

"I commend your intentions, Cael," Bayton says, "but if I may make a suggestion, rather than shut the harbor down, you may wish to legitimize it. A properly regulated harbor shipping authorized Monkworks products will allow you to dump those slow, antiquated carts the Abbey still uses to sell its devices. You could increase your sales exponentially using a modern shipping and distribution system."

"Spoken like a true shipping magnate," Cael says, laughing.

Bayton smiles. "Still, you should consider it. And if there is ever something I can do to help you and your companions with this, please ask."

"Thank you," says Cael.

262

"By the way," Bayton says, "and please forgive any intrusion. But I noticed your boot and you mentioned your twisted foot. I wonder if you know that Portus Sironika is the home of a medical institute famed throughout the Three Kingdoms for its advances in treating problems of the foot. I know for a fact that they have great success there with people who have similar conditions."

"You know for a fact?" Cael asks skeptically.

Bayton points to his right foot. "Until I went there," he says, "I walked with crutches. It's why I never got to go to sea back in the day, even though it was my greatest desire. They take a science-based approach, using only rigorously tested and proven therapies. One of the people you will meet tonight is a large donor to the institute, Veronika Neel. If you are interested, she can provide you with more information, and even make introductions."

"I am interested," Cael says. "Maybe science can do what magic cannot. And I would like to speak to this member about it. But I'm afraid I have a lot to do first before I can properly look into it."

"I understand," says Bayton. "But don't wait too long. It gets harder to fix."

Then we hear voices, and members start climbing up the stairs. We stand and begin the chit chat stage of our evening.

We both get introduced around, and Cael is immediately in the thick of discussions. I stand on the periphery of several conversations, listening. Much of the talk is about the possibility of war after at least a century of peace. The merchants seem unconcerned about attacks on shipping and, in fact, seem to believe a Kingdoms-wide wartime economy will be very profitable for them. Already orders are up as governments move to stockpile grains, vegetables, weapons, and raw materials like metals and wool. These smug bastards better hope the Keep doesn't come up with a ship-killing construct, I uncharitably think.

Cael is waving me over now as the evening gets down to business. I sit at one of the small tables, with the magician on my right and Bayton on my left. Standing in a circle around us are the Guild members, eager to see what they have heard so much about. Mika and the others move in a little from the sides.

Bayton is explaining that, for purposes of this demonstration, the cargoes of two ships at sea have been marked by a magical stamper shaped like a mermaid, a copy of which Cael holds up. "Cael and Egon will now show you how their device, called *Freight Finder*, will revolutionize all of our lives." There is some applause and whistles.

I take the small black box from the velvet bag and put it on the table in front of me. "So with this Finder," I say, "the Guild can track your goods wherever they are in the Kingdoms at any time you need to know. It will alert you to delays or catastrophes immediately, and it will record any depletions in inventory as it happens. If a ship is pirated, it will follow the progress of your stolen goods back to the home ports of the perpetrators."

"Show us," someone commands, and the others laugh.

I pick up the box and twist the top and bottom in opposite directions, and it transforms into its upright tracking surface resting on the solid black base. I press an indentation on the base and an overhead map-like image of the room we are gathered in appears on the display. The Guild members jostle around until each has a good view. I press again and the town and harbor appear, a little fuzzier, with us very tiny in the center. I press again, and a chunk of Nir and the Eastern Sea appear. My next press exposes a larger portion of Nir and the Eastern Sea, along with a part of the Great Southern Sea upon which are two glowing dots.

A window opens up above each dot, and both ships can be seen in lifelike detail with full sails and flying spray under triple moonlight. I hear gasps. Under one image it says, 'Carrier: The Golden Phoenix.' "That's mine," someone shouts. Under the other image it says, 'Sorceress,' and a woman says, "Oh my gods." Then the manifests appear, itemizing the entire cargo in each ship, regardless of attempts to scatter unlike goods throughout mismarked crates. "That's beyond ingenious," someone says.

"And there you have it," Bayton says, standing up. "The Guild will now be able to track your ships and goods in real time and notify you of progress or unexpected deviations. When we roll it out we will be selling the stampers, customized for each buyer, with proceeds going to repay the purchase of the device, which will be a significant outlay."

They start to chew over all of that as Cael and I stand up as well, our evening pretty much over. Cael goes to talk to a woman who I guess may be the foot institute donor, and I walk over to Mika.

"I checked with our escort, and they've made camp just outside town on the road to our next test," she says. "After Cael and Fletch leave, the rest of us will head over there."

"Sounds good," I say. "I'll go check on Cael."

Cael sees me coming and politely excuses himself.

"You about ready?" I ask.

"Let's just say goodbye to Bayton," he says, "and we're out of here."

The Guild Master is thrilled with how the evening has gone, and thanks us for our 'performance.' Then all of us escort Cael and Fletch to the roof and waiting Gryphon, and they take off for their new Haven, between Portus Sironika and our next stop, Jakarina. Then the five of us remaining, plus Snout, make our way down to the coach for a short ride to what turns out to be an uneventful overnight.

TEN: I WOULD HAVE HAD SEX WITH HIM

Next morning, we travel north along the coast through grasslands towards Jakarina, and our final mission test. Cael told us that the entire hierarchy of the Jakarene faith is there to elect a new Caliph. There will be many speeches and many rounds of voting before the new leader is elected. Our device, *Friend & Foe Finder*, will be used to allow all candidates to gauge their relative popularity in the moment, so as to adjust their message as the voting progresses.

By late afternoon we reach a fishing community with a welcoming seaside inn. Mika and I get an airy room upstairs, with a balcony overlooking a small harbor filled with fishing boats of every imaginable type. We have tangy seafood stew in a pub on the ground floor, take a stroll with Snout along the docks at sunset, and retire to our room.

"I want a baby, Egon," Mika announces as we get into the big, four-poster bed.

"We have Cael," I say, before realizing it came out wrong. "I mean, we're risking our lives to protect Cael right now. This isn't the time for a baby."

"I don't think you understand the situation, daddy," she says. Uh oh, last time she said something like that my life was on the line. At least, in a manner of speaking.

"What situation?" I ask, cautiously.

"The situation," she says, undoing the knot in her robe, "is this, Egon. You have proposed marriage to me tonight, a very serious step. So I will consider it carefully and then we will get married at the first reasonable opportunity. I will immediately dispense with Monkworks preventatives, and we will endeavor to create a baby together. Her name will be Aurelia."

"You realize I've said nothing about getting married," I say, as though it might remotely matter.

"A technicality," she says.

"You realize I no longer have a home?" I ask.

"We will soon have a new one," she says.

"You realize I have no money?" I ask.

"You're friends with someone who conjures it," she says, undoing the knot in my robe.

"I'm feeling all of my mighty defenses crumbling," I say.

"Then I accept your proposal, Egon," she says, reaching for the one part of me that is making any kind of proposal.

"You may kiss the bride-to-be," Mika whispers.

Later that night, after Mika falls asleep, I get on my ring for an emergency discussion with Cael.

The next day we're on the road early through grassy, rolling hills. We get about an hour out of town before we're attacked. It is the last thing I am expecting. I have completely let my guard down. I've been acting, I don't know, happy, since I got up. What a fool.

So anyway, Snout alerts, my ring stays silent in the face of a human threat, and arrows start thudding into our carriage. Horses are screaming now, and a wild ululating cry rises all around us. I look to see the tall grass erupting with waves of attackers with shaved heads and light purple robes. I recognize the Swin Jin Ree, Cael's would-be assassins courtesy of Immobilin Keep.

I find out later that the first flight of arrows killed 7 of our 100 Ranger escort, with more wounded. But unlike me, they were prepared for hostilities. Two rangers have unlimbered their bows and are already shooting from the roof of the carriage. We suddenly rocket forward as the driver tries to get us out of the kill zone, but our archers are somehow unaffected. Rangers behind us lower their lances and attack into the mass of sword-wielding attackers coming down the slope towards the road. Rangers on either side and ahead of us string their bows as they ride, in an incredible display of competence, and are firing in the blink of an eye.

Up ahead, a tree falls in our path. We slow down and a squad of riders races ahead to the tree while the rest prepare to defend the nearly stopped carriage. Meanwhile, our lancers on the slope are decimating the Swin Jin Ree fighters on foot. I use my ring to contact Cael, and communicate that we will need his healing abilities if and when we can secure the scene enough to make it safe.

I look up to see that there is a second ambush set up at the fallen tree, and riders to the front of our carriage race forward to support the squad moving the tree. A hidden cadre of purple robes use that distraction to charge our carriage. Arrows are singing out above us in response as I toss a rippler through the open window. It's an awkward throwing angle, so I hurtle through the door, the rest of the crew emptying the carriage behind me.

I start throwing ripplers to good effect as the others fan out around me. Caton takes a cleric on his sword and kicks him off with his boot. Mika kicks another in his balls, and I have reason to feel a momentary pang for the ambusher. Rangers are screaming for us to get back in the carriage now, which we immediately do as they drag the tree away.

The carriage takes off and we are suddenly out of the fray. When we finally slow down, a squad stays around us and the rest of the Rangers go back to join their comrades, who are mopping up the attackers and protecting the wounded. Cael drops in then with Fletch, whose augmented bow is strung. The seven of us race back towards the fight, Snout in the lead and our protective squad surrounding us.

When we get there, Cael immediately goes to work, as Fletch assists with triage and helping the wounded with medicinal Monkworks devices. The captain of the Rangers is interrogating a prisoner who, instead of answering, is chanting in a language I don't recognize. As we approach, the captain lifts the cultist's head by his hair and slits his throat. He sees us and says, "There all like this," and walks away in apparent disgust.

All told, 11 of our escort are dead. Cael saves five more, and there are 18 walking wounded that Cael and Fletch soon have on the mend. Then Cael, the Captain and I talk for a moment and agree to proceed to Cael's Haven to recover, before proceeding on in to Jakarina tomorrow morning.

Once at the Haven, Cael provides meals and drinks for the Rangers, who camp outside it in a protective ring. Then he uses his pad to brief the Sultan and commend the bravery and competence of the Rangers.

Later, around the Haven's fire, Caton says, "Who were those guys and why did they come after us?"

"They're a religious cult opposed to Monkworks devices and funded by Rusk," I explain. "I can only guess at why they attacked us. It could be they thought Cael was with us and they wanted to make good on their previous failed attempt to kill him for the

Keep. Or maybe they thought to take the rest of us out so Cael would be more isolated and vulnerable in the Holy City. It could even be that they have their own reasons for not wanting him to reach Jakarina."

"An attack on the road by someone almost had to happen sooner or later, unfortunately," says Mika. "Still, your strategy, Egon, of moving Cael to the Havens has worked beautifully, keeping him safe and mostly reducing the pressure on us."

"I got complacent and wasn't prepared," I say, and then I realize that there could have been a more heinous reason for the attack. "In fact, it just occurred to me that I got downright stupid by bringing Cael out of safety to the scene of the battle to heal the injured. That could have been their plan to get to Cael all along."

"Forget it, Egon," says Cael. "Not even the Guardians saw it coming, and they've been out overflying your route looking for this kind of trouble. The Gryphon that just flew us communicated sorrow, and that some of the Swin Jin Ree live out in the grasslands and have ways of moving through it that are all but undetectable."

I shrug. The fact is that beating myself up is a luxury I can't afford right now. "Ok, it is what it is" I say. "So let's talk about what we're facing in Jakarina."

"It sounds to me like a religious form of our Aurelia test," Cael says. "Your coach pulls up at the Grand Mosque, and their version of Var greets you and takes you to see their officials. Later, you gather up Fletch and me on the roof, and together we go to meet Umam Hani den Jakarina, the one who is running the election. After that we will allow any candidate to use our *Friend & Foe* device to monitor changes of opinion during the course of the proceedings. Each Umam will be allowed to try to head off negative momentum before it can affect the next vote. There will be many votes before a consensus on a new Caliph is reached."

270

"Ok," says Mika, "it sounds like Fletch and Caton should stay at the landing site to secure the exit and serve as backup. Meanwhile, Neenah, Brik, Egon and I will escort Cael. We all stay in touch by bracer. Sound right?"

She looks around and we all nod.

I get up to refill my vest at the Rowan tree, and Cael comes over. He hands me something in a silk pouch.

"After you contacted me last night," he says, "I had a lot of fun developing this for my favorite mercenary, who lacks for nothing except her taste in men."

I laugh out loud. "You know, Cael," I say, "for once I have to agree with you."

I tug open the drawstring and upend the pouch into my hand. The ring is a simple band of entwined white gold delicately grasping a dazzelite gem of gasp-inducing beauty. It is so intense, its moving images so brilliant, that it must have held more magic than a unicorn.

"I don't have words, Cael," I manage, shaking my head. "It is so beautiful."

"Why, thank you, Egon," he says, "but, just like Mika, it is so much more than beautiful," he says, grinning. "I protected it so that it can never come off, unless she takes it off. And, it's been blessed by the Guardians so it has all the powers of the rings they gave us. Oh, and, one other thing. If you are both wearing your rings you will always intuitively know where to find each other, anywhere in the Three Kingdoms."

I look at him. "How do I even take this, Cael?" I ask. "It is so much more than I can ever repay."

He smiles. "That's the thing, Egon. You've already repaid me, more than you'll ever know. You made this journey possible, and you valued me, and you showed me how to value myself. It's me who can never repay you."

Ahhh shit. You know that there's only one thing left to do following a speech like that, so we hug, in a very manly way of course. And guess what? I'm the one who blushes. Then I ask him to be my best man. He agrees.

Later, in our Cael-conjured luxury tent, on a bed that literally floats like a cloud in the air, Mika wants to know what 'that scene' was earlier between Cael and me.

"Oh nothing," I say. "He just finally admitted that I was right all those years about his devices being defective."

Mika looks at me, indisputably unconvinced. "I'll tell you who's defective around here," she says, threateningly.

"Ok, Ok," I say, giving in. "He congratulated me on my engagement, and asked if he knew the lucky girl."

Mika halfway reaches for her sword. "Final warning," she growls.

"Well alright," I say, "if you must know, what Cael actually said, by way of congratulations, is that you lack for nothing but taste in men."

"Now that I can believe," hoots Mika triumphantly.

"Yes," I say, sadly, "he also made me see that I mishandled the whole engagement thing, and that unless I correct it, our marriage will be doomed from the start."

"Correct away," Mika says, coyly, "although I think it was handled to my complete satisfaction."

I blush again, godsdammit. This better not become a habit. "Why, thank you," I say, "but I believe there is always room for improvement."

"What do you have in mind?" she asks.

Have you ever tried to get down gracefully onto one knee from a cloud bed that is floating around randomly? Then I had to hold the bed in one hand to keep Mika from floating to another part of the room, while using my other hand to dig the silk pouch out of the pocket of my robe. She looks over the edge of the bed to find out what I'm doing.

"Mika," I say, finally slipping the ring out and holding it up to her. "The truth is that I can't imagine my life without you. I am so totally in love with you, and I need for us to always be together. So I'm wondering, and hoping, will you marry me?"

It's her eyes I'll always remember. They shine with a flood of sudden tears that literally leap out onto her cheeks. Then she falls off the edge of the floating bed and into my arms.

"I didn't realize it would be so much better if you did the asking," she laughs, crying.

The ring fits perfectly, of course, and I tell her about its properties as she moves her hand every which way to catch the light. Honest to gods there is a lightning storm going on inside the stone at this moment, as if in celebration.

"So that scene by the tree? Cael gives you this ring and all you give him back was a hug?" Mika asks in utter disbelief. "At the very least, I would have had sex with him."

"That's why you didn't get the deluxe model," I say. "You should see what that can do."

She laughs out loud. "Ok, studly," she says, "let's see what you can do."

And we properly engage.

ELEVEN: THEY'VE FUCKING GOT HER

Next morning, the seven of us are eating breakfast when the Kingdoms start to come apart. First, the Captain tells us by bracer that the escort is being recalled to Aurelia as soon as Cael completes his work in Jakarina, because Sultan Anseem Hawarri is about to declare war on, of all places, Floendahl Abbey. We can accompany the escort back to the capital if we so choose, but we must hurry. What the fuck?

At almost the same moment, Janx contacts me by ring, to communicate that the Abbot is upping the charges against us all to treason, for conspiring with Nir against the Abbey. He has placed a huge bounty on our heads for our capture and return to the Abbey to stand trial. Janx warns us to stay away and trust no one. We are now exiles.

Then another ax blow falls. The Sultan contacts Cael by pad to say that Abbot Tenebrus is formally accusing the Kingdom of Nir of illegally protecting wanted fugitives, and is declaring the existing treaty, including its tribute payments to Nir, null and void.

"The Sultan just told me," Cael says, looking up from his pad, "that in response he declared war against the Abbey last night for reneging on its treaty obligations. Enduron, he says, is coming in on the side of Nir in accordance with their alliance. Both Kingdoms are massing troops on the trade route to the Abbey, one from the east and the other from the west."

Then it gets even worse.

Cael looks down at the pad again and holds up a finger. Then he says the Sultan is communicating word-for-word the Abbot's statement in response to this joint declaration of war. Cael pauses and then starts to recite:

> '...the shameless exploitation of arcane practitioners by the ungifted is over. From this day forth, magical Floendahl Abbey and the alchemist Kingdom of Rusk, in holy brotherhood, cease all sales of devices and Ky constructs to Nir and Enduron. We throw off the shackles of our unappreciated toil, and will instead join hands together in mutual defense to protect ourselves from the aggressors...'

Cael stops talking, apparently shocked into silence.

It's all out in the open now. It's not magic *for* the masses anymore. Tenebrus is trying to turn magic *against* the masses, in a world turned upside down.

Our brains are exploding, so of course Mika pulls us together. "Ok, let's take it from the top: First, our escort," she says.

"We're dead meat out here without them," Brik says.

"You're right," agrees Cael. "You all need to go back when they do."

"You have to come with us too, Cael," Neenah says.

"I have to finish this," Cael replies quietly. "The Abbot is evil. The second site is a chance to get it right, and prove to humanity once again that magic is a force for good."

"Ok, ok" says Mika. "I get it. So here's how we are going to finish it. Egon, you fly with Cael to the second site right now, to see what's what. Neenah, Brik, Caton, Fletch, me and Snout go with the escort into Jakarina according to plan, to set up security. That will keep the escort with us long enough for you to figure out your next steps, Cael. Then you meet back up with us in Jakarina, and we do the testing. After that, all of us go back together to Aurelia under escort so you can explain to the Sultan why now is a good time to annex some of his land. Thoughts?"

Mika is amazing.

"That is unbelievably great," Cael says emphatically, looking around at each of us in turn. "You've all given me more than I ever could have hoped for. You know I love you guys, right?"

"Oh my gods," explodes an exasperated Caton. "What kind of mercenary cutthroats *are* you people?"

Everyone laughs. "Ok, ok," says Mika, moving us along. "Next up: We're traitors now."

"Join the club," Caton says dismissively.

"Fine," says Mika, "nothing to be done. So let's talk about the fact that there's a war on, magic and alchemy against the rest of us, and two thirds of the Three Kingdoms is cut off from magical devices and labor saving constructs."

"Tenebrus wants that to be the narrative, that this war is 'magic and alchemy against the rest of us,'" I say, "but let's not let him. The war is between some evil renegades and everyone else. They represent no one and nothing but themselves. We need to show the Kingdoms whose side Cael is fighting on, or magic and the Abbey will never recover. We need to get back to Aurelia fast, before the chance to make things right is lost."

Little did I know we would not see Aurelia any time soon.

Our meeting breaks up after that and once again I find myself high in the air on the back of a Guardian, Cael on a second

Gryphon flying next to me. It takes about an hour to reach the outskirts of Jakarina, where we will turn left up the coast to the site.

From the air, the clerical city is a far cry from the other prosperous cities we have visited in Nir. The first thing we see is a sprawling, ramshackle outdoor camp of thousands of people outside the main city gates. We circle lower, and see squalor everywhere: shredded tents; no hygienic facilities of any kind; babies playing in dust without any shade; and apparently only one source of water, a hand-cranked well.

I know what's coming next, regardless of the urgency of his mission. Fucking Cael, you've got to hand it to him. We land by the well, alongside a man clad in a Jakarene cleric's saffron robes. He, and others dressed like him, appear to be the organizers of a long line of people waiting for water to fill their random assortment of containers.

"Who are you?" the cleric demands as we climb off the Guardians, unintimidated by our airborne arrival on creatures from mythology. The other people back off.

"I am Brother Caelum Venarius from Floendahl Abbey, and this is my colleague, Egon Brodie. We are here to help."

The cleric looks massively unmoved. "You make a dramatic entrance," he says drily, "but unless you also make food, water, clothing, shelter and sanitary facilities, it won't do us much good."

"I guess all I can do is try," Cael says. He turns to the well and does that thing with his arms. There is a pop and a long hiss as the well expands into an immense stone fountain in the shape of a Jakarine falcon, a stream of water cascading from its beak into an enormous basin shaped like a nest. Then he conjures three more of them. The crowd surges forward as the basins start to fill.

278

I start working in the camp itself, throwing Monkworks devices for bathing, sanitation, tents and children's toys. Around me and throughout the camp I see small groves of trees suddenly spring up, and I hear Cael tell the cleric that they will always remain fruit-bearing no matter how much is harvested. There are date palms, orange trees, olive trees, mango trees and more. Most ridiculous of all, there are bread trees filled with hanging loaves. I mean, what is magic for?

Then, tents and facilities start springing up everywhere in orderly rows, making my efforts seem feeble. Then Cael makes four huge tents, one stocked with clothing, one stocked with food, one for religious services, and one that's a medical facility. I meet him at the medical tent, where people start bringing in their sick, elderly and disabled. Saffron-robed clerics organize the bedding and supplies, and start treating who they can. Cael walks among the rows of cots and fixes the worst cases.

The cleric we first met is there as well. He looks at Cael appraisingly. "I am Umam Kasseem den Jakarina. You must be the magician that Umam Hani den Jakarina - may the Falcon God destroy him - is bringing in to fix the leadership vote," he says pointedly.

"I am the magician that has been asked to assist the process of fairly reaching consensus," Cael says.

"Maybe you believe that," the Umam says, "but what you see here are outcast citizens and devoted pilgrims, faithful Jakarenes all, who have been utterly betrayed and abandoned by the leaders you plan to assist. It's been very bad here for some time but, since the Nir garrison was recalled, Umam Hani and his Purple Robe rabble have unleashed all of their depravity upon us. The city itself is no better off than we are out here, except for the few. The few do very well in Jakarina, and you will help them."

"Maybe you believe that," says Cael back at the Umam, "but I am not here to influence the vote in favor of any one side. I will promise you, though, that I will bear in mind what you have said when I get in there."

"Then so be it," Umam Kasseem says in dismissal. "I can do nothing more than trust in your word. In any case, I thank you for relieving our suffering, if only for a while."

We leave then and resume our flight. I am trying to figure out what he means by 'only for a while.' But then I shake it off and start to get excited about finally seeing the second source of magical *Floe*.

Which, as it turns out, doesn't freaking exist.

We fly north up the coast for two hours beyond Jakarina. Cael is following the original map from Janx's mission report, and we land on a promontory which is supposed to overlook a scene of piled up supplies and busy personnel. Instead, there is nothing. We fly in widening circles for a while, before re-landing on the promontory. We find a couple of boulders to sit on, and then both of us try Janx on our rings and connect simultaneously, something I didn't know the rings could do.

"We've reached the second *Floe* site," Cael begins, "and there is nothing here."

Janx radiates consternation. "The second site?" Janx asks. "Why in the gods' names are you there?"

"I'm on a mission that you started," communicates Cael tensely, "and again, there's nothing here."

"Of course there's nothing there," Janx mentally roars into his ring. "There never was anything there. The site finder device was a failure."

Cael's face turns ashen.

"The Abbot told me you confirmed the second source five years ago, Brother Janx," Cael projects, "and that we've been preparing to build a new Monkworks here ever since."

"He lied," Janx communicates flatly. "He lied to me as well, I realize now, since he told me you were on a test and repair mission to speed up the manufacturing and revenue process for the prototypes."

We talk it over a bit more but, crestfallen and infuriated, we finally break contact with Janx. Cael looks at me, as we try to absorb the enormity of the Abbot's double dealing.

"Do you have any idea what's going on, Cael?" I ask.

His face is as tight and grim as I have ever seen it. Slowly he nods his head, up and down.

"I believe I finally do," he says. "This whole mission, everything, has been a mirage, just like the second site. The fight on the ridgeline, the fights at the bridge and the Notch, it was all the Abbot making early moves in a bigger game."

"What game?" I ask.

"He was already conspiring with the alchemists of Rusk to both kill me and build an alliance," Cael says. "Oh my gods. All of it. The Twins. The Inn. Aurelia. The Purple Robes. Everything. Everything we went through. It was just a phony mission designed to get me out of the Abbey, with a single Tester for protection, so he could have me killed."

"But why the fuck, Cael?" I ask, mystified.

"Because Tenebrus knew I'd never go along with an alliance with the flesh farmers of Immobilin Keep against the humans of the other Kingdoms," Cael says grimly. "And because Tenebrus desperately needs that alliance."

"I don't get it," I say. "Why does he need the alliance?"

He looks at me then like he's put it all together and I'm not going to like it. "There's something you don't know, Egon," he says. "Something I couldn't talk about before on my oath as a *Floe* magician. But after what Tenebrus has done, there is no oath to him that can bind me."

"Then let's finally hear it all, Cael," I say quietly.

I guess he hears an undertone in my voice. "I know, Egon, sorry," he says. "You deserve better from me. But the fact is, *Floe* is running dry. Maybe not in five years, maybe not even in 10. But unquestionably the volume of *Floe* from the source below Monkworks is past its peak and diminishing significantly every year. It will eventually run out, and with it will go the Abbey's prestige and the Abbot's power."

"So everything that's going on right now in the Three Kingdoms is part of his strategy for dealing with the depletion of *Floe?*" I ask.

"Yes," Cael says. "He has cut off Nir and Enduron from magical devices on the pretext of war, but I think it's really about conserving *Floe* as much as possible. He must be expecting a strong backlash to this cut off that could threaten the Abbey, thus the need to bring in Rusk and its military as allies. And my guess is that he is beginning to build a stockpile of *Floe* at the Abbey he needs to protect, so no matter what he will always have a supply to power his personal magic for the rest of his life. No room in that scenario for two magicians."

"So not only have you uncovered the Abbot's corruption on this trip," I say, "and not only do you stand in the way of his grand plan to selfishly cling to power at all costs, but you also could threaten his personal supply of stockpiled *Floe.*"

"Yes on all counts," Cael says.

"Do you think Janx knows about the loss of *Floe*?" I ask.

"He didn't sound like it just now," Cael says. "No reason Tenebrus would tell him. But I do know, and I've been such a fool. I refused to see the obvious. Like the Abbey could need money, when the Abbot and I can make our own gold. None of it made sense. I should have seen what he is doing. Do you know how many people died for this? For me?"

He is distraught, pacing now, running his hands through his hair. "And you, Egon," he says. "If you didn't ignore his advice about the Havens," he says, "if you didn't call in reinforcements, if you didn't outthink him every step of the way, I surely would be dead by now. All of us would be. You are the one wildcard he didn't count on."

At that moment, the Sultan contacts Cael by pad again, and when he's done he shakes his head. "This is weird," he says. "The Sultan is asking me why we've decided to stay without an escort in Jakarina." Dread is descending over me. "I'm telling him that's not so," Cael continues as he writes on his pad, "that our plan is to return to Aurelia with the escort." There's a pause and then he looks up at me. "He says Umam Hani den Jakarina released them, telling the escort captain that we all wish to remain behind."

Which is when my world explodes.

Mika flows into my mind using her new magical engagement ring. "Food drugged…" she communicates, "…fading…leaders here are all Purple Robes…don't come ba…" Then she is gone.

I resurface and Cael is looking at me quizzically.

"What's wrong, Egon?" he asks.

"The engagement ring," I grit out. "Mika. They've fucking got her. Fletch and the others too, all drugged. Hani den Jakarina and his Swin Jin Ree Purple Robes."

Then we race to the Guardians. 'They've fucking got her' is a repeating, screaming mantra inside my skull. Anguish shoots through me like an arrow on fire. My breath comes in harsh rasps. 'They've fucking got her' repeats itself maliciously, relentlessly, until it finally unleashes in me a rage so explosive it obliterates all thought. Cael and I mount our Gryphons and head away from one trap into what we know is another. What those purple-robed fuckers don't realize is that the trap just closed on them.

PART 3: *THE BALANCE*

ONE: WE'RE TOO LATE TO STOP IT

We fly directly to the Grand Mosque, where my ring lets me sense Mika is being held, and whose turrets and balconies are bristling with the Purple Robes of the Swin Jin Ree. We circle around and then head back to the refugee camp outside the city walls. We land beside what was the medical tent. Its walls are blackened by fire, its cots shredded, its patients laying untended in the dust. Cael's groves are burnt to the ground, his fountains smashed. Everything he created is destroyed.

Umam Kasseem den Jakarina is standing by the destroyed medical tent when we alight.

"What happened here?" cries Cael, striding forward.

"Your employers happened here," says a bitter Umam Kasseem. "Right after you left they came on horses with lances, axes and torches, in their pious purple robes. These are the rulers who seek the legitimacy of a phony vote made possible by your magic."

I see Cael reach his limit then. He whirls and, within the time it takes his outstretched arm to pass in a complete circle, he restores what was just destroyed.

"This," he says, his finger in the Umam's face, "is what my magic makes possible. And I will make more of this possible very

287

shortly, if you will get off your sanctimonious high horse and help me."

"What do you want," the Umam says, either outraged or cowed, I can't tell.

"I want for you to show us some entrance to the city that the Purple Robes will not be expecting us to enter by," Cael says, his anger still blazing. "We have people in there held against their will, and we are about to destroy the Purple Robes to get them out – although maybe you will insist upon a vote first? Consensus? No? I thought not. Well buckle up, because you and your followers are about to have free reign to do a better job of governance if you can. Now get us in there."

I can see that it is definitely outrage the cleric is feeling. Cael's angry words are stoking Kasseem's own anger issues to new heights of indignation. "Given the chance," he thunders, "I will rebuild this Church in the spirit of the Jakarine; holy, just and ever faithful to those ever faithful to the Church." He pauses. "And if that means consorting with the likes of you and your devil-spawn magic, than I will do it." What a surprise.

Umam Kasseem turns and starts issuing orders to the other nearby clerics. They scatter, but one comes back almost immediately holding saffron robes, which Kasseem tells us to put on. Then we follow him towards the edge of the camp and closer to the city walls. Soon, other saffron-robed clerics surround us, disguising us with their numbers, and together we enter the city through a small gate. "This is the route assigned to voting Umams during this process," Kasseem says. "The door we use to enter the mosque itself usually has only two guards."

"If you come in with us," Cael says to him, "there will be no going back for any of you."

"We are past caring," the Umam says.

I turn around and see hundreds of camp inhabitants beginning to follow in our wake, all of them seeking an overdue reckoning with the Purple Robes.

The two guards at the door make it easy for me by wearing their purple robes, thus declaring their allegiance. I take out both of them with my sword. I know from the power of her ring that Mika is 'up,' so Cael and I race ahead of the Umams and up the stone staircase that winds around the inner curve of the mosque. We are unopposed until about halfway to the ceiling, when side doors start opening above and below us. Purple Robes with swords and lances erupt onto the staircase, while arrows start bouncing off the protective aura of our medallions.

I sprint up the stairs towards our attackers while, behind me, Cael starts unleashing controlled explosive bursts that send dozens of the pursuing fanatics to their doom. When I get close enough, I start throwing ripplers along the curved mosque wall to my left, and purple robes start flying over the balustrade and into thin air. I burst into the attackers' reeling front line, slashing with the magically-enhanced power of my sword. I clear space around me and throw more ripplers ahead. Additional bodies fly, and the whole attacking force crumbles. I bound further up the stairs, slashing at the too slow, and reach the top. But even as I do, I sense that Mika is now moving down on the other side. I sprint around the arc of the dome unopposed, my rage and heartbreak spiking.

Cael races up behind me, having devastated the trailing Purple Robes. Together we reach the staircase on the other side, only to find it blocked by a company of fanatics who have hastily erected makeshift barriers of furniture and whatever. Beside me, Cael goes to work. Barriers explode from his magical discharges, and the first line of Purple Robes evaporate.

"C'mon," I shout to Cael. "They're taking her down somewhere." We tear through the defenders, but they are so many,

289

and more and always more come from rooms off the staircase, and it's taking precious time.

We might have caught them nevertheless, except as I pass one of the open doors I hear a pitiable whimper. It's a sound I've never heard from her before but still instantly recognize. Snout, in agony. I run into what seems to be a dining room, and there on the floor is my precious slaughtered friend.

I kneel next to her in a pool of her blood, cupping the back of her head. "Oh my gods," I say, "what have they done to you?" One leg is nearly severed. There are slash marks all over her body, as though they tortured her with their blades. Her flank is cut so deep I can see ribs. Her protective medallion is gone, apparently taken after they drugged her like the others. They must have attacked her for sport when she came to, and next to her are three dead Purple Robes with their throats open. In the end, Snout learned to fight.

But it isn't the end. She whimpers again and I realize she is still alive. Cael is there, then, and abruptly shoves me aside. "Guard the door," he barks, and goes to work. I go to kill.

I kill everything above me on the stair, and then everything below. I go into rooms and kill. I kill Purple Robes who are already dead. I am blind with unquenchable rage. It takes a yelp to finally snap me out of it.

A barely limping Snout comes out of the dining room, followed by a blood-soaked Cael. I run to her, burying my face in her bloody fur. "Good, good girl," I say softly, and she is licking me.

By now, Mika has been transported to the bottom of the mosque, through the city, and outside the city walls. Cael drapes Snout around my shoulders and we continue our pursuit. We run into Umam Kasseem, whose followers are tearing through rooms looking for Purple Robes to kill.

"What is in that direction, outside," I ask him, pointing.

"The harbor," he says.

Oh shit, shit, shit. We race as fast as we can without hurting Snout, trying to catch up, sometimes fighting, mostly just moving forward. We pull up on a dilapidated wharf in time to see a galley being rowed out but we're too late to stop it. I see its sails go up and it turns south, taking Mika, Fletch and the others with it.

TWO: I HAVE BEEN DOWNRIGHT WONDERFUL

"Gods-fucking-damn it," I scream in frustration. Then sudden realization strikes. South. Of course. The Great Southern Sea, and then around to the west. Umam fucking Hani den Jakarina and his lowlife band of thugs are heading for the Abbey's secret harbor, there to turn over their prisoners for the Abbot's bounty. I wonder now if that was the purpose of the earlier attack on the road. I scan the docks looking for something we can commandeer to follow them, but there is nothing remotely its size or speed.

"Egon," says Cael, "we can contact the Gryphons and fly out after them."

"The Guardians can't do it," I say, frustrated. "The earth is their domain, and the source of their power. They literally cannot go out to sea and still magically function."

"Well what the fuck," says Cael.

Then it hits me. "Cael, you are fucking brilliant," I exclaim.

"What?" he asks, bewildered.

"You're right about contacting the Gryphons. We ask them to fly us to Portus Sironika. I'm sure Bayton Nayby will be able to get us a vessel and crew that can catch them."

"Let's do it," Cael says.

The Guardians agree to the transport when I contact them, provided we stop first at the Haven to change magical mounts. I use the stop as an opportunity to rearm my vest. We are back in the air in minutes, and that's when Mika touches me again.

"Egon, I'm ok, we're all ok," she communicates, but I sense her disorientation. "They have us chained up, those Purple Robe fuckers. They drugged us, took our medallions. I think we're in the hold of a ship. It's dark, rocking, cold; we're all together except for Snout, unharmed but groggy."

"We're coming to get you," I communicate, "and Snout's with us." I tell her about the non-existent second site, the end of *Floe*, the fight at the mosque, her galley prison, and our race to Portus Sironika. She takes it all in, but I sense her fading, needing sleep. I tell her I love her, and everything will be alright. And then she slips away. I use my ring to reach Cael on the Gryphon flying next to me, and communicate my exchange with Mika. I can sense he feels some relief.

In total it takes us a day to travel from Jakarina to Portus Sironika. I feel Mika's nearness, but she is passing us by as her captors keep their galley well out to sea. I am tight with frustration and worry.

Bayton laughs out loud when Snout, Cael and I come down the stairs from the roof and into the big open reception room. He's having drinks and cigars with two others, and he jumps from his chair and strides towards us in welcome. "I meant to do something about that lock upstairs," he says, smiling, "because you never know what ruffians will drop in." He's scratching Snout's ears but the expression on my face gives him pause. "What's wrong?" he asks.

"We're sorry to intrude like this," I say, "but can we speak to you alone for a minute?"

293

"Certainly," he says. "follow me." He leads us towards the door to what turns out to be his office, excusing himself to his guests as we go. He closes the door behind us and immediately gets down to business. "What can I do for you?" he asks.

Cael tells him we are pursuing Swin Jin Ree kidnappers, most likely heading for the Abbey's smugglers harbor. He asks Bayton for a fast craft and reliable crew so we can overtake them.

"Can't do it," he says sadly, shaking his head.

"Why not?" I ask, my hopes plummeting.

"Oh, I can get you the ship and crew," he says, "just not in time to catch your kidnappers before they reach the Abbey. And, anyway, no commercial captain here will agree to risk his ship, crew and license boarding another ship at sea under fire. Your best option is to quietly follow them to the Abbey, then take them unawares once they land."

I feel another obstacle go up between me and Mika, but I know Bayton is making sense.

"Ok, I get it," I say reluctantly, my sea rescue suddenly turning into an Abbey invasion. "So we need a vessel to drop us off at the harbor, then wait out at sea for a couple of days in case we need a pickup. And something else now, to be on the safe side: space and provisions for another 10 or 15 of us."

"I take it you're expecting violence?" Bayton asks.

"Only after landfall now," I say. "We're not asking the crew to participate."

"Still, it sounds hazardous," Bayton says, "and a crew will want extra."

"Done," says Cael. "When can we get underway?"

294

"Let me get to work," Bayton says. "I will try to get you out of here on tomorrow afternoon's tide. Meanwhile, take your old guestrooms for the night."

Later, Cael asks about the extra people I spoke of to Bayton.

"This rescue has become an assault on the Abbey," I say. "So, once again, we are going to need reinforcements. Only this time, we are going to be the ones on the attack."

Cael smiles for the first time since I don't know when. "Speega," he says, pulling his pad from his pack.

"That's right." I say. "Speega Somes and her Killer spARROWS, plus any of Mika's mercenaries still available where we left them at the Nir & Far Inn."

He writes 'SPEEGA SOMES' on a page, which begins to glow when the pad senses a connection. We reach Speega like before, and brief her on the kidnap, our rescue mission, and the need to pick up her and her cohorts at a harbor between the Inn and Portus Sironika, if she is willing.

"THOSE FUCKERS," she writes. "YOU BETTER BELIEVE I'M WILLING."

She also knows a harbor we can meet at, and Cael tells her he estimates it will take three days for us to get there. We end the communication, promising to keep her updated.

Bayton rejoins us then, and he's smiling. "You're in luck. I have arranged a galley for you with a captain I trust and who, more importantly for this transaction, trusts me. He has begun securing provisions and crew."

"You are the best," I say to Bayton, and mean it. "Are we still good to go tomorrow?"

"The captain says you should be on board at midday tomorrow in order to catch the outgoing tide," Bayton says. "His name is Darion Creedmont, and I think we should go now to say hello to him."

We meet Captain Creedmont on the wharf. He's bearded, weathered and dour. "We'll be ready at change of tide tomorrow," he says, "and we'll be provisioned for ten days. Up to 15 passengers. I just need to know where we're going and what we're doing there."

"Very well," I say. "There are lives at stake here, so we'll reveal our ultimate destination tomorrow on our way out to sea, along with a stop we're making on the way to pick up more of us. As for what we are doing at our final destination, we wish you to drop us off then stand offshore for two days in case we need you to pick us up. After that, you're free to go."

"I trust Bayton here, so I'll play along for now," Creedmont says. "But anything I don't like, I turn us around."

"You're the captain," I say, and he nods.

After that, Bayton goes back to his duties, and Cael and I walk the harbor. The fact that I can't rescue Mika immediately weighs on me, is crushing me.

"I'm dying," I say to Cael.

"Me too," he says. "This is really hard."

"Fletch is going to be ok, Cael," I say.

Cael puts a hand on my shoulder. "Mika's going to be ok, too, Egon," he says in his earnest way. "I think there's time to figure this out."

"Why?" I ask.

296

"The hostages – because that's what they are - are worth gold to those clerical fuckers," Cael says. "They are probably hoping the Abbot can return them to power in Jakarina as well. As for Tenebrus, he needs our people as bait to lure us in. So maybe we can't rescue them at sea, but we can use the time to outthink the bastards."

I'm trying to calm myself down, and Cael is helping. I realize that the galley was outfitted and ready to sail as soon as Mika's attackers got there, or we would have caught them. And that means this was a kidnapping plan all along, though bungled in the end. I'm sure they wanted us all, drugged and transported, but that fell apart when Mika, Fletch and the crew arrived first to Jakarina without us. Then they went ahead with a partial kidnapping, figuring either it would make it easier to capture Cael and me when we arrived at the mosque, or that our people could be used as bait to force us to come to them. But then Mika warned me through her ring, and their plan – and their religious reign of terror - fell apart. Costly mistake, you fucks.

"Ok, you're right," I say. "Thanks." This is going to take some time, but maybe we have some time.

Back in a guest room at the Guild Hall, Cael and I reach out with our communications devices. He reaches out to the Sultan and I contact Janx. I communicate the kidnapping, pursuit, and the plan to enter the Abbey through the smugglers' tunnel.

"I'm sorry about this, Egon," Janx communicates. "I'll do all I can to help. They haven't arrived yet, or I think I would have heard about it. When they do, I'll try to find out where they are being held."

"Thanks, Brother Janx," I communicate. "What's the situation at the Abbey?"

"Mirren has brought in his own Abbey Guard from Immobilin Keep," Janx communicates, "all of them human-like constructs.

297

Programmed somehow to be loyal only to him, Tenebrus, and the alphas who control them. They have replaced our regular militia guards inside the Abbey buildings and tunnels. They wear red uniforms and they all carry explosive and incendiary devices, along with construct daggers, swords and crossbow bolts. *Floe* magic won't hurt them but conventional weapons will, as you know."

"None of it surprises me," I send. "How goes the war?"

"There are some breeders from the Keep inside Monkworks consulting with Tenebrus and Mirren," Janx communicates, "along with some Rusk military advisors. There are thousands of Rusk troops out on the plain, including both humans and constructs, but the Abbey's main 'M' gate is shut as though the allies don't fully trust one another."

Janx then agrees to get back in touch as soon as he has word of the hostages, and we break contact.

I'm done at the same time as Cael, and we compare notes. "The Sultan says his troops have fought their way up to the Notch against Rusk troops, plus alphas and constructs," Cael says, "on both the trade road and the upper trail. Heavy fighting, significant losses. He says the Three Kingdoms is a hard place to have a war, because there's basically only one connecting road through the mountains to everywhere. He says Enduron is having the same problems."

I think about this for a minute. "Maybe after we take care of our own business at the Abbey, we can find a way to help both Nir and Enduron break through."

"How?" Cael asks.

"Don't know. Have to think about it," I say. "Did you tell the Sultan about the kidnapping?"

"Yes," Cael says, "but only that we're in pursuit. No details. He expressed his regrets again about the escort mix up. He also communicated that Umam Kasseem den Jakarina has been declared the next Grand Caliph of the Jakarina, promising reform. He thanks us for our efforts on behalf of the new Caliph and against the Swin Jin Ree."

"I actually like Kasseem a little," I said, "even if he is a rude son of a bitch."

Cael smiles wryly. "I guess he has a right to his anger. I wish him well."

About then, Mika connects with me. "We're ok," she communicates, "but our accommodations cannot be compared to the Sultan's Lake House."

"But there are pirates," I communicate, "and moonslit seas."

"Even so," she transmits, "it's all oddly unsatisfying."

I laugh out loud. Maybe the best laugh I will ever have, so great is my relief that she remains herself. "I see not even a kidnapping by cutthroats can keep you down," I communicate.

"I miss you so much, Egon," she communicates. "It's by far the worst part of this."

I tell her about our pursuit galley then, and Speega and her old mercs, and how we will be together in just a few days.

"Was it a dream, Egon," she asks, "or did you actually tell me before that the second site was empty and *Floe* is running out?"

"Yes. The whole mission was so Tenebrus could get rid of Cael so he could manage the looming loss of his power."

"Oh my gods," she says. "That fucker. I'll tell the others."

299

We communicate some more and I tell her I will always love her, and finally there is nothing left to say.

When I resurface I tell Cael that Fletch and the others are doing ok. "I assumed as much," he says glumly, "watching you laugh."

I realize I'm the asshat again. "Sorry, Cael" I say. "I wish you could speak directly to Fletch too."

"I'll have to design a ring for him before the next kidnapping," he says ruefully.

Next morning we're up early and kill time fretfully, until it's time to say goodbye to our host.

"I'll never forget your help, Bayton," I say.

"Nor will I," Cael says.

"Well, it's true," Bayton says, smiling. "I have been downright wonderful. And I won't even ask you for another measly year's exclusive on your *Freight Finder* device in return, even though I'll be regretting it forever."

We smile, and Cael reaches into his robes. "Take the prototype," he says. "I have more."

Fucking Cael. What a softie.

Bayton is beside himself. Sputtering. "Thank you so much," he manages.

"Don't mention it," says Cael.

"Good hunting," Bayton says to us as we leave.

THREE: MAGIC GONE MAD

Down at the wharf, Captain Creedmont has the galley ready when we arrive. We float out with the tide, and the crew begins rowing. I tell the Captain our first stop is Grax Harbor, and he orders sails raised. Out of the mouth of the harbor we head south. The trip to Grax to meet Speega will take two interminable days.

Snout is having a blast chasing seabirds off the galley. I find Cael sitting on a huge coil of rope and tinkering with several devices. "What are you up to?" I ask, sitting down next to him.

Cael gestures to the devices. "Fixes, adjustments, surprises," he says, "fiddling with *Friend & Foe*, toying with the enhanced bows, trying to get prepared for whatever we will face at the Abbey. I keep trying to remember that whatever I do to them, the Abbot can do to us."

"Meaning what, exactly?" I ask.

"Meaning, for instance, that if I can blow up medallions, so can he," Cael says.

"Yikes," I say. "Looks like we go in medallion free, then. The good news is that his constructs and alphas can't use them either."

"That's right," he says. "How about you? Have you come up with a rescue plan?"

301

"Too early to call it a plan," I say. "Or even an idea. I'm just not feeling it yet."

"Well, keep picking at it," Cael says.

"Yeah," I say. "I hope Janx has more information for us as we get closer."

So we sit there on the rope coil for a while longer, Cael tinkering and me brooding. I can feel our ship slowly getting closer to Mika but way too slowly, and instead of calming me my anger and anxiety are rising as the distance shrinks. One of my feet is tapping the plank deck spasmodically, and my fingers are scratching at the thick rope we're sitting on. So much can go wrong, and there's so much to lose. I'm a mess.

"You know," Cael says about then, "you never did tell me the full story of how you met Mika." Good old Cael, I think, knowing I'm fretting and trying to distract me.

It works. "Well, like I told you," I say, recalling it instantly and vividly, down to the ale and sawdust and sweaty body smells, "she was recruiting for her crew at this pub in Aurelia. It was half empty when I walked in, but the half that was there was downright scary. Mercs, soldiers of fortune, out of work guards, militia, cutthroats, and random muscle. I was in there testing a new personal protection device, a medallion, which had failed before but which absolutely 'could not miss' this time, according to my esteemed Section Leader, Brother Jinx."

"Testing the device there in Aurelia?" asks Cael. "Or there in the pub?"

"In the pub," I say. "I was looking for a fight to see how the medallion would hold up, and that pub was well known for its fights."

"Gods," says Cael, "you Testers really do risk your lives. And here I'm thinking it's all bullshit."

At least he's smiling.

"So anyway," I continue, "I see Mika right away because she's such a beauty in there among the beasts. She's in this alcove playing Necks & 'Nads with this grotesque collection of monsters, all of them dripping in weapons and gauntlets and tattoos."

"Necks & 'Nads?" Cael asks.

"It's a knife-throwing game," I explain, "where the object is to throw two knives at once and hit a human-shaped target in the neck and testicles simultaneously. Very popular in merc pubs."

"So Mika is actually doing this?" Cael asks.

"And winning," I say. "As I'm watching her, she hits on four throws in a row, and is raking in the mercs' gold. So that's when I see my chance to test the medallion and impress the girl."

"You didn't," Cael says.

"Yup," I say, "I walked over there and told her she had no talent, and that if she could handle a little wager I would prove it to her."

"You are flat out insane," Cael says.

"Oh, it gets better," I say. "Everyone is expecting a one-on-one knife throwing contest between us, but instead I wager that I will stand in for the target and she will not be able to hit me, no matter how many times she throws."

"Oh my gods," Cael says.

"The place goes crazy," I say, "everybody screaming that if Mika doesn't throw her blades at this asshat, then they will. But Mika, she just looks at me for a long moment, and then she asks, 'Do you know what you're doing?'

"So I walk over in front of the target, smile at her, and just nod," I say.

"She doesn't go through with it, does she?" Cael asks.

"Oh but she does, fast as a viper," I say. "Then four more times, each thrown perfectly, and each absorbed and deflected by my medallion."

"You are one lucky bastard, Egon" Cael says.

"So after her last throw," I say, "Mika smiles, picks up her knives off the floor, and returns them to their sheaths. She come towards me slowly, still smiling, and I open my arms up in a conciliatory gesture and, like you've seen before, she springs in and gives me a massive kick in the testicles. As you know, thrown knives and whatnot get deflected and their energy dissipated by the medallion. But when someone kicks you between the legs, there is just no place for that energy to get deflected to, except up through you. So, also like you've seen before, I go flying back, but unharmed, and wipe out the target behind me. And, of course, when she offers a hand to help me up, I drag her down and threaten her with a hickey if she doesn't have a drink with me."

"Unbelievable," Cael says.

"So that's it," I say, "the strange and romantic tale of how I won Mika's heart while certifying a Monkworks device."

"Well wait, did she take the hickey or the date?" Cael asks.

"The date, of course," I say. "She hates hickeys."

That night, communicating with Mika by rings, I tell her how Cael wanted to know how we met. "He was shocked to learn about your skill at Necks & 'Nads," I communicate, "and even more shocked that you threw your knives at me."

"Oh, I knew you were up to something," Mika communicates. "I just wanted to find out what."

"So what you're saying is that I intrigued you," I communicate.

"Definitely," she sends. "I knew the moment I saw you at the bar, snuggling puppy Snout in your arms, that we were going to hook up. The knife throwing and balls kicking were just to set the proper tone for our new relationship."

"And here I thought the relationship was my idea," I send.

"You never had a chance," she communicates.

Ahhhhh, my Mika.

Next day, Cael and I are back on the rope coil, sea gulls calling, a salty breeze filling the sails. I'm not in the mood for it. I feel Mika getting closer and I should be encouraged, but I'm not. I think it's because Cael has done a great job of solving tactical problems we will face when we land, but I haven't done any kind of job of putting a strategy together.

"I need to get on top of this, Cael," I say.

"What are you thinking so far?" he asks.

"Well, it's all a jumble in my head right now," I say. "I guess the first fact we are facing is that this rescue operation is different than blasting into a mosque in the middle of nowhere and taking out a bunch of corrupt fanatics."

"How so?" Cael asks.

"When we go into the Abbey," I say, "we will be at the absolute heart of a war the Three Kingdoms hasn't seen in over a century. Our presence and our success could affect the outcome of that war, and I think we have to talk about it as though our actions have a greater purpose, and are not just personal and incidental."

"Do you have something specific in mind?" Cael asks. "Besides just rescuing our people?"

"I guess I do, Cael," I say, "even though all I really want to do is grab Mika and Fletch and the rest, and kiss the Abbey goodbye forever. It's just that we owe other people as well. We owe the SenSen Twins, Brik's people, and Speega's spARROWS; we owe the guard who died for us at the Inn, and the dead palace guards in Aurelia; we owe all the women and men and their loved ones that we've learned were brutalized by someone they should have been able to trust; and we owe all the people dying in a war that one corrupt degenerate started."

"I couldn't agree more, Egon," Cael says. "So what exactly are you saying?"

"I'm saying Tenebrus needs to die, Cael," I say. "We may be the only ones who will ever get a chance like this again."

"I guess I have to agree," Cael says quietly.

" And there's something else," I say.

"What?" Cael asks.

"It's your time, Cael," I say. "It's time for you to take charge of Floendahl Abbey, to lead it with your honor and decency. You are the Three Kingdoms' only chance of regaining its balance."

"That's impossible," Cael sputters.

I look at him, my honest, moral, modest friend, and smile. "Like a great magician once told me," I say, "so what? You do the impossible every day."

Cael is not having it. He jumps up from the rope coil and starts pacing the deck. He's alternating between rubbing his hands together and running them through the stubble on top of his head. "Who am I to do this, Cael?" he says, in denial. "I have no experience, no following, no nothing."

"Not true," I say. "You are Monkworks only other magician; you are friends with the Sultan of Nir; the Grand Caliph of the largest religion in the Three Kingdoms owes you a favor; and your parents are the King and Queen of Enduron. I say you are the only one with the credentials for the job. But more importantly, Cael, you are what the Abbey needs right now, simply because you are good. You are a genuinely good person."

Cael sits down again. "Godsdammit," he finally says. "You're exploding my brain."

"I know," I say. "It's what has been bugging me, and I had to get it all out to make sense of it. We need a bigger strategy than snatch and run."

"Ok," Cael says, "then let's get down to it. How do you see this thing unfolding?"

"It starts," I say, "with three big assumptions: Tenebrus is not expecting us from the harbor side; he's not expecting us this soon, so is unprepared; and we land unopposed."

"Those are big assumptions," Cael says.

"Remember burning your Abbot communications pad?" I ask. "Before we got to Jakarina?"

"Yes," says Cael. "You think that stopped him from directly tracking us?"

"Yes, I do," I say. "I'm sure he heard about what happened at the mosque, but I don't believe he knows we flew back to Portus Sironika, hired a galley, plan to pick up reinforcements and invade the Abbey. I doubt he even knows we know about his harbor. Returning to the Abbey by land from Jakarina would have taken us two weeks or more, and that may be the timeline he's working with."

"Plausible," admits Cael. "And landing unopposed?"

"It's all part of the same thing," I say. "I don't expect it to be more heavily guarded than usual, and maybe Janx can help us with that from his end."

"Ok," says Cael, "you've convinced me. What's the plan?"

"Well, assuming I'm right about this," I say, "I think our mission is all about surprise and speed. Hitting before they know we're there, being where they don't expect us when they counterattack, using misdirection to cover our moves."

"Sounds good so far," Cael says.

"But the thing is," I say, "as soon as we arrive on shore we have to race down that first long tunnel Caton talked about to get through the mountains and under the Abbey proper."

"What about it?" Cael asks.

"Well," I say, "it's just too little a problem to ask a magician of your enormous talents to solve."

"Ok, asshat," says the thoroughly not flattered magician. "Spit it out."

"The tunnel is way too long," I say. "We have to get through it in minutes not hours, or we lose all momentum, and that's our edge. You need to make it happen."

"Oh sure," Cael laughs scornfully, "just a little abracadabra and razzamatazz, and Cael just hands you your against-all-natural-laws solution."

"Yes," I say emphatically. "Exactly."

Cael looks at me, thoughtfully this time. "Well I suppose," he says slowly, "I could do something with the galley's longboat."

"I'll speak with Captain Creedmont," I say. "Consider it yours."

"Hmmm," he says, "ok. Interesting problem."

"You'll solve it, I'm sure," I say. "So now we land, scramble to the tunnel with the longboat, and power through the tunnel under the mountains in no time flat. On our way, we get a briefing from Janx and pick the best route to reach our people."

"What then?" Cael asks.

"Speed, speed, speed," I say. "We go before they can react."

"What happens when we reach our people?" Cael asks.

"We free them, arm them, and go on the attack," I say. "If we kill Tenebrus and Mirren, we may end the war."

"Sooner or later, they'll discover us," Cael says.

"You're right," I say. "That's when total chaos explodes all around us."

"What kind of total chaos?" he asks.

"No idea, my friend," I say grinning. "I need you to surprise me, surprise everyone, with an unmistakable disruption, a diversion so mind-blowing that it will capture the attention of everyone in the abbey."

"Oh right," he says. "I see. Someone with my magical talents and blah blah blah."

"Well said," I say.

"So what happens if we're successful?" Cael asks. "If we manage to kill Tenebrus and Mirren?"

"Then we ask Janx to talk to the Abbey militia about recognizing you as the next Abbot, while you talk to the Abbey Governing Board about the same thing. After that, who knows?"

Cael nods, and we sit and think about all of this for a bit. "It's good, Egon," he finally says. "It could work. But there is one other thing you need to do in the Abbey."

"What's that?" I ask.

"Find your father," he says.

Hmmm. He's right. Mika is all I can think about since the abduction, and I completely forgot that *Friends & Family Finder's* map will pinpoint the location of dear old dad once we get into the Abbey itself. But then, it's more than my concern for Mika that has kept me from thinking about my lost parent. "It's funny, Cael," I say. "Who he is has obsessed me all my life. But now, with everything that we've been through, and everything we're facing, somehow it's just not that important to me any longer."

Cael smiles. "I think that's probably for the best," he says. "I think it means that knowing or not knowing can't hurt you anymore."

I think about that, and all that has changed for me, and all that I have, and all that I'm doing. "You're right, Cael," I say. "I guess I am still curious, like wondering how a story ends. But deep down where it counts, I'm over it."

"Ok, then," Cael says. "It will happen or it won't."

That night I keep it upbeat with Mika, who is bored and angry and anxious. "We pick up Speega and company tomorrow," I communicate. "It won't be long before you are getting your revenge."

At mid-morning of the next day we reach the port where we are meeting the mercs. As we approach, I see Speega standing on the dock. She waves at me and then runs off. By the time the galley is secured to the mooring she is back with 11 others, including six of her spARROWS, with their enhanced bows and cartons of arrows, and all of the remaining five from Mika's mercenary band. I'm gratified; whether it's for gold or for Mika I don't care.

As soon as they all board, the Captain has the crew row us back out, trying to beat the incoming tide. I meet him by the wheel, and tell him we're now headed for the hidden harbor behind Floendahl Abbey.

"Figures, looking at you lot," he says, scornfully. "I'm not taking any contraband onboard."

"Understood, Captain," I say. "We're here to rescue our comrades, who were abducted and are being forcibly held at the Abbey."

"I see," he says skeptically. "And once we get there?"

"I'm expecting our way in to be clear," I say. "If it is, then you'll drop us, and head back out to sea. Wait like I told you for two days in case we need a pick up, and then your obligation ends." I hand him a bracer and show him how it works. "I'll signal you with this," I tell him.

"What if the way isn't clear?" he asks.

"We stop the landing and rethink it," I say.

"Sounds ok," the Captain says, grudgingly.

Next, I head to Speega and the others. Speega sees me coming and runs across the deck to hug me.

"I'm so sorry about Mika, Egon," she says, "but we'll get her back. Her, Fletch and the others."

I smile at her. "Thank you so much for helping us again, Speega," I say. "I can't tell you how grateful I am."

"Hey," she says, "I knew Mika from way before you got lucky and she got blind."

I laugh, and it feels good.

"I would be here no matter who asked," she says, "and the others feel the same way. We're going to do this thing, Egon, so man up and stop thanking me."

"Holy gods," I say. "Here I am thinking Mika is one of a kind. Seems there's at least two of you."

She grins. "Now that's saying something, Tester man," she says, "knowing what a wild one that Mika is. Now come on, let's say hello to the others and then catch us up."

Cael is already with them and together we tell the tale, the whole tale, with caveats about keeping it to themselves.

"So it was all the Abbot's doing, in order to remain in power," Speega says when we finish, shaking her head.

"That's right," I say. "With *Floe* running out he makes moves to preserve it. He begins to stockpile it, and ends production of *Floe*-thirsty devices for Enduron and Nir. He knows that these Kingdoms will react strongly to the cut off, and to the cut off of related tribute payments, so he makes an alliance with the flesh farmers of Rusk for their military protection. But the Abbot knew Cael would oppose his sick alliance plans became, you know, Cael."

We all laugh and Cael blushes.

"Not to mention that Cael the magician was helping to use up dwindling *Floe* supplies," I continue. "So he sends him on a phony mission outside the Abbey walls where he is most vulnerable, and asks Immobilin Keep to kill him."

"And the plan would have succeeded," Cael says, "if it wasn't for all of you."

"Well," says Speega, "payback time is coming, master magician. When you're in charge I expect an exclusive warrant for me and the spARROWS to guard foreign dignitaries traveling to and from the Abbey, until we get tired of it and want something else from you."

Is she kidding? Knowing her, she's not.

Cael seems to take it at face value and pauses, frowning. He puts a hand to his chin, thinking it over like he's really having trouble getting to yes on this one.

"C'mon Cael," I say, "give the lady her due."

"Geez," he says, grimacing, "I just don't know."

I can feel everyone tensing up a little, the warmth and camaraderie of a moment ago starting to fade.

And then Cael just flat out laughs. "Hah," he roars. "I had every last one of you going." Then we start laughing too. "You people think you know me so well. Good old Cael. Well let me tell you, you don't know me at all. I can be as evil as the next guy, even eviler, the most evilest guy in the Kingdoms. So watch out."

And with that he walks off, leaving us gasping for air.

The land to our right, starboard I think, started out as rolling hills but is rapidly rising into imposing ice and snow-covered mountains. The rescue party is checking weapons, sharpening blades, trying to stay loose while killing only time. We get together to run through scenarios, options and tactics. Then Cael works on adding ripplers to some of Speega's already deadly arrows, to get multiple detonations at distance, which he's calling sizzlers. The explosions are magical so they will not kill the *Ky* constructs or alphas directly, but in the confined spaces of the tunnels they will unleash ordinary stone shrapnel and rock falls that will do the job nicely.

Another day drags by. The air turns colder and the water choppier. I sense Mika has reached the Abbey. Cael and I give a final brief to the mercs on the plan for the assault, what we expect to encounter, and the surprises Cael has developed to counter the opposition.

The night before we reach the harbor, I contact Janx.

"Mika and the others are here," Janx communicates, "and they're holding them in this abandoned section of the tunnels they once used as a jail."

"Who's guarding them?" I ask.

"Mirren's Red Guards constructs," Janx sends. "They control everything inside the Abbey now are manning the Abbey's outside walls. Our militia is confined to barracks. "

"What about you and the other Testers?" I ask.

"Testers are also confined to quarters," Janx sends, "but we have access to some tunnels the Abbot doesn't know about. At least not yet. So we have some limited mobility."

"Then I have a big favor to ask," I communicate. "A favor that could have fatal consequences. Can you and your colleagues make sure the harbor and long tunnel are free of Red Guards when we land tomorrow?"

"Of course, Egon," Janx communicates. "I'm in this with you, and all of my people have had it with the Abbot's bullshit. I need two hours' notice and it will be done."

"Outstanding," I say, gratefully. "I won't ever forget this, Brother Janx."

We break communications and I contact Mika. "We landed and are in new cells," she sends. "The clerics are gone and we have new, red uniformed guards. Rough, surly bastards, not that the others were sweethearts. Facial twitches and the like, too, like the pretender in Aurelia."

"Yeah, they're constructs from the Keep that Mirren and Tenebrus have contracted for to replace the normal Abbey militia," I communicate. "Meanwhile, Janx has you pinpointed in an abandoned section of the tunnels under the Abbey that used to be used as a jail."

"So far," she sends, "we haven't seen Tenebrus."

"Let's hope it stays that way," I communicate. "We'll be there tomorrow."

"Thank the gods," she says. "By the way, tell Cael that Fletch sends his love."

"Will do," I send, and I can tell her spirits are lifting.

I find Cael on deck, just looking out to sea, and I give him Fletch's message. He nods and smiles. "He's a lot tougher than I am," he says. "All of them are."

"I actually don't know anything about Fletch," I say, "other than I've always liked him since I started hanging out with Mika and her crew."

"He's like us in some ways," Cael says. "He grew up hunting game with a bow in Rusk's frozen forests. Harsh country and tough hunting. He was orphaned at 14 by a plague that hit his village. He and some of the other kids who lost their parents banded together into a feral gang to survive. He got spotted and recruited into the Abbey at 16, and then left with Mika when she left, and was a founding member of her merc crew."

Well," I say, "I'm glad you two found each other."

"Me, too," Cael says with feeling.

The night drags on, and then half of the next day. Finally, the captain notifies me that we're about two hours from landfall. I get his agreement to borrow the longboat he tows behind the galley, which involves a little wrangling and a lot of gold. Then I pick a quiet spot to concentrate on Janx while looking into my ring stone. I feel immediate contact and excitement.

"We're in the tunnels, ready to go," Janx communicates. "There are Red Guards here but no more than usual. They don't appear to be expecting you from this direction."

"Go get them," I communicate. "See you on shore."

I brief Cael, then together we go off to gather our rescue force, 14 strong against only a whole freaking world of magic gone mad.

FOUR: PAYBACK IS A BITCH

The minutes inch by until we pass one final ice-covered headland and the smugglers harbor comes into view. "Ok, everyone," I say, "time to deactivate your medallion if you have one. Remember, don't turn it back on unless it's life or death."

I see several piers but only two ships: One is the galley we've been chasing, and the other is a sleek-looking black schooner I somehow know belongs to Tenebrus. On the wharf is a solitary figure.

"We're good to land," I yell to the captain.

Brother Janx stands quayside, waving us in. "Are those empty," I yell across the water to him, pointing at the docked ships. He gives me a thumbs up. I turn to Cael but he's ahead of me. Waterline explosions hit both vessels, followed by fireballs.

Meanwhile, Creedmont does an expert job of putting us gently against an open pier, and some of the crew quickly secures us. Others beach the long boat. "Two days," I yell to Creedmont, who nods uneasily, disturbed by Cael's magical display. Then I scramble off the ship along with Snout and the others.

Cael somehow flicks the 30-foot wooden boat up the rocky shore to the tunnel mouth while I hug Janx – did I really just hug Janx? – and ask him if the tunnel is clear.

"Yes, all the way through," he says, as five more monks materialize around the longboat from the tunnel. "I've brought those guys, section leaders like me, and one more at the other end."

"Then let's get onboard," I yell, already running up the slope. "We can catch up as we travel."

Clearly, Janx has no idea what I'm talking about, but he and his men follow us on board the longboat.

"Grab some solid shit to hold onto," shouts Cael. Then he does that wave thing he did at the Notch to build the earthen embankment, only this time he's using the air. The boat is picked up off the ground and shoved forward into the tunnel and we are off, 20 of us and a dog, armed to the teeth and absolutely flying down a stone corridor in a boat. Magic sure can be wonderful.

I try to get Janx's attention to learn if anything has changed, but he is not ready to chat. He, like the others, is just having too much fun. I mean, we are positively scorching down the tunnel, faster than we have ever moved before. Shipping boxes, stone walls and Monkworks magical torches streak by, Cael standing up at the prow like a figurehead. Within 10 short minutes we slow, already through the mountains and under Abbey grounds, and approach a monk standing over two prone Red Guards constructs.

The boat comes to a stop within inches of them, and we all jump out. Two of Speega's killers, enhanced bows up, run past the monk and out to the first intersection ahead. Cael sets up *Friend & Foe Finder* and Janx starts to talk.

"There are Red Guards in the tunnels," Janx says, "but not currently in large numbers except where they are holding Mika and the others. The rest of the Abbey grounds is crawling with the bastards. Tenebrus and Mirren are set up at the top of the Monkworks tower with Rusk military advisors, some Ky breeders, plus those clerics who did the kidnapping. The Abbot has completely sidelined our own militia, disarming them and confining them to barracks."

"The 'M' Gate is still closed?" I ask.

"Yes," Janx says. "But Floendahl Heights and the plains beyond are full of Rusk military, constructs and alphas."

"How goes the war?" I ask.

"Seems like a stalemate to me," Janx says. "Enduran and Nir can't break through on the trade routes and Rusk can't break out."

"One other thing," I say. "Is there anyone in the tunnels who wears a medallion and who is either neutral or a friendly?"

"No," he says. "Why?"

"It's possible Tenebrus could try to blow up medallions the way Cael did at the Notch," I say.

"You think he heard about that?" Janx asks.

"Maybe yes, maybe no," I say. "But I recommend you and your people turn your medallions off."

"I'm good to go here," Cael says just then. The display appears in midair, the monks gasp, and we see a complete map of every level of the tunnels and towers of the entire Abbey complex.

"What IS this?" Janx asks in amazement.

"One of those prototypes you gave us to test," I say. "*Friend & Foe Finder.*"

"I needed to make some improvements since we started out," says Cael, "but now it can show us where all the good guys and bad guys are located in any part of the Abbey, and the best route to get to the hostages."

"Outstanding," Janx says, moving over for a better look.

"I'm guessing this is the jail complex," says Cael, looking at five solid green figures among a host of red outlined ones.

"That's right," says Janx. "We need to be careful inside the jail itself, because there is only one way in or out."

Cael presses on one of the figures and the caption 'Mika Marianis, Aurelia, Nir' appears in the air above her shape. He quickly does the same for our other missing companions, and they are all there.

Elsewhere, the tunnels themselves are a mishmash of intersecting corridors and various-sized rooms, and there are three levels. There doesn't seem to be any stairs anywhere, but rather zigzag switchbacks connecting the levels.

"I've never seen half of this," Janx says.

Groups of red outlined figures, both constructs and alphas, move through the subterranean complex, apparently on patrol. Here and there are stationary guards, keeping watch in particular areas for unknown reasons. Aboveground, red outlined shapes and green shapes are sharply segregated. Militia, Testers, Engineers, administrators and the like – almost all green, but some neutrals and reds - are clustered together in barracks, dormitories and living quarters. Red outlined shapes are on the walls, patrolling the grounds, guarding buildings, or stationed on various levels of the Monkworks tower. There is a more complex cluster of hostile colored forms on the top floor of Monkworks, including many solid reds, some gray with red outlines, and some black with red outlines.

Cael presses on some solid red shapes and finds Tenebrus and Mirren. "They're both up there," he says.

Then he presses a button on the cube and a glowing route forms between us and the hostages. Janx studies it hard and nods. "We'll hit some opposition – no route will be completely undefended down here – but if we get lucky we can eliminate anything we face without raising an alarm."

"Before we go," I ask Janx, "do you and yours have some combat devices you can share with the group?"

"Almost forgot," he says, and he and his monks begin disgorging explosive, gaseous and projectile devices from their robes.

"Load up," I tell the others and, being mercenaries, they are eager to comply.

Then I ask Speega to study the route to our people. "You and most of your Killer spARROWS take the lead, with Snout out in front," I brief her. "Just behind you will be Brother Janx and his monks guarding Cael and his *Friend & Foe* device. I'll be behind them with the rest of the mercs, with your two remaining archers bringing up the rear to protect our backs. If you become unsure about the route, just look to Brother Janx and Cael for directions. Expect opposition, and try to take it out as quietly as possible."

"You got it, Egon," she says with a downright jaunty grin, and after about a minute of study she is back out to the corridor and directing her people. We move the dead Red Guards to the side, and Cael does something to try to disguise their presence. Then he pushes the boat a little ways back down the long tunnel to make it less conspicuous. Then, we set off in formation, Cael keeping the device display up as we go, watching for any changes.

We move fast, crossing numerous intersections, the stone corridors all lit by fake Monkworks magic torches and often packed with shipping crates. We are only a few minutes into our route when Snout freezes and Cael looks up from the display. Everyone stops.

"There are Red Guards in corridors all around us," he whispers, circling an upraised finger.

We start off again, but slowly, trying to keep quiet.

A minute later, Snout and Cael both stiffen again. "Six of them plus an alpha are heading right for us, unless they turn off," Cael whispers. "Maybe one minute out."

"Standard patrol," Janx whispers back.

I look to the display. "Here," I say, pointing. "We take them when they march around this bend, where they won't see us until it's too late. Speega, you're up." The spARROWS at the front of our group deploy across the tunnel about 20 strides before the bend, out of sight of the approaching patrol. I nod to Speega and she gives a thumbs up.

I finger rippler and trippler explosives in my vest, in case the arrows fail. Cael keeps focused on the display and the others look forward and backward nervously, no one making a sound.

We can hear the patrol moving towards us and then they appear from around the bend, loose formation, not alert, expecting nothing.

Speega and her spARROWS release as the last of the patrol comes into view, and they all collapse without a sound. I am on them in a heartbeat with my sword drawn, and finish off two who are trying to rise despite arrows in their throats. The others are already dead.

"Let's move them to the side," I whisper.

When we're done, Cael camouflages the bodies with magic. "It's a race now," he says. "Either someone will stumble over them or someone will miss them when they fail to show up."

"Anyone alarmed?" I ask him.

"No unusual activity yet," he says, looking at the display.

"Ok, let's keep moving."

We move out again in the same order, go down two levels, and jog for another few minutes before Snout and Cael again raise the alarm.

"Patrol," Cael hisses. "Moving left to right across our path. Let's see if they just continue through the intersection and ignore our tunnel." They do, and after a pause we move forward. But just as we get past the intersection Snout alerts again, and the display shows a patrol in the corridor in front of us, and moving our way.

"Back to the intersection we just passed and hide in the side tunnel," I whisper. "Maybe this patrol goes straight too. "Be ready in case, Speega."

We tense up as we hear them approach but they, too, go straight. "They'll stumble over the bodies," I say. "We have only minutes before the alarm sounds, so let's get to the cells on the double."

We move out running, Speega in the lead, intersections rushing by, until the tunnel narrows and curves off to the right. Snout alerts again and Speega puts her hand up, and we all stop. The archer edges up to the bend and peaks around the corner, then swings out into the middle of the corridor and releases two arrows blindingly fast. She waves and we rush forward around the bend.

The corridor ends at a three way intersection, the massive wood and iron door of the old jail in front of us, and corridors branching off to our left and right. Two Red Guards lay on the ground, blood pooling on cold stone.

Cael is about to blow the door when suddenly an odd series of drumbeats erupt behind us.

"They're signaling," says Janx, listening intently. "They found the bodies and...He listens some more and grins. "They also found the boat, and they just can't figure out how it got there."

"Tunnels are filling up with Red Guards," Cael says softly. "They don't seem to know where we are yet, but pretty soon they'll guess we're after the hostages."

"Speega, Brother Janx," I say, "you know what to do. You and your people hold this intersection while the rest of us go in for our people. Sizzlers and ripplers. Make them count."

They all nod and split up to cover the three-corridor intersection. We're hearing sounds of running feet and clanking metal now from the stone corridors in front of us and to either side. Janx's monks lob magical devices down the three corridors, and jagged stone barriers like so many tombstones erupt from the ground, providing cover from incoming weaponry but allowing for angles of fire above and around. Speega and her crew nock their arrows and draw their enhanced bows. Mika's mercs prepare to storm through the jail door when Cael blows it. Drums continue their booming conversation and the display shows red outlined shapes closing in on us from three sides.

I turn to Cael. "Moment of truth," I say, and he blasts the jail door inward.

That's Speega's signal to open up. Arrow-mounted sizzlers streak down three corridors and multiple explosions rip stone shrapnel through the oncoming ranks of Red Guards. Some get through and are running at us, only to be cut down by old-school arrows from enhanced bows.

I'm first through the blown jail door, hard and fast, followed by Mika's mercs and Cael. Immediately inside there are scattered bodies of guards who were caught in the door-busting discharge. Left and right are corridors lined with barred cell doors, which I ignore because I know from Cael's display that the hostages are in cells at the end of the corridor in front of me. Red Guards race towards me, and at least one projectile whizzes by my head. I close with them before they hit me, though, and go to work with my sword, its magical enhancements stifled by Ky protections but still entirely lethal. Adrenalin replaces magic to give me unmatchable speed and jarring force, so for the moment I am a killing machine.

Mika's crew are right with me with pikes leveled, and they hit the mass of oncoming guards around me with devastating impact. I should be hearing the sounds of battle but I am oblivious now, lost in a maelstrom of cutting and parrying and shoving and thrusting. Faces, limbs, swords, and spears flash by me until I am out the other side, covered in blood, seeking more targets.

The rest of the corridor is clear, though, and I run down it, searching, scanning cells, and finally I find five fired up and cheering companions.

"Get us out of here," yells Mika. "There are some asshats who need serious killing."

I grin, and behind me Cael comes through and lashes out. Locks burst and cell doors open.

Mika is in my arms then, and I swear to gods I'm crying. So is she. I finally look up in time to see Cael disengaging from a crying Fletch, and Mika's mercs are all over Neenah, Bric and Caton. Then they are handing out weapons and devices to the newly rescued.

"Back to the intersection," I shout, and we move out fast, all business again. Speega, Janx and their crews are still fragmenting the corridor walls with sizzlers and lobbed ripplers, but the Red Guards are beginning to fight back more effectively. Alphas are hurling a more systematic barrage of explosives towards us that don't quite reach but which are pinning us down. The explosions also bring down chunks of rock from walls and ceilings that add to the debris that the constructs are now using for cover. They are creeping ever closer and their crossbow bolts and projectiles are getting more dangerous.

Suddenly one of the monks is hit and goes down among the barriers the monks erected in the left hand corridor. Janx dives in after him and drags the injured monk behind cover, but is under heavy fire. Cael lashes out with the same kind of air pressure wave he used to propel the longboat. I see Janx and the injured monk go up and then settle safely down as the wave gathers force towards the Red Guards. The wave collects cobblestones and boulders and is now hurtling down the confined space of the corridor. It hits the Red Guards with irresistible power and the firing from that direction instantly ceases.

Cael reaches the fallen monk to heal him, and the spARROWS keep firing down the other two corridors, supported by the other monks and now Mika's mercenaries. Cael returns to the center of our group and kneels down behind their screen of protection. He sets up the *Friend & Foe* display again, me kneeling next to him. Speega, Janx, Mika, Neenah, Brik and Caton form a circle around us.

"You all know what to do," I say. "We bust through this corridor and, when we're clear, we split up." I'm pointing at the display showing the corridor to our right. It's straight for 100 strides, filled with red-outlined forms, but then clears of guards and separates into many corridors.

"Cael," I continue, "let's show Brother Janx and his companions a possible route to the militia barracks." Cael touches the barracks on the display and a glowing route appears linking it to our current position. "If you can convince them to join us," I say, "wait for Cael's disruption before you advance on the Monkworks tower."

"What disruption?" Janx asks.

"Oh, it will be impossible to miss," Cael says, grinning wickedly, but offering no specifics.

"Speega," I say, pointing at the display. "here's your route to the Perches. Mika's mercs are with you. Remember, wait for Cael's disruption, then do your thing. The mercs will bust down a Perch door and blow out the front window. Then you and your people fire two sizzler volleys at the Monkworks tower and get out fast, before Tenebrus retaliates. Head to another random Perch and repeat. Keep it up until you see my move, then go join the militia."

"Got it, man-with-the-moves," she says, and Mika laughs.

I look at the rest of us: Cael, Fletch, Mika and Snout. "That leaves us," I say, "and when Cael lets loose, we go for Tenebrus." The five of us touch knuckles, Snout included.

I stand up and look around at my 25 raiders and a reluctant killer dog, friends all. "Good luck," I say. "See you on top of Monkworks."

We grab our gear as Cael starts lobbing fireballs down the two corridors still manned by Red Guards, even though they can't be hurt by them. But it's enough of a distraction that when he sends the air wave thing down the breakout corridor the constructs and alphas have no answer. "Go, go, go," I shout, and we all take off with Speega and her spARROWS again leading the way.

There is almost no opposition left, and we regroup for an instant where the tunnels branch off.

"Ready?" I ask, and everyone starts fist-pumping and hooting and laughing. "Then," I say, "in the words of a cranky old Section

Leader I know: 'Give 'em guts, muscle and steel.'" And we're off, Janx laughing, three different directions for all of us, one outcome in mind.

Cael, Fletch, Mika, Snout and I race along our route, rising up two levels, encountering some patrols, mostly Fletch responding with sizzlers and unadorned arrows. Finally we reach the place it all began for Cael and me, the tunnel leading to the eastside exit towards Nir.

I turn to the group. "Just before we exit," I say, in words Cael instantly recognizes, "I'll launch a distractor and we'll follow it out. But where the path goes straight we'll go hard right and up the cliff. Be right on my ass. Don't stop for anything. Here we go."

As I did before, I reach into my vest and pull out a coin with a runner engraved on both sides. I throw it through the tunnel entrance and run after it, Snout at my side and Mika, Fletch and Cael on my heels. Again I see the coin hit the ground and basically explode into a running replica of a Monkworks Tester in full mission gear. I watch it race straight up the trail hurling smokers and noisemakers, and disappear around the bend. The expected bedlam erupts.

We turn sharply right, moving quickly, obscured by smoke, and after twenty strides I see the goat path that winds up the cliff. I reach into the vest again and pull out a tiny squirt bottle. "For the bottoms of your boots," I whisper to the group, "and then the palms of your hands." I squirt each in turn. Then I do the same for Snout and me. Together we climb to the top of the ridge overlooking Floendahl Abbey.

Waiting for us are the four Guardians from the nearby Haven, and I go over to connect with them. Meanwhile, Cael sets up the *Friend & Foe* display, and when I get back to him he points out Red Guard concentrations in the plaza in front of the Monkworks tower, in one of the three barracks that they have apparently commandeered, on the top floor of Monkworks, and on the floor just below that.

"I take it you are about to surprise me, good buddy," I say.

"Oh yes, yes, yes," he says gleefully. "And I never again want to hear another of your asshat comments about my magical abilities."

I laugh out loud. "We'll see," I say, Tester to the last.

Cael moves toward the edge of the cliff then, slightly limping now after a grueling day, robe billowing on his slight frame, and as always I don't see what he does.

In all, there are 22 iron Gryphons atop the archery towers built on the defensive wall around Floendahl Abbey. In unison, 22 bases shatter, 22 sets of iron wings unfold, 22 sets of lion haunches bunch, and 22 mythical predators spring into the air. They form up into a circle above the Abbey, screeching deafeningly through iron eagle beaks, spiraling higher and higher, drawing the eyes of Red Guards, of Brother Janx, of the Abbey militia, of Speega and all the raiders, of Tenebrus and Mirren and all the scum with them; and no one has any doubt that something unbelievable is about to happen.

Fletch, Mika and I stand in awe, watching the show from the most spectacular viewpoint in the Three Kingdoms. Then I see Cael's rising arms pause as the iron killers reach some pinnacle of their flight. Suddenly, Cael's arms slice down and the Gryphons tip over into a vertical dive. Then they separate into four smaller groups, and I understand.

Four metal predators each slam into the top two floors of Monkworks, talons extended, ripping, smashing, biting and raking through everything and everyone in there. We hear alchemical and magical explosions as the scum up there fight back. But I know to my core that they have no chance. Then the eight Gryphons reappear in a shower of glass, as they break through the windows of the opposite wall and fly back up into the sky.

Simultaneously, two groups of seven gryphons fly into the plaza in front of the tower and the barracks beyond, rending through Red Guards with their deadly metal beaks and talons. Then they, too, launch themselves back into the sky.

Something of a silence descends on the shocked complex then, interrupted by the occasional clang of metal falling off the tower, or cries from the injured. Overhead, the iron Gryphons circle and occasionally keen. Oddly, the tower's ball of light continues its jaunty, repetitive journey up through the core of the building, sparks exploding now at the top around twisted metal and shattered glass.

"How's that for disruption?" a downright cocky Cael asks.

Then things start to happen fast. A window blows out from a cliffside Perch, and seven explosive arrows streak towards Monkworks and burst into the top floors, bringing down bubbles and balconies and more glass. Then another seven, blasting wood and metal shrapnel everywhere. At the same time, scores of Abbey Militia explode out of the two remaining barracks and charge towards the tower, Janx and his crew plainly visible leading the charge. Another window blows out of a Perch, and another volley of sizzlers streak towards Monkworks.

"Mount up," I yell, and we each jump on an actual flesh and blood Guardian, Snout riding with me. We jump off the cliff together and go into a long glide that takes us straight through a blown open wall and into the top floor of the Monkworks tower. We land four abreast amid complete devastation. Walls and furniture are on fire. There are body parts strewn about. In a corner, the body of a Purple Robe is burning. We stay mounted and slowly move forward.

An alpha appears out of the smoke and throws canisters of alchemical flame at us before we can react. The Guardians don't even flinch, their magic more ancient and powerful than anything that can be aimed against it today. The firestorm simply stops in front of us, rages momentarily, then dies out in wisps of smoke. Fletch skewers the *Ky* handler with an arrow and we move forward.

I see Mirren next, held upright somehow on top of a table against a wall, torso and head only, his lower limbs shorn away. His mouth is open like he was in the middle of a sentence when tons of avenging iron tore him apart.

Tenebrus is alive but bloody, and his robes are in tatters. His back is to us as he looks through blown out windows at the Abbey grounds, the city that sprang up from it, and the militarized plains beyond. Snout growls then, and the Abbot spins around and lashes us with tremendous magical force. The stone floor before him explodes towards us in a burst of overwhelming destruction. Only it never reaches us. Instead, the roiling mass is sucked down beneath the gryphons' feet, and then out to the sides. And then, in a display of consummate magical precision, the Gryphons curve the flying rubble back to where it came from, solidifying it back in place to complete an astounding repair.

Tenebrous looks at the floor, and then he looks up and takes in the four of us humans. His medallion, I see immediately, is gone. He is tall, imposing, imperious and pissed off. Incandescently angry. His black eyes are fierce, his hands like claws. And he knows he is defeated.

He settles his gaze on Cael.

"Well if it isn't Big Foot and company," he mocks in a low growl. "A fool and his puppets. You and I could have owned the world, Venarius, for decades, for centuries, even after *Floe*, if you had just been smart. But you were always a whiny, pathetic, insecure little prig who will wither away as *Floe* does. You just always lacked the vision necessary to grasp greatness when it was laid in front of you."

Cael looks at him for a moment before speaking, a mix of emotions on his face, from pity to sadness to distaste. "Vision isn't one of my problems now, actually," Cael says quietly then. "I finally see you quite clearly as the corrupt, depraved egomaniac that you are."

Tenebrus slowly shakes his head. "Yet still blind to your own sanctimony," he says, before turning to Fletch.

"Ah," he says, "you must be Big Foot's boy toy. Is he the best you could do?"

"Why, yes," Fletch says. "He's the best anyone could do."

Tenebrus doesn't respond, just sneers and turns to me.

"Well, well, well," he says, "welcome home, sonny boy. Is this how you imagined our sweet family reunion would go? Did you ever dream of you, me, and your insignificant twit of a mother living happily ever after? Well, just know that if it wasn't for that meddler, Janx, and his Gryphon friends, I would have been rid of you long ago."

I have to ask Janx about that last part, I think. But to Tenebrus – dear old Dad - I say, "You completely overvalue your presence in my life. I stand with my mother's sweet memory, and Brother Janx, and these friends; and with them and without you I will live happily ever after."

"You stand for nothing," Tenebrus says, dismissing me and turning to Mika.

The Abbot bows. "Greetings, bitch," he says. "Yet another Janx reclamation project, and for what? You were a no-talent nothing with big ambitions who ran from the biggest opportunity of your life."

Mika grins. It's a very evil grin. "That's not entirely correct, Abbot sir," she says. "I do have one extraordinary talent."

Maybe I should have seen it coming. Certainly I know that grin. But the truth is I would have done nothing to prevent it. Faster than the strike of a deadly snake, faster than anything, Mika draws and throws her pair of daggers, and both smack to the hilt in their intended targets: Abbot Ichanor Tenebrus' neck and 'nads.

The Abbot rocks back and staggers, refusing to go down, unable to scream, blood spurting from grievous wounds. Calmly, Mika slides down from the back of her Gryphon, and walks toward the stricken magician. She reaches out with both hands and yanks back her blades. Again, Tenebrus staggers but does not go down.

"Payback," she says, "is a bitch."

And then she kicks him in what's left of his balls so hard that he launches backwards and out into thin air, no final sound escaping his lips. She calmly walks back to her magical steed and remounts. She looks at us. "Shall we move on?" she asks.

Man, you've got to love her.

FIVE: YOU ARE A DEAD NUTS GENIUS

Janx arrives then as we dismount, and he is a bit winded from the climb up the staircase that winds around the core of the Monkworks tower. With him is the head of the Abbey Militia, General Hiraam Barko, who looks out of sorts and out for bear.

"General Barko," Cael says, "good to see you again."

"If I had known you were going to save my ass I would have paid more attention to you before now," he growls.

Cael laughs. "Well just as long as you pay attention to me from now on," says the Three Kingdoms' only surviving *Floe* magician.

The General snaps to attention, salutes, and says, "Yes, sir."

"At ease, General," Cael says, "and come say hello to all these other ruffians."

Cael turns then to Janx. "Outstanding work, Brother Janx," he says. "None of this would have been possible without your help."

"Well, let's not get ahead of ourselves," grouses Janx, looking around at the devastated Great Room. "We still have plenty to do. So far, we've retaken the walls, we're searching the tunnels for Red Guards, which will take time, and Monkworks is secure, at least what you've left of it."

Cael grins at the classic Janx grumpiness, and does something. The keening and screeching of the iron Gryphons overhead stops, and out the shattered windows we see their circle descend to our level and then below. We rush to the edges in time to see all 22 slam down to retake their places atop the archery towers they came from, as if they'd never left.

Then the room starts to retake its shape, walls heal, glass unshatters, bodies disappear. Fallen balconies reattach themselves and light bubbles continue their journeys without interruption. Across the compound, broken Perch windows reassemble themselves and catch the setting sun.

"I share your irritation, Brother Janx," Cael says. "It's long past time for magic to repair the damage that it does."

Janx nods, and then does something I don't expect. He walks over to the Guardians, and one by one they lower their heads to him and he presses his forehead against theirs. When he finishes, the big monk has a smile on his face. I'm not having it.

"What's going on," I say to Janx, "with you and the Guardians, me and my mother, Mika and Tenebrus? What?"

"It's too long a story," Janx says, "stretching back decades."

"So give us the short version," Mika says.

Janx nods reluctantly. "Well, ok," he says. "You deserve to hear it, of course. So, at around the time you were born, Egon, the old Abbot became aware of the true depravity of Tenebrus. He sent me from one end of the Kingdoms to the other, to reach out to women, and men too, who Tenebrus had harmed, and try to make amends. I met your mother shortly after you were born in her cabin on the outskirts of Kinor, in Enduran. But she was indignant, and wanted nothing to do with any 'charity' from the Abbey. She sent me packing."

"I could see her doing that," I say with a smile.

"Yeah," says Janx, smiling too. "I remember her as dignified, fierce, and beautiful. She would be proud of how you turned out, Egon."

Suddenly, and for some moments, I can't say anything. Mika reaches over and grabs my hand.

"Well anyway," Janx continues, "I took to checking on you guys whenever I passed through over the years, never showing myself, just leaving a little gold or some useful device on the paths around your cabin, where one of you was sure to find it. When I heard your mom died, Egon, I went looking for you because I knew you would have few options. That's how I came to bring you back to the Abbey."

"Tenebrus said he wanted to get rid of me," I say, "but that you and the Guardians stopped him."

"Yeah," Janx says. "That was the old Abbot's doing too. He couldn't just get rid of Tenebrus, because he was the only other *Floe* magician at the time. So he tried to contain him. One thing he did was to put me in touch with the Guardians, who gave me this ring and asked me to contact them regularly about what Tenebrus was up to. They thought him to be a magician without character who could unbalance the Three Kingdoms with his depravity and ambition. That is truly what the Guardians guard, the balance between easy magic and true achievement in the Kingdoms.

"So I've been in touch with them ever since," Janx continues, "pretty much every week, and they turned out to be right. Tenebrus wanted to use magic as a drug to addict and subjugate the Kingdoms, and suppress innovation and progress. Our devices are doing that very thing, because they solve so many problems so conveniently. But even that wasn't fast or grand enough for Tenebrus. He wanted to be obeyed and worshiped as a god."

"So Tenebrus knew about your connection to the Guardians all along?" I ask.

"I made no secret of it," Janx says. "In fact, when he threatened you, and Mika, and others, I made it clear I would take his actions to the Guardians for judgement, and for a long time he feared that. Until all of this happened, I still believed he did."

"I guess he just feared losing *Floe* more," I say.

Janx quickly turns to me. "What do you mean?" he asks.

"Well, Brother Janx," Cael answers for me, "there's something I don't think you know."

"I had a feeling," Janx says.

"The one big thing that puts all of Tenebrus' actions in perspective is that *Floe* is running dry. Not right away, but inevitably, and the Abbot knew that his power would go with it."

"Oh my gods," Janx says, a new understanding in his eyes. But then I see something else occur to him. He says, "But you know, you may be wrong."

"How so?" Cael asks sharply.

"I don't think it's running dry," Janx says. "I think it's being throttled." Then he turns to the four Guardians and points. "By them."

And suddenly I get it. "You're saying that in order to preserve balance in the three Kingdoms, and to rein in Tenebrus, they began to place limits on magic," I say.

"That's my guess," Janx says. "Smart move."

"But with unintended consequences," I say.

"Maybe, maybe not," Janx says thoughtfully.

Cael walks over to his enigmatic mount, the Gryphon quietly watching him come. He places his forehead and ring on the Guardian for a minute, then they break apart and Cael turns to us.

"Brother Janx is right," Cael says. "The Guardians saw magic spinning out of control, saw it replacing all human initiative with easy convenience, and saw Tenebrus scheme his way towards human subjugation. They acted according to their purpose."

"They must not have foreseen the Abbot's extreme response," Fletch says.

"Or they counted on it," Cael says, "so responsible parties would act."

"You mean like us," Mika says.

Yes," Cael acknowledges. "But also Enduran and Nir. It could be one reason the Guardians have been of such help to us. Oh and, guess what, they've returned *Floe* to full strength as of right now."

Practically everyone breaks out in grins but not me. Grimly, I try to figure out who *didn't* use us on this mission.

Janx just shrugs off the news. "It's all water under the bridge," he says. "We have to deal with the here and now."

"Meaning what, exactly?" Cael asks.

"Well, first," Janx says, "we secure the Abbey and we announce to the world that Tenebrus is dead, you are about to be named the new Abbot, and there will be no further cooperation with the North. Then the militia, the engineers' guild and the Abbey Governing Board need to declare you the new Abbot. After that, we need to secure the town. Then we have to end the war and restore peace to the Kingdoms."

"Is that all?" an amused Cael asks.

"That's just tonight," Janx says, dead serious.

"Well, in that case" says Cael, "I am naming you my Acting Chief of Staff, since I'm naming myself Acting Abbot for now, and my first order is to ask you to get all the people we need up here right now, in order to figure out how to do the things you just listed. Also, food and drink for everyone please; it's going to be a long night."

"On my way," Janx says. But, as he goes, Cael walks with him to a newly-repaired bubble and asks him something privately. He smiles, nods, and is gone.

Then, other bubble doors open and Speega and her spARROWS, Mika's mercs, and Neenah, Brik and Caton bust out into the big room. The four of us scramble over to greet them, as Snout slobbers on his particular favorites. For a few minutes there's laughter, back slapping, hugs and handshakes as we all take a moment to realize that we're somehow still alive, and the impossible is really possible.

At some point, Cael and I have the same thought at the same time, and we connect with the mute Guardians. After receiving our thanks, they walk over to an open balcony and fly off, presumably back to the local Tester's Haven.

I put a hand on Cael's shoulder. "You are pretty amazing, Cael," I say.

"Right back at you, brother," he says.

Then Janx returns trailing a group of mostly monks, plus one woman, all of whom Cael knows already. I am introduced to Madame Mercanor Rews, Chief of the Abbey's Diplomatic Corps; Brother Danal Omendall, Chief Engineer and head of the Abbey's

Engineering Guild; and Brother Mustering Dobus, Chairman of the Abbey's Governing Board.

After further introductions all around and some chit chat, Cael magically repairs a long table and chairs, and asks everyone to take a seat. He takes the chair at the head and looks at each of us, completely comfortable and in charge.

"Thanks you for being here to help me undo the damage wrought by my predecessor," he begins. "I won't go into that now, because tonight we have urgent business that must be attended to immediately."

"Who put you in charge?" Brother Dobus demands, before anything can move forward.

Cael nods and smiles. "That's on tonight's agenda, Brother, and we will get to it in due course," Cael says calmly. But then he leans forward. "However, the short answer is that you, Brother Dobus, will put me in charge in short order, if you have any hope of Monkworks continuing to operate."

Then, without waiting for a reply, Cael turns to Mika. "Like you have done for us every step of the way, Mika," he says, "start us off."

If Mika feels any surprise, she shows nothing. "Let's take it from the top," Mika, says, and I can't help but smile. "First off, let's discuss securing the Abbey. What's our status, General Barko?"

"We control the walls and tunnel exits, the storehouses and warehouses, the various Abbey buildings, and all Monkworks manufacturing and *Floe* source floors," the General enumerates. "We are scouring all levels of the Abbey for Red Guards as we speak, but that could take weeks, especially in the tunnels. Finally, we are in the preliminary stages of forming a tribunal to investigate the former Abbot's abuse of his office, smuggling activities, the attempted murders of Acting Abbot Venarius and his party, plus other criminal acts, and to determine who among us aided and abetted him."

"Very good, General Barko," Cael says. "Please add to your duties the securing of all the shipping crates we saw this morning in the tunnels, and a listing of their contents. Also, I have a device that may assist in your Red Guards search."

The General nods . "Very well, sir," he says.

"Now tell me this, General Barko," Cael says. "What is your assessment of the likelihood of the Rusk forces outside our gate attacking and overwhelming the Abbey, once word gets out that Tenebrus is dead?"

Remarkably, given the disparity between their forces and ours, Barko is clearly dismissive. "We are impregnable," he states flatly. "An enemy may be able to contain us in here, but any assault on our walls will fail."

Cael looks at him with surprise, as others around the room murmur. "Impregnable?" he asks. "Please explain."

"Sir," the General says, "the Abbey is protected by both active and passive defenses built into the very structures and foundations of the complex during construction, using Gryphon magic. They are activated whenever the 'M' Gate is lowered, which in effect makes our walls one large protective medallion. Nothing can touch them, and no attack can penetrate, even from above or below. I can control some of the defensive options from the 'M' Gate's archery tower, but mostly they are automatic. However the main thing is, sir, the defenses are sentient."

The murmurings become gasps of astonishment then.

"How do you mean?" Cael asks.

"Our defenses," the General continues, "have awareness. They just know, for lack of a better term, who the enemy is, what their threats are, what defenses to deploy and when, and how to avoid friendly fire."

"Why have I never heard of this before?" Cael asks.

"The Abbot kept the information close," the General says, "but to be fair, we've been at peace for so long the subject rarely comes up."

"So how do you know about all of this, General?" I ask.

"Two ways," the General says. "First, service in the Abbey Militia is often generational, and many of us have knowledge that's been faithfully passed down from the distant past. Second, we have the records and reports from the last war, when the defenses were last activated."

"Please give us examples of these defenses," Cael says.

The General unexpectedly laughs. "Well," he says, "I can tell you that your flying iron Gryphon maneuver is an actual defense, only it is meant to be aimed outside the walls and include explosives. Oh, and with far less tearing metal."

"Holy shit," Cael says. "I hope I haven't damaged their usefulness."

"No worries," the General says. "The defenses are self-maintaining and self-repairing."

"I think I need to up my magical game," Cael says, shaking his head.

"It's pretty amazing," the General says. "There are fireball throwers hidden in the walls, alarms and traps at all the tunnel and wall access points, and the tunnels are able to flood if invaded. The list goes on and on."

"We invaded the tunnels this morning," Speega says, "and there was no reaction."

"Lucky for you," the General says, "our defenses think. They clearly approved of your presence or you wouldn't have survived."

"Holy shit," Cael says again. "This has been an education, General, and I haven't even started yet."

"Speaking of which," Mika says, "let's get back on track. We need to get the word out to our allies that Tenebrus is dead, Cael is about to succeed him, and all former cooperation with the Northerners is over."

Cael turns to the Chief of the Diplomatic Corps. "Madame Rews," he says, "good to see you again. Can you help us out here?"

"Of course, Abbot Venarius," Rews says, boldly ignoring Cael's interim status. "We are always in touch with Enduran and Nir, using diplomatic communications pads. I can actually do it now, from here, as our meeting continues."

Cael smiles. "Very well, Madame Rews," he says. "A pleasure doing business with you, as always."

Rews nods, smiles back, and starts writing.

"What's next?" Cael asks.

"Officially naming you the new Abbot," Mika says.

The old Cael would have haltingly asked about the process, expressed his reservations about his qualifications, and shown everyone how uncertain he is about the whole thing. Well, that was the old Cael.

"General Barko, do you have any reservations about my candidacy?" Cael asks.

"None whatsoever, Sir."

"Will you follow my legal orders with complete devotion to duty?" Cael asks.

"I will, sir."

"And how about you, Brother Omendall?" Cael asks the Chief Engineer. "Will you and your Guild support me?"

"We will, Abbot Venarius," Omendall says, "with pleasure."

Cael looks next at Madame Rews, who is still scribbling. "And for the record, Madame Rews," says Cael, "what say the diplomats?"

"I just told the world of your ascendancy, Abbot Venarius," she says. "I'd look a fool to change my mind now, and I'm no fool."

Cael laughs. "No, you most decidedly are not," he says. Then he turns to the head of the Governing Board.

"And now we return to you, Brother Dobus," Cael says. "I am asking you for the authority to act on behalf of the Abbey both in this time of crisis and in the time beyond, when we will need to undo the damage that Tenebrus has done to the stability of the Kingdoms. Will you give it?"

"I will bring the matter to the full Governing Board as soon as we are able to meet," Dobus replies, "and we will render a prompt decision. If the vote goes in your favor, I can see a naming ceremony in a week to 10 days."

Before Cael can reply, the entire tower shakes, and some unsecure items around the Great Room fall. Everyone looks around warily. A few even suspiciously. "In case you're wondering, Brother Dobus," Cael says, when it stops, "that wasn't me, nor because the building was damaged earlier."

"It was the building itself, Brother Dobus," says General Barko. "Apparently it feels entitled to an immediate vote."

"Oh, bullshit," Dobus exclaims with unholy bluster. "We have rules, and the Governing Board will not be stampeded by either magical theatrics or superstitious claptrap."

The building shakes again, this time for longer.

When it stops for a second time, Cael leans forward. "Then let me appeal to your honor and sense of responsibility, Brother Dobus," Cael says. "Our namesake town, Floendahl Heights, is beyond our gates and undefended. It is full of our people, Brother Dobus, who will more than likely die gruesome deaths once our enemies find out that their agreement with our former leader is terminated; an agreement, I might add, that you and your Board must have signed off on. According to the rules of the Governing Board, the only person with the authority to order our militia into action is the Abbot. So unless you want the blood of our townsfolk on your hands, I am asking you, Brother Dobus, to uphold your rules, follow your conscience, and save our people. Only you can do it."

That is brilliant, I think. And Dobus must think so too, because he folds his losing hand. "You force me to acknowledge the extraordinary situation we find ourselves in, Brother Venarius," Dobus sighs, in full retreat. "My duty requires me to protect our people above all else, and I will not fail them. So, as Chairman of the Abbey's Governing Board, and in consultation with the powerful interests represented at this table, I name you Abbot Caelum Venarius, long may you lead us in peace."

"Lead us in peace," some of the others murmur, as if it is a standard response on such occasions, and then everyone breaks out in smiles, cheers, hugs and general relief. I never did ask Cael about that whole tower-shaking thing, but I have my thoughts.

Of course it is Mika who refocuses us. "Next up," she yells, to settle us down, "how do we save the town?"

"We can't defend it with our militia alone," General Barko says. "We're too few and the enemy is too many."

Cael looks to Janx and smiles. "I seem to remember that our tunnels extend under the town," he says.

Janx smiles too. "It's a popular route," he says, "for young monks and Testers looking for an unregulated evening's relaxation."

"Then I'm thinking you are the one to organize an evacuation," Cael says. "Starting tonight, if you can. Keep it as quiet as possible, but have a company of militia with you in the tunnels, ready to cover you."

"Can do," Janx says. "General Barko, let's coordinate when this meeting breaks up."

"Of course, Brother Janx," Barko says. "But, the truth is, this will take days, days the townsfolk may not have."

"Maybe the Guardians can help," I say.

"What are you thinking?" Cael asks.

"Well," I say with a smile, "the Northerners out on the plain saw a lot of weird and destructive shit involving Gryphons today. Maybe it made them a little wary. And maybe we can use that to buy the town some time."

"How so?" Mika asks.

"We ask the actual Guardians to overfly the town for the next few days," I say, "a regular patrol. As if they will do to the Northerners what Cael's iron Gryphons did to Tenebrus and company."

"Will the Guardians fight?" Cael asks.

"Not directly, no," I say, grinning. "But I have a feeling they are willing to bluff."

Barko is grinning, too. "I love your devious mind, Egon," he says. "It could work, at least for a while."

"Great," says Cael. "Please try to set it up when we're done here. Mika, what's left?"

"Our final issue tonight," Mika says, "is to figure out how to win the war."

Dobus snorts. "You people? Tonight? You can't be serious."

Mika ignores him. "What's the main holdup, General Barko?" she asks.

"The passes from Enduron and Nir," says Barko, "are clogged with alphas, constructs, and regular troops from Rusk. There is no room for us to maneuver and, at present, they are unmovable."

"Can we attack them from the rear?" Neenah asks.

"How so?" Mika asks.

"Troop ships from Nir and Enduron to the Abbey's hidden harbor. Then a surprise attack on the troops outside our gates, followed by an attack on the passes."

"Not bad," Brik says.

"I like it to," Cael says, "but I'm not willing to risk all those Nir and Enduron troops inside our walls. I don't know our allies' full intentions yet. Besides, it could take longer then I think we have."

That crushes a good idea, I think, but Cael's right.

"Has it occurred to you all to negotiate?" Dobus offers, condescendingly. "We simply pay more in tribute and everyone returns home."

I don't think any of the rest of us likes that idea, or thinks it's that simple. Too much blood has been shed. Rusk needs to pay for their crimes, not the other way around.

"There will come a time for negotiations," says Cael. "And not just about the war. It will have to be about restoring a new balance in the Kingdoms, one that can maintain the peace for many decades to come. But I don't think we're ready for that yet."

"Well, I think the answer is staring us in the face," says Speega. "And it's proven to work."

"Do tell," Cael says, grinning, "and maybe I'll reconsider your warrant request."

"Reconsider hell, oh maven of magic," Speega says. "That's a done deal already, as you well know, and after I solve the whole war thing for you, hell, me and my spARROWS will be asking for a lot more."

"Ok, ok," Cael says laughing, "let's hear it then."

"Well, here you go," says Speega. "It's the sizzlers with enhanced bows. There is nothing like them on the battlefield. The arrows alone are effective against *Ky* trash and regular troops from long distance, particularly because of the speed and accuracy our bows provide. Then, the added Floe explosives devastate regular troops at long range, and kill Ky trash as well – indirectly but effectively – by creating lethal shrapnel in the narrow stone corridors of the trade route. Plus, you don't need training to fire them accurately. And most importantly, now that we have Monkworks we have the ability to manufacture enhanced bows and explosive arrows in vast quantities, and fast. No more improvised fixes on existing equipment."

There is utter silence when she finishes. Then I clear my throat. "Holy shit," is all I can think of to say.

"I think she's right," Fletch says.

"You are a dead nuts genius, Speega," says Mika.

"Sizzlers?" asks a bewildered General Barko.

"Sizzlers," Cael explains, "are arrows married to our Monkworks ripplers that explode multiple times on contact, and are fired by bows that hit harder, faster and more accurately than any we've had before."

General Barko smiles. "I love it," he says.

Cael looks to each of us in turn. "I think we have our answer," he says. "Egon, please check with Bayton Nayby in Portus Sironica about launching a flotilla to ship bows and sizzlers from our harbor to Nir and Enduron troop concentrations. We'll need them ready in, say, 10 days." He looks to Brother Omendall for confirmation on the manufacturing timing, and the Chief Engineer nods. Then Cael turns back to Speega with a nod. "The Abbey's treasury is yours, er, within limits of course."

Speega is positively beaming. "Suddenly," she says, "I can see me and the girls taking a brand new ownership position in the Nir & Far Inn."

We laugh and chatter, and it takes a minute for Mika to call us back to order.

"One last thing, everyone," she practically has to shout. "We need to get Enduran and Nir on board with a three-way simultaneous offensive featuring our new weapon."

"The four of us should coordinate on this," Cael says to General Barko, Madame Mercanor and me.

We nod.

Cael stands up. "Thanks, everyone. Let's meet here late tomorrow afternoon to review progress."

Everyone scatters then, but not before Cael rounds up all of us recent comrades in arms, thanks us again, and suggests we all meet for an early breakfast, where he has planned a surprise. We all agree, interest piqued.

Later, Mika and I lay down on a canopied bed in a room in the tower usually reserved for visiting dignitaries rather than Tester types, finally alone and together again. We've bathed away the grime of days, and let go of our tensions and frustrations and anxieties.

I'm looking over at Mika, who is toweling off her wet hair. "I can't help but feel," I say, "like you've been neglecting me lately," I say.

"*I've* been neglecting *you?*" she asks calmly, never pausing in her toweling.

"That's right," I say, fearlessly plunging on. "It's like, ever since you got the ring, there's been a distance between us."

"I see," she says, still toweling, deciding where to take it. "And you believe that clerical cutthroats and kidnappings and insane rampages through fiery tunnels is no excuse for my dereliction?"

"None whatsoever," I say. "You are soon to be a respectable married woman, and I can't condone your recent activities or the rabble you associate with."

"Well," she says, putting her towel aside, and unfastening the belt to her robe. "Is there anything I can do to make it all up to you?"

I sit up in the bed, cross legged, and pivot around to face her. She smiles then, and swings around to sit on my thighs, her ankles behind my back. I ease the robe off her shoulders. She does the same for me.

Dropping her eyes, and then grasping me with both hands, she says, "I see you have a suggestion."

I sigh. "You know," I say, "this is not something trivial I can heal from quickly. It will take patience and repetition and perseverance far into the future."

"I see," she says, her hands in slow, rhythmic coordination.

I run my hands down behind her thighs. I guide her up, over and around me. Our arms grasp each other's backs and we look into each other's eyes. "I was dying without you, Mika," I say. Tears well in her eyes, and she holds me tight.

"I love you so fucking much," she whispers fiercely, pressing the side of her head into my chest. "I don't ever want to be apart from you again."

She moves a little then, slow but emphatic, to punctuate her emotions. We make it last, long into the night.

SIX: THE REST IS A SLAUGHTER

Next morning we sit down for breakfast: Mika and me, Cael and Fletch, Speega, Janx, Neenah, Brik and Caton. The spARROWS and Mika's mercs have been heartily thanked and heavily compensated, and they are already casting around for new adventures.

Cael has a heavy schedule of meetings and blah blah blah ahead of him today which, among other things, will determine the governing structure of the Abbey going forward. He also has to allay the fears of the engineers with the news that *Floe* is resurgent. Meanwhile, most of the rest of us will be busy with our own assignments. So we dig in fast to the hearty meal.

About then there's a knock on the breakfast room door, and a young monk enters and whispers something to Janx. He nods to Cael, who clears his throat.

"Caton," Cael says to our long mistreated companion, "there are people here to see you, waiting in the next room."

Caton springs up, hope on his face, and sort of staggers out of the room. We hear, "Mara," then, "Son," then a shouted, "Dad," and the sound of running feet. I don't know what happened next exactly, but I am pleased that Caton does not rejoin us at breakfast.

After the meal, everyone leaves to pursue their tasks, but Cael asks Mika and me to stay. General Barko and Madame Rews join us, apparently by prearrangement, and Cael pulls out a communications pad, positions it where we all can see it, and contacts Sultan Anseem Hawarri of Nir.

"Congratulations, Abbot Venarius," the Sultan writes after contact is made, "on your survival and elevation. Also on your ending of the pact between the Abbey and Rusk. I have some hope, now, that a strong and lasting friendship can be rebuilt between our two houses."

"As do I, your majesty," returns Cael. "I will do my part to address the issue of balance, which you made me aware of in our first meeting."

"I am glad to hear you have thought about our discussion," the Sultan communicates, "and maybe there is still time to put things right. Unfortunately though, this war has unleased forces that will be hard to control. We are, the Abbey and Nir, still at war technically. Anger, envy, fear and resentment drive opinions and decisions these days, rather than any kind of practicality or rationality."

"I have ideas I wish to share with you about that, your majesty," Cael communicates, which is news to me. "But first, we have reached out to you to discuss ending the war."

"You have a plan?" the Sultan asks.

"We do, your majesty," he communicates. "We have both a plan and a new weapon which we are certain will break the stalemate in the passes." He goes on to describe the advantages of the sizzler, our 10-day shipping goal to Nir's port of choice, and the need for a simultaneous attack on the Northerners by Nir, Enduron, and the Abbey.

Sultan Hawarri is clearly intrigued by the sizzler, but suggests that the Abbey begin the attack before Enduron and Nir, to force Rusk to draw forces back from the passes to the plain. General Barko immediately draws his finger across his throat, signaling a deal breaker. No way we want to go into battle outnumbered and with no assurances that our allies will join us.

Cael picks up the discussion smoothly. "My advisors," he communicates, "feel we must avoid a situation where the North can fight us one at a time. A combined strike gives us superior numbers along with the new weaponry." Whether the Sultan was trying to take advantage of an inexperienced leader is unclear, but he has the grace to back off.

We conclude the contact on a positive note, and the Sultan agrees to reach out to us in a few days with his final answer.

"You were right to keep the Sultan's force out of the Abbey," I say afterwards. "He is clearly hinting that anti-Abbey forces are building within his palace."

"We have sins to atone for," is all Cael says. He turns to Madame Rews. "Are we ready to go?" he asks.

Madame Rews produces a communication pad and nods. "King Leander and Queen Miran of Enduran are in their palace in Kinor," she says, "and are awaiting your communication." Cael takes the pad and begins writing. The contact mostly follows the pattern set by our conversation with the Sultan, although more brisk and businesslike. There is no hint by either party that they have anything other than a governmental relationship. The preliminaries are over swiftly; the royal couple are seemingly impressed by the new weapon; they make no attempt to alter the simultaneous attack plan; and they promise to get back with final approval in good order. Then the conversation becomes more pointed.

"The previous Abbot did serious damage to our alliance," the Queen writes. "Shaken our trust. Awakened us to the ongoing threat magic poses to the Kingdoms."

Cael is smooth. "Sadly, I am aware," he writes. "The previous Abbot's actions have disrupted the harmony and balance in the Kingdoms, and I have a plan to satisfy your concerns. But first, we must win the war with Rusk. Afterwards, let's sit down and hear each other out."

What the hell does Cael have up his sleeve. I hope he's not just winging it.

We end our contact then, hoping to hear back from them soon with a positive response.

"Our allies are not happy," Madame Rews observes. "You will have to fill me in, Abbot Venarius, on your plan to make things right."

"We have a war to win first," is all Cael will say about it.

A military aid comes in then, and hands a note to General Barko. "There is a delegation from Immobilin Keep at the 'M' Gate," he informs Cael and the rest of us. "They demand to speak with Abbot Tenebrus and their own advisors in Monkworks, in order to be assured of their safety."

We all ride a bubble up to the Great Hall, and through its clear glass walls I can see the Guardians flying vigil over the town. I point them out to the others. "They're on station," I say.

We take up positions on either side of Cael, all of us remaining standing, and we don't have long to wait. The attaché returns with two *Ky* breeders and two uniformed military officers from Rusk. They are closely watched by Abbey guards. Three of the contingent stop a few strides away from us, while one of the breeders continues forward and stops in front of Cael.

"Unfortunately, you are very hard to kill, Brother Venarius," he says without preliminaries, apparently unsurprised by the absence of Tenebrus.

Cael doesn't respond right away, apparently debating his options. He looks at the other three visitors, and then goes eye to eye with the breeder. "I recognize you from the Sultan's succession event," he finally says. "You were the ambassador being escorted out of the hall at the time, so I didn't catch your name."

"I am Leutgar, now commander of the Rusk forces you see outside your walls," the warlock says, "which your Abbot Tenebrus requested. What have you done with our ally?"

"The Gryphons on our archery towers rather forcefully removed him from office yesterday," Cael says. "They found his new friends distasteful."

"And what of my colleagues?" the warlock demands. "They were here in friendship at the request of the Abbot with full diplomatic protection."

Cael laughs in his face. "Show me the agreement," Cael says, "that gives you and yours protection as you try your hardest to kill me and mine?"

"I think that what we can agree on, Brother Venarius," the *Ky* commander says icily, "is that you are trapped in here, while your city out there is completely vulnerable to destruction. Live up to the terms of our alliance or your people will die."

"As Abbot here now," Cael says, "I reject any possibility of an alliance with you, and I invite you to reconsider your assessment of Floendahl Heights' defenses." Then he points out an open window, where the four Guardians are circling. "The Gryphons are impervious to your alchemy, Leutgar, and what happened to Tenebrus yesterday can just as easily happen to you."

"You will pay for this betrayal," Leutgar says icily.

"It is time for you to march your troops home, Leutgar," Cael says evenly, "while they are still able to."

Leutgar spins around then, and the delegation storms off.

Cael says, "Did he buy the bluff?"

"For now, I think," General Barko says, "but I don't know for how long."

In late afternoon, the full group of us meet up again to review the day's progress.

"The evacuation got off to a good start last night," Janx says. "We got out about a quarter of the population, and we'll do better tonight."

"There was no visible reaction from the enemy," General Barko adds.

"Excellent," says Cael. "How are we housing everybody?"

"We are using our devices to build a tent city on the parade grounds in front of the barracks," Janx says. "Other devices supply food, water, sanitation, diversion and what not."

"Very well," Cael says. "Where do we stand on sizzler production?" he asks next.

Brother Omendall, Chief Engineer, clears his throat. "We have completed the designs for a Monkworks-produced sizzler and enhanced bow," he says, "and have assembled and tested prototypes. We are on track to hit our 10-day shipping target for Enduran and Nir forces."

"You are a marvel, Brother Omendall," Cael says, beaming.

"Well, then you will really like this," Omendall says smiling. "We've also developed a reasonably effective non-magical sizzler, which will kill the *Ky* on the plain directly, without the need for shrapnel off narrow stone walls."

"You amaze me, Brother," Cael says with feeling.

"Many thanks, Abbot Venarius," says the head engineer. "General Barko will have a limited supply of these non-magical weapons in two days for Abbey security, with more to follow quickly. We're calling them sparklers."

"Sparklers it is, then," says a delighted Cael. "Outstanding initiative, Brother Omendall."

"I'll pass your positive comments along to my crew," the engineer says. "We've made similar non-magical adjustments to a supply of tripplers and ripplers, too."

There is lots of excited chatter then, and among the most pleased is General Barko. "This is a game changer," I overhear him saying.

Cael gets us back on track finally. "Where do we stand on production of explosive devices and medallions?" he asks Brother Omendall.

Suddenly, Brother Omendall looks unsettled. "Well, Abbot Venarius, I went to ramp up production this morning, only to find out, to my embarrassment, that Abbot Tenebrus ordered mass production several weeks ago, without my knowledge."

"Why would he do that?" Cael asks.

"I can only assume that he wished to give, or sell, them to his new Rusk allies for the use of their regular troops," Brother Omendall says.

"The crates in the tunnel," I say.

Cael nods. "General Barko, please prioritize securing and inventorying the crates. They may be extremely useful to us, and scary if placed in the wrong hands."

"Yes sir, right away," the General says.

"Also, please work with Brother Omendall to see if you can figure out if any explosives or medallions have already been distributed to our enemies."

"Yes sir," the General says again.

"And finally," Cael says, "I want us to start using *Freight & Asset Finder*, a new device that will help us keep track of every device we manufacture, both within our walls and on through to final destination. Brother Omendall, General Barko, please check with my personal lab to implement a program of stamping and tracking our new devices as well as anything we have warehoused or in the tunnels."

Brother Dobus looks pained. "Abbot Venarius," he says, "such a drastic change to our procedures and controls must come before the Governing Board for review."

"Then come it shall," says Cael agreeably. "We welcome your input. But we will not delay implementation while our weapons may be falling into our enemy's hands."

Dobus looks pissed, and I'm beginning to wonder why.

Cael moves on. "General Barko, how goes the hunt for the Red Guards?"

"Completed and successful, sir," he says, "thanks to your *Friend & Foe Finder* device. "We've cleared all of the complex, above and below ground, of all possible combatants. We did discover through interrogations, however, that one or more of the Purple Robe kidnappers were outside the Abbey at the time you attacked, so they've slipped through our hands."

"Can't be helped, then," Cael says. "What of the plan to defend the town in the event our bluff fails before the evacuation is complete?"

"Even with the new sparklers, any determined attack will eventually overrun anything I can prudently put in the field," the General says, "because of the overwhelming numbers of the enemy. However, if there is an attack, I think I can buy the town some hours of additional evacuation time if you, Abbot Venarius, assist our troops with your legendary iron Gryphon maneuver."

Cael smiles. "I would be delighted," he says, "provided the builders of this place don't launch their own attack before I do." Then he turns to me.

"How's our good friend Bayton Nayby?" Cael asks me.

"He's eager to help," I say, "and is mobilizing his Guild members. They'll be ready to go when they get the word, all for what he calls a 'modest' amount of gold."

Cael laughs. "There's nothing modest about Bayton," he says. He looks around. "What else'" he asks.

Fletch leans forward. "I've got something," he says. "Speega, Neenah, Brik and I have experience in battle with the enhanced bows. General Barko put us in touch with his people, and we are working out how to integrate the sizzlers into existing military tactics to maximize effect."

"Great thought," Cael says.

"We think that when the time comes," Fletch continues, "the four of us should split up and sail with the weapons shipments to

Enduron and Nir, so we can advise their troops on what we've developed."

"That's terrific, you guys," Cael says. "Do it, and let me know if I can help. Ok, that does it for today, everyone. See you tomorrow afternoon again."

And so it goes. We get closer and closer to ship date, and each day we check off our assignments. Janx completes the town evacuation and no attack materializes. General Barko finds the crates in the tunnels to be full of medallions, ripplers, and tripplers. Apparently none were ever distributes to Rusk. Formerly destined to go to our enemies for the right price, they are now destined for our allies.

Enduran and Nir both formally agree to a simultaneous attack, tentatively scheduled for one week after we ship the weapons. They keep up the pressure in their respective canyons, however, to keep Rusk from suspecting any impending change. Meanwhile, the Guardians begin nighttime overflights for us of the Rusk camp on the plain in front of the Abbey, and we learn the locations of command tents, concentrations and types of constructs, and general troop dispositions. General Barko and the rest of us hone our plan for the attack.

On the 10th day the sizzlers ship from the Abbey's harbor; Bayton's flotilla is right on time. Our acting advisors, Speega and Fletch, accompany a shipment to Grax Harbor close to the Nir & Far Inn; and Neenah and Brik sail to Enduran's capital of Kinor.

Six days after that, the Sultan of Nir and the King and Queen of Enduran communicate that they are ready. Mika and I spend a tense night with Cael in the Great Hall. Advisors come and go with reports and orders. After midnight, General Barko and his militia start to crowd into the tunnels in preparation for their dawn emergence from the exits in town. The tent city for evacuees is on edge and alert with anticipation. Non-combatants gather in groups around the complex to share rumors. There's a late service in the cathedral, which remains open throughout the night.

The sky is just lightening in the minutes before sunrise when an aid comes in to say that General Barko is ready. Cael goes to a window overlooking the plain, and once again wrenches the archery tower Gryphons from their bases and wills them into the air. They circle the Abbey once and then race towards the unsuspecting enemy army.

Cael does something then and they separate. Eight dive towards command tents, including one sheltering Rusk Force Commander Leutgar. Ten target concentrations of *Ky* constructs, two apiece. The remaining four fly low to the ground, aiming for the densest rows of troop tents, intending to hit the line at their highest speed and let their fatal momentum carry them deep into the encampment.

Then, from our vantage point atop Monkworks, we see General Barko and his militia erupt from their tunnels and race towards the center of the enemy camp. The Northerners are beginning to react now, but chaotically, our attempt to decapitate their command structure apparently working. Our archers come into range of the enemy and begin to sow terror and destruction among the disorganized force.

For nearly the first hour, everything goes our way. Their destructive work done for now, the iron Gryphons have returned to the sky, and are circling the battlefield along with the four actual Gryphons. But slowly, inexorably, the thousands of confused Northerners congeal from chaos into a fighting force once again, and our hundreds of militia fighters begin to be pressed. General Barko orders the retreat, and the riskiest part of the whole operation begins.

The archers fire a massive barrage of new sparklers and then run back behind a convex semicircle of pikes and swords, dropping non-magical tripplers as they go. Pursuing Rusk troops, alphas and a variety of grotesque but deadly constructs are slowed as some trip the explosive devices. Alphas open up with explosives and flame, enemy troops fire their crossbows, and we take losses, while our archers suppress them as best they can with withering fire. But, soon enough, the enemy covers the distance and slams into our pike line. Somehow we absorb it, and our archers manage to prevent flanking or envelopment for now.

Then our pikes and swords disengage and run back through the archers, who again level a shattering barrage of sparklers at the fast approaching enemy. Then the archers take flight and the whole cycle repeats. The plan is working.

Professionally and in an orderly fashion, our retreat is drawing the enemy towards the Abbey. At just the right moment, the 'M' Gate is lifted to the height of a trooper, and our militia streams in. The howling mass of enraged Northerners, who are closely following, get the massive gate slammed down in their faces.

They spread out along our walls, into the dry moat, looking for weaknesses. A group of a half dozen or so fyrboren constructs, backed by an equal number of alphas, open up on the 'M' Gate with everything they have. Fire and explosives in a continuous torrent splash against the impervious gate. As if finally losing patience with an irritant, our sentient defenses react by opening a square segment of road beneath the attackers' feet, and they vanish. Nearly instantaneously, the empty road reappears, assuming its prior position with no apparent change.

The rest is a slaughter.

Hidden ports in the Abbey walls disgorge a torrent of flame on the invaders, a flame of such ancient magical origin that no *Ky* can stand against it. Then the walls shudder and there is a whoosh sound, and thousands of steel darts explode from the fire ports, ripping into the reeling, burning, chaotic mass of attackers. Finally, water from underground storage is disgorged into the moat, washing away whoever is left standing in a flash flood.

The Rusk combatants are decimated, and any who survive turn and run. The rout is so murderous that we let them go. Cael returns all 22 iron Gryphons to the top of the archery towers, as the Abbey's automatic defenses fall silent.

SEVEN: I HAVE THE MAGIC AND YOU DON'T

The next week is a blur. On the first day after the battle, our patrols report the plain is clear, and cleanup begins. By the end of the day, we hear from the Sultan of Nir and the King and Queen of Enduran that their assaults were a success and the enemy routed. By day six we see remnants of the defeated Rusk armies exiting the trade routes from Enduran and Nir and limping north across the plain. They are clearly no threat and we don't pursue.

The next day, lead elements of both victorious armies push through the trade roads and out onto the plain. They set up encampments, apparently planning to stay awhile. Cael orders the 'M' Gate to remain closed.

Then we get word that both the Enduran royals and the Sultan of Nir and his heir are coming to the Abbey in a week for a so-called peace conference. No mention is made for the moment that they are still officially at war with the Abbey. Meanwhile, representatives from Immobilin Keep have been summoned to submit their formal surrender.

I assume it is because the invitation wasn't ours that Cael makes no plans to host the peace conference, other than to occasionally huddle with Madame Rews. In fact, Mika and I don't see him much over this entire two-week span. General Barko tells me at one point that he is spending all of his free time in his private lab, presumably doing magical things. Mika and I spend our time talking about the future and making plans for when things settle down in the Kingdoms.

The night before the heads of state are due to arrive, Cael invites us to join Fletch and him for dinner. Fletch is just back from his advisory mission to Nir with Speega, who has opted to return to her friends at the newly reopened Nir & Far Inn for now.

If Cael has any anxiety about the upcoming conference, he shows none. In fact, he and Fletch are in a great mood when Mika and I arrive, because they are sporting new matching engagement rings. After hugs and congratulations, Cael proposes we have a dual marriage ceremony after the conference and we accept.

Then we toast each other, eat, drink and toast some more, and generally have a great time.

At some point I say to Fletch, "It seems like your advisory mission was a big success," and we toast to that.

After he drinks, he laughs. "Yeah, it turned out well," he says. "The key was getting the Nirians to make an all-out assault on the ridgeline trail first. Once we started pushing the Northerners back there, we began shooting sizzlers down into their massed army in the canyon below. They couldn't really move to avoid the barrage at first. It was carnage. By the time Nir's troops on the canyon floor began their own attack, the enemy was already running."

Cael claps him on the back. "Great work, Fletch," he says.

Next morning, the four of us meet up again for breakfast. As we are finishing up, an advisor comes in to say that King Leander and Queen Miran of Enduran's House of Morr have arrived and would like to pay their respects before the start of formal events.

"Please show them up to the Great Hall," Cael says to the aide, "and make them comfortable. We will arrive shortly."

"This should be interesting," Cael says to us.

"Do they have any idea who you are?" I ask.

"None, as far as I know."

We take the winding staircase up to the top of the tower then, and the King, Queen and a young man are picking at refreshments in a seating area when we arrive. The three of them stand up to greet us, and Cael leads us forward. I notice the Queen notice Cael's slight limp and enlarged boot. All of them appear ill at ease.

Introductions are made, and it turns out the young man is Crown Prince Corum Morr, heir to the throne of Enduran and closely related in appearance to Cael. King Leander gets right to the point.

"The Abbey and Enduran have enjoyed many years of peace and prosperity together," the King says, "but Abbot Tenebrus broke our treaties and worse, broke our trust."

Cael starts to respond but the King holds up a hand.

"I wished to see you personally before this conference begins," the King continues, "out of respect for the years of our alliance, and because of your personal actions, Abbot Venarius, to bring about our victory. That stated, I want to be clear that recent events are neither forgotten nor forgiven. The Abbey has a price to pay, as does Rusk. Indeed, magic itself has a price to pay."

"Then pay it we shall, Your Majesty," Cael says. "I take full responsibility for the former Abbot's actions, and I am prepared to propose remedies at the upcoming discussions."

"Then be warned, Abbot Venarius," he says, "that Enduran and Nir have come prepared with our own remedies."

Cael smiles. "I suppose that explains why your armies still occupy the plain."

"The actions of Floendahl Abbey explain why our armies are still here," the King says harshly. "We will not tolerate the continual instability caused by magic, nor will we risk another betrayal."

"Then we will have much to talk about," Cael says. "What else are peace conferences for, Your Majesty, than to air out family grievances?"

There is a sharp intake of breath at Cael's words from the Queen. The King glances over to her and waits a beat. She stirs uncomfortably but says nothing. The King seems to decide he's said what needed saying, and starts to stand up. It's Cael's turn to raise a hand. "Please," he says. The King sits back down.

"As long as you're here, Your Majesty," Cael says, pulling from his robes the *Family Finder* prototype, "I am wondering if you heard about our recent trip to Aurelia, and the assistance we were able to lend to Sultan Hawarri related to a succession problem he was having?"

"I heard about it, yes," the King says. "Your exploits in Nir have assumed legendary proportions."

"Well, I thought you might enjoy seeing a demonstration of the device we used to prove the Crown Prince was the Sultan's first born son," Cael continues.

This time the Queen flat out gasps, and her eyes lock on Cael. I see Cael looking at her, as does everyone else. The King, appearing perplexed, finally breaks the silence.

"There have been no succession challenges in Enduran," the King says, "so this device is of no interest to me."

The moment hangs then to an almost awkward degree. I see Cael glance again at the Queen, and she is flat-lipped and tense, her eyes absolutely pleading and pitiful.

Cael hesitates for just a moment longer, before putting the device away and nodding.

"Of course, King Leander," Cael says. "No matter."

The King stands up then, and the Queen and Prince follow. The King and Prince enter the bubble first, but the Queen turns to look at Cael.

"Thank you," she mouths silently, and then they are gone.

Fucking Cael. He never fails to surprise me.

"There's a story there," says Mika.

Cael is smiling ruefully. "You bet," he says. "I didn't have the heart to expose her, so we may never know for sure."

"That may be the least of our problems," I say, "based on the King's warning."

"No worries, Egon," Cael says. "They'll all leave happy and we will have peace in the Kingdoms once again."

"I don't know how you can be so sure," I say.

"I'm a magician," he says, and laughs.

An hour later Sultan Hawarri arrives with the Sultana and Crown Prince. In contrast to the Enduran visitors, this group seems happy to see us.

"Ah, my dear friends," the Sultan says, after the formalities. "I am so happy to see your good fortune. Many times lately I have worried over your safety."

Cael smiles. "And are you still worrying, Your Majesty?" Cael asks.

"Betting against you is a fool's game, Abbot Venarius," the Sultan says, laughing. "Although, if it was anyone else but you I would be very worried. There are powerful forces in the Kingdoms now who are calling for the end of the occult, magic and alchemy both, and I'm not talking about just the clergy. They scent an opportunity to gain back the power they feel they have lost to you."

Cael nods. "I hope to show them an alternative that even the most power hungry among them will support," he says.

"Then that will be your most amazing magic trick ever," the Sultan says. "In any case, we are set to meet tomorrow morning in a big Monkworks tent on the plain. There were many who didn't want to meet in the Abbey, since they feel like they are the victors and so get to name the time and place. In any case, I personally guarantee the safety of you and yours on the life of my beloved wife and first born."

"You are a great friend, Your Majesty," Cael says, "and I appreciate it."

Next morning, we assemble in the tunnels for our trip into town and then out onto the plain. Abbey guards lead us, followed by General Barko, Neenah and Brik, Mika and I, then Cael and Fletch, Madame Rews, and Brother Omendall. More guards bring up the rear. About halfway to the conference site we pick up a military escort from Nir, the Sultan apparently making good on his promise of safety.

Brother Dobus, Chairman of the Abbey's Governing Board, is not with us and, indeed, is no longer in the Abbey. When he learned last night that he was to be excluded from the conference, Dobus angrily confronted Cael, as Mika and I looked on.

"You are the Abbot, not the King," he shouted at Cael. "You have no right to exclude the Board from important matters of governance."

"You are correct as always, Brother Dobus," Cael answers, "which is why I have appointed Mika and Egon as the Board's newest members."

Dobus starts to protest but Cael cuts him off with a gesture.

"Enough," he says, and damn if Dobus doesn't shut up.

Then Cael reaches into his robes and pulls out the *Fact Finder* prototype. He dangles the solid gold 'M' from its chain and looks at Dobus.

"This device detects lies, Brother Dobus," Cael says. "It has been tested and is infallible. You have a choice to make."

Dobus has gone from indignant to wary in a heartbeat.

"You can gather your things and leave the Abbey within one hour, never to return, or you can answer my questions in the presence of *Fact Finder* about your involvement in Tenebrus' device smuggling operation."

Dobus swings back to indignant. "This is outrageous," he shouts. "I will not be treated like a common criminal by some opportunistic little shit like you."

Cael looks at him calmly, then nods to two guards at attention against a wall. They respond instantly, taking up positions on either side of the infuriated and about-to-be-former Board chairman.

"What will it be, Brother Dobus?" Cael asks. "The device or the door?" Cute.

For a second it looks like Dobus is going to reply. But then he abruptly spins around and leaves, flanked by the two guards. They are back in less than an hour, reporting that they escorted Dobus to his quarters and then through the tunnels and out to the town.

Meanwhile, Cael looks at us. "Welcome to the Board," he says, before we all say goodnight.

When we arrive at the large peace conference tent, everyone else is already there. I can see immediately the adversarial nature of the proceedings. We are directed to the left side of the tent, where the delegation from Rusk's Immobilin Keep is seated. To the right of the tent and facing us are the delegations from Nir and Enduran. In the middle between the opposing groups is a plain wood table. A cleric in saffron robes sits on one side, across from empty chairs on the other. It turns out that he will serve in the role of prosecutor as Nir and Enduran put the rest of us on trial. Cael looks completely unperturbed.

After we sit, our guards posted around us, the cleric gets up to speak.

"I am Umam Vorka den Jakarina of the Grand Mosque of Aurelia," he announces. "I have been designated by the victors in the War Against the Occult to assess the damages the conflict has caused, determine appropriate penalties, and set the terms of the new order to be established in the Three Kingdoms."

If I have any illusions left that we are on the side of the righteous, they are gone by the end of that little speech. 'War Against the Occult?' So it's *Floe* and the flesh farming alchemists lumped together against humanity? And it just keeps getting worse from there.

For the next two days, Umam Vorka calls a parade of people he labels 'victims of the occult' to the table at the center of the tent. Each has a tale to tell of injury they or those they represent have suffered because of magic and alchemy. And they aren't wrong.

Trades people come forward to say they are losing work because construction, maintenance and repair are increasingly handled by magical devices and alchemical constructs. Merchants say they are losing business because they can't compete with the

373

devices Monkworks produces. Civil authorities complain that criminals increasingly use illegal weapons smuggled out of Monkworks. Bureaucrats decry the complete lack of regulation when it comes to devices and flesh farming. Clergy complain their messages of all powerful gods is increasingly ignored by populations grown used to everyday miracles. Philosophers argue that whole societies are losing their wills to invent, innovate and problem solve. Government ministers tally up the cost to their treasuries of the recent war. Diplomats complain of the destabilizing effects of magic and alchemy on their relations with the other Kingdoms. And family members describe the utter despair they feel after losing loved ones in the conflict. The list goes on and on.

In the irony of all ironies, a breeder from Immobilin Keep declares that he and his kind are also Monkworks victims. He bitterly describes the loss of prestige and revenue caused by the Abbey's sale of popular magical devices throughout the Kingdoms that compete with their constructs for business. It's a speech delivered with no sense of shame or absurdity whatever.

On the third day, the accused are asked to respond. Immobilin Keep's defense is that it had been lured into an alliance with Floendahl Abbey that they felt they had to accept, or they would eventually be crushed by the Abbey's ascendancy. Then it is our turn.

I see Cael nod to Madame Rews, who has replaced the Umam at the center table. She introduces herself and says she will be calling witnesses to tell their own stories about magic. She's clearly been busy. She starts to call her first witness, when she is interrupted.

"What the fucking fuck," says a familiar voice from the entranceway of the tent. It's the cart man from the Notch, his wife at his side, and he is looking around belligerently at the crowd of staring muckety-mucks. "What the fucking fuck," he says again.

Madame Rews comes forward then and ushers them into chairs at the center table. She thanks them for coming, and then points to Cael and asks if Cart Man knows him and the people he's with.

"I know him alright," Cart Man says. "He's the only one who could read those stupid Monkworks directions for the device that fixed my cart. Those other two over there," he says, pointing to Neenah and Brik, "couldn't make heads nor tails of them."

Cart Man goes on to tell the story of how he lent some staves to Cael and how, in return, Cael helped set him up in his own business.

After they were done, Madame Rews asks Neenah to come forward. She describes in piercing detail how she was left gutted and dying by a *Ky* construct from Rusk, only to be saved by Cael's astonishing magic.

Then the Captain of our Nir desert military escort tells the story of Cael saving the lives of wounded troopers after an attempt on his life by the Swin Jin Ree, a cult funded by the breeders of Immobilin Keep.

When his turn comes, Fizo Ali, Chief of the Guard at Oanhe Palace in Aurelia, tells a similar story of a miraculous recovery from a wound he received at the hands of the pretender to the Nir throne, who was actually another *Ky* construct. He also credits Cael with saving his guards who were gravely wounded in the same fight.

General Antin Miza, Former Commandant of the prison in Gume, testifies that Cael's device uncovered corruption within his command, and also righted a terrible miscarriage of justice. Caton Welty follows, declaring that he was the victim of that miscarriage of justice at the hands of Abbot Tenebrus, and that Cael and General Miza saved him, with the help of a Monkworks magical device.

Bayton Nayby, Guild Master of the Seafaring Merchants, testifies that Cael has revolutionized the worldwide shipment of goods with a device that tracks cargoes and sailing ships in minute detail, and helps apprehend thieves and pirates that prey on shipping.

Encos Var is at the table next, and confirms to Madame Rews that he is speaking with the full knowledge and approval of the Sultan. First he describes how Cael solved the Sultan's succession crisis with an irrefutable demonstration of a new device. Then he tells the story of how Cael developed the weapons that ended the war, and sent them free of charge to Nir. He said the whole initiative for the final attack came from Cael. He also thanks Cael for sending military advisors who demonstrated the effectiveness of the weapons and revealed the tactics that would drive the Northerners from the trade route.

"Would you say," Madame Rews asks then, "that *Floe* magic is a positive force is Nirian life?"

"Our cities would die of thirst or choke on waste without *Floe* devices to manage our water supplies," Var says. "*Floe* devices are transforming our transportation services, and improving the lives of our citizens in countless ways."

It is surprising to me that all of these witnesses are able to make their statements without interruption or objection from those in the audience. But that changes when Grand Caliph Kasseem den Jakarina of the Holy City of Jakarina is called to testify. He tells the story of how Cael and Egon dropped out of the sky on winged creatures, twice, to save a multitude of pilgrims and Jakarina citizens from starvation and disease, after their abandonment by Umam Hani den Jakarina and his purple-robed cult.

He tells of the subsequent unholy kidnapping for ransom of members of Cael's party by Umam Hani, at the behest of the late

Abbot. He describes the fight in the mosque to rescue the hostages, and Umam Hani's cowardly flight.

At that point, prosecutor Umam Vorka jumps to his feet, looking scandalized and angry.

"You admit in front of all your unholy communion with the ungodly magic makers," he shouts. "You violate the first principles of our religion and are unfit to lead."

It is a stunning attack, and the tent falls deadly silent. Grand Caliph Kasseem remains calm.

"On the contrary, Umam Vorka," Kasseem replies. "I have done nothing but uphold with my life the very first tenets of our religion, which are to guide, protect and nurture our Jakarina flock. That is what I did and I owe you no explanation. However, I will say this: Because of Caelum Venarius, I have learned that the religion of the Jakarines and *Floe* magic can coexist in harmony and peace."

Another stunner of a statement.

Then, shockingly, Madame Rews calls on Queen Miran of Enduran to testify. The King looks indignant but the Queen shuts off protest by standing up and walking to the center table. She looks tense but resigned.

"I have but one question, Your Majesty," Madame Rews says. "Did Abbot Caelum Venarius provide Enduran with the weapons and military advice which broke the stalemate on the trade route and led to the rout of Rusk forces there?"

"Yes," the Queen states.

"Thank you, Your Majesty," Madame Rews says, and the Queen returns to the audience.

The next to last witness to speak is Brother Janx. He describes the long-term corruption of Abbot Tenebrus, and the prior Abbot's efforts to contain the problem. He tells of Tenebrus' vision of a supremacy of magic that would make the citizens of the Three Kingdoms merely exploitable pawns in the new order. He describes the deception of a phony mission that Tenebrus used to get Cael out of his way. And he tells of the plot to murder Cael that the traitorous Abbot hatched with his Rusk allies, and the many failed attempts.

"There can be no honest linkage," Janx concludes, "between the criminality of Abbot Tenebrus and the righteous behavior of our new Abbot."

Madame Rews stands up as Janx departs, and addresses the audience. "I have one last witness to call," she says, "Abbot Caelum Venarius."

There is complete silence as Cael walks to the middle of the room. He doesn't sit down, just calmly stands in the center, facing his accusers.

"Magic," he begins, "is messy. It disrupts. It has victims, some of whom we've heard from these past few days. But we have heard another side as well. Magic transforms, it eases, and it heals. Your citizens want it, for the most part. A few are hurt by it. And you, the leaders of our Kingdoms, are left trying to ride a rising wave you feel is becoming uncontrollable. I have sympathy for that position and will rectify the situation today."

There are murmurs from the audience at that.

"So let us talk now about what this gathering is really all about," Cael says, and pauses to calmly look around at all the rich and powerful judging him. "We are here today because I have the magic and you don't, and it is transforming the world without you."

Now the murmurs grow louder, some denying, some agreeing, all angry.

Cael walks over to the tent flap and pulls it aside. Through it we can see the Monkworks tower, with its continual pulse of light and bursting sparks on top.

"That," he says, pointing to the lightshow, "is *Floe*. It bubbles up from underground and escapes out the top of our tower, where it eventually gets distributed across the Three Kingdoms, albeit in weakened form. It is everywhere. It is why my magic works no matter where I travel. I can always feel its presence, its eternal power. I can always shape and channel it. And from today on, you can too."

There are gasps now.

Cael is still holding the tent flap open, and he nods to someone outside. An aide pushes a cart into the tent bearing a replica of the Monkworks tower. It is the height of half a man. Behind him come more aides, bearing trays covered in cloth. They arrange the replica on the center table with the covered trays all around it.

Cael comes back to the center of the room again, and again he takes time to slowly look at his audience.

"This is my latest device," he says quietly. "It is a Monkworks Magic Machine, and with it anyone anywhere can magically charge a properly engineered device. From this day forward, any person with this machine can make their own magical devices, with no help from the Abbey."

There are more gasps, everyone talking at once. "Impossible," someone shouts.

"I understand your skepticism," Cael says, "but think of it this way. *Floe* is basically a universal power source that is intelligent, even sentient some might say. But what it lacks is intentionality. It needs to be directed, to be given a purpose. That's what I do with my magic. So what I've built here might be called, instead of a Magic Machine, an Intentionality Machine, because that is what it does."

"Show us," someone yells from the now raucous crowd.

"Yes," Cael says, "I will show you. And then any of you who wants to can come use this machine themselves."

Cael takes the cover off one of the trays, which contains ordered rows of standard Monkworks devices. He picks one up and presses it, shakes it, twists it and throws it on the ground. Nothing happens.

"These are newly engineered children's toys," Cael says. "But they lack the power of *Floe* to bring them to life."

He presses something on the side of the Magic Machine. A pulse of light travels up the core of the replica tower and explodes into sparks on top that shoot out like lightning and strike each of the devices on the tray. They visibly vibrate and spin.

Cael picks up two newly charged devices from the tray and squeezes them. A pair of pink bunnies jump from his hands and start running around the room, much to the delight of the audience.

"They last a day and go away," says Cael, with what sounds like a jingle from Marketing. "Each is identical to the others, so if a child wants her bunny again you can always have another one on hand, without the bother of caring for a live pet."

There are smiles on some in the audience now.

"Now," asks Cael, "who will be first to try this out?"

The Sultana of Nir is the first up, and she intentionalizes a tray of exquisite crystal goblets that are designed to vanish at the end of an evening's festivities without the need for cleanup. The Sultan draws a tray of Shrinkers, which will shrink anything for travel and then reinflate it with a specific sequence of taps. The King of Enduran energizes a tray of walnut-sized snow kits, each of which will disgorge full-sized snow shoes, a walking staff, instant heat pads, flint and steel to light fires, travel food, gloves and a hat. Others come and go until the trays run out, each marveling at the experience.

Finally, the Sultan clears his throat. "So what are you imagining, Abbot Venarius?" he asks. "How would this work?"

"I'm suggesting that the Abbey goes out of the magic business while we help you get into it," Cael says. "We will lease these Magic Machines to anybody your regulators say is permitted to operate one, on a five year basis, including maintenance and repair. After five years, if you choose to continue, we will replace your old one with a new one. Some devices will be powerful enough to build a complete factory around; others will be small and portable for personal use."

The room is once again stunned into complete silence, and calculations and ramifications are sorted.

"This is quite extraordinary," the Sultan says.

"In addition," Cael continues, "we will charge a fee for our engineers to teach your engineers how to design and manufacture devices that can be intentionalized by *Floe,* and how to invent entirely new ones. And we will run workshops for your creators and innovators, so that they can use the capabilities of *Floe* magic to their maximum potential. You, the leaders of your Kingdoms, can tax and regulate this new industry as you see fit, while the Abbey phases out our device production and tribute payments."

"No tribute?" someone in the Enduran camp asks, sounding indignant.

"From now on, all of us will create our revenue in different ways," Cael says. "You will control device manufacturing, and can produce income through device sales, taxes on sales, physical gold and coin production, and much more. Meanwhile, the Abbey will cease device production, clearing the way for you to enter that market. At the same time, we will lease, maintain and repair the Magic Machines; sell our engineering and manufacturing expertise to you; and create innovative new designs for devices which we will offer to you at a negotiated price, and which you will manufacture yourselves."

"What do you hope to achieve by this?" King Leander asks.

"Balance again in the Three Kingdoms," Cael says. "A balance held in place by mutual self-interest."

"What of the Northerners?" the Sultan asks.

Cael shrugs. "I'm sure everyone has thoughts about that. But if you see value in what I am proposing here, than I guess I do have something to say about their punishment."

Cael looks around for reactions, but everyone is silent until King Leander says, "Let's hear it."

"Ok, then," says Cael. "I think Rusk should be monitored for 10 years by representatives of Enduran and Nir, onsite. Rusk should not be allowed to participate in the *Floe* revolution for a period of 10 years, at which time you can assess their worthiness to rejoin the new order. In addition, the breeders of Immobilin Keep must forever be prohibited from using bioalchemy to produce constructs or any other forms of quasi life. In fact, their alchemy must never be used again for any dark or destructive purpose."

"And after 10 years?" a breeder asks sourly. "How do you propose that Rusk gets its fair share of device revenue, since we don't interact with *Floe* magic?"

"Your citizens do," Cael shoots back, "just like the other Kingdoms. It's time for you to let them join the party."

"And the alchemists in Immobilin Keep?" the breeder persists angrily. "Do you just expect us to just disappear?"

"I believe," Cael says, "that you should turn your skills back to their purest state and highest value to humankind."

"And what might that be?" the breeder asks.

"Medicine," Cael says. "The biological sciences. It is a fundamental part of *Ky* alchemy, to understand biological growth, and to see and understand the processes and constituents that control our health. I propose that you use your talents to establish healing centers and research institutions throughout the Kingdoms, with the goal of lengthening healthy lifetimes through your knowledge, experience, and alchemical powers."

The Sultan of Nir stands up then. "I must say," he declares, "I think this is a brilliant proposal, Abbot Venarius. Oh, our advisors will spend hours, days and months wrangling over the details. But I, for one, want to see this happen."

And incredibly, that's pretty much how it goes down.

Later, back in Monkworks Great Hall, we all sit around reviewing the previous days' events. Chief Engineer Omendall looks to be in shock.

"We're not making devices anymore?" he asks again.

"It's really for the best, Brother Omendall," Cael says, trying to placate him. "We will sell your new designs all over the Kingdoms at great profit, and won't ever have to sweat the production details again."

"Except for the Magic Machine," Omendall says.

"That's right," Cael says. "Those we design, innovate, build, maintain and repair, the works."

"But what will I do with all my extra time?" he asks.

"You'll become a worldwide celebrity," Cael says. "You will be feted and compensated throughout the Kingdoms for your expertise."

"Well holy shit," the now bemused engineer says.

EIGHT: FUCKING CAEL IS SITTING UP

The Sultan is right, and the wrangling is intense. Madame Rews serves as the Abbey's lead negotiator, and proves herself to be fearless, tough and fair. Within a week, the Enduran and Nir armies have left the plain and are heading home, as official peace is declared. Tension is easing dramatically among the remaining diplomats and royals, as the new age of balance in the Kingdoms takes shape.

Meanwhile, Cael, Fletch, Mika and I have moved on to a less world-changing but vastly more important activity: planning our double wedding. Which turns out to mean that Cael and I have surprisingly little to do. We are told in no uncertain terms to show up at the appointed hour and perform as directed.

So we kind of hang out in the Great Room for a few days, Cael signing the occasional historic order or world-altering document, me just shooting the shit with my friend.

Like at one point I say to Cael, "You know, this whole marriage thing is unfair."

"How so?" asks Cael.

"Let's say you get into a big fight with Fletch and he's upset," I say. "You just conjure up some flying coach and ride across the moonslit skies to an empty beach and make up. But me? With

Mika? I have no magic. I just have to grovel and beg, be patient and understanding, and listen intently. Everything I'm no good at."

"Not true," Cael says. "I've already done the flying coach thing," Cael says. "And the cozy lodge atop the highest mountain thing. Not to mention the undersea glass palace thing. But sooner or later, even a magician has to face the work of a relationship."

"Wow," I say. "I had no idea you were such a romantic."

"Yeah," says Cael, blushing as usual, "Fletch and I had a lot of free nights alone at the Havens in Nir, remember. And the Guardians taught me some things about magic I didn't know were possible."

"Like what?" I ask.

"The main thing," Cael says, "is that when I'm inside a Haven I'm in a space where my *Floe* magic can make almost anything happen. So every night we went somewhere exotic without actually ever leaving. Just like at the Lake House. But you always have to come back to reality and deal with whatever needs dealing with."

"Well, then, I'm glad to hear you're in this with me," I say. "I'd hate to think of you just magicianing you're way out of everything."

Yet I have to say that, even during this downtime, interesting things keep happening. Bayton Nayby visits one day with a woman he introduces as Queetan Marcasin, Founder and Director of the Marcasin Medical Devices Institute in Portus Sironika.

"Bayton tells me," says Marcasin, "that you suffer from a condition that my institute can cure. With your permission, and with the use of Monkworks fabrication facilities, I can start your treatment today."

The treatment turns out to be surgery that Cael performs on himself with the guidance of Marcasin, followed by a new boot, custom designed to gradually realign Cael's club foot without further discomfort.

Cael is ecstatic when he is fitted. "When I made my boot," he says, "I didn't know what I was doing so I just magicked it for less pain and more mobility. That mostly worked, but I didn't know that the problem has a permanent fix."

"I guess science beats magic," I say.

"Maybe," Cael says, "but both is better. And that reminds me." He consults with Janx for a moment and sometime later both Marcasin and Grand Caliph Kasseem den Jakarina arrive.

Cael thanks them both for coming on short notice, and then cements the new balance in the Kingdoms with one stroke. "You represent morality in the Kingdoms," he says, speaking to the Grand Caliph, "while you, Director Marcasin, represent science. The three of us bring together the forces of morality, science and magic, and I want us to form a global institution that finds ways to strengthen balance in the Kingdoms and improve the lives of everyone everywhere. Maybe even in time, bring in the alchemists."

It's a mind blowing idea, and both visitors agree on the spot. They set a date for one month hence to hold their first organizational meeting.

Our next visitors are Sultan Hawarri and Encos Var. They congratulate Cael on his plan for magic, and give us some perspective on the talks. The Sultan also congratulates us both on the upcoming wedding, and offers his Lake House for our honeymoon.

"Take it for as long as you like," he says. After checking with our respectives, we happily accept.

The most riveting visitor is Queen Miran of Enduran, Cael's mother. She comes alone, and is nervous. Before she speaks she looks at me, but doesn't ask me to leave.

"I wanted to thank you," she finally says to Cael, "about keeping my secret the other day. Leander, your father, never knew what I did."

Cael is calm, gentle even, and asks the Queen to tell him what happened.

"I was young," she says, "and new to the court, and I wasn't the preferred choice for Queen. Leander married me for love, against the wishes of his parents. And so..."

She pauses then, a trickle of tears beginning to flow down her face.

"...and so," she continues, "I did a terrible thing, because I was afraid. I was terrified that if I didn't deliver a perfect firstborn male child, it would be used against me in the palace, maybe even to drive me out of it. I panicked when I saw your poor little foot, and I sent word to Leander that you had died at birth. I hid you and your nursemaid away until I could have you smuggled out of the palace. Then I arranged to have you sent here. I'm so very sorry, Loel. That's who you were supposed to be. Prince Loel Morr. I've thought of you, and hated myself, every day since."

So then Cael does what Cael does. He walks over to the seated, sobbing Queen, and holds out his hand. When she takes it, he lifts her up into an embrace.

"It's all good now," he says. "We have all the time in the world to get to know each other, mother."

I leave, then, to get out of their way, so I don't know what happened exactly. But Cael is happy when I see him again, which is good enough for me. I wonder, though, if there are any plans to tell his dad.

Finally the big day arrives, and I'm not talking about the treaty signing, which happens the day before. Cael and I are dressed in the morning by attendants, of all fucking things. We have had no hand in selecting the outfits, and certain parts of them we don't even know how to put on. My Testers vest is not permitted, it seems, but I sneak a couple of things in my pockets anyway. Neither Cael nor I wear our medallions but, what the hell, we're among friends.

There is a breakfast, and some ceremonies, and some signings, and then a lunch, and all the time we are kept separated from our betrothed. Which is annoying. But what's fun is that everybody is there, at one event or another. All who testified for Cael at the peace conference, all the royalty from Enduron and Nir, Speega's crew and Mika's people, Neenah and Brik, some of Mika's friends I don't know yet, some of my Tester buddies, Brother Janx, General Barko, Madame Rews, Brother Omendall, and a pile of Monkworks friends and colleagues. I don't see the cursing cart man and his wife, but I know they must be here.

Then Cael and I are marched out to the open 'M' Gate, musicians playing well and loudly, fireworks exploding around the sparks at the top of Monkworks. Far above that, four Guardians patrol the skies, as if offering their protection and giving their blessing. How did they know the wedding date?

Waiting for us is Grand Caliph Kasseem den Jakarina, smiling and offering us his congratulations in the moments before he performs the marriage rite. Behind him is a horde of townsfolk, most of them Monkworks workers just here to wish us well. Finally, the music changes and Cael and I turn to see our brides approaching, with a crowd of colleagues and friends behind them. Speega Somes is escorting Fletch, and Mika is on the arm of Brother Janx. Fletch looks handsome in some sort of formal black and white get up, but I really see only Mika. Gone are the leather mercenary duds and lethal weaponry. She's in white, carrying flowers, her black hair shiny and falling in waves around her bare shoulders. She looks ravishing, and I still can't believe she's marrying me.

She comes to me then, smiling, and Holy Gods, crying, and takes my hand. Then the four of us face the Grand Caliph. He says a lot then but I don't hear it. Finally, the big moment is here, and Mika and I exchange magical wedding rings supplied by Cael, although it occurs to be now that I don't know what the magic does. I see Cael and Fletch going through the same motions. Then I kiss Mika as the ceremony ends, and feel as though no one anywhere can possibly be as happy as I am right now.

When we finally disengage, smiling at each other, I see that the crowd of friends, colleagues and well-wishers has moved in to surround us, clapping, shouting congratulations, spreading the cheer. There are so many faces around us that I know and like and even love, that I feel no premonition at all.

Yet, I guess instincts never sleep, because I catch just a flicker of out-of-place movement from the townsfolk side of the crowd, and just the quickest hit of recognition. Instantly I reach for my vest and just as instantly realize that what I need is now in a pants pocket instead. And that is all the delay it takes. Umam Hani den Jakarina - kidnapper, murderer, betrayer of his faith and flock, out of his purple robes but unable to conceal his murderous intent - descends on Cael like a voracious desert falcon. Three times he raises his bone white construct knife above the magician and plunges it home before I can draw, aim, and fire my projectile weapon.

The crowd is screaming as Fletch eases Cael to the ground and Hani gasps his last. Mika and I rush towards them, Fletch crying now and Cael's lifeblood spraying everywhere. His eyelids are fluttering and I can see he is trying to say something to Fletch, but he doesn't manage to get it out. He slumps in Fletch's arms, his eyes roll back, and his head drops to the side. Fletch is screaming

Cael's name, and the faces around me are stricken with horror. How can this possibly fucking be, I think. How can this great, great heart just stop?

And then a massive rush of air flings us all aside. Later I learn from some on the scene that the four massive Guardians patrolling the sky above the Abbey went into a screaming dive as Hani made his move. They smack into the ground around Cael and cover him in their eagle's wings. For long seconds nothing seems to happen, and then the Gryphons step back onto their lion haunches and launch themselves into the sky. Behind them, beyond miraculously, fucking Cael is sitting up.

NINE: WE DEFEATED MAGIC TO SAVE IT

Fletch reaches him first and helps him to his feet. The militia moves in to push back the crowd. Mika, Fletch and I crowd around Cael, trying to be of help where no help is needed.

"I'm fine, fine," Cael is saying, seemingly embarrassed rather than hurt. He starts shrugging his shoulders, shaking his limbs, checking himself out. "Matter of fact," he says, "I feel better than ever." He's smiling now and so are we.

Someone in the crowd starts up a 'Hail, Venarius" chant as we walk back to Monkworks. Is that a thing? Cael waves as the music restarts and the celebration fires back up. The four of us head down into the tunnels below the tower, straight to the long tunnel under the mountains. A newly engineered iron and glass cylinder awaits us there and we pile in. A magical blast of air that Cael no longer needs to conjure propels us towards the hidden harbor in solid comfort at breakneck speed.

We burst out onto the beach and into sunshine and, practically before I can catch my breath, Mika and I are alone in a luxurious private stateroom aboard a sailing ship supplied by Bayton Nayby. I see chilled wine, fruits, cakes and a huge open window looking back at the hidden harbor and towering mountains. We sail off on our honeymoon.

The four of us take three days to reach Grax Harbor close to the Near & Far Inn, and never leave our staterooms. We find out almost immediately the value of Cael's magical wedding rings.

For lack of a better word, they are sexplosive. Sex with someone who wears the same ring is a pleasure so great that minstrels and poets will never catch up to it.

When we reach port the four of us blink and stumble our way on deck as Captain Darion Creedmont looks on disapprovingly.

"Gangplank's that way," is all he says.

On the pier is a horseless coach sent by the Sultan, and it whisks us to the Inn for a fun night. Next morning, the same carriage takes us to the Lake House, which today looks like a quaint mountain village in the fall. We find plenty to do, and when we're not doing, we're talking about our future.

"We're sort of unemployed," I say.

"Glad I didn't marry you for your prospects," Mika says.

At the end of a week we again board the coach and speed towards Pagan's Notch. We arrive at sunset, where a party is already in progress under a huge Monkworks tent pitched on the grassy meadow near the river. Neenah and Brik are there, along with Speega, plus all the spARROWS and mercenaries who fought with us at the battle of the Notch. Janx is also there, along with Caton and his wife and son.

It's a bittersweet night for me, because I know that in the morning we all will scatter to pursue the rest of our lives. I was a rootless Tester who left the tunnels not so long ago on a routine mission with a naive monk, and find myself now amongst a new family who I've come to love. Magic is great, but everyday living has a magic all its own.

It seems like everybody has made plans. Neenah and Brik have bought the mercenary bar where Mika and I met in Aurelia. Speega now owns a piece of the Nir & Far Inn, and has a lucrative armed escort contract from the Abbey. Her spARROWS and the rest of Mika's mercs have joined forces to fill up the ranks of the new outfit, called Speega's Guardian Services.

I congratulate Janx on his official new position as Cael's Chief of Staff. He congratulates me on being the last official Tester, all the others at the Abbey having converted to being traveling experts helping the rest of the Kingdoms with the device manufacturing process.

"And by the way," he says as he moves off to mingle with the others, "you're fired."

Caton has moved back home with his wife and son. They are working out some issues, of course, but from what I see tonight they are a happy family.

Later in the evening, Cael gives a little speech outlining the new balance in the Kingdoms and thanking everybody for their help. Then he hands out beautifully made purses of gold to everyone in the room, each with the recipient's embroidered initials.

"The thing about these purses," he says, "is that they will refill on the anniversary of this day year after year for the rest of your lives. They symbolize the fact that my gratitude to you is bottomless, and if you ever need my help in the future, you only have to ask."

There are cheers and tears then, as the party ends.

Next morning we watch as Cael conjures a bronze memorial to those who lost their lives at the battle. It is composed of oversized statues of each of the fallen, arranged in a semicircle, the SenSen twins in the center, all linked together by the placement of arms over shoulders of those adjacent. He places it at the edge of the meadow with their backs to the river and their eyes on the road.

"You stood with me," Cael says to us, the living and the fallen, "and together we defeated magic in order to save it, and in order to save the Kingdoms."

We all agree to meet once a year on the same date at the Memorial, and then we say our goodbyes for now. Cael, Fletch, Mika and I hop back into the Sultan's carriage for the multi-day ride up the trade road to the Abbey.

Somewhere in there, Mika and I reveal our plans to return to the area of my home in Enduran, outside of Kinor, to open a residential school for orphaned teens looking to find a place in the world.

Cael almost cries. "I wanted us to always be together at the Abbey," he says. "But I guess I should have known that Abbey life is not for renegades like you two. So I wish you well, and I think your idea is wonderful."

"It won't be so bad, Cael," Mika says. "We have to come back every three months to vote on this stupid Governing Board you've saddled us with."

Cael grins mischievously. "Oh yeah, and I forgot to tell you, it's a lifetime appointment."

Back at the Abbey there are no big goodbyes. We'll all see each other again soon, and everything that needed saying has now been said. But Cael has two more surprises up his sleeve as we get ready to leave for Enduran. He gives us a horseless coach of our own which we can drive ourselves. And behind it is the cart man and his wife in a new, much larger cart, and it's filled with tools, equipment and all manner of magical construction devices.

"They'll follow you down at their own pace," Cael says, "and they'll supervise the construction of your new school."

Ok, ok, so this time there are tears in *my* eyes. Mika's too. I hug Cael then.

"I love you, brother," I say.

"I love you too, Egon," Cael says. "I love you both."

After the farewells, Snout, my trusty not-much-for-war dog jumps up into the carriage, and Mika and I follow. We wave to Cael and Fletch, then drive out of the complex and turn left, Mika at the intuitive controls. I am still choked up a while later when Mika pulls over to the side of the road and puts her arms around me.

"You're even more studly when you cry," she says, and kisses me like I've never been kissed before. Did I mention how those wedding rings work? Fortunately, Cael supplied us with a comfortable back berth in the coach, along with soft bed, cozy blankets, and a plush little alcove for Snout. That Cael thinks of everything. Somewhere around then we hear the cursing cart man pass us on the road. "What the fucking fuck," he says, and Mika and I laugh until we cry.

The End

Acknowledgements

I finally realized that one thing nobody can afford to be is a 72-year-old procrastinator. Thus this book. I am so grateful to those people who helped make it happen, including:

Fred, Jill, Robin, Todd, and Tom T. for your rave reviews and invaluable suggestions;

Joan, for perfecting a cheery mumble/nod to withstand my incessant and unsolicited updates on the progress of this book, along with your always honest reactions;

Pat and Rick, my early readers, for your thoughtful and helpful feedback;

Juliette, Ayla and Elliott, for giving me a forever bright and happy space in your hearts;

My fishing family – Bob, Bud, Bud, Dennis, Michael, Phil, Rob and Tom B. - for your friendship and encouragement despite your lifelong struggles with illiteracy;

Kihm, for your publishing insights;

Karen, Martha and Nancy for believing I could;

Fran, Joe, and Mike for lighting the way;

And finally, retirement, without which this book would not have been written.